LORD OF
WICKED INTENTIONS

A LESSON IN SEDUCTION

She placed her hand in his. Hers seemed so tiny, and when he closed his fingers around it, she was incredibly aware that he could easily break her with very little effort. She was surprised by the coarseness of his flesh. These were not the hands of a gentleman. He drew her up, then expertly moved her arm behind her back, somehow snagging her other wrist until both were held within his firm grasp. With his free hand, he cradled her face, stroked her cheek with his thumb.

"You will learn to do things as I like them done," he said softly, in a voice that promised pleasures. His eyes captured and held hers, and she thought that even if he wasn't holding her, she'd not have been able to break away. "I have particular needs. The first is that you are to never wrap your arms around me."

"Why not?" she whispered.

"Because it's what I require." He lowered his lips to hers . . .

LORRAINE HEATH

LORD
OF
WICKED INTENTIONS

AVON
An Imprint of HarperCollinsPublishers

AVON BOOKS
An Imprint of HarperCollins*Publishers*
10 East 53rd Street
New York, New York 10022-5299

Copyright © 2013 by Jan Nowasky
ISBN 978-0-06-210003-0
www.avonromance.com

First Avon Books mass market printing: May 2013

Avon Trademark Reg. U.S. Pat. Off. and in Other Countries, Marca Registrada, Hecho en U.S.A.
HarperCollins® is a registered trademark of HarperCollins Publishers.

Printed in the U.S.A.

10 9 8 7 6 5 4 3 2 1

Prologue

Yorkshire
Winter 1854

Lord Rafe Easton waited, unmoving.

Perched on a boulder in the center of the abbey ruins, he was immune to the discomfort of the hard rock. The icy winds howled around him, the snow fell gently from the heavens, but he did not stir. He allowed no memories of happier times to intrude. He was not *anticipating* his brothers' return. He refused to anticipate it. He was merely awaiting their arrival.

Ten years earlier on this very night, they'd left him. As though he were rubbish, as though they weren't brothers, as though they didn't have the same blood coursing through their veins. They'd left him with the promise to meet up here on this particular night in order to gain revenge against the uncle who had meant them harm, the one who wanted the dukedom of Keswick. The one who had planned to kill them.

Rafe had found ample opportunities through the years to do in the blighter. He'd watched from the shadows while Lord David strutted about, and enjoyed the fruits of his misguided scheme. He knew he should feel unmitigated anger at the fool, but it was his brothers who garnered his wrath.

Especially Tristan, who had called him a baby. Then Sebastian for not seeking to reassure him that everything would be all right.

Rafe had been barely ten. Terrified beyond measure. They were four years older, blasted twins, who knew each other's thoughts, each other's fears, each other's ambitions. He'd not heard a word from either of them since they'd abandoned him at the workhouse and ridden off together. Yes, he'd cried, blubbered, begged . . .

It shamed him now to think about his behavior on that horrid night. Since then he'd dammed up his tears, dammed up his emotions, dammed up his heart until he felt nothing.

He welcomed the numbness seeping through his body until it matched his soul, didn't bother to extend his gloved hands toward the wildly dancing flames of the small fire. He would not even consider that they were not here because they were dead. They must see how well he'd done for himself. He hadn't needed them. In all the passing years, he hadn't required their assistance in order to survive. He certainly didn't need them now.

At the workhouse food was short and punishment in abundance, particularly for a lad who wasn't very agile. Admittedly, he'd been a bit of a

roly-poly back then. He loved his sweets. They were his secret indulgence now, but not often. He would never again be slow to action. A number of men had learned how quick he was—and deadly.

Eventually he'd managed to escape the work-house and made his way to London. He'd lived on the streets, scavenging and scrounging, until he'd fallen in with a fellow who knew all of London's darkest secrets. Now they belonged to Rafe.

By the time the sun was easing over the horizon, the fire had long since turned to ash, the cold had made its home in the depths of his bones. He finally unfolded his body and made his way over the scattered debris until he reached the remnants of a window.

They're not coming.

He should have known. He didn't want to acknowledge the small kernel of disappointment that threatened to blossom into rage and hurt, and something that resembled loneliness. They meant nothing to him anymore. He wouldn't allow them to mean anything.

He sincerely hoped they were writhing in hell.

His features set in a stoic mask, he spun away from the window, his greatcoat flaring out around his calves. He tugged hard on his finely crafted leather gloves, even though they were already perfectly positioned. "Wait here until they show."

"For how long, sir?" his man asked from the corner in which he'd been standing guard through the night.

How long indeed? How long was long enough?

"Until they show," he repeated.

"And if they don't?"

He wouldn't contemplate the possibility of that happening. He wouldn't consider that they were indeed truly dead. That they would leave him totally, completely, absolutely alone. That they would deny him the ultimate pleasure of telling them he didn't need them in his life. That they were nothing to him, less than nothing. Rubbish, just as he'd once been to them.

"They will."

He strode to his horse and mounted it in one easy practiced movement. He urged his black gelding into a gallop, its hooves beating out a steady rhythm that caused the words to reverberate through his soul: *You're alone. You're alone. You'll always be alone. You deserve to be alone. That's why they left you behind.*

Chapter 1

London
April 1859

Please don't go. Please don't leave me.

Evelyn Chambers merely thought the words. She didn't say them. To do so would be most cruel. Her father had been in excruciating pain for some time now, slowly dwindling away until he was a mere shadow of the robust, boisterous Earl of Wortham whom she loved so terribly much.

Sitting in a chair beside his bed, she held his withered hand, one too weak to squeeze her own. So she did the squeezing, trying to impart with her touch what she could not bring herself to utter with words: *It's all right to let go.*

Because once he left her, she had no idea how she might manage. She shoved back the terrifying realization. She would not make his parting more difficult, but the truth was that she hadn't a clue how she would survive without him. But she would face the uncertain future as best as she could. For now, her only concern was to bring him comfort.

He'd done little more than study her for hours now. It was late into the night. The bustle of the city had quieted. Only the most senior of the servants stood vigil outside the door, waiting for orders. A lamp burning on the bedside table illuminated his sallow complexion, his sunken eyes. With a slow blink, he turned his head slightly, focusing his attention somewhere near the foot of the bed. "Geoffrey?"

The word was barely a whisper, scratchy and rough, as though it had taken all his effort to form the syllables.

"Yes, Father."

His son stood there, leaning against the bedpost, arms folded over his chest, his strikingly handsome face showing no emotion whatsoever. He might as well be one of the many porcelain dolls that the earl had given Evelyn when she was a mere slip of a girl.

"Promise me . . . you'll see her . . . well taken care of."

"I give you my word that she shall have all she deserves."

For some reason which she could not fathom, a shiver coursed quickly up her spine. Geoffrey Litton, presently Viscount Litton, had never been cruel to her, but then neither had he ever been kind. He had, for the most part, simply ignored her. She thought it sad that they knew so little of each other, especially as now they would have only each other for comfort.

The earl nodded once, before giving her a weak smile, his eyes no longer glittering with the pride

and joy that they usually did when he gazed on her. They simply appeared incredibly weary. "You're as beautiful . . . as your mother."

Tears prickled, threatened to roll down her cheeks. "You'll see her soon. She's waiting for you, you know?"

"It's the only thing . . . makes leaving you not quite so painful—to see her again." His gaze wandered to the canopy above his bed as his smile softened and a distant look came into his violet eyes, eyes she'd inherited. "Ah, how she did make me laugh. That's the secret to love, Evelyn. Laughter. Remember that."

With his words, he seemed to have regained his strength, and she considered that perhaps the physician had been wrong, that his leaving would not come tonight. Still, she couldn't chance not letting him know how much he meant to her. Had always meant to her. He would have been within his rights to pretend she didn't exist. Instead he had made her to feel like a treasured princess. "I shall remember every word you've ever spoken, every smile you ever gave me, every laugh we shared, everything about you. I love you so much, Papa."

His tired gaze settled back on her. "You were always the light of my life."

"As you were mine."

Then the light was gone. One second it was there, the next it was simply gone.

"Father?" She pressed her lips to his hand, allowed the tears she'd been holding at bay so as not to upset him to silently scald her cheeks. Her chest felt as though a massive rock was pressing down on it.

"Go to your chambers, Evelyn."

Snapping up her head, she twisted around and stared at Geoffrey. He'd not moved a muscle. He appeared no different. It was as though nothing at all had happened. As though death had not made a visit, as though everything in their lives had not suddenly changed for the worse. The clock on the mantel continued to tick. Someone should stop it. All clocks needed to be stopped. A house in mourning did not have ticking clocks. Suddenly, irrationally, it became very important to her that the blasted clocks cease their infernal ticking.

"Go to your chambers," he repeated in a flat emotionless voice, "and wait there until I come for you."

"I thought to help prepare him." To wash him, to dress him in his finest clothes, to comb his hair, to give him the dignity in death that his illness had stolen from him during the final days of his life.

"The servants will see to it."

"Then I would at least like another mo—"

"No."

"Geoffrey—"

"It's Wortham now, and you will do as I command. Go to your room willingly, or I shall drag you there."

She wanted to ask why he was being unkind, what she'd done to garner his lack of sympathy during this devastating moment, but she knew the answer. She'd been born.

She gazed at her father, so pale, so small, so fragile. His hand was lax in hers. She slipped hers from his, stood, and studied his quiet frail features. He hardly looked like himself. She did hope her mother would recognize him.

"Evelyn, you are testing my patience."

With only the tiniest bit of rebellion, she delayed her parting, determined to have the few seconds she so desired. She combed her fingers through her father's snowy white hair, then leaned over and pressed a kiss to the wrinkles that had begun to mar his forehead of late. "Good-bye, Father. Be at peace."

I doubt that I shall ever be, now that you are gone. You were my safe harbor, and suddenly I feel as though I am cast out to sea, adrift.

Without looking at her half brother, she slowly wandered from the room. She'd never felt so lonely, so sad, so wretchedly alone.

A week passed. She'd discovered rather quickly that leaving her bedchamber was not an option. He'd locked the blasted door.

Evelyn didn't shout, cry, scream, pound her fists on the thick wood, or kick against it as she wanted. She maintained her dignity. She simply sat and waited, gazing out the window onto the glorious garden that continued to flourish. Should it not be draped in black? It seemed disrespectful for it to remain so brightly colored, but then she supposed it was simply demonstrating that the world carried on. Tears dried, hearts healed. Things would never again be as they were, but that didn't mean that all wouldn't be good.

Geoffrey had promised that he would see she was taken care of. She was not overly concerned, as promises were not to be broken, especially the ones made to someone who was dying. In spite of the fact that he did not seem to favor her in the least, he would provide for her.

But surely he didn't intend to do it by holding her prisoner for the remainder of her life. Perhaps he simply wanted to spare her from seeing him grieve. He was such a proud man, so reserved. Much like his mother, he never revealed how he felt about anything.

Her lady's maid, Hazel, brought her meals, but spoke sparingly. She informed Evelyn that the earl had been laid to rest. Evelyn wished that the earl's son had allowed her to see him one more time. What would it have hurt?

But she forgave him his inconsideration because she knew how difficult it must be for him to bury his father, take on the mantle of earl, and find himself charged with her welfare as well as that of the estates. Besides, he'd really done her an immense favor with his inconsideration as she was forced, for comfort's sake, to rely on her memories of her father while he was alive, rather than holding the image of him in stillness within a casket. He would always remain vivid and vibrant in her mind. Tossing her in the air, laughing boisterously, wrapping his larger hand around her smaller one. Kneeling before her shortly after her mother died, and assuring her that everything would be all right. She had loved him more at that moment than she thought it possible to love anyone.

It was early afternoon, on the seventh day, when she heard a key turn in the lock. Too soon for tea. She rose from her pink velvet chair at the window as the door opened, and Geoffrey strode into the room dominated by pink frills and lace.

Unlike her, he did not appear to have lost weight as he mourned. His gray eyes were not shadowed by grief. His blond hair was combed back, every strand in place. His black jacket, waistcoat, and trousers were pressed. His white shirt and cravat pristine. Only the black armband signaled that he had lost a family member.

He bore so little resemblance to his father. He took after his mother. She had been a cold woman who had done little more than look at Evelyn as though she wished she would fade into nothing. When in her ladyship's presence, Evelyn often wished she could make herself do exactly that: disappear.

"I'm having a few friends over this evening." He marched to her armoire, opened the door, and began riffling through her gowns as though he owned them. "I shall expect you to entertain them."

"We're in mourning," she reminded him, abhorred by the notion of his going about as though this was not a house that had suffered a recent loss.

He pulled out a gown of lush purple silk and held it up for his inspection. She wanted to snatch it from him. He couldn't just come in here and start pawing through her things. Even if he was now the earl. "This should do nicely."

He tossed it negligently onto the bed before making his way toward the door. "Be ready at nine."

Aghast at his callousness, she drew back her shoulders and said as forcefully as possible, "Geoffrey, I'm not entertaining."

He came to an abrupt halt, but he did not look over at her. Rather he kept his gaze focused on the hallway. "I've told you before. I'm Wortham now. Don't make that mistake again."

"I don't understand why you're behaving so—"

"So *what*?" He spun around then and she saw the fury darkening his eyes, the hard set of his jawline. It took everything within her not to step back, not to give any indication that he frightened her. "You are his bastard. He brought you into this home, right beneath my mother's nose, and flaunted the fact that he did not love her, but loved another woman. Do you think she died so young because of illness? No, she died of a broken heart. You are a constant reminder to me of all that she suffered. All I suffered. He didn't love me either. Not once did he ever say that he loved me. Yet he poured those words over you as thick as honey."

Her heart twisting for his pain, she took a step toward him before she recognized by his glower that her touch would only serve to worsen matters between them. Therefore, she filled her voice with all the empathy she could muster. "I'm so incredibly sorry for any hurt that you've suffered because of thoughtlessness."

"I don't want your apologies or sympathies. I gave him my word that I would see you well cared for. The first step in that endeavor is to introduce you to some lords. Tonight. So please make yourself presentable. Be charming. Flirtatious. Let them see that you are made of stern stuff, even when grieving. Convince them that you would be a satisfactory companion."

"You intend to see me married off so quickly, even though I am in mourning? It's not proper."

"Proper? Dear girl, believe me, you are considered anything but proper. They will overlook the impropriety. Now then, be a good sport about it. If not for me, then for Father. If he can look down from above, he will be most pleased to know you shall never want for anything."

With that, he strutted from the room and slammed the door in his wake. Hearing the grating of the key in the lock, she sank back into her chair. Her chest ached, her throat so thick with tears that she thought she might suffocate. She had lived such a blessed life, spoiled and pampered. She knew not all by-blows were fortunate enough to be treated as warmly and kindly as she'd been by her father.

She supposed she couldn't blame Geoffrey—she couldn't bring herself to think of him as Wortham, not yet. That name belonged with her father—for wanting to be rid of the burden of caring for her. He would be searching for his own wife soon. Best to see his father's daughter well situated first and out of the household. She suspected once she left here, she would rarely see him—if at all.

He was right, of course. She wasn't exactly proper. She hadn't had a coming out, a Season, and certainly not a presentation to the queen. She'd never attended any balls, although she'd often fantasized about doing so and capturing some handsome lord's fancy. But she'd not been saddened by her lack of a social life, because her father had always had a way of making her forget exactly what she was.

Geoffrey now carried the weight of her nonexistent place in Society on his shoulders. At least he wasn't striving to foist her off on some common man—a merchant or a tradesman or even a servant. He was seeking to find her a lord to marry. He was attempting to secure for her what her father had failed to accomplish: a place in Society.

That he was doing it so abruptly and soon . . . well, she would be grateful that he was doing it at all. She didn't think she would be able to carry off being flirtatious this evening, but she could be charming.

In memory of her father, of his great love for her, she would assist Geoffrey as much as possible in securing herself a fine husband.

Chapter 2

The invitation came because of a debt owed. Owed to him. All debts were owed to him, while he owed no man anything. Not his friendship, not his loyalty, not his kindness. And certainly not his hard-earned coin.

But the Earl of Wortham, a man of little *worth,* Rafe Easton thought snidely, did owe him a good deal of coin, which was the reason that he was allowed into the earl's magnificent library. He wondered briefly how long it would be before it was stripped of all the former owner's prized possessions. He had left his son with little, and what remained had been quickly gambled away in Rafe's club.

The man wanted his credit extended, and so for tonight he pretended a friendship with the Rakehell Club's owner.

Drinking fine Scotch that the earl could scarce afford, Rafe lounged insolently in a chair near the fireplace while the other lords mingled about, chuckled, chatted, and downed far too much liquor. They were a randy lot. He could sense their eagerness and anticipation hovering thickly about the room.

The young earl had a sister, although he didn't recognize her as such. No, more precisely, she was his father's daughter, born on the wrong side of the blanket. But on his father's deathbed, he'd given his word that he would see to her care, and that was what tonight's gathering was about.

Finding someone willing to see to her care.

Wortham swore she was a virgin, and that knowledge had some of the lords salivating, while others had sent their excuses. Rafe didn't give a whit one way or the other. He did not bother with mistresses. They tended to cling, to desire baubles, to lead a man down a merry path, only to eventually grow weary of the bed in which they slept and seek another.

He didn't do anything that even reeked of permanence because anything that hinted at forever could be snatched away, could leave him, *would* leave him. Even his gaming establishment—he took no pride in it. It was simply a means to coins in his pockets. It could be taken away and he could walk from it without looking back, without a measure of regret. He had nothing in his life that meant anything at all to him, that would cause him the least hurt if he should lose it. His emotions ran on a perfected even keel, and he liked it that way. Every decision he made was based on cold calculations.

He was here tonight to watch these lords make fools of themselves as they vied for the lady's attention, to measure their weaknesses, and to discover means of exploiting them.

He'd heard that his brothers had been invited. That was a waste of ink on paper. They were both married and so disgustingly devoted to their wives that he couldn't see either of them straying, not even an inch. But then what did he truly know about his siblings?

They'd finally returned to England two years later than they'd promised. Tristan a few months earlier than Sebastian. Rafe's man had been waiting and ensured they made their way to the gaming hell. Rafe had greeted their arrival with little more than a glass of whiskey. He'd provided them with rooms and food until they'd secured Sebastian's place as duke. He'd seen little of them since.

His choice. They invited him to join them: for dinners, country visits, and Christmas. He declined. He didn't need them cluttering his life. He liked things exactly as they were. He was his own man, responsible to no one beyond himself.

From somewhere down a hallway, a clock began to chime the hour of nine. Conversations ceased. The lords stilled, their gazes riveted on the door. Sipping his Scotch, Rafe watched through half-lowered lids as the door opened. He caught sight of a purple hem and then—

He nearly choked on the golden liquid, as he fought not to give any reaction at all.

He suddenly had an acute understanding of why Adam was so quick to fall from grace when confronted with the temptation that was Eve. Wortham's sister was the most exquisite creature Rafe had ever seen. Her hair, a shade that rivaled the sun in brilliance, was piled up to reveal a long graceful neck that sloped down to alabaster shoulders that begged for a man's lips to make their home there. She was neither short nor tall, but somewhere roughly in the middle. He wasn't exactly certain where her head might land against his body. The curve of his shoulder perhaps. She was not particularly voluptuous, but she contained an elegance that drew the eye and spoke of still waters that could very well drown a man if he were of a mind to go exploring within their depths.

Which he wasn't. He was content to appreciate the surface. It told him all he needed—all he desired—to know.

Glancing around, she appeared confused, her smile uncertain, until Wortham eventually crossed the room to stand beside her without looking as though he was with her. Two people could hardly appear more different. Wortham stood stiff as a poker while she was composed, but emitted a softness. She would be the sort to touch, hold, and comfort. Rafe almost shuddered with the realization.

"Gentlemen, Miss Evelyn Chambers."

She dipped elegantly into a flawless curtsy. "My lords."

He'd expected her voice to be sweet, to match her smile, but it was smoky, rich, the song of decadence and wickedness. He imagined that voice in a lower pitch, whispering of naughty pleasures, curling around his ear, traveling through his blood. He imagined deep throaty laughter and sultry eyes, lost to heated passion.

"Visit with the gentlemen," Wortham ordered.

Again she gave the impression of one confused, but then she straightened her lovely shoulders and began making her way from one man to the next, a butterfly trying to determine upon which petal to light—which would be sturdy enough to support her in the manner to which she was accustomed.

He caught glimpses of her face as she worked the

crowd of a dozen men. A shy smile here, a bolder one there. Furrowed brow when a gentleman rested a hand on her shoulder or arm. Fluttering eyelashes as she expertly glided beyond reach without offending. He wasn't quite certain she understood the rules of the game she was playing. Could she be that innocent?

Her mother had been the earl's mistress. Surely she knew what her mother's role in his life had been—to warm his bed, to bring him pleasure, to keep him satisfied.

Sometimes she seemed to have confidence, to know exactly what she was doing. Other times she seemed baffled by the conversation. Still, it was as though she were ticking off a list, speaking to each man for only a moment or two, before moving on. Never returning to a man once they were acquainted.

Come to me, he thought. *Come to me.* Then he shoved the wayward thoughts aside. What did he care if she didn't notice him? He was accustomed to living in the shadows, to not being seen. The gossamer depths offered protection equal to the strongest armor. No one bothered him there unless he desired it.

He didn't desire her, yet he couldn't deny that he wondered what her skin might feel like against the tips of his fingers. Soft. Silky. Warm. It had been so very long since he'd been warm. Even the fire by which he sat now couldn't thaw his frigid core. He liked it that way, preferred it.

Nothing touched him, nothing bothered him. Nothing mattered.

She matters.

No, she didn't. She was an earl's by-blow, on the

verge of becoming some man's ornament. A very graceful ornament to be sure. An extremely lovely one. But she would be relegated to the same importance as a work of art: to be looked upon, to be touched, to bring pleasure when pleasure was sought.

She glanced around, appearing to be lost within a room that should have been familiar to her. Then her gaze fell on him, and his body tightened with such swiftness that for a heartbeat he felt light-headed, dizzy. He should look away, tell her with an averted glance that she was nothing to him, that he had no interest in her, and yet he seemed incapable of doing anything other than watching as she hesitantly strolled toward him.

Finally, she was standing before him, her small gloved hands folded tightly in front of her. With her this near to him, he could see clearly now that her eyes were the most beautiful blue. No, more than blue. Violet. He'd never seen the like. He imagined them smoldering with heated passion, darkening, gazing at him in wonder as he delivered pleasure such as she'd never experienced. An easy task if she had indeed never known a man's touch.

But just as he had no use for mistresses, so he had none for virgins. He had not been innocent in a good long while. He had no interest in innocence. It was a weakness, a condition to be exploited, a quick path to ruin. It held no appeal.

She held no appeal.

He rethought the words in an attempt to convince himself of their truth. But as her eyes bore into his, he was left with the realization that she was not only innocent, but very, very dangerous. A silly thought.

He could destroy her with a look, a word, a caustic laugh. And in destroying her, the tiny bit of soul that remained to him would wither and die.

It was an unsettling realization, one he didn't much like.

He watched her delicate throat work as she swallowed, her bosom rise with the intake of a long breath as though she were shoring up her courage.

"I don't believe we've spoken," she finally said.

"No."

"May I inquire regarding your name? The other gentlemen were kind enough to introduce themselves."

"But then I am not kind."

Two tiny pleats appeared between her brows. "Why would you say something of that nature?"

"Because I *am* honest, at least."

"But surely you have a name. Is it a secret? You steal children from their beds? Rumpelstiltskin perhaps? I would be hard-pressed to see you as Prince Charming."

Fairy tales. She'd been brought up on fairy tales, and she seemed to have no awareness that she was wading through a nest of ogres.

"Come. It can't be that horrible of a name. I'd like to call you something."

He considered suggesting Beelzebub, something to unsettle her, send her scurrying away, but for reasons he couldn't fathom, he simply said, "Rafe."

"Rafe," she repeated in her smoky voice, and a fierce longing fissured through him with an almost painful prickling. "Is that your title?"

"No."

"Are you titled?"

Perhaps she wasn't as innocent as he'd surmised. She wanted to ensure that she was well cared for, was going to be particular about whose bed she warmed. He supposed he couldn't hold that against her. She was on the hunt for a man to please, one who would serve as her protector. She had a right to be particular.

"No," he finally answered.

"I see you're a man of few words." She gnawed on her lower lip, which served to plump it up and darken its red hue. He wondered how often she'd been kissed. Had she ever let a man press his mouth to hers? Had a man ever touched her skin, trailed his fingers along her high cheekbones, folded his rough hand around her neck, and brought her in close? "What are your interests?"

"None that would amuse you."

"You might be surprised."

"I doubt it. I'm a rather good judge of character."

"A quick judge it would seem. I'm left with the impression that you don't think very highly of me."

He slid his gaze over her, admiring the curves, the dips, and swells. He couldn't deny that she was a fine piece, but she would require a certain . . . gentleness and care, neither of which was in his repertoire of behavior. "I've not yet decided."

"Unfortunately, I have, I'm afraid. I don't believe we'd be well suited. I hope you won't take offense."

"I would have to give a care what you thought to be offended. I don't."

She opened her mouth—

"Evelyn, you're done here," Wortham said as he grabbed her arm and began madly ushering her toward the door.

Almost tripping over her small feet encased in satin slippers, she appeared to be attempting to shake off the earl. She was gazing over her bared shoulder at Rafe as though she was determined to have the final word, but she was no match for Wortham's strength as they both disappeared through the open doorway. It was some minutes before Wortham returned. Rafe was surprised Miss Chambers didn't barge in behind him. No doubt he'd dissuaded her, convinced her to lay low so as not to discourage any of the lords from having an interest in her.

"All right, gentlemen," Wortham said, rubbing his hands together. "Does anyone wish to bid on her?"

So that was how he was going to handle the matter, Rafe mused. He'd wondered. He didn't know why the manner in which Wortham was proceeding caused a chill in his bones. The girl meant nothing to him. It might prove interesting to see what sort of value the other lords placed on her. Especially if he could determine a way to use that knowledge to his advantage.

"I say, Wortham," Lord Ekroth sneered, "I'll give you five hundred quid for her, but I've a mind to examine her first and ensure she is a virgin as you claim."

A round of raucous laughter accompanied the ribald suggestion. Rafe suspected those who laughed the loudest were striving to cover the fact that they weren't quite comfortable with the direction in which the evening was going.

"By all means, each of you may examine her," Wortham said callously as though he were offering little more than a mare for purchase. "Then I shall entertain further bids."

"Excellent. I'll go first, shall I?" Ekroth and Wortham headed for the door.

Rafe envisioned Ekroth's pudgy sausage-like fingers traveling over her silky thighs, ripping at her undergarments, shoving into—

"I'm taking her." Rafe could hardly countenance the words that burst from his mouth with such authority that Ekroth and Wortham stumbled in their tracks, while the other lords gaped at him. Obviously, he'd imbibed a bit more than he'd thought, but it didn't matter now. The challenge had been spoken, and he never recanted his statements.

Standing, he tugged on his black brocade waistcoat that suddenly felt far too tight. "If any of you touch her, I shall separate from you the particular part that touched her. Wortham has assured us that she is pure. I don't want her soiled by your sweaty hands or anything else. Have I made myself clear?"

"But you were only here to watch, to ascertain—" Wortham cut off his sentence and stepped nearer, lowering his voice, "—to ascertain my ability to cover my debt."

"When have I ever confided my plans in you?"

"Then you'll pay me the five hundred quid that Ekroth was willing to pony up?"

"I'll allow you to continue to breathe. We'll call it even, shall we?"

"But the terms of this meeting were that she would go to the highest bidder."

"What value do you place on your life? Do you think anyone here can match it?" He waited a heartbeat. "I thought not."

He downed what remained of his Scotch before striding to the desk, lords leaping out of his way.

If he were not a stranger to laughter, he might have at least chuckled at their antics. He found a scrap of paper, dipped a pen in the inkwell, and scratched out the address of his residence. Placing a blotter on it to keep it in place, he turned and headed toward the door. "My address. Have her there at four tomorrow. Good evening, gentlemen. As always, it's been a pleasure to be in such esteemed company."

He was in his carriage, traveling through the London streets, before it resonated within him exactly what he'd done.

"Good God," he muttered, even though no one was about to hear. What the devil had he been thinking? Obviously, he hadn't.

He glared out the window at the fog-shrouded night. His taking her had nothing to do with the fact that she was in effect being abandoned, because she wasn't. She was being given to someone to care for her. She wouldn't go hungry, she wouldn't be smacked about, she wouldn't have to work until her fingers bled and the small of her back ached so hideously that she feared she might never be able to straighten. She would lie in silk on beds and fainting couches, and wait for a man to part her thighs. She would eat chocolates and plump her lips. She would run her tongue around those lips, and gaze at her benefactor through half-lowered lids.

And he was her benefactor. Damnation.

He should have allowed Ekroth to have her. His fingers weren't all that pudgy. He could call on him in the morning, barter, let him take her.

But then he'd appear to be a man who didn't know his own mind.

So he was stuck with her. For a time anyway.

Perhaps it wouldn't be so awful. She'd never had a man. He could guide her toward pleasing him in the manner he required. She would have no other experience, so she would know nothing different, and therefore, she would not be disappointed.

The possibilities began to have merit. He didn't have to care about her. He wouldn't care about her.

But he could damn well make use of her.

Chapter 3

Evelyn had never been quick to temper. But Geoffrey was testing her patience beyond all measure. In spite of her protests, he'd dragged her up the stairs and locked her in her bedchamber again. She'd wanted to tell that Rafe fellow that he was impossibly rude. Why would he say such a horrid thing? Why would he deliberately attempt to make her feel as though she was nothing?

Sitting at the window, she gazed out on the garden and wondered if the gentlemen were still at the residence. She contemplated tearing off strips of her sheets and fashioning a rope so she could climb out the window. She would march into the library, confront Rafe, and . . . say what exactly?

That he was the most refreshingly honest man there?

That was the thing of it. The other gents had been so . . . oddly behaving. Of course, having never attended any sort of formal—or informal for that matter—affair where lords were attempting to impress a lady, she wasn't quite certain how they should

behave, but she'd thought they'd be more compli-
mentary, more flirtatious, would seek to engage her
mind. Instead, it seemed as though they expected her
to compliment *them*, to shower them with praises, to
make them feel good about themselves.

All except Rafe. It was as though he couldn't be
bothered with her at all. Perhaps he wasn't there
looking for a wife. He'd certainly made no effort
to approach her. Maybe he was simply Geoffrey's
friend, and he'd been in attendance for some other
reason.

But if that were the case, why had she felt his
gaze on her from the moment she'd walked into the
room? It had unsettled her, knowing he was watching as she introduced herself to one man and then
another. Was he judging her, considering her, intrigued by her?

She couldn't tell. What she did know was that he
was the handsomest devil she'd ever clapped eyes
on. His hair, black as midnight, was unfashionably
long, but it framed his face and made his pale blue
eyes more noticeable. They reminded her of a frozen
lake she'd once walked across as a child. The water
that had appeared so blue in summer had seemed
faded when peered through a shield of ice. Standing
on the frigid banks, she'd shivered, just as she shivered standing before Rafe tonight.

She saw no softness in his features, no gentleness in his manners. She was rather glad she'd not
appealed to him. She didn't want him sending her
flowers or reading her poetry or taking her on walks
through the park.

Although if she was quite honest with herself, she
wasn't certain that she wanted those considerations

from any of the gentlemen she'd met tonight. They'd made her feel as though she were a prized mare they were contemplating purchasing rather than a woman that they wished to woo to the altar.

Perhaps that was how courtship began. She felt so uneducated in that regard. She had not attended a girls' preparatory school, but had been tutored. Her only friends had been her father and a few of the younger maids. She was familiar with so little of the world beyond the walls of the residence. She knew only that her father had taken great pains to protect her from it, even as he'd sought to prepare her for it with various lessons in etiquette and proper comportment. She understood everything in theory, and so little in practice. She didn't want to find fault with him, but she did wish he'd seen her settled before he died.

She suspected Geoffrey would see her married to the first man who offered for her hand, rather than determining if he was the man who would make her the most happy.

But then happiness was relative. Being released from this room would bring a great deal of happiness, even if it involved marriage to a man she barely knew.

With a sigh she set her elbow on the windowsill, her chin on her palm, and tried to run through her mind the faces of all the other gentlemen, but each one morphed into someone with coal black hair and ice-blue eyes.

Late the following afternoon, freed from her lovely prison, Evelyn couldn't recall a single time when she'd ridden in a carriage with Geoffrey. It was odd to have him sitting across from her, staring out the window at the darkening skies. It would no doubt be raining by nightfall. The air felt heavy and damp, as though it were simply waiting to unburden itself. She didn't even know where they were going, although she recognized the area as they'd not yet traveled far from their residence.

When he'd come to her room and commanded she ready herself for a ride, she'd almost told him to go to the devil. He'd left her to languish all night, wondering if any of the gentlemen had hinted at an interest in her. But she'd been too desperate to leave the residence to chance upsetting him by revealing that she was out of sorts with his behavior and lack of regard for her feelings. So she'd simply donned a black walking dress, matching pelisse, and hat. She hated appearing so docile as to give the impression that she was someone upon whom he could wipe his muddy boots, but the truth was she had so few options.

She had no money to speak of. She supposed she could sell the jewelry her father had given her, but she didn't know its value or how far it might take her. She was beginning to realize that her father, bless his soul, had done her a disservice in not preparing her adequately for his departure, in making her dependent upon Geoffrey's kindnesses—of which he appeared to possess so very few.

Wondering how to properly broach the subject of last night's endeavors, she quietly cleared her throat before taking a stab at it. "Were your friends adequately amused last night?"

Geoffrey's jaw tightened, his gray eyes narrowed,

and she suspected he looked frightening to anyone who caught sight of his features as the carriage rolled along. "Yes."

Yes? That was it? She wanted to reach across, pinch his nose, and order him to expand on his answer. She squeezed her hands together. "Did anyone in particular express any sort of interest in me?"

"Rafe Easton. We're off to his residence now."

So his last name was Easton, was it? Not that it meant anything to her. Why had he been so mysterious about it? "Oh?"

Geoffrey looked at her then. Did she actually see regret in his eyes?

"Is he a good friend then?" she asked.

"He's not a friend at all. He owns a gambling establishment. I am in his debt."

"I see." Only she didn't. Marrying a gambling den owner would be far worse than marrying a merchant. As a matter of fact, it would be quite scandalous. She was surprised he was allowed entry into polite circles. "He mentioned that he wasn't titled."

"He's the third son of a duke, although he rarely acknowledges it."

"So he's a lord," she murmured. She supposed that explained his presence the night before.

"He doesn't fancy being addressed as such. You should probably simply call him 'Mr. Easton.' At least until he informs you differently."

It still made no sense. If the man had been resting in a casket, he couldn't have expressed less interest in her than he did last night. So why would he wish to spend more time with her? "It's a bit early to be dining. Will we be going for a walk about the park? Will this be the start of his official wooing of me?"

Geoffrey squinted, blinked, squinted again as though his mind were stuttering along, unable to process the words she'd spoken. He returned his gaze to window. "I doubt he has plans to woo you."

"Then I don't understand why we're going to pay him a call."

"You'll . . . see after things for him."

What a strange turn in the conversation. And then it dawned on her—

"You mean I have been employed to manage his household?"

"I am not certain exactly what your duties will entail, but you will see to his needs."

Why didn't he look at her? Why didn't he meet her gaze? Why was he being so blasted mysterious regarding her purpose? Was he embarrassed that he had found her employment rather than a husband— that his own place in Society had not allowed him to do more for her? She didn't wish him to feel as though he had failed in his promise to her father, but still this was rather odd going.

The carriage turned onto a cobblestone drive. In spite of her best intentions, she leaned over and peered out the window. A grand residence, larger than Geoffrey's, loomed before them. She could not help but be impressed. "He must be incredibly wealthy to live in a place such as this."

"Embarrassingly so."

She heard the resentment then, the anger. Geoffrey had said he owed him. Was she to work for Rafe Easton as a way to pay off her brother's debts? Surely this arrangement would be only temporary, until someone spoke for her. "How long will I work here?"

"As long as he wants you."

The carriage rattled to a stop. A footman opened the door. Geoffrey leapt out as though his seat had suddenly caught fire. The servant handed her down.

"Geoffrey, I'm not quite sure I understand."

"It'll all be explained. Come along." He dashed up the wide sweeping steps.

She contemplated climbing back into the carriage, but if she were being paid for her services, she might have the means to see after herself until she could find a proper husband. She supposed the least she could do was listen to the terms of the arrangement. Lifting her skirts, she walked up the stairs. At the beginning and end of them sat the most hideous stone gargoyles. They seemed to fit their owner. Based upon her limited interaction with him, she couldn't imagine him suffering through cherubs dancing about.

As soon as she reached the top, where Geoffrey waited, a butler opened the door and she glided through, aware of Geoffrey following in her wake. The inside was even more impressive, with frescoed ceilings, exquisite artwork, and statuary standing about. But she saw nothing personal. No portraits. All the paintings were landscapes: stormy seas and dark forests. Everything was arranged perfectly, too perfectly, as though it was all for show.

"Miss Evelyn Chambers to see Mr. Rafe Easton," Geoffrey said. "She's expected."

"Yes, my lord, as I am well aware, but regretfully the master is not yet home. However, I have been instructed to see to Miss Chambers's comforts until he arrives. Miss, if you'll follow me to the parlor?"

She'd taken a mere half-dozen steps when she realized that Geoffrey was not accompanying her.

Turning to face him, she asked, "Geoffrey, are you not coming?"

"No."

"You're leaving me here?"

"Yes."

"But you'll be returning for me?"

"Easton will explain everything." With that, he placed his hat on his head, spun on his heel, and walked out the front door.

When she took a step forward to follow and question his odd behavior further, the butler gently touched her arm. "It'll be all right, miss."

He was not terribly old, somewhere in his thirties, she suspected. He had dark hair and kind brown eyes. His clothing, like everything that surrounded them, was immaculate.

"I fear Geoffrey has told me very little. I understand that I'm to manage the household."

"I have no doubt that all the servants will heed your wishes."

"What is your name?"

"I am known as Laurence." He bowed slightly, extended his hand. "Please allow me to escort you to the parlor."

She gave a brisk nod and followed a half step behind him. "How many servants are there?"

"Twenty-five."

They walked into a room of burgundy and dark paneling. It seemed Rafe Easton was not one for cheery colors. A large globe rested on a pedestal in a far corner. A low fire burned in the hearth. Suddenly chilled, she went to it and extended her gloved palms toward the small dancing flames.

"May I take your cloak?" Laurence asked.

She rubbed her warmed hands up and down her arms. "No, not yet, thank you."

"I shall have tea and biscuits brought."

"Thank you." She turned, wishing she didn't feel so unsettled. "When will Mr. Easton return home?"

"I'm sorry, miss, but that I cannot say."

He left her then, and for reasons she couldn't explain, she wished she was still locked in her bedchamber. It suddenly seemed a far safer, more comforting alternative.

Lord Tristan Easton stood in the open doorway that led into his brother's office at the gambling hell. He couldn't recall ever seeing the door closed. At his desk, his brother poured diligently over his ledgers, his dark head bent in concentration, just as he'd been the first time that Tristan had seen him after twelve long years of separation. Rafe's giant of a man had been waiting at the abbey ruins and he'd brought Tristan here, to this very doorway.

His grip tightening on the large package he held, Tristan shifted his gaze to the shelves on the far wall where Rafe kept his assemblage of assorted globes. He'd once told Tristan he collected them because they gave him hope of there being a place better than where he was. Tristan was saddened to see that his brother had acquired a new one. After Rafe had helped him right a wrong he'd done to Anne before she became his wife—when he had no expectation of her ever becoming his wife—he had thought they might be on their way to closing this rift between them. But it seemed his hope was as pointless as Rafe's.

"I hear you've taken a mistress."

Rafe jerked up his head, his eyes—the same crystal blue as Tristan's—hard, his mouth set in a thin line. "I've not seen you in months and that's how you greet me?"

Tristan almost blurted that turnabout was fair play. After not seeing Tristan in twelve years, Rafe had merely reached back, grabbed a tumbler, poured whiskey in it, and set it at the edge of the desk. His face had held no expression, his eyes had been as calm as the sea before a storm. There had been no surprise, no rising from his seat, no embrace. His first words? *Sebastian has yet to show.*

"I would have thought you'd learned by now that I believe in getting to the point," Tristan said, giving his brother what he knew was a devilish smile that would only serve to irritate him. "So who is she?"

Rafe grabbed two tumblers and a bottle of whiskey. He began to pour as Tristan ambled over and took a chair, then pushed the full tumbler toward him. "I don't see that it's any of your concern."

Tristan lifted the glass, inhaled the fumes, and took a small sip. His brother did have damned good taste in whiskey. "Is she pretty?"

Rafe narrowed his eyes. "Thinking of taking her when I'm done with her?"

Tristan belted out a laugh. "God, no. Anne damn near kills me with her desire for me. I could hardly keep another lady satisfied." He relished another sip. "Besides Anne is everything to me. When you have everything, you neither need—nor want—anything more."

"Spoken like a poor besotted fool."

"You don't believe in love?"

Leaning back in his chair, Rafe took a good long swallow.

Not going to answer, Tristan thought. But then he hadn't really expected him to. He knew Rafe had yet to forgive him and Sebastian for leaving him behind. They'd had no choice. Separation had been the best chance of ensuring at least one of them survived to manhood in order to reclaim the dukedom.

"Don't suppose I can blame you. I didn't believe in it either, not until Anne graced my life."

"Do take your leave before you begin spouting poetry. I have no stomach for it."

Tristan disliked that Rafe was becoming more difficult and more of a recluse—at least where he and Sebastian were concerned. He accepted none of their invitations, but he wasn't yet ready to give up on him.

"You know," Tristan began, eager to change the subject, "most fellows would at least inquire as to what a man was holding if he walked into a room carrying a large box."

Rafe shifted his gaze over. "I would have to care to ask. I don't. It's your box."

"Actually, it's not." Tristan set it in the center of the desk. "It's yours. Well, not the box really. But what's inside. Although you're more than welcome to keep the box."

He didn't know why he was rambling on stupidly. He wasn't anxious regarding what Rafe might think of his offering. He'd battled the sea, tempests, pirates, and sharks. He had no worries here. Still he watched as Rafe eyed the package as though he thought it might attack him.

"What do you mean it's mine?"

Tristan wondered once again, as he often did,

what sort of life his brother had led since the night they escaped Pembrook. None of them ever talked about their years apart. Sebastian had left half his face on some godforsaken battlefield in the Crimea. Tristan bore the scars of a lash that had flayed his back. He suspected, had always suspected, that Rafe bore scars as well, but that they ran much deeper than the skin, and he had little doubt that made them much harder to heal. "It's a gift."

"Why?"

"No reason in particular." He knew he should have said *because you're my brother and I love you*, but the words were as difficult for him to speak as he suspected they would be for Rafe to hear.

Rafe set his tumbler aside and pulled the present nearer. He removed the lid from the box, tipped it cautiously toward him—

Jerked his gaze up to Tristan, who squirmed, feeling a bit self-conscious. "I know it's not perfect. I carved it during the two years I was at sea, after Sebastian again had his title."

Slowly Rafe stood, reached in, and withdrew the wooden globe attached to a stand in such a way that his brother could spin the world as he pleased.

"Although I'm not so nimble with a brush, I thought about painting the land masses green and the ocean blue—"

"I like it plain." Rafe was trailing his fingers over every indention and relief, studying them as though they were of great importance.

"Do you? Like it, I mean?" Tristan asked.

Rafe nodded. "I didn't know you carved."

There's a lot you don't about me, Brother, and I suspect even more that I don't know about you.

"One gets bored on a ship. Unlike working here, in a gambling den."

"It gets boring, looking at ledgers and such all the time."

Tristan grinned. "What do you do when you get bored?"

Rafe looked at him as though he'd asked if he could fly. "I continue working. Boredom is not an excuse not to work."

"Do you ever go sailing?"

Rafe returned his attention to the sphere. "No."

"I've started a business of designing yachts, having them built. The first, I just finished, is mine of course, but I thought the second could be yours."

"I have no need of a boat."

Tristan fought not to clench his jaw. A yacht was not a *boat*. Especially the ones he was designing. By God, the luxury built into his own vessel was appalling. "You might be surprised. The sea can bring calm to the soul."

"If one has a soul, but still it's not something on which I wish to waste my hard-earned coin."

"I wasn't going to have you pay for it. It would be another gift. God knows I don't need the money, and I enjoy designing something that so closely resembles a ship."

Rafe studied him. "What are you doing here, Tristan? We're not friends, acquaintances, or even brothers, really."

Tristan shoved himself to his feet. "We *are* brothers."

"Why? Because we came from the same mother, had the same father? Being a brother is more than that."

"Why will you not let go of the past? It's tearing Sebastian up that you've yet to forgive him for leaving you at that blasted workhouse. Do you really think he had a choice?"

"We all have choices."

Tristan knew this discourse was pointless. Rafe was beyond listening. Tristan took some comfort in the fact that Rafe hadn't flung the globe across the room. He sighed. "I'm going to christen my new yacht in two weeks. I thought you might like to go sailing with us."

"I shall be too busy."

"Enjoying your new mistress?"

"She's none of your concern."

"Bring her."

Rafe's brow furrowed. "You're joking. She's the by-blow of an earl. I'm sure her presence would offend the sensibilities of your wife."

"If you think that, then you don't know my Anne very well. And I wish you did. She's a remarkable woman. You'd like her. Anyway—" Tristan set his empty glass on the desk. "—the invitation is open should you change your mind. Two weeks from Friday, be at Easton House at eleven."

"Sebastian's invited as well."

"Of course he is. He, his wife, and his heir."

"My schedule is full."

"Your loss."

Tristan turned on his heel and marched from the room. He wouldn't give up on Rafe, not yet.

Rafe had never expected to be glad of a visit from his brother, but for a few moments he'd been spared thoughts of Evelyn Chambers. She'd been haunting him all day, and he knew that as of twenty-two minutes ago—if Wortham were punctual at all—she had arrived at his residence. Laurence would show her to her bedchamber, introduce her to the maid—Lila—who would see to dressing her, fixing her hair, and whatever else ladies' maids did. Servants would assist in unpacking her things. They would see that she was settled and comfortable as she waited for his arrival.

Spinning the globe, he suddenly wished he was somewhere else—someone else. If his brothers ever learned the truth about the sort of man he truly was, they would want little to do with him. He shoved back the rancid thoughts.

Mick, his main man, stepped through the doorway. His slender physique hid a well-toned body that often gave Rafe a good going over when they sparred in the boxing room hidden away downstairs.

"I thought you should know that Lord Wortham has settled his accounts."

Rafe fought not to look surprised. "Where did he get the money I wonder?"

"I can ask around."

"No need. It's not important." The reckless way he played at cards, he'd be back in Rafe's debt soon enough. "Has Ekroth made an appearance?"

"About an hour ago."

As a general rule, Rafe didn't allow cheating in his establishment. Not from his customers and certainly not by those hired to oversee the games. But sometimes exceptions were needed. "See that the games don't favor him tonight."

Mick arched a thick dark brow. While he might

have been hoping for an explanation, he knew better than to insist upon one. "I'll arrange it."

"You may also inform him that he is barred from spending any time with the girls."

"He'll take his business to another club if he's not satisfied here."

"I'll ensure no other club will have him."

After Mick left, Rafe set the globe on the corner of his desk and gave it one final spin. He'd not relegate it to a shelf. He wasn't quite certain how he felt about it. Grateful, but not quite comfortable with the gratitude.

It was nearly four hours later before he left his office and made his way to the back stairs at the rear entry of the building. He'd never had a guest at his residence, few knew where he lived. He didn't know why he had given Wortham his address instead of simply sending for the girl. For some reason, the night before, his ability to think coherently had left him completely for a time. Thank goodness it had returned.

He climbed into his carriage. He was not avoiding what awaited him at the residence. He simply had a great many items at the club that required his attention: bills, deliveries, cheaters.

It was dark, a light drizzle falling, by the time his carriage clattered to a stop in front of the monstrosity that he owned. He didn't know why he'd bothered to take it for payment of a debt owed, except that at the time he'd wanted it and he'd felt that a man of his wealth should own a residence. Even if he seldom spent any time here.

He preferred his apartments at the club. They weren't as quiet. The walls thrummed with the ac-

LORD OF WICKED INTENTIONS   43

tivity that took place on the floors below. He could be in a room alone, but not feel lonely. Here, the servants were so blasted quiet that they might as well be ghosts.

Like some ominous harbinger of ill winds, lightning flashed as he stepped out of his carriage and strode up the steps. It was chilly tonight, but he would have a woman to warm him. Already he was reconsidering his misgivings about this arrangement. She would come in handy after all.

Before Rafe arrived at the landing, Laurence was opening the door. Sometimes he thought the butler did little else except stand at the ready to open the door for him. He handed over his hat and coat. He began tugging off his gloves. He wanted to go to his room and remove everything but that would have to wait. "Is she here?"

"Yes, sir. Waiting in the parlor, but I'm not sure . . ."

His voice trailed off. Rafe stilled and gave him a hard glare. "But what, man? Spill it."

"I'm not quite sure she understands her purpose in being here. She seems to believe she is to manage the household."

Rafe shrugged. "She can do that if she wishes."

Laurence scowled. "I am given to understand that she believes it is to be her only duty."

Rafe swore harshly. Wortham, the stupid little sod, wouldn't explain things, would he? It was his lack of guts that characterized his losing at the tables. What did she think last night was about?

"She brought her things, did she not?" he asked, slapping his gloves into Laurence's waiting palm.

"No, sir, I fear she brought nothing save herself.

Lord Wortham made quite the hasty retreat. It left her a bit flummoxed."

"No matter. I'm sure she knows why she's here." And that he would be providing everything she required. He headed for the parlor.

"What time will you be dining, sir?" Laurence asked.

"Give us half an hour." That should be all the time he needed to set things right with her, to lay out her duties, his expectations.

Opening the doors to the parlor, he strode in, staggered to a stop. She was in profile, standing by the window, gazing out on the rain, looking as forlorn as the weather. She turned slightly at his entry. She was wearing black, a hideous color. It made her look ill. He wanted to see her in blue, a deep blue that would enrich the shade of her eyes. It appeared she was baring very little skin, that her dress buttoned up to her chin, but it was impossible to be certain because she was wearing a cloak.

"I see Laurence didn't adequately see to your comfort, didn't bother to take your wrap."

She brought it more closely about her. "No, he offered, but I've been chilled, even with the fire."

"Scotch should help there." He went to a table in the corner and poured a generous amount into two glasses, concentrating on his actions because for some damned reason his hands were shaking. It had nothing to do with the notion that he would soon be touching her, stripping her clothes from her body, ordering her to lie on his bed—

Later, that would all come later. He'd been fighting all day not to think about it. Lust. It was all lust, animalistic, barbaric needs that a man possessed, that consumed him. He shoved aside all thoughts of what secrets might be hidden from him beneath her clothing, picked up the glasses, and crossed over to where she waited beside a chair near the fireplace. At least she'd moved away from the window.

He could not mistake the wariness in her eyes as she took the glass he extended toward her. She was right to fear him. He wouldn't abuse her, he would never willingly hurt her, but he had little doubt that eventually he would cause her pain. Even the women he paid for his pleasures suffered some because he gave them nothing beyond the physical, and women, bless them, seemed to need more than that.

He simply didn't have it to give. Which was the reason that he'd avoided feminine encounters for a good long while now, because he couldn't stand the disappointment that always seem to punctuate his leaving. He did not hold, he did not cuddle, he did not allow them to hold him.

Taking a chair by the fire, he indicated the one opposite him. Slowly, gracefully, she sank into it. Both her gloved hands circled the glass. Such small hands. He imagined them circling him. He'd barely know they were there. Perhaps—

He forced away the thoughts because his body was reacting and the last thing he wanted to do was frighten her. He sipped slowly on his Scotch while she studied the fire. Finally she brought her gaze to bear on him.

"Geoffrey—" she began.

"Geoffrey?"

She gave him a small smile. "Lord Wortham. I'm afraid I've not quite accepted that my father is gone. Anyway, he said I was here to manage your household, but quite honestly it appears to be well managed already, so I'm not quite certain what I could contribute."

"I'm certain you can contribute quite a bit." He savored another long sip. "What were his exact words?"

Her delicate brow furrowed, she looked back at the fire. "That I was to see to your needs."

"*My* needs," he emphasized. "Not those of my residence."

Her gaze swung back to him, the furrow deeper. "I'm not sure I understand. Do you not have a valet to see to your needs?"

"I have a valet."

"Then I can't see that I would have much to do."

She was too innocent, far too innocent for the likes of him. He should send her back to her brother, but unfortunately for Evelyn, he had decided that he wanted her. He wasn't quite certain when it struck him so forcefully that he did. Perhaps when he opened the parlor door and saw her waiting there. Waiting for him. When had anyone ever been waiting for him?

"What did you think was the purpose of last night's . . . entertainment?"

"To secure me a husband."

He nearly choked on his Scotch. The very last thing he would ever contemplate was marriage. If she knew him at all, she'd know that. But therein resided part of the problem: she didn't know him, and he preferred to keep it that way.

"I was most surprised," she continued, "to find myself arriving at your residence when I was left with the distinct impression that you found me hardly worth a thought."

Hardly worth a thought? How he wished that was true. He'd been unable to stop thinking about her since he'd first seen her. She invaded his dreams, inhabited his thoughts, occupied his mind.

"To be quite honest," she carried on, "I suspect I will not be here long before someone offers for me. I doubt it is worth it to either of us for me to be in your employ."

While he didn't relish the thought of shattering her naiveté, he didn't much like this dancing about either. Best to just get it said. "You're not to be in my employ. You're to be in my bed."

She blinked, blinked, blinked. Opened her mouth, closed it. Blinked again. "I beg your pardon?"

"Your brother was seeking to find a man to take you as his mistress, not as his wife."

She shook her head slightly as though she were almost frozen in disbelief, as though working out what he'd said was taking all her energy. "That can't be. He promised Father that he would see that I was well taken care of."

"Mistresses are often treated better than wives. At least I have no wife on the side, which is more than I can say for a few of the gents who were in attendance last night. As my mistress—"

"You can't possibly want me to be your mistress. You don't even like me."

"I don't have to like you to bed you. Truth be told, it's better that there be no sentiment between us."

She came to her feet in such a rush he was surprised she didn't stumble. However, she did drop her glass. It fell to the carpet, spilling his extremely expensive Scotch.

"You're wrong about last night," she announced,

her eyes welling with tears. "About Geoffrey's intentions. He wouldn't have brought me here if he'd known what you assumed, what you planned. He promised. He promised Father . . ."

Then she fairly raced from the parlor. He heard the front door slam, could almost feel the walls trembling with the impact. Swearing harshly, he tossed back his Scotch.

He supposed he could have handled that a bit better.

Chapter 4

Evelyn ran. And ran. And ran.

Her legs churning, her chest aching as she fought for breath, the tears blurring her vision. The rain pelted her, seeped through her clothing. Somewhere along the way she lost her hat, her pins. Her hair tumbled down around her shoulders, absorbed the wetness, weighted her down.

It was lies. It was all lies. Geoffrey wouldn't be so cruel. In spite of the fact that he had never given her leave to think that he liked her overly much, he was innocent in this debacle. He'd not known what that horrid Rafe Easton had assumed, had planned. When she explained to Geoffrey what the man said, what he expected of her, Geoffrey would call him out. He would insist upon pistols at dawn. In honor of his father, he would protect her reputation. He would not allow her to be completely ruined.

Although he had never given her cause to believe that he would champion her, he was enough of a gentleman that he would not stand by while some cur took advantage of her.

All she had to do was get home. Thank God it wasn't that far. She remembered the way. One street, and then another and another, and she would be there. The few people she passed stared at her as though she were a mad woman. But it was Rafe Easton who should be carted off to Bedlam.

Geoffrey would apologize for the misunderstanding, and then he would make everything all right. Years from now they might even laugh about it. When she was married and had children and a husband who loved her. He *would* love her. Maybe not at first, but in time.

What Rafe Easton proposed was so hideously horrible. How could he be so cold, so harsh, so uncaring? How could he think she would welcome his touch?

She wouldn't. She would die first. She would scrub floors, she would . . . she would—

She couldn't think, but it didn't matter. Geoffrey had made a promise. He would keep it. He would see that she was well cared for.

Drenched to the bone, she turned up the long drive. The gaslights were lit along the path, guiding her. Her entire body was aching now. It was becoming harder and harder to pull air into her lungs. She stumbled, landed hard on her knees and hands, jarring her bones, rattling her teeth. Pushing herself to her feet, she staggered on and trudged up the steps.

She expected the door to open. A footman was always standing there to open it, but then they weren't expecting her, were they? Grabbing the handle, she pressed it and pushed on the door—

It didn't open. It was locked!

She banged the knocker. Over and over. Harder

and harder, with the crash echoing around her. No one came.

"Geoffrey!" Oh, God, surely he wasn't out of sorts about *that*. "Wortham! Wortham! My lord!"

She heard a click, the door opened slightly, and the butler peered out, barring her entrance.

"Manson, thank God. Let me in."

"I'm sorry, miss. His lordship has forbidden me to allow you entry into the residence."

"What? No, you're mistaken. He wouldn't—"

"I'm sorry, miss. But we have our orders."

His expression as bland as unseasoned food, he closed the door. When she tried to open it, she found it once again locked.

She banged, kicked, screamed until she was hoarse. Her knuckles were bruised, her toes ached. Dejected, horrified, terrified, she unceremoniously crumpled onto the landing, all her strength zapped from her. The rain pelted her unmercifully, but surely he would eventually open the door if she just stayed here long enough. He had misunderstood his orders. Surely.

She became vaguely aware of someone crouching before her. She lifted her face. Through the haze of her hot tears, she saw Rafe Easton. His black hair was plastered to his head. He appeared to be as wet as she.

"Come with me, Evelyn," he said, his voice calm, even.

She shook her head. "They won't let me in. There's been a mistake. He wouldn't do this to me. He promised Father. He promised."

"You're soaked through. You're going to catch your death."

"I don't care. He can't be cruel enough to cast me

out like this." Why was she even talking to this callous man? He didn't care about her. He only wanted use of her person. Her stomach roiled. She thought she might be ill. Shudders wracked her body. She didn't know if it was the cold or the sobbing that almost had her convulsing. She'd never felt more dejected in her life.

A fog of grief snaked through her, settled around her. She was shaking so badly, her teeth chattering, that she could barely think. Where could she go? She had no friends, no one who would offer her sanctuary until she could determine how to resolve this dilemma. She had no funds. Everything was in her bedchamber. What had he said when he'd come for her? "We're going for a ride." And she'd been so grateful that she'd not questioned him further. Now she had nothing, no one. She wrapped her arms around her middle, trying to contain the pain.

"Damnation," Rafe Easton growled.

There it was: more proof that he thought so little of her that he would use profanity in her presence. He considered her a guttersnipe. A wanton. Someone unloved. And now she was. She wanted to curl into a ball—

His arms came around her. She was vaguely aware of his holding her against his broad chest, lifting her as though she were little more than a sodden pillow.

She had a strong urge to protest, to let loose a scream that would wake the dead, but all she seemed capable of doing was sagging against him. She wished he were kind. She wished he had spoken for her, that he sought marriage, that his intentions toward her were not so wicked.

He wanted to ruin her, to take away her chance at happiness, a proper husband, and children. He wanted to dally with her, soil her reputation, then toss her aside. Wasn't that what men did with mistresses? Her father might have even done that with her mother had she not died so young.

Her entire life she'd known exactly what her mother was: good enough to bed, but not to wed. Her father had always made her feel as though she were somehow better than that. Her brother made her realize that she wasn't.

Beneath the roar of the pounding rain, she became aware of Rafe Easton's muttering, "One more step, one more step. Almost there."

She didn't know why he was urging her on like that. She wasn't the one taking the steps. Perhaps he thought his words would be reassuring, but she knew what would happen when they were finally *there*.

He would take the one thing left to her that mattered, that was of any value. She couldn't allow that to happen, yet neither could she simply wander the streets. She would find the strength to fight him. She would find a way to barter, to bargain, to regain some pride and dignity.

She was vaguely aware of his climbing steps, of a door opening, of light washing over her.

"Good God," a voice she recognized as belonging to Laurence said.

"I want a hot bath prepared for her. Rouse the maids to see to her care. She's like ice. Hasn't moved a muscle since I picked her up."

Hadn't she? She'd thought she'd been protesting, but perhaps it was all in her mind. She was conscious of him going up stairs. The wide sweeping ones that had so impressed her when she'd first stepped into the residence, before she'd known exactly why she was here.

She could hear other footsteps rushing by them, those of a servant perhaps. They reached the landing. The click of a door opening. He swept through the entry, his progress muffled by thick carpets before he set her on the bed. He grabbed her wrists, unlocking her arms from about his neck. When had she clutched him so? Why had she?

He stepped away without a tender touch, a word of kindness, a whisper of reassurance.

"Get her warm," he barked. "Find her something dry to wear."

Then she became aware of gentle hands urging her to care, to ignore the fact that the remainder of her life would be spent within the bowels of hell.

Hell and damnation!

As soon as Rafe was in his bedchamber with the door slammed behind him, he began tearing at his sopping clothes before they suffocated him. Buttons went flying, brocade and linen ripped. He was fighting to draw in breath, had been ever since he'd made the ghastly decision to cart the woman back to his residence. He knew it was a mistake the moment she wound her arms about his neck and clung tenaciously to him.

He couldn't very well drop her at that point, no matter how desperately he'd wanted to be rid of her cloying hold. So he'd urged himself on with a mantra: *One more step, one more step. Almost there.*

Knowing all the while that he was lying to himself, that he had a good distance to travel. Why the devil hadn't he taken the time to have his carriage brought round? He'd been almost certain where she was going. Instead, like a blundering idiot, he rushed out into the rain after her to ensure that she reached her destination without being accosted.

He'd wanted Wortham, the worthless blackguard, to tell her exactly what his plans for her had entailed, that he had purposely set out to ruin her, to turn her into what her mother had been. Rafe had intended to lead her back to his residence with the assurance that he would forgive her unconscionable behavior, but he would not tolerate it in the future.

Instead, he had watched as she'd banged on the locked door, had heard her exchange words with the butler when he finally appeared to her summoning, had seen her crumple into a shattered heap.

Damn Wortham for being the coward he was!

With his clothes finally strewn about his bedchamber, Rafe marched to the fireplace, set match to kindling. When the fire was finally going properly, he stood. The flames licked at the air, but the warmth barely reached him as, legs spread, head bowed, he grabbed the mantel and stared into the writhing precipice. Finally able to breathe again, he gasped in great draughts of air.

Anger swirled through him. Anger at Wortham for his insipid handling of the situation; anger at the woman for looking at him in abject despair. Images of his own caterwauling at the age of ten had rushed through his mind. It was disconcerting to feel completely helpless, to not know how to right things for her. He'd wanted to shout at her to stop blubbering, buck up, be strong, stop being a *baby*—

He pressed his head to the hard edge of the marble mantel, welcomed it digging into his brow. Was that the reason that Tristan had lashed out at him, called him a baby all those years ago? Because he'd felt helpless, maybe even terrified himself, had feared that he was on the verge of tears as well?

It had unnerved Rafe to see her reduced to a lifeless heap, especially when the evening before she'd been daring enough to inform him that they didn't suit. As though he wanted them to be well matched, as though it mattered to him.

He should have left her on her brother's front stoop, but by God, she was his now. He had claimed her, whether she liked it or not. Whether *he* liked it or not. He had put a great deal of effort into building a reputation as being someone who was dangerous, who got his way at all costs, who was not to be trifled with. What would happen to his reputation if word got out that he'd allowed her to escape him?

The aristocracy's fondness for gossip was astounding. That he and his brothers were often the center of the gossip was beyond the pale. Why anyone cared what they did was outside his comprehension, but care they apparently did. Ever since the brothers disappeared on a cold wintry night in the year of our Lord, 1844. Rumors abounded regarding what had truly happened to them. When they returned to Society, the gossip worsened. They were viewed as barbaric, just because Rafe had held a pistol on a servant who had refused to announce their arrival at their uncle's ball, and Sebastian had very nearly choked their uncle to death when he'd first clapped eyes on him. It had not helped matters that several months later their uncle died mysteriously.

So it was with certainty that Rafe knew a good many people were well aware he had taken on a mistress. Which meant, by God, that she would serve as his mistress. Whether she wanted to or not. Whether *he* wanted her to or not.

He was not a man known to waver when it came to decision making. He set his course, traveled it, and Lord have mercy on anyone who sought to block his path or prevent him from reaching his destination.

He didn't know how long he stared into the fire arguing with himself, convincing himself that the arrangement regarding Evelyn—a name that didn't roll easily off his tongue—had been made, and that he would follow it through, regardless of cost, when the rap on the door brought his scathing diatribe up short.

"Yes?"

"The lady has finished her bath, sir. She is presently drinking tea." Laurence spoke through the door. Every servant knew that no one was admitted into Rafe's chamber. No one. They thought him eccentric. If they knew the truth, they would believe him mad.

"Very well, that's all," he replied before shoving himself away from the mantel. He had a blinding headache. He combed his fingers through his unruly hair. It was dry, so he must have been waiting for her to be ready to receive him for some time now. When he was lost in thought, minutes could slip away without him realizing it. He didn't allow clocks to govern his life. He did what he needed to do when he needed to do it.

Now he needed to speak with her, make sure they came to an understanding regarding this situation.

He didn't bother to ring for his valet. No need to dress formally. Trousers, loose shirt was about all he'd need.

He glanced at the door that separated his room from hers. He wouldn't use it tonight. For her sake he would enter through the hallway, but after their discussion, she would understand that no barrier had the power to keep him from her.

The room was warm, the fire crackling, and yet sitting in front of the fireplace, Evelyn felt as though she were carved from ice. Her own clothes a sodden mess, she wore one of the maids' nightdress and dressing gown. She had soaked in a tub of hot water for what had seemed like hours. Her hair was washed and braided. She curled one bare foot over the other. She should strive to determine what she was to do about this unfortunate circumstance, but she seemed incapable of managing little more than staring at the yellow and orange flames.

Geoffrey's strange behavior in the carriage, his cryptic words—she was quite amazed that he had been able to meet and hold her gaze at least once. If she sought to destroy the very fabric of his being, she'd not be able to face him.

A mistress, not a wife. That was what she was to become, what he expected for her future, what he sought to give her. Not love, not a family, not a place in Society. It was not to be tolerated.

What were her options? Literally, all she possessed were the clothes on her back. Well, the clothes she'd been wearing on her back earlier. The clothes she now wore were not hers. She wore them only because of the kindness of servants.

She heard the door click open, without a knock, without warning. She might have assumed it was a servant, but the very air in the room seemed to shift and change as though a mighty gale had suddenly swept through it. The fine hairs on the nape of her neck and arms rose. The footsteps were almost silent, and yet she knew to whom they belonged. Breathing became a chore, but she forced herself to do it because she refused to swoon. It was bad enough that he had witnessed her unconscionably weak and falling apart.

She concentrated on the fire. But even it seemed to have grown smaller in submission.

"Here, you'll find this will warm you more efficiently than tea."

A large hand holding a thick tumbler came into her field of vision, very nearly kissing her nose. Long, thick, powerful fingers. She imagined they could wrap easily around her neck and choke the life from her body. Inhaling, she recognized the scent.

"Do you think Scotch is the remedy for all ills?"

"You'd be surprised by the answers you can find in the bottom of a bottle. Take it."

It was not an invitation, so much as a command. As much as she didn't want to obey, she knew she needed to pick her battles. Keeping her hands steady, she set the teacup and saucer on the small table beside the chair, then took the offered glass.

She'd ignored the contents earlier in the evening when he'd given her a tumbler. This time she took a small sip. It burned, but he was right. It also warmed as it went down, the heat spreading out to her fingertips.

He moved away, placed himself by the fireplace, rested his forearm on the mantel. She wondered if he was as cold as she after their journey in the rain. His hair was much curlier now, as though he'd not bothered to tame it. His white shirt was loosely fitting, buttoned only to midchest. Black trousers fit snugly over his legs. His boots were polished to a shine, and she thought he would see his reflection in them if he glanced down.

Instead, his gaze was focused intently on her. He, too, was holding a tumbler, and when she lifted hers to take another sip, he did the same, his eyes never straying from her. He was a large man. She had felt his corded muscles beneath her fingers, pressed against her body, as he'd carried her here. He'd never paused his rapid steps. He'd never struggled for breath. He'd seemed unbothered by the pelting rain.

She suspected he was a man very much accustomed to having his way. And he wanted his way with her.

"I'll fight you, you know," she said. "I shall kick and scream and claw out your eyes."

She thought she saw a twinkle of humor light those very eyes that would feel the scrape of her fingernails, but it happened so quickly she couldn't be sure. His throat worked as he took another long slow swallow of his Scotch. She couldn't recall ever seeing so much of a man exposed: his neck, the narrowing V of skin down his chest. She saw strength there, potency that Geoffrey didn't possess. Neither had her father. Before his illness, his form had been robust but it had not exuded power. Food, rather than anything of an exertive nature, had shaped him. Rafe Easton obviously did not lie around all day doing nothing more than ordering servants about.

"I'm not in the habit of forcing women, Evelyn," he finally said. "But I am pragmatic. If you do not become my mistress, what recourse is open to you?"

Ah, there was the rub and well he knew it. She fought not to let her shoulders slump with her despair. "He didn't let me take anything, not even the jewelry my father gave me. I could have sold it—"

"And how far do you think you would have gotten with it?"

She shook her head, hating to admit, "I don't even know where I would have sold it."

"With me," he said, "you will have a roof over your head, food in your belly, a clothing allowance to rival the queen's, as well as jewelry, trinkets, baubles. You will never want for anything that is within my power to purchase."

"But I must give you my body."

Another long swallow of Scotch, a slow nod, a half closing of his eyes in acknowledgment.

She was suddenly unbearably cold again. She took a big gulp of her drink, but it failed to warm her. "I want a husband, a family."

"How do you expect to acquire that? By sitting out on the street in your hideous black gown until someone walks by and thinks, 'By jove, I'd like that lovely for a wife.' How will you eat? Where will you find shelter? Be realistic, Evelyn. You have nothing. You have no one. You have no options."

"I could work for you. Oversee your household as I thought—"

"I have someone who sees to my household. Shall I dismiss her, toss her out on the streets because you don't want to warm my bed?"

She shook her head, wishing she was of a selfish bent, content to think only of herself. "No, you're right. That's not fair either. Perhaps you would be kind enough to allow me to stay here for a few days until I find employment—"

"What skills have you?"

She wanted to blurt out something, anything, but the truth was that she wasn't certain she could even manage a household. She'd never helped with the servants. She knew only that tables were never dusty, fires were always ready to be set, floors were always polished, her clothes were always pressed. She was horrendous at stitchery, her penmanship was not precise, and numbers were not her friend. They never added up the way they should. She could read, very well in fact, but who would hire her to read?

It also seemed she was very good at drinking Scotch. She downed the last of the liquid in the glass and set it aside. With smooth unthreatening movements, he exchanged his glass for hers. Did he have to be so graceful, so masculine, so utterly gorgeous?

"Geoffrey informed me that you own a gambling establishment. Perhaps I could work there."

"The women who do wear very little clothing and spend a good bit of their time sitting on gentlemen's laps. Do you prefer to spread your thighs for many men rather than only one?"

Her mouth opened, her eyes widened. If she were

a true lady, he wouldn't speak to her of such raw, carnal things. But then if she were a true lady, she wouldn't be in this predicament.

Crouching, he added a log to the fire and stirred it. His trousers outlined his muscular thighs and firm buttocks. She imagined guiding her hands over them. Was that what she would do if she was his mistress? Touch him, caress him, tell him how marvelous he was even though at this precise moment she hated him with every breath she took?

She reached for the almost half-full glass of Scotch and tossed back nearly half of it. It fairly scalded her as it traveled through her. But it made her limbs feel as though they were no longer part of her. If she drank enough could she lie beneath him and pretend she wasn't truly there?

"I know what it is, Evelyn, to have no options." He was still stirring the fire, not looking at her. "To think: this cannot be my life. It is not where I was headed, and yet . . . it is where I have arrived. To survive, you learn to make the best of it. It's not easy. It's not what you want, but you can still own it, make it yours."

He unfolded his magnificent form, placed his arm back on the mantel, and studied her with those icy blue eyes. "Your brother sought to humiliate you, to degrade you, to give you a place in Society that is no place at all, where you would not be seen or acknowledged. What better revenge than to become the most infamous courtesan in all of London? I won't hide you away. I'll flaunt you. I'll teach you to manage your money. When our time together comes to an end, as long as the ending is of my choosing, you may have the residence and everything within it. You won't be forced into becoming any other man's mistress. You can select your paramours, be choosy if you wish. Seems a rather fair trade to me."

"Fair? I will be ruined."

"You were ruined the moment you were born."

Her stomach lurched at the truth of his words. Her father had protected her from the gossip and rumors, and in doing so, he'd given her false expectations. She thought she would marry a lord, and now she was discovering she wasn't worthy of a guttersnipe.

Studying this man, she saw no kindness in his features, no compassion, no sympathy. Yet he had come after her, had carried her through the rain. Because he thought he owned her, or was it because as he'd said, he knew what it was to be where she was? But how could that be when he was the third son of a duke?

"I'll have your answer now," he said.

"You won't even allow me the kindness of sleeping on it?"

"I told you last night that I am not kind."

But she could see that he was strong, implacable, confident. If she could learn from him to be the same, perhaps no one would ever be able to take advantage of her again. It made her stomach roil to realize that all the men last night had been contemplating entertaining themselves at her expense. Their lascivious gazes made a great deal more sense. She suspected that one or two of them would have already had her on her back by now.

"If I say no?"

"I'll have the servants return your damp clothes so you are free to take your leave."

And go where? Do what?

"You've only given me the illusion of choice," she said.

This time, she couldn't mistake the appreciation that lit his eyes. "I knew you were a woman of keen intelligence."

"You promise to help me ensure that Geoffrey regrets what he did?"

"I have a talent for making men regret what they've done."

She wasn't quite certain that it was a talent to be boasted about, but she had little doubt that he was a man of his word. He could have taken her already. He could have barged in here and had his way with her. For all her bravado about fighting him, she knew he could conquer her, quite easily if he set his mind to it. That he hadn't already told her a good deal about his character, when it came to women at least.

"I suppose this *arrangement* will begin tonight."

"Not tonight. It's late. You're undoubtedly tired. I'll give you a few days to become accustomed to the notion, to become more comfortable with me. I don't want you dreading what is to happen between us. But make no mistake that if you spend tonight here, you will spend other nights in my bed."

She heard a cold ruthlessness in his voice. A gambling hell owner. A man to whom Geoffrey owed a debt. A man who had sat alone the night before, that all the other lords watched warily from a good distance away.

"Have you a coin?" she asked.

He furrowed his brow. "A coin?"

Her stomach gathering into little knots, she

nodded. "It's something my father taught me, when I had a difficult decision to make, and wasn't quite certain which way to go. I flip a coin."

She thought she saw the barest twitch in his lips. "You're going to allow chance to decide so grave a matter?"

"You should appreciate that—being a gambling house owner."

"Fate is seldom a friend."

"At this moment, it may be the only friend I have. A coin?"

He took a long breath, studied her, looked as though he might comment further, but finally reached into a small pocket at the waist of his trousers, removed a silver coin, and offered it to her.

Taking it, she skimmed her thumb over Victoria's profile, inhaled deeply, tossed it, and let it fall to the carpet. "Heads," she said quietly. "I stay."

He narrowed his eyes. "You're supposed to announce before you flip what you're associating with each side."

"My father taught me that I didn't have to do it like that."

"Not much of a gambler, your father."

She shook her head. He never spoke of gambling. "A fortunate thing, as he gambled on Geoffrey seeing after my welfare. A rather unfortunate wager."

Leaning over, he snatched up the coin and slipped it back into his pocket. "That remains to be seen. You stand to gain a great deal."

"But at an unconscionable cost."

"Still, you agree to the terms?"

As much as she didn't want to, she nodded. She had decided her course, she would see it through.

Stepping forward, standing in front of her, he held out his hand. His large, long-fingered, ungloved hand. She must have somehow managed to swallow a bird because there was intense fluttering just behind her breastbone. "You said you wouldn't bed me tonight." Her voice sounded small, fearful. She hated it.

"I'm not. I'm merely going to help you to your feet."

She placed her hand in his. Hers seemed so tiny, and when he closed his fingers around it, she was incredibly aware that he could easily break her with very little effort. She was surprised by the coarseness of his flesh. These were not the hands of a gentleman. He drew her up, then expertly moved her arm behind her back, somehow snagging her other wrist until both were held within his firm grasp. With his free hand, he cradled her face, stroked her cheek with his thumb.

"You will learn to do things as I like them done," he said softly, in a voice that promised pleasures. His eyes captured and held hers, and she thought that even if he wasn't holding her, she'd not have been able to break away. "I have particular needs. The first is that you are to never wrap your arms around me."

"Why not?" she whispered.

"Because it's what I require." He lowered his lips to hers, and she realized that if he hadn't manacled her wrists that her arms would have twined about him of their own accord, simply to ensure that she remained standing when her knees grew so weak.

His tongue toyed with her mouth, painting it, outlining it as though he wanted to be intimately familiar with it. Then he was urging her lips apart and delving into the depths of her mouth with an urgency that astounded her. He might not like *her*, but it was becoming plain enough rather quickly that he was quite fond of her mouth. He explored every inch of it, every nook, every cranny, every hidden corner. When she dared to meet the thrust of his tongue with a thrust of her own, he groaned low and pressed her against his broad chest. Through the thin linen of his shirt and the maid's well-worn nightly attire, she could feel the thudding of his heart, sense its increase in tempo.

When she tried to break free of his hold, his hand clamped harder on her wrists, just shy of causing pain. She relaxed her shoulders, relaxed her arms. Why couldn't she hold him? She'd held him in the rain as he'd carried her home. Had she hurt him? Was she stronger than she thought? Had it been unpleasant?

She didn't know what to make of his rule, his demand, and she wondered if he would have many. She suspected he would. She was agreeing to allow him to do whatever he wanted with her, and yet if his kiss were any indication of the pleasures she might find with him, she thought that perhaps he was right—it would not be such an awful trade.

The kiss deepened, grew hungrier. Her sighs were now mingling with his groans. She felt guilty for enjoying the way he played with her mouth. She should be ashamed, but perhaps she was more like her mother than she realized. Her mother had not required marriage in order to lay down with the earl. And here she was coming to understand that her regrets regarding this arrangement might not outweigh the benefits.

Breaking away, he stared down at her, his icy blue eyes not quite so icy, a heat there that astounded her.

"I think you'll do rather nicely," he said. Releasing his hold, he walked from the room before she could gather her wits about her to reply.

She sank back into the chair, brought her legs up, and wrapped her arms tightly around them. His comment left her empty. Suddenly her brother wasn't the only one she wanted to have regrets regarding his treatment of her.

She wanted Rafe Easton to regret having taken her as a mistress instead of a wife.

Chapter 5

Kissing her had been a colossal error in judgment. Her lips were like silk. Her mouth, smoky with his Scotch, had tasted particularly inviting. Her sighs were as low and throaty as her voice. The sounds had sent desire shooting through him.

As a general rule he didn't misjudge his actions, but from the moment she had walked into his life, he'd been having a time of it when it came to rational decisions.

He'd claimed her for his mistress.

He'd trotted after her into the rain like a misbegotten fool.

He'd carried her home, knowing the torment that would entail.

He'd promised to give her time instead of sinking into her molten heat tonight as he desperately wanted.

He'd kissed her.

And now he was heading to Wortham's.

At least this time he'd had the good sense to have the carriage brought round. He tugged on his waistcoat. He hated that he had to display himself fully dressed in order to properly throw around his weight. Clothing always made him feel as though he was suffocating. He could trace his aversion back to his experiences living at the workhouse.

His arrival at Wortham's stopped him from having to travel that particular path of memory. It was not pleasant, and he'd not thought of it in years. He'd shoved it into the back corner of his mind, just as he shoved everything upon which he did not wish to dwell. No good would come from taking it out and examining it further—other than to stir up the resentment he felt toward his brothers for abandoning him.

He stepped out of the carriage, bolted up the steps, and slammed the knocker, once, twice, thrice. The butler responded with a slowness that would have had him relieved of his post if he were in Rafe's employ. It didn't matter that it was half past midnight.

As soon as the door opened a crack, he barged past the butler. Eve should have done the same. She shouldn't have allowed him to block her way. She'd been too polite by half. She might not carry the title of lady, but by God she was one. Too good for the likes of him, but that didn't make him want her any less.

"Where's Wortham?" he snapped.

"He's not at ho—"

Rafe swung around and pinned the man with a hard-edged glare that he had honed to perfection during the years he had worked as a debt collector for someone on the shady side of the law. He knew it spoke of punishment and retribution. It put the fear of God into large brawny men.

The slender butler did little more than stammer, "The library, sir."

He'd been there last night, so he had no trouble finding it. He didn't bother to soften the stamping of his large feet. He wanted Wortham to be well aware that hell was arriving.

Rafe burst through the door. Wortham bolted to his feet. He'd been behind his desk, studying something. Ledgers perhaps, it didn't matter.

"Changed your mind about her already, have you?" Wortham asked with a sneer. "I knew she wouldn't measure up."

"Your father gave her jewelry. I want it."

Wortham looked as though Rafe had punched him. "That was not part of the bargain."

"You dropped her off at my residence with nothing more than the clothes upon her back."

"Because she's yours to see after now. Everything else my father purchased. That makes it mine."

"Not the jewelry. Hand it over and you'll continue to breathe."

"I'm growing quite weary of that threat. I don't owe you anymore. So I see no need—"

Rafe rounded the desk with remarkable speed, wrapped his hand around Wortham's throat, and shoved him against the wall. "You see no need for what? To heed my words?"

Anticipating that he might have to resort to a show of force, he'd not worn gloves. He knew precisely where to press his thumb to cut off air, to cause pain. Wortham's eyes bulged. He gasped. He dug his fingers into Rafe's wrist. He'd have marks there tomorrow, dammit. If he wasn't striving to make a point, he'd simply snap the man's neck. But

Wortham didn't deserve death, and of all Rafe's sins through the years, killing a man who didn't deserve it was not one of them.

Wortham gagged. Nodded.

Rafe loosened his hold. "You had some wisdom to impart?"

"Sold it," Wortham rasped.

So that was how the weasel had paid off his debt earlier that evening. Releasing him, Rafe stepped away to avoid the possibility of encountering a mess, as it appeared Wortham was on the verge of tasting his dinner for a second time. "To whom?"

Wortham rubbed his neck, shook his head. "Don't know. Some fence."

"Describe him."

"Small, black hair, black teeth. Has a kinship with some rodent I imagine. Met me at a tavern."

Rafe arched a brow. "The tavern have a name?"

"The Golden Lion."

"Good." He considered ending Wortham's membership at his club, but he'd rather have the man where he could see him. Besides, it made it easier to torment him, and he was a man in need of tormenting. "Should I discover that there is anything else here that your sister longs to have, rest assured that I shall return to claim it."

"But I'm selling things."

"Do not sell anything else of hers until you've heard from me."

"That was not part of the arrangement."

"I'm restructuring the arrangement."

Wortham's face turned a mottled red. "You have no right to order me about. I am an earl."

"Take care with your words, Wortham, or next

time, I might not release you until you're shaking hands with the devil."

On that note, Rafe spun on his heel and strode from the room. He was quite familiar with the Golden Lion, although in his opinion, it would have been more aptly named the Tarnished Scrawny Cat. Its clientele were not the best that London had to offer. Because of that, Rafe would be quite at home there as he searched for the man who had the jewelry he sought.

Evelyn awoke feeling as though a heavy thunderstorm had taken up residence in her skull. That she had slept at all was a miracle. She tried not to think about the bargain she'd struck. With the pale morning sunlight easing in through the window, she considered dressing, then quietly leaving, seeking sanctuary somewhere else. Surely some shelter existed for women in her circumstance, but even as she had the thought, she knew he wouldn't let her easily go.

He would find her. He would make her pay for staying in his residence through the night. She had no doubt of that. He was a man of his word. She was beginning to understand why the other lords had avoided him as though he harbored the plague. If he dealt with them as he dealt with her, he would have few friends. No one liked a bully.

Rolling over, she came up short at the sight of a young maid standing there. The girl curtsied.

"Good morning, miss. I'm Lila. I've brought your clothes, freshly pressed. The master was hoping you would join him for breakfast."

As though he'd suddenly walked into the room,

all the air left and she could find none to draw into her lungs. "He's still here?"

"Yes, miss."

Silly thing to be disconcerted over. He lived here. She would see him. She just hadn't thought she'd see him until tonight. "All right then."

She would pretend this was what she wanted. She would make the best of it. Someday, she would make two men regret their taking advantage of her circumstance for their own gain.

She was quite surprised by the maid's expertise at readying her, and she didn't want to contemplate that she wasn't the first mistress in this residence. But then what did it matter how many he'd had? She didn't want to consider it, to know anything about him. She would simply do what she had to do, until she was in a position that she could do what she wanted.

After she was dressed, her hair pinned up, she followed Lila through the hallways, even more impressed with each room they passed. The residence and all it contained had to be worth a massive fortune.

A tall liveried footman stood before a set of closed double doors. As they neared, he opened one.

Lila smiled. "Enjoy your breakfast, miss."

As the girl hurried away, Evelyn couldn't help but think that enjoying anything today was not on her schedule. She would endure because she had no choice. But she would certainly not enjoy.

Taking a long deep breath, she straightened her shoulders before striding into the dining room. Rafe Easton was sitting at one end of a long table, reading a newspaper. He set it aside and stood.

"Good morning, Eve. I trust you slept well."

How could she have forgotten how incredibly handsome he was? He was properly dressed, with waistcoat, jacket, and cravat. His black hair was tamed. She missed the curls. They softened him a bit. But this morning nothing about him appeared soft.

"It's Evelyn," she informed him, trying to regain her bearings, trying to convince herself that she could handle the monstrously unappealing task that lay before her.

"Evelyn doesn't suit me."

"It doesn't suit you?"

"I will be providing you with a home, food, clothing, jewelry, servants . . . everything about you will suit me. You will spend your day planning for my arrival. You will amuse me with discussion, entertain me with pianoforte. You shall read to me."

What price would she pay if she left this instance, simply turned on her heel and walked out of the room, walked out the front door?

He was studying her intently, and she had a feeling that he knew exactly what she was thinking. Perhaps he was right that a change in name was in order. Evelyn was a far different woman than the one she would become. Evelyn had been loved. She doubted Eve ever would be—certainly not by this man who seemed incapable of harboring any emotion at all.

With a wave of his hand, he indicated the sideboard. "Tell Andrew what you'd like and he'll prepare your plate."

She turned toward the footman. Of course he would be tall and handsome as well. The most desired footmen were tall and in good form. It seemed Rafe Easton only went with the best. She wandered over to the sideboard. She selected poached egg, toast, ham. Not an abundance, but then she very much doubted she'd be able to eat. All this wonderful food would go to waste.

Andrew carried her plate over to the foot of the table. Setting it down, he pulled out her chair. She sat, watched as Rafe did the same, picked up his newspaper, and shook it. She reached for her napkin, froze.

Resting on the white linen was the sapphire encrusted necklace and matching bracelet that her father had given her for her nineteenth birthday. Gingerly she touched them, hardly daring to believe they were truly there.

She fought not to weep. Lifting her gaze to Rafe, she caught him watching her before jerking his attention to the paper as though he couldn't be bothered by her reaction. "How did you get these?" she asked.

He didn't look at her. Simply narrowed his eyes as though he was having difficulty making out the letters he was reading. "Paid a call on Wortham last night. If there is anything else you wish to have from his residence, let me know and we shall stop by there on the way to your seamstress this morning." He lowered the paper. "Who is your seamstress, by the way?"

She shook her head. "Her name is Margaret, but she always came to the residence. I don't know where she worked or how to contact her."

He sighed. "I shall have to make inquiries then, regarding where I should take you for your clothing. I want to see you in only the best."

His words hardly registered. She was still too stunned by the jewelry. "I can't believe you did this, went to such bother."

"Did I not explain that you would never lack for anything that was within my power to purchase?"

"You paid Geoffrey for these?"

"No, I paid the little rodent he'd sold them to. I'm relieved to know that he didn't try to swindle me by giving me the incorrect pieces."

"I can't imagine anyone daring to swindle you."

He bent his head to the side slightly in acknowledgment of her words. "It has been a good long while since anyone has tried to get the better of me. Do you read?"

She started at the abrupt change in topic. "Yes."

"Good. You may read to me." He folded the paper, signaled to the footman. The man brought it over, set it beside her fork.

"Why would you want me to read the news aloud?"

"Because I enjoy the sound of your voice."

She released a tiny laugh. "Geoffrey once told me I had a man's voice."

"I believe we've already ascertained that he's an idiot."

Carefully, she eased the jewelry off her napkin, fluffed the linen in the air, and settled it across her lap. "How did you come to own a gambling establishment?"

"What does it matter?"

She toyed with the egg, darted a glance to the footman. Servants were discreet, she suspected his more so than most, but still this was awkward. "It just seems that I should come to know you, to understand you, before . . . that things will be more comfortable between us, that I will be able to more easily determine what you need."

"I'll tell you what I need."

"Everything?"

"Everything."

"Oh, I see." She sliced off a piece of ham. "I enjoy riding."

He looked at her as though she'd said, "Did you notice I have four arms?"

"I thought it might prove helpful if you knew something about me," she offered.

"I know all I need to know."

It was going to be so incredibly sterile, this arrangement between them. She didn't know if she'd be able to stand it. She picked up the paper. "Where shall I begin?"

She hated that her voice quavered, that it threatened to reveal her doubts and her burgeoning regrets.

"Did you have a horse?" he asked, his voice flat, emotionless, as though he couldn't be bothered to care, as though he didn't really desire an answer.

But she provided one anyway. "Yes. A mare. I called her Snowy, because she is so white. She's at the country estate. I don't suppose I shall ever see her now."

"Do you want her?"

She stared at him.

"If you want her, all you have to do is tell me, and I shall obtain her for you."

"I don't want to be further in your debt."

"In our arrangement there is no *depth* of debt. You give me what I require. Whatever items you want, you may have. Do you wish to have the horse?"

She wished to be free of him. In the light of morning, her decision to stay seemed rash. "Geoffrey would never give her up. She's a thoroughbred, incredibly valuable."

"Trust me, Eve, Wortham provides no obstacle to anything you want."

She tiptoed her fingers over the jewels. Was she really contemplating asking for something? Once she started down this road, he would well and truly own her. "There is a portrait of my father, in the study of the London residence. I would rather have it than the horse."

"You shall have both." The chair scraped over the floor as he pushed it back and stood. "We shall delay your reading to me as we've spent what little time I had available with conversation and I must go to my club for a bit. This afternoon we'll see to your wardrobe."

He began heading for the door, came to a stop beside her chair, tugged on his waistcoat as though it had grown too small while he'd eaten. "Last night I told you that you will never want for anything that is within my power to purchase. Do not hesitate to ask me for items that you want. Because I promise I will not hesitate to take what I require of you."

As he strode from the room, those words continued to echo through her head, her heart, her soul.

The table was too blasted long, but even with the great distance separating them, he'd seen the joy light her eyes when her gaze fell on the jewelry. He could only imagine how bright they'd been when she'd first been given them. She'd have not expected them. She seemed not to expect anything.

Mistresses were supposed to be demanding, by God. She should be demanding things of him. She shouldn't make him urge her to accept things; she shouldn't make him want to stop off at a jeweler's to find a set of stones that more accurately resembled her eye color. The sapphires were close, but a shade too blue, a little lacking in violet. Amethyst perhaps. No, that would not have enough blue. Pity he didn't have the power to create stones.

He shook off the thought. What was this mooning about?

His carriage came to a halt in front of Easton House, his oldest brother's residence. After alighting, he marched up the steps. He'd not been here in some time. Still, he knew Keswick and his lady were already in London for the Season that would soon be upon them. The door opened before he could knock.

"Thomas," he said succinctly, addressing the butler.

"Lord Rafe, it has been a while. If I may say, you're looking fit."

"You may say. Is the duchess about? I need a word with her."

"I'll let her know of your arrival."

While he waited, Rafe wandered over to a portrait of Sebastian and Tristan when they were boys. Uncanny how alike they looked, although Tristan did have a bit of the devil in his eye. Their uncle had destroyed most of the family portraits. There were none of Rafe as a boy, none of him with his brothers. It was for the best. No need for reminders of what had been stolen from them.

Hearing the light footsteps, he turned as Mary glided toward him, her red hair piled perfectly on her head, her green eyes dancing, the smile on her face so large that he was amazed her jaw managed to stay hinged. Before he could move away, she'd grabbed his hands, pulled him down, rose up on her toes, and pressed a kiss to his cheek. Were he any other man, he would find her need for closeness charming. As it was he suffered through it because he would not do anything to hurt her.

If not for her, they'd all be dead. She had helped them escape from the tower in which their uncle had imprisoned them. She was two years older than he. He'd never known a braver girl or woman.

Although Eve was certainly showing backbone. He'd not truly expected her to be in his residence that morning. He'd thought she'd try to slip away in the darkness. He'd stayed up all night, sitting in the shadows at the end of the hallway, watching. He still didn't know if he would have let her go or forced her to remain.

"It's so good to see you," Mary said, squeezing his shoulders, his upper arms, his hands as though she were trying to assure herself that he did in fact exist.

It was with a great deal of guilt that he stepped beyond her reach. "I can't stay. I just have a question—"

"I won't answer it if you won't at least sit with me in the parlor for a bit and enjoy some tea."

"I fear I don't have time."

"Suit yourself. It was lovely to see you, Rafe." She spun on her heel and began walking away. He'd forgotten what a stubborn wench she could be.

"One cup," he ground out.

She pivoted back around, her eyes filled with teasing and victory. He remembered when he'd first seen her again, after his brothers had returned. She'd been engaged to someone else. She'd not looked this happy. He supposed Keswick was good for her. He knew he was good *to* her. What man wouldn't be?

"Splendid."

She reached for him again, as though she would entwine her arm around his, but he managed to gracefully sidestep by leading the way into the parlor. This had been his home when he was a boy and the family would come to London. He should have been comfortable in these surroundings. Instead he simply wanted to leave.

"Keswick's not here," she said softly, studying him as they settled into chairs by the fire.

He shrugged. "His whereabouts are of no concern to me. I didn't come to see him."

"I wish you would . . . come to see him, that is."

"Now that Uncle is dead, we have nothing in common, Mary."

"You might be surprised."

"I doubt it."

"You are a stubborn—"

He suspected she was going to say *fool*, but the arrival of the tea cart interrupted her. He watched as she prepared the brew, but it was Eve's fingers that he saw. Small, delicate, arranging things so slowly. He'd wanted to watch her eat. What a silly thing to desire. He considered returning home straightaway, after he was done here, but it would not do to make her think that he was anxious to be with her. Because he wasn't. But he did want to get the clothes situation taken care of, as he abhorred her in black.

Mary extended the cup toward him and he dutifully took it. "I was wondering who sews your clothing."

She peered at him over the rim of her teacup as she sipped. She didn't seem surprised, and he suspected she, too, knew he had taken a mistress. "I frequent Madame Charmaine's on St. James."

"Splendid." That would be easy enough to find. He set aside his untouched tea. "Thank you, Mary."

She looked up at him. "You're not leaving."

"I have much to which I must attend."

"I wasn't asking, Rafe. I was stating that you are not leaving."

"Mary—"

"Tell me about this girl, the one for whom you need a seamstress."

He scowled. "It's hardly appropriate conversation. She's my mistress."

"Would I like her, do you think? We should have you both over for dinner."

"You're mad! This is the home of a duke. You don't bring a mistress in here."

"If she's important to you—"

"She's not."

She puckered her brow into tiny pleats that had to be painful. "Then why make her your mistress?"

Why the bloody hell did she think? She was married. She knew a man had needs.

"I'm not discussing this with you. Have a good day."

Before she could aggravate him further, he

charged from the room. Eve was no one's business save his own. He wanted to keep it that way.

"**I** think this girl might mean something to him," Mary said as she walked through the garden with Keswick later that morning.

"Men do not marry their mistresses."

"I'm not implying he should marry her, but she might be able to reach that part of him that still belongs to Pembrook."

"You do have fanciful thoughts, sweetheart."

She tightened her hold on his arm. She walked on his unscarred side only because he wouldn't be able to see her otherwise. The heavy scars that marred his face did not bother her. They never had—except for revealing that he had suffered greatly. She had loved him as a child. She loved him still. She always would.

"He's still there, you know. The boy he was. It's only that he's lost."

Keswick stopped walking and took her in his arms. "I hope you're correct about this woman, then. Because I know what it is to be lost. And I know what it is to finally come home. You are my home."

He kissed her then, deeply and urgently. She would never tire of the passion that swelled up between them. As he lifted her into his arms and began carrying her toward the house, she laughed. It seemed he would never tire of it either.

Chapter 6

Evelyn wandered through the corridors and rooms. Rafe could not possibly have meant that he intended to gift her with this residence. He must have meant that he would purchase a smaller one, maybe even a cottage somewhere. This place had been built to accommodate a large family, someone who entertained often. There were salons with crystal chandeliers, and she imagined the light from the candles flickering over dancers. The library contained numerous sitting areas and walls of books. Chairs and draperies were dark burgundy or hunter green. Everything was exquisite.

No, he could not possibly intend to give her this dwelling.

What truly fascinated her was that every room contained a globe, or a picture of one. She strolled to the window of a small sitting room and gazed out on the luxurious gardens. She could well imagine the lady of the house doing the same thing, finding herself filled with peace and comfort.

Closing her eyes, she fought not to open the

nearby doors, step out, and keep walking through the garden, to the mews. She would have a very fine life here, but the cost to her soul—

She couldn't even imagine the price she would ultimately pay.

Opening her eyes, she set her jaw. She would make certain Geoffrey paid more, in one way or another. She had never considered herself to be one for revenge, but at that moment she despised him. That he would do this. What sort of creature was he? It was difficult to believe they shared the same father.

She suddenly felt overwhelmed with exhaustion.

Turning on her heel, she strolled from the room. The residence was so large that, in spite of the many servants, it felt incredibly empty and lonely. She thought she might go mad with nothing to do except wait for Rafe's arrival. Her stomach clenched, for when he did arrive—

She didn't know how she would manage to give herself to him without making a spectacle of herself, weeping for all she was losing.

She pulled herself up the grand staircase. At the top she turned in the direction of her bedchamber. As she passed a door, she stopped.

It barred entrance to his bedchamber. Last night, she'd heard movement in there as the maids had been undressing her and attempting to warm her quickly. Then it had grown eerily quiet.

Was a globe in that room as well? His bed was there, the bed she would share with him. She wondered what it looked like. Large. Thick sturdy wood. Dark wood. She supposed the canopy would be draped in the burgundy he favored. The room would smell of him. Sandalwood and bergamot. And Scotch. Although that was more taste than fragrance. On his tongue, in her mouth. Licking her lips, she could almost taste that devastating kiss that he'd bestowed upon her after they'd come to terms near midnight.

A tiny shiver swept through her. In that room, in that bed, he would do a good deal more than kiss her. She would be uncomfortable enough with him. She should be familiar with the room, be at ease within it. She reached for the knob—

Strong fingers wrapped around her wrist, pulled her to the side, and she found herself brushing up against Rafe.

"You seem to have lost your way," he said. "Your room is next door."

She swallowed down the lump of fear that had risen in her throat. "I've been touring the residence. I just wanted to see your room."

"You're never to go in there."

Confused, she blinked. Dare she hope that he had changed his mind? "Then how will I get into your bed?"

"I'll come to yours."

No reprieve. Blast him. That knowledge pricked her temper. "But you said I would be in *your* bed."

"It's an expression, although technically your bed is my bed since I own it."

"But you're giving it to me, along with the residence and everything in it. Did I have that correct?"

He narrowed his eyes. "Yes, but not until I'm done with you."

"Then it is to my advantage to displease you."

The smile he gave her was one of a wolf on the

verge of eating its prey. "You do *not* want to displease me."

"You're hurting me."

He glanced at her wrist as though he'd forgotten she possessed one. Slowly he unfurled his fingers. "My apologies. Fetch your wrap. We're going to the dressmaker."

"I see." Dear God, she was taking another irrevocable step. Once he bought her clothes—but what choice did she have? She turned on her heel.

"Eve?"

Stopping, she spun to face him. He was concentrating on tugging his gloves. "As you are now familiar with the house, in which room did you wish Laurence to have your father's portrait hung?"

She could do little more than stare at him. "You have it already?"

He gave her but one brisk nod. He was certainly not one to let moss grow beneath his feet. Compared to him, Geoffrey went through life much like a sloth.

"In my bedchamber, I suppose."

"Do you truly want to see his face when you and I are . . . intimately engaged?"

Her heart nearly dropped to her toes. "Ah, no, you're quite right. The front parlor? No, wait. That little sitting room that looks out over the garden. I should like it there."

He studied her as though he could envision her in that small room. "I shall see that it's done while we're gone. By the by, bring your jewelry."

"Why?"

"Because it would please me for you to do so. Now hurry along. I don't like to be kept waiting."

With that, he spun on his heel and headed down

the stairs. She was tempted to open the door to his bedchamber, simply because he'd said she couldn't. What was he hiding? It was only a room.

She also considered making him wait, but she had yet to discern how volatile his temper might be. For now she hurried into her bedchamber, gathered her jewelry, slipped it into a skirt pocket, and snatched up her wrap. Back in the hallway, she considered escaping down the servants' stairs. Instead, she squared her shoulders and marched to meet the devil.

The skies were overcast. As the carriage rumbled along, Rafe watched the shadows weave in and out, dance over and around her as she gazed out the window. And blast it all if he didn't envy their ability to touch her so lightly. She'd rubbed her wrist— the one he'd held with his powerful grip—a couple of times now, and it was all he could do not to take her hand, peel off her glove, and press a kiss to where he'd felt her pulse thrumming earlier.

He didn't know why he'd reacted as he had. The door to his bedchamber was locked. She'd have not been able to enter anyway. His hold had tightened with the talk about beds and her in them. He imagined her there, sprawled over the sheets, her loosened hair spread out around her. How long was it? The braid she'd worn last night only hinted at its length.

He'd almost laughed when she'd given him the daring look and said that it was to her advantage to displease him. When was the last time he'd laughed? He couldn't recall. He didn't want to be intrigued by her. One moment she seemed vulnerable, and the next she was standing up to him. Displease him, would she? He doubted it very much.

"You don't really intend to give me the residence, do you?" she asked in that raspy voice that seemed a bit rougher since last night.

"I said I would."

She peered over at him. "But it and everything in it must be worth a fortune."

He shrugged as though it hardly mattered, because in truth it didn't. He purchased items because he could, but he took no pleasure in them or the act of obtaining them.

"How can you value it so little?"

"Perhaps the better question is how can I value you so much?" As soon as he heard the words, he wanted to suck them back in. He didn't value her, not at all, but he knew what awaited her with him. Guilt prodded him to give her what he could so she would forgive him for the things he couldn't.

She opened her mouth slightly, pinched her bottom lip between her teeth. "That is a good question. I've not given you any reason to place such a high value on me. So why are you?"

"Mistresses are supposed to take what they're given and not question it."

"Is that the law? Is there a law of mistresses somewhere, a book that solicitors study?"

It seemed the farther they traveled from a bed, the bolder she became. He wondered how she might react if he informed her that he could bed her without a bed, that the plush cushions of his carriage would do just as nicely. And yet, he couldn't bring himself to silence her. She made him want to smile, a real smile, not the wolfish one practiced over the years to imply victory before a battle was even fought.

"Yes, I believe there is."

She angled her chin haughtily, her pert little nose going up ever so slightly. "I should like to see it. I suppose you know all the laws where mistresses are concerned."

"The important ones."

"How many have you had?" she asked.

"Laws?"

She scowled. He suspected she imagined that she looked quite ferocious. Instead, she looked kissable. Utterly and fascinatingly kissable. "Mistresses."

He considered lying. But what would he gain? Nothing. He reserved falsehoods for when they were useful to obtain what he sought. "You shall be my first."

Her eyes widened. "Why me?"

Why her? That was the question, wasn't it? The one he'd asked himself a thousand times since that night in Wortham's study.

"Ekroth wanted you. I don't much care for Ekroth."

"I seem to recall he has jowls and pudgy fingers."

"Quite."

She glanced out the window. "I didn't like the way he looked at me. I didn't like the way any of them looked at me. As though I was beneath them. But you didn't." She looked over at him, gave him a sad smile. "I thought you were incapable of caring any less about me. Yet, here I am with you. What if Lord Berm had spoken up for me?"

"He has rancid breath."

She gnawed on her lower lip, and he thought she did it to stop herself from smiling. It irritated him that she might laugh at him. "Lord Pennleigh?"

"He has too many years on him. He's bound to be wrinkled in places where he shouldn't be wrinkled."

She studied him intently, and he fought not to squirm. Why weren't they at the blasted dressmaker's yet?

"Who would have been acceptable, do you think?" she asked.

Any of the other lords, sweetheart. Even Ekroth, Berm, and Pennleigh, truth be told.

"It hardly matters," he said. "You're with me now."

The carriage came to a stop. *Thank God.*

"And we're at the dressmaker's. Let's see about getting you some proper clothing."

Proper clothing? As though what she was wearing wasn't proper.

But when she stepped into the shop, her irritation with him dimmed. She'd been in shops before, but never a dressmaker's. Two well-dressed ladies were at the counter, obviously making their purchases. Another elegant woman was sitting in a plush chair in a corner studying what appeared to be drawings of patterns.

A large woman bustled toward them. "Sir, how might I be of service?"

Rafe tugged on his waistcoat. "I wish to be attended to by the proprietor."

"I am she. Madame Charmaine."

"I expected a French accent."

She smiled, her teeth straight and white, her lips as red as cherries. "I excel in providing my customers with the unexpected."

Rafe seemed to be taking measure of her. She remembered that he said he was a good judge of character. She wondered what he thought of so bold a creature. "Miss Chambers is in need of a wardrobe. Everything."

Madame Charmaine arched a brow, and Evelyn imagined she was creating a mental list of what *everything* might include, and how profitable this endeavor might be.

"She will require only the finest of materials," Rafe said before walking over to a table burdened with bolts of brightly colored cloth.

Evelyn traipsed after him and whispered, "I'm in mourning. I should wear black."

"You may when I'm not about, but when you are in my presence it will please me to see you in colors."

He selected them: rich blues, purples, crimson. Bold strong colors. She'd always worn pale shades, pastels, so that she blended in, wasn't truly visible. Except for the one purple gown Geoffrey had selected for her to wear. She'd had it made as a dream, something to be worn if she ever attended a ball.

All the while Madame Charmaine slowly raked her gaze over Evelyn, and she knew the moment that the woman deduced exactly what she was to Rafe—or what she would become to him. She thought she might die, that her heart would cease beating, her blood flowing, her lungs drawing in air.

"I want a dozen dresses for her within the week," Rafe said, distracted by his perusal of the fabrics.

"I fear, sir, that my schedule is quite full. You might have better success at another shop."

Rafe stopped riffling through the fabrics and faced her. "My sister by marriage, the Duchess of Keswick, assures me you are the best."

"I am, sir, but—"

"My lord."

"Pardon?"

"Apologies for not introducing myself earlier. Lord Rafe Easton. I don't imagine the Duchess would continue to shop here if I informed her I was turned away."

"It is only that to meet your deadline with my current workload—"

"Yes, I quite understand, but here's the thing: Miss Chambers requires clothing due to an unfortunate circumstance that left her with nothing save the dress she is now wearing." His voice grew lower with each word spoken until Madame Charmaine was leaning toward him in an attempt to properly hear. "A sad state of affairs indeed for a lady to have to go about with only one dress to see her through, wouldn't you agree? What will it cost me to have you open up your schedule for her?"

"My lord, it's quite impossible. I have an incredible number of orders to fulfill—"

"Shall we say double the outrageous amount you were going to charge me anyway?"

The woman glanced at the fabrics, the ceiling, the floor, and Evelyn could see her calculating. "I suppose I could see my way clear to complete an item or two within the week."

"Splendid. I so admire the rare woman who exhibits good sense. I've no doubt that we shall get along famously. I shall want to approve all designs and fabrics."

"An unusual request. Most gentlemen don't care, but I'm sure I can accommodate. I shall need to get some measurements."

"Excellent."

Evelyn had watched the entire encounter with a measure of horror. Did he think the moon and stars revolved around him? That only his wants and needs mattered? What of her other customers?

He turned to her. "I have some things to see to. I'll return for you within the hour. Enjoy your time with Madame Charmaine."

The bell above the door tinkled when he went out. How could it sound so innocent when someone so determined passed beneath it?

"The elusive Rafe Easton. I daresay I'd never expected to cross paths with him," Madame muttered. "However did you manage to find yourself tangled up with one of the lost lords of Pembrook?"

Evelyn turned to her. "The lost lords?"

"Do you live beneath a rock?"

Evelyn fought not to start laughing maniacally. "No, just in a residence, protected by my father, the Earl of Wortham."

"Ahhh." Madame looked at her with sympathy. "I've heard a bit about that. The good news I suppose is that you've landed with a man who will do everything to protect you."

"But he was so insistent that you put everyone else's needs aside and see to mine."

She scoffed. "Negotiations, my dear. I'll charge him triple. He won't know the difference. And you shan't tell him."

"I'm not certain I would try to cheat him."

"Oh, he may bark very loudly, but I don't think he bites women. Not if the way he looked at you is any indication. Now come along to the back room. You'll need to remove your clothing so I can get proper measurements."

"Why did you call them the lost lords?" Evelyn asked as she followed Madame into a small room.

As Madame helped Evelyn out of her clothing, she said, "Now that's a story. When they were lads, they disappeared after their father died. Rumors abounded. Some said they'd fallen ill. Some that they were murdered by gypsies. Some that they were eaten by wolves. Then I suppose it was . . . what, three years ago? Something like that. I remember because Lady Mary—who is now the Duchess of Keswick—had just come to London, and I'd made her a ball gown. Anyway, the lords appeared at the ball. Caused quite the stir."

"Where were they all those years?"

"Keswick was in the army, fought in the Crimea. Ghastly business that. Lord Tristan returned as captain of a ship, so I assume he was on the sea. Lord Rafe was about here somewhere. Not much is known of him. He shuns Society, or perhaps it shuns him."

Evelyn thought of the empty feeling of his residence, the way he had sat alone during her *coming out,* his gruff manner, his rule that she could never hold him. She wondered if his claiming her for a mistress had nothing at all to do with Ekroth, but with his own loneliness.

Leaving his carriage near the dressmaker's, Rafe strode with purpose down the street. He needed a sweet, a nice, hard, sugary sweet. He couldn't recall the last time he'd had such a craving. He wanted something to make him feel good instead of like a rotten bastard.

Whatever had overcome him to press the dressmaker as he had? It was Eve, dammit all. The look of mortification and a wish for death that had crossed her face when she realized that an inconsequential shop owner had determined her purpose in Rafe's life—and disapproved of it. Who was this woman to disapprove of anything he did?

He was providing Eve with a sanctuary. Yes, she had to pay a price for it, but then nothing in life came free. Not even freedom. It was the highest price of all.

To make matters worse, he'd fallen back on his heritage to get the respect he wanted for Eve. Lord Rafe Easton. He'd not referred to himself as lord since Sebastian's place was secure. He couldn't be more disappointed in himself. He was his own man. He didn't need to tie himself in with his brothers to gain what he desired.

But he had been angry, so very angry that Eve was feeling as though she was less than she was, that she appeared to be on the verge of tears. But she had been strong enough not to shed them, and that had made him want to take a lash to himself.

Finally, to his immense relief, he caught sight of a sweet shop. He opened the door as two ladies were coming out. He tipped his hat and as soon as they were through, he charged inside. Some little imp of a girl was standing beside an older scruffy-looking lad, holding his hand, trying to decide what she wanted. He could see a penny clutched in the boy's grip. A penny's worth of candy. How long was this going to take?

Children. He would never have any. Didn't want them, wouldn't know what to do with them. Still, this girl drew his attention, a blue ribbon holding her blond tangled hair from her face while it flowed down her back. He imagined Eve at that age. Had she ever held her brother's hand, had he ever looked out for her? Why had her father not arranged to see that Eve was properly taken care of after his death? Surely he was not blind to the fact that his son was lacking in character.

Perhaps he thought leaving her to her brother's care would force the man to grow up, to assume responsibility, to learn to put someone before himself. Instead, he'd followed his nature and selfishly rid himself of her as soon as possible in a way that profited him, selling off her things. He wished she'd asked for more than a portrait and a horse, because he'd have acquired the whole blasted house if she'd wanted it. Not because he cared for her, but because it would have been the right thing to do. It had been a long time since he'd wanted to do anything simply because it was the right thing to do.

Last year sometime. When Tristan had needed his help to locate the man everyone thought should marry Anne. And two years before that when he'd

attended balls that he didn't want to attend, in order
to ensure Sebastian's rightful place in Society. And
since then he'd cared only about what he wanted.
Maybe he wasn't that different from Wortham. The
thought sickened him—that he might have anything in common with that scapegrace.

The child was sucking on her finger now and
dancing on the tips of her toes. The clerk behind the
counter gave him an I'll-be-with-you-in-a-moment
look that truly meant I may never be with you.

"Come on, Lizzie. Pick sumfink," the lad said.

Yes, Lizzie, Rafe thought. *Pick something.*

"Dunno. They're all so pretty."

The clerk sighed, pursed his lips. "May I help
you, sir?"

"A dozen peppermint humbugs."

As the clerk scooped the light and dark brown
striped hard candies into a sack, Rafe's mouth began
to water. He'd gone too long without the indulgence.
As soon as the clerk handed over the sack, Rafe
dug out one of the hard nuggets, popped it into his
mouth, and savored the sweetness.

The girl looked up at him with wide blue eyes,
not the shade of Eve's, but still a color that would
draw men to her as she got older. He extended the
bag toward her. "Here, you may have the rest."

The boy pulled her nearer to his side, and put his
arm protectively around her narrow shoulders. "We
dun know ye. Wot ye be wantin'?"

Street children then, old enough to already have
learned not to trust. It was a hard lesson, one Rafe
had not excelled at quite quickly enough. He'd innocently taken food offered by a fellow named
Dimmick, and before he knew it he became one of

Dimmick's lackeys, doing what he was ordered to do because the man's punishments generally involved mutilation of some sort.

"Nothing, lad. I simply misjudged how hungry I was. The clerk can't take them back once he's handed them over. I'm not of a mood to toss them in the garbage bin. Do you want them or not?"

He could see the boy struggling, the fingers of the hand not holding the coin twitching. He wanted to reach for the offering, but he feared the price.

"I loike Wellington sticks," the lass said. "They're pretty."

Their red, blue, and yellow stripes were colorful, but then most hard candy was brightly colored. Rafe had been intrigued by it all as a lad. He would sit for hours sucking on one after another.

"A dozen Wellington sticks," Rafe told the clerk.

"Very good, sir." He pulled the lid off a jar. With each stick he removed, the girl's eyes brightened further.

When the sack was full, the clerk held it out. Rafe took it and offered it to the girl. She lacked her brother's reserve. She snatched it with tiny hands. With an arched brow, Rafe again offered the humbugs to lad.

He skewed up his mouth, grabbed the bag and the girl's hand, and darted for the door. Suddenly the girl was back, her scrawny arms wrapped tightly around his leg. His breath caught as he stiffened, fighting not to kick her off, not to send her flying across the shop, through the large window that looked out on the street. She couldn't weigh more than a feather and yet he was immobilized as though heavy metal chains had been wrapped about him. The world began to retreat as darkness hovered at the edge of his vision. He ran his tongue over the hard candy in his mouth and concentrated on the sugar. Sweet, sweet sugar.

"Come on, Lizzie!" the boy yelled.

Yes, go, Lizzie, for God's sake, go.

She released her stranglehold and raced out the door, followed by the lad.

Rafe forced out a long slow breath, fought to calm his racing heart as mortification threatened to swamp him. How could a mere slip of a girl unman him so?

"So is that it for you today, then, sir?"

The voice came from far away, through a tunnel. He couldn't go out into the streets yet. He'd be staggering on unsteady legs.

He managed to turn toward the clerk, to hold his face in a mask of boredom. "No, I'll take a large box of chocolates as well."

The clerk gave a nod and reached for a dark brown box. "The large box holds twelve pieces and we offer a variety of twenty-four. Which would you like?"

Something to concentrate on. Good. He was beginning to feel more like himself. He looked at the display case and the assortment of chocolates. The various shapes, the tiny decorations on each of them. "Doesn't matter."

The clerk reached for a dark square.

"No, not that one," Rafe said. "The one in the shape of a leaf." Eve would like that one. It was intriguing with all the little lines carved in it.

"Very good, sir."

"Then the clover . . . and the diamond-shaped one. But not the heart." Wrong message would be sent there. He ended up selecting all the pieces because it seemed the clerk was a poor judge of what would appeal to a lady. He wasn't certain when he decided the chocolates would be for Eve, or why it was important to him that the box contained the proper pieces for her. She might not even enjoy chocolate.

With box in hand, he strode from the shop and headed back toward the dressmaker's. They should be finished by now. The farther he walked, the heavier the package became. It wasn't something she'd asked for. Why did he even think she might desire it? She might misinterpret its purpose. Think he'd begun to develop feelings for her, or worse, that he cared.

Whatever had he been thinking to spend fifteen precious moments selecting bits of chocolate?

He spotted a bedraggled woman curled in a corner, pressed against some steps. He hardly broke his stride as he bent down and set the box beside her.

"Thank ye, kind sir!" she yelled after him.

Kind? If he was kind, he'd let Eve go. But then if he was kind, he never would have taken her to begin with.

When Evelyn heard the bell above the door tinkling, she knew it was him. She didn't know how she knew. It should sound the same no matter who opened the door, and yet she knew.

Madame had just finished helping her dress—for which she was grateful. She suspected he wouldn't care if she was clothed or not. If he wanted to see her, he would barge into the back room and see her.

Madame arched a brow. "You think it's him."

"How do you know?"

She smiled. "A little shiver went through you. Is he a good lover?"

She felt the heat of embarrassment swarm over her face, over her body.

"How can you be so innocent?" Madame asked.

"I should probably go." She didn't know why she walked with such purpose, why she didn't linger. Being back in his company meant she might indeed discover if he was a good lover—tonight. How much of a reprieve was he giving her?

It *was* him. He was studying the bolts of cloth again. He held his hat in one hand, had removed his glove from the other, and was rubbing red silk between his fingers and thumb. His movements were so incredibly slow, as though he was savoring the sensation of each thread as he touched it. Would theirs be a leisurely mating? Would he relish the feel of her skin as much as he did the cloth?

Ever so casually he glanced over, his lids half lowered as though he wanted to shutter his thoughts, not that she would have been able to read them anyway. "Are you finished with the measurements?"

"We are, my lord," Madame said, and Eve could have sworn that Rafe cringed, although the change to his expression happened so quickly that had she not been focused on him, she'd have not seen it.

And why was it that she seemed incapable of taking her eyes from him?

He was as handsome as ever, but something had changed. She couldn't quite figure it out. It had to do with his mood. Angry? Frustrated? Disappointed? Would she ever learn to read him, to determine what he thought, what he felt?

"I have some designs in mind for your lady—"

And again there was that quick contortion of his features.

"—that I could share with you now," Madame said. "If you have the time."

"Yes, I'd like to get this matter finished as quickly as possible."

Madame brought over sheaves of paper, and while they discussed patterns with their back to her as though her opinion was of no importance, she wandered over to the chair before the window where a true lady had been sitting earlier. She glanced out on the street, on people bustling by, going places, doing as they pleased, making their decisions.

Her father had told her to never envy anyone anything because she would never know what price they had paid for whatever she was envying. But at that moment it was very difficult not to covet the freedom to go about life as one pleased. She had no control over what she would wear, what it would look like, the shade of the material. She had no choice as to where she would live. She had no say in when she would be bedded—or even *how* she would be bedded, because he had rules. He governed all.

Perhaps she *would* be disagreeable. At the very least she could be unenthusiastic.

"I'm ready to leave."

Startled, she looked out on the darkness and wondered when night had fallen. Glancing up at him, for a brief moment, she could have sworn that he looked as sad as she felt.

With a nod, she rose. He didn't offer his arm, but merely led her out of the shop. She wasn't good enough to touch in public. Perhaps she would be fortunate, and he would decide she wasn't good enough to touch in private either.

The footman assisted her into the carriage while Rafe spoke to the driver. The carriage rocked as he climbed inside, sitting across from her. Then the conveyance was rattling along. She stared out the window, much safer than staring at him. She didn't want him to think that he intrigued her with his quicksilver expressions, his caustic moods, his ability to know exactly what he wanted and to never doubt himself. She doubted so much. Doubted that she could do this.

"She intends to charge you triple," she said quietly.

"I thought she might."

She'd expected anger not amusement to accompany his reply. She peered over at him. "You don't sound at all bothered by it."

"I can hardly blame her when I practically forced her into doing my bidding at the expense of some highborn lady who might very well find herself without a new gown to wear to a ball."

"She referred to you as a lost lord."

He was the one to look out the window now. With the little bit of illumination filtering in from the gas-lights, she could see his jaw clench, his eyes narrow. "We shan't talk about that, Eve."

She interlaced her fingers. She wanted to know about his past, to know what had shaped him into the man he was. Why did his servants not refer to him as my lord? Why did he have a gambling establishment? He should be like Geoffrey. A man of leisure.

Then she thought, *Thank God he isn't like Geoffrey.*

"What shall we talk about then?" she asked.

"We shan't talk at all. That's not why you're with me."

"But if we don't know anything at all about each other, it's going to be incredibly awkward, don't you think?" She didn't want to sound mulish but she didn't want her body to be the only thing about her with which he was familiar.

"I shall ensure it's not awkward."

"How can you do that when simply riding in a carriage together is awkward? And I don't like the red that so fascinated you. I shan't wear it."

His gaze landed on her so swiftly and so heavily that she could have sworn she heard a thud. "You will."

"I won't."

"You seem to have forgotten the terms of this arrangement."

She clutched her fingers until they ached, until the pain traveled up her arms to her neck. "I don't think I can do this. I don't think I can be your mistress."

"I know."

"You know?"

"Did I not tell you that I was a good judge of character?"

She swallowed hard. Was he not going to force her into this? "I can give you my jewelry to pay you back for the bed you gave me last night." She started to reach into her pocket—

"Keep it."

What did he mean by that? Keep it because he

wasn't going to let her go, or because he was and she would need it?

The carriage rolled to a stop.

"We're here," he said succinctly.

"Where is that?"

"The life you think you'd prefer."

Chapter 7

He was mucking things up. Royally. He couldn't remember the last time that he had handled a situation so poorly. Perhaps when his brothers first returned. He remembered the hearty hug that Tristan had given Sebastian, and he'd ached because the thought of being wrapped that tightly by such strong arms had forced him to distance himself, to shove whiskey into their hands, to give no indication that he desperately wanted to share in such a joyous reunion. He'd been angry with them then. He still was, but it was the fear of what they might realize, what they might understand of his past that held him back.

He was having a difficult enough time as it was allowing Eve to cling to his arm as they strolled through the rookeries. But he couldn't risk anyone thinking that she wasn't with him. He had a reputation down here. He didn't come often anymore, but legends grew with absence, and enough people would remember him that he knew they wouldn't be accosted.

He had come to understand at breakfast that she wasn't fully committed to being with him. He had sensed at the dressmaker's that she was mortified by her place in his life. In spite of her father's love for her, he had hidden her away, had made her more of a prisoner than Rafe ever would. Her brother had wanted her out of sight. Rafe had promised to flaunt her. She had to understand the price that entailed.

She also needed to understand the price of leaving. She needed to want to stay because he didn't want her to go.

He wanted to see her in the red gown that she swore she wouldn't wear. He wagered she'd change her mind when she saw it. He wanted her at his table during breakfast and dinner. He might even return to the residence for a midday meal.

He wanted to catch wafts of her rose fragrance as he walked through his residence, as he strode up the stairs to find her. He wanted her eyes to widen when she looked up and realized he stood beside her. He wanted her lids lowering when he bent in to kiss her.

He wanted her in his carriage laying out her terms, even knowing that he was the rule maker. He didn't want to break her, but compromise had never been his strong suit. He had learned early that compromise signaled weakness, that men would take advantage. One's guard could never be lowered.

Even she, as sweet and innocent as she was, would take advantage, would ruin him, would leave him. She didn't much like him. He had expected that. He'd never cared one way or the other if anyone fancied him. He was a loner. It suited him.

But she made him feel not quite so lonely. So he wanted her to stay, if only for a while, and then he would let her go.

Evelyn was horrified by what she saw. People in bedraggled clothing hovering near small fires. Children so thin that their eyes were enormous in their fragile faces. Barefoot children in the chilly night. Dirty. Filth everywhere. The rancid stink made her want to gag.

Rafe walked through the narrow alleyway—with poorly constructed buildings squatting on either side—as though he owned it all, as though he weren't bothered in the least.

"Where are we?" she asked.

"St. Giles."

"These poor, wretched people." She wasn't completely innocent. She knew of the impoverished. Her father had mentioned them once. Had said something needed to be done. Apparently nothing had.

Rafe stopped walking, looked to the side. She followed his gaze toward the dark alcove. She could barely make out the shadow of a woman flattened against the wall, a man rocking against her, grunting. Surely they weren't—

"Can't you stop him from treating her like that?" she asked.

"I would if she were struggling against him, but she's not. It's her choice." He turned about and began escorting her back the way they'd come. "He'll probably give her a coin, or part of his meal, or maybe warmth through the night."

"Is that what it's like?" she asked quietly. "Being bedded."

"For some. Not with me."

Not against a wall, but in a bed. With him over her, rocking, grunting. Once Geoffrey had shown her his dogs "making puppies." She'd been too young to truly understand.

Rafe stopped walking again, and she dreaded knowing what he was going to show her this time.

"Do you see that gent standing against the wall over there, watching us?"

Gent? He reminded her of a mouse the cat had once brought her from the stables. He was hunched over as though he didn't want to be seen, or perhaps he carried invisible burdens. Still, she nodded.

"He'll give you a hundred quid for your jewelry. But don't let anyone see him handing it over to you. They'll try to take it after you walk away. In that building over there—" He nodded toward a place that had a single lantern hanging by the door. "—you can get a bed for the night for a couple of pence. You'll share it with others, of course. Hopefully none of them will have lice."

She jerked her gaze up to him. "You're leaving me here?"

"If you wish to be free of me. Last night you stayed because of fate, because of the flip of a coin. Tonight, if you climb back into the carriage with me, I want you to do it because you truly understand it is the better option. It does not come without a price. I know that. Even if I take you to a less seedy part of London and leave you there, eventually I fear fate will lead you here."

She looked around, trying to envision herself in this squalor.

"I am not fool enough to believe you will be happy with me," he said, "but I do have hope that you can be content during the short time you will be with me."

Hope. She had never considered him to be a man who would hope, who would voice that word. Her mother had been a mistress, and an earl had fallen in love with her. Would this man come to love her? She very much doubted it.

She would not be happy in the rookeries, of that she was certain. She would not be content. She would be cold, hungry, and dirty. And very much alone.

She angled her chin haughtily. "I'm not certain why you felt compelled to bring me here. I gave you my answer last night."

"I must have misunderstood. I thought you were having doubts."

Tightening her fingers on his arm, she shook her head.

"Good."

He led her back to the carriage. After he had handed her up, he said something to the footman, then climbed in and took his place opposite her. He tugged on his waistcoat as though it had become askew.

"Why are we not leaving?" she asked.

"My footman is spreading around a few coins."

She suspected it was a good many more than a few. Eventually, the carriage bolted off, thank goodness. It was awful of her, but she felt the need for a bath.

"I'm surprised we weren't attacked," she said.

"They know me there."

"Because of your kindness?"

He chuckled low. "No. Because it is where I lived for many years during that time when I was *lost*, as Madame so romantically put it."

She tried not to look surprised. She wondered if she would ever be as skilled as he was at revealing so little. "Why were you here? Why didn't you leave, like your brothers?"

"Because they didn't take me with them." She heard the bitterness in his voice. "I was only ten. Our uncle wished to possess the dukedom, but three heirs stood in his way. So off we went until we were old enough to reclaim what was ours."

She wanted to wrap her arms around the boy he'd been. As innocent and trusting as she had been until yesterday evening, he must have been more so. A duke's legitimate son. He would have been pampered by all. "That's the reason you know what it is to be me."

"I don't know what it is to be *you*, Eve. I know what it is to be where you are. To be without anyone or anything. To be hungry, to be cold, to be unsheltered. I know what it is to do things that you'd have rather not done, but you do it because you must. You come to accept it. To live with it. In time, perhaps to even admire yourself a bit. That you survived when no one thought you would." He cleared his throat as though punishing it for speaking such revealing words, and turned his attention back to the window. "I'm glad you didn't stay there."

She thought at some point she might look back and be as glad—

"It would have been a colossal mistake," he added.

She almost laughed. Had she ever known a man as pompous and self-assured? Surely not Geoffrey. Not even her father.

"I still shan't wear the red."

He flashed a grin, brief and white in the shadows. She didn't know why it thrilled her to know that she was responsible, even if the smile didn't last longer than the blink of an eye.

"Oh, I think you will."

Arrogant man. She held the words back because she didn't want to ruin this moment of . . . she wasn't quite certain what it was. Understanding, acceptance. Perhaps after a time they might even become friends.

The tension within the carriage had abated, until it seemed almost pleasant. She tried to imagine what it might be like to have a gentleman court her, take her about in his conveyance. Of course there would be a chaperone. She supposed she really needed to give up on those childish thoughts. On the other hand if he truly gave her his residence and all it contained, she could become a powerful woman, one with enough independence that a gentleman might be willing to overlook her unfortunate beginnings. It was a heady thought.

The carriage turned down the drive. She didn't want to acknowledge the sense of relief that washed over her. Although nerves quickly followed. She'd made her commitment to him clear. Perhaps tonight would be the one when he came to her, when he claimed her as his mistress.

They jostled to a stop. A footman opened the door. Rafe stepped out, then handed her down, releasing her as soon as her feet touched the pebbles.

"Are you hungry?" he asked as they walked side by side, not touching, toward the steps.

She realized with a suddenness that she was famished. "Very."

"I thought we might enjoy a late repast on the terrace."

"I'd like that, yes."

"Good."

They went up the steps. The door opened.

Laurence bowed. "Welcome home, sir. Miss."

"We'll be dining on the terrace," Rafe informed the butler.

"Very good, sir."

Rafe turned to her. "I shall see you on the terrace in half an hour. No need to dress formally."

Without waiting for a reply, he jaunted up the stairs, taking them two steps at a time. Not that there was anything for her to say, but she was going in the same direction. They could have gone together.

"He always requires a bit of solitude after returning home," Laurence said kindly.

She snapped her attention to him. "Have you been with him long?"

Laurence looked up at the ceiling. "Six years now, I believe. Ever since he took the residence from Lord Laudon."

"Purchased it from him, you mean?"

He pursed his lips. "I don't think so. Lord Laudon was notorious for his gambling habit. I believe the residence settled his debt."

"So you were employed by Lord Laudon."

"No, miss. Until Mr. Easton brought me here and saw that I was properly trained in my duties, I had the misfortune of living in the squalor of St. Giles. Now, if you'll excuse me, I must see that dinner is prepared."

She watched him walk off, then glanced up the stairs where her . . . what was the word for a man who had a mistress? Her lover? Her paramour? Her protector? Whatever he was, he was a mystery. Brute or savior? Or a combination of both?

What would he eventually be to her?

Chapter 8

He'd wanted to dine on the terrace with candles flickering because it provided more shadows than light, and he'd already given away far too much. He didn't want her studying him, trying to decipher him. He also didn't want the formal attire that was required in the dining room—although it being his home he could wear, or not wear, whatever he wanted.

He was in a loose white linen shirt. His frock coat, waistcoat, and neckcloth were on the floor of his bedchamber. She was still in the hideous black, but she'd removed all the pins from her hair and secured it with a black ribbon. The golden tresses reached the small of her back. It was a vision that would haunt him tonight when he returned to the club. He couldn't remember the last time he'd spent so few hours in a day at his establishment. Odd that he'd not given it any thought until that moment. She had been his focus for much of the day.

He studied her over the rim of his wineglass, imagining her in the clothing that the dressmaker was no doubt already busily sewing. The black would be gone. He could scarcely wait.

She had been inordinately quiet while enjoying the soup, and then the pheasant. Now he caught her fingers shaking when she reached for her wine.

"It won't be tonight," he said quietly.

She peered up at him.

"The bedding," he continued. "I told you it wouldn't happen until you were comfortable with me."

He didn't much like the gratitude that swept over her features. He should just take her and be done with it. Then she wouldn't be nervous, although she might be a good deal more uncomfortable with him.

"Do you like chocolate?" he asked.

She smiled softly, sweetly. He wondered how long he could keep her without her losing that particular smile.

"Who doesn't love chocolate?"

He regretted now that he'd given it away. He hoped the old woman had savored it, rather than gobbling it down.

"When did you begin living with the earl?" he asked.

She picked up her wineglass, and he was grateful to see that she held it steady.

"When I was six, after my mother died of the scarlet fever. His wife passed away four years after that. Then it was just he, Geoffrey, and I. For the longest I didn't understand his having a wife. He was my papa. I thought he was married to my mother. Do you know how to ensure that we don't have children?"

He nearly choked on his wine. When would he learn not to drink when she was about?

"I shouldn't like to have children out of wedlock,"

she continued. "No matter how much they might be loved, it's not an easy path for them."

He almost told her that if they had children, he'd not leave them unprotected as Wortham had, but had he not thought that very afternoon that children were not for him? "I know methods that increase the unlikelihood of children."

"I thought you might. How long does a mistress generally stay with a gent?"

"Depends on the gent. Depends on the mistress."

"My father loved my mother. I don't think he would have ever turned her out."

"But she left him."

She jerked her head back. "Not by choice. Death took her."

"But it must have hurt."

"Of course it hurt, but that is part of life, is it not?"

Not his life, not if he could help it.

"You may redo the rooms if you like," he said.

She blinked at him. He knew it was an abrupt change of subject, but he didn't want to follow the conversation she was leading.

"May I? Some of the rooms seem rather dark. Did you decorate them?"

"The house is as it was when I acquired it. But I like the dark rooms. If you don't"—he shrugged—"change them. I don't spend much time here. I have rooms at my club."

She set down her wine, studied him. Thank goodness for the shadows. He didn't want her to guess that even for tonight, he didn't want to leave. He wanted her to play the pianoforte for him. He wanted her to read to him. He wanted her to just sit in the garden with him. He wanted her to spread out on the bed and welcome him. He would hold her hands to keep her from reaching for him, but then he would kiss her slow and deep, just before he pounded into her. He wouldn't be able to hold back. He knew that. Already his body was aching for her.

He thought about going to a prostitute tonight, but she wouldn't satisfy him. From the moment he had seen Eve, he had known no one would satisfy him save her. He could blame Ekroth for having pudgy fingers all he wanted, but the truth was that he had desired her from the moment he'd gazed on her profile.

"Then I won't see much of you," she said, her voice sounding more raspy.

"Only late evenings usually. Once things begin between us."

"Haven't they already begun? Surely there will be more between us than just the rutting in bed."

No, no there won't be hung on the tip of his tongue. But he'd already hurt her enough by not being the man she desired—a man who would marry her. So he held back the words that would upset her. He'd never considered himself deliberately cruel. What he liked most about her was that she wasn't cynical. She would be in time, the longer she was with him. He would let her go shortly before then.

As though realizing that no answer would be forthcoming, she asked, "May we take a walk about the garden?"

He finished off his wine, got up, and pulled out her chair. She rose so gracefully, and it was all he could do not to plow his hands into her hair, cup the back of her head, and kiss her with every ounce of passion he possessed.

As they walked side by side, the lit gaslights guided their path past the rhododendrons, pansies, and roses.

"I don't understand why you would want to bed me when you don't even want to touch me."

Not want to touch her? He wanted to touch her more than he wanted to breathe, but that would invite her to do the same, and therein resided the problem. In spite of his loose shirt, if she wound her arms around him, he would feel as though he were suffocating, he would shove her aside, possibly hurt her.

"I understand your rule about not embracing you, but we could at least hold hands, don't you think?"

Before he could respond, she'd slipped hers into his, her palm pressed flat against his, her small fingers threaded through his larger ones, curling around to rest against his knuckles—knuckles that had battered faces for money owed, not to him, but to the man he'd worked for when he was younger. He'd done what he needed to do in order to survive. He didn't make excuses for it, but it seemed wrong for her to be clasping his hand as though it were worthy of her touch.

But he couldn't bring himself to pull free. Nor could he bring himself to talk. His throat had clogged with an emotion he didn't recognize, couldn't name.

"When I was a child, my father would give me dolls," she said softly, as though the journey through reminiscences required a reverence. "When I was sad, when I was happy. When I was ill, when I was well. It didn't seem to matter. They were so beautiful. I would have tea parties for them. They were my friends. They kept me from being lonely.

"Then one day, I found a path through the hedgerows, to a wooden fence. There was a small hole, and I could peer through and see the neighbor's garden. I saw a girl, not much older than I was at the time, and she was playing with another girl. They were talking and laughing and frolicking about. Dolls can do nothing except sit. I threw a tantrum and broke all my dolls. It wasn't the least like me. Father was terribly disappointed. That's when I began to suspect that I was a secret."

"I've told you that you won't be a secret with me."

"Yes, but I'm left to wonder if it will be better or worse. I still shan't have friends. I won't be respectable."

He would not feel guilty for his role in shaping her life. If not for him, she'd already be bedded, of that he was certain. She'd have no choice at all. "Respectability will not keep you fed, warm, clothed, or sheltered."

"Have you friends?"

"No. I need no one save myself."

"But you have your brothers."

"And you have yours."

Within his, her hand jerked. "Are yours horrid as well then?"

"No, they are good men."

"I don't suppose they'd approve of me."

He stopped walking and faced her. He was grateful for the shadows that cloaked her features, hid the blue of her expressive eyes. "It makes little difference what they approve. All that matters is what I think."

And what he thought, by God, was that he couldn't go another second without tasting those succulent lips again. She was still holding his hand, so he very smoothly moved her arm behind her back while he snagged the other hand and brought it round to meet its mate. He could feel her steady gaze on him, even if he couldn't see it.

"You don't have to hold me captive. I'm quite capable of following your silly rule."

Silly, was it? It was a rule that would save her. He released his grip, brought up his hands and cradled her face as he'd longed to, with both hands, his thumbs stroking her cheeks, slipping down to caress the corners of her mouth. He wanted her to smile for him. He plowed one hand into her hair before lowering his mouth to hers. He tasted the wine, a rich bouquet that only became richer on her tongue. She wasn't quite as timid tonight. She parried, danced, challenged. He liked when she didn't fear him.

He didn't relish knowing that she had grown up alone and that with him, she would continue to be so. He would hire a companion, someone to visit with her during the day. He would hire a dozen if it would make her smile.

She kept her promise, bless her. She didn't touch him. She didn't run her hands up his torso, she didn't tangle her fingers in his hair. But she didn't need to do either of those things in order to bring him to his knees. She sighed huskily. She circled her tongue around his mouth. She explored as he did—hungrily and deeply. He had no doubt that she would be all he required in bed. She would learn quickly, she would—

Lie there and take what he gave her. Keep her hands fisted at her side as they were now. He felt the tension radiating through her as she fought for her own enjoyment while not breaking his blasted rule.

What would it hurt if she settled her hands lightly on his shoulders?

He dare not risk it. He couldn't give her power over him. He couldn't relinquish control. He couldn't take a chance of her discovering the truth about him.

He marched forward, forcing her to step back—once, twice, half a dozen times—until she was pressed against the brick wall. He could take her here, lift her skirts, bury himself to the hilt. But if he did that, she might as well have stayed in the rookeries. He could take her down to the grass, let the verdant green serve as their bed. But she deserved better than that sort of barbarism.

He had promised her that he would wait until she was comfortable with him. While her lips played wildly with his, he knew she wasn't yet ready for more. Or perhaps it was that he feared how he might hurt her the first time. The taking of a virgin came with responsibility. He couldn't simply plow into her as he did with other women. He had to take more care.

It would be different if he weren't going to see her again, but she was living in his blasted residence. He would see her. Unless he took her once, then walked away and left her with everything, as he'd promised. He wouldn't have to see her disappointment or sorrow or regret. Perhaps that was the best way to handle this situation: take her, be done with her, let her move on with her life.

But already he knew that at the very least he would desire another kiss.

He drew back, not surprised to see that he was correct. Her fists were clenched. He stroked his thumb over her damp and swollen lips, felt her tongue dart out and touch his skin.

"I must get to the club." His voice sounded rough and raw, as though he'd not spoken in a century.

She merely nodded.

"I don't know when I'll return." Nor did he know why he felt compelled to say that. His schedule was his. She would conform, would wait for him.

Turning on his heel, fighting everything within him that demanded he make her well and truly his mistress, he left her there in the shadows of the garden.

She waited several heartbeats, taking in shallow breaths, working to regain her composure. She unfurled her hands. Her nails had dug into her palms. She'd come close to drawing blood. When she thought she no longer needed the wall for support, she walked on trembling legs to the table, lifted the wine bottle, and began pouring what remained into her glass. She was quite glad he was gone. Or so she told herself. The alternative was to wish he'd stayed, and had he stayed, she had little doubt that things between them would not have ended with the kiss.

If not for his silly rule, she would have melted against him, entwined her arms around him, might even—to her immense shame—have begged him to carry her to his bedchamber. He was so skilled at stirring heat and passion, such torrid heat and passion. Considering his stiffness, his distance, his aloofness, she had not expected him to send her senses ablaze.

Perhaps in the bedchamber was where he unleashed everything. If so, he might reduce her to a heap of cinders. She didn't know whether to anticipate it, or be terrified.

Setting aside the bottle, she lifted the glass, tipped it toward lips that were still tingling with his assault.

"Will there—"

She released a tiny screech at Laurence's voice intruding from the darkness. The wine sloshed over the sides, onto her hand and, she imagined, her gown. She cradled the bowl of the wineglass with both hands, to steady it as much as herself.

"Apologies, miss. I didn't mean to frighten you."

"No, I'm sorry. I wasn't expecting you." She released a self-conscious laugh. "Which I suppose is obvious."

He smiled. It wasn't quick or feral or predatory. It didn't hide secrets. "I saw the master leave. I came to see if there was anything else you required."

"No, I think I shall just enjoy the garden for a bit."

"As you wish. I shall retreat to the shadows and keep watch."

Her fingers tightened on the glass. She was surprised it didn't shatter. "No need to inconvenience yourself so. I'll be fine."

"If anything happened to you because of my negligence, the master would beat me to within an inch of my life."

Surely he jested. "At least he won't kill you."

"Killing would be merciful."

Her heart lurched. "Are you saying he's not merciful?"

"I'm saying that he's very skilled at making his

enemies or those who disappoint him live with regret."

"Has he many enemies?"

"I've said far too much. You are quite easy to talk to. I should learn to hold my tongue around you."

"You're quite safe. I won't tell him what you tell me."

"He has a way of finding things out. Enjoy the garden."

He slipped away into the darkness, but she could sense him still watching her. She sat in the chair and looked out on the foliage. The gaslights glowed, but fog was beginning to seep in. She could see the mist trailing around the lamps. She should go in, and yet she couldn't quite bring herself to do so yet. Beyond the fragrance of the flowers, she could still detect his lingering scent. He was a man whose presence remained, even after he left.

"Are you afraid of him?" she asked, knowing Laurence was hovering near enough to hear.

"No."

"But you said he would beat you."

"Only if I disappoint him. Then, yes, I would be afraid of him. Very afraid."

Sipping her wine, she realized her lips were no longer swollen from his kiss. She skimmed her tongue over them. She'd lost the taste of him. "Is he a bad man, then?"

Silence stretched between them. She wished she hadn't begun this conversation. She needed to draw her own conclusions regarding Rafe, not base them on someone else's opinion. It was just that he was so difficult to characterize.

"I once thought he was," Laurence finally said, so

quietly that Evelyn almost didn't hear him. "It's the reason I tried to kill him."

Jerking around in her chair, she couldn't see him. She could hear a slight breeze rustling the trees, hoped it masked her stuttering breath. "Why would you try to kill him?"

"Once again I've said too much." The disappointment in himself riffled through his voice. She thought if she persisted, he would eventually tell her. Instead, she turned back around and sipped on her wine.

Obviously Laurence had not succeeded in killing Rafe. She wondered how close he might have come. She couldn't deny the spark of admiration that flitted through her, because Rafe had not only fended off the attack but had converted Laurence into someone he trusted to look after his things. He'd provided him with something much better than what he'd obviously had in St. Giles.

Was he not doing the same for her? Begrudgingly, to be sure, and completely on his terms, but still he was offering her things no one else had. She wondered how different her life might be this evening if Ekroth had won out and taken her as his mistress. Would she be sitting in the garden enjoying the night? Or would she be waiting for moments to pass while he took his pleasure with her?

Would he have kissed her? Would he have gone to the bother of finding her jewelry? Would he have claimed her father's portrait and had it displayed in the morning room?

She wondered how her mother had come to her father's attention. Had she fallen in love with him before she became his mistress, or had the falling happened slowly, over time? She could not claim to love Rafe Easton, was not certain she ever would.

But she was beginning to be very glad that he had carried her through the rain, and not abandoned her on Geoffrey's stoop.

Chapter 9

She'd left a lamp burning by the bed. Rafe wondered if she suffered from nightmares, if monsters visited her in sleep as they did him. But then he suspected the existence of monsters was a recent discovery for her. Soon she'd add him to the list, if she hadn't already.

She appeared so innocent in sleep. On her back, but not completely, twisted a little to the side, her hip raised slightly, one bent leg resting over the other. One of her hands lay near her head on the pillow, fingers curled. So trusting, certain he wouldn't come to her tonight, wouldn't claim what he was owed.

He didn't know why he was here and not at his club. He'd planned to work until dawn, until he was too exhausted to think of her, to want her. Instead the clock had barely struck midnight when he left. Like some misguided fool, he'd hoped to find her sitting in the morning room, staring at her father's portrait, sipping wine or rum or Scotch. He'd hoped she'd not yet retired, but then she was still not a woman of the night. Her habits would change, would begin to mirror his as she learned to wait for him, to be ready to receive him whenever he was ready to have her.

He wanted her now, dammit. He didn't understand this pulling he felt to be with her. It was her specifically, not just lust. Or perhaps it was lust for her. He knew no other woman would satisfy this craving, and it was a craving. He thought of her constantly. Once he had her, all these ludicrous longings would melt away like fog before the sun. If she knew the stranglehold she had over him, she could demand so much.

That she didn't demand at all was partly responsible for his obsession.

Her eyes fluttered open and his chest tightened so swiftly and so painfully that it was almost as though he still wore his jacket, waistcoat, and cravat, but he'd removed them as soon as he'd arrived. Not finding her about, he'd gone to his second bedchamber, the one into which servants were allowed to enter, the one where his valet saw to his needs, and ordered a bath be drawn. He'd fought to distract himself from what he wanted—to look in on her, to gaze at her. It seemed wrong. When had something being wrong ever stopped him before?

"You're back," she murmured in her smoky voice that spoke of secrets shared. She smiled softly, so softly, so innocently. Then her eyes widened. Fully awake now, she scrambled back, sitting up, pulling the covers over her until they were tucked beneath her chin.

He much preferred her alarm to her innocence. His chest began to loosen.

"Is it to be now?" she asked, breathing harshly,

her knuckles turning white as she clutched the sheets.

"No, I just wanted to make certain that you were all right."

Her brow furrowed. "Why wouldn't I be?"

He didn't want to admit the complete truth, so he negligently lifted a shoulder. "I didn't know if you had difficulty sleeping."

She shook her head. "Not usually, no, but then I don't expect to awaken to company."

With a sardonic twist of his lips, he leaned against the bedpost. "But then you've never before been a mistress."

"Is this another law of mistresses? That you can spy on me at any time?"

"I can visit you at any time."

"I should have some hours of the day that are mine and mine alone."

This was why he'd come. He liked her cheekiness, telling him what she should have. She wasn't afraid of him at least, but as she still had a death grip on the covers, neither was she completely comfortable with him. "Carve out two hours during the day when I'm not to disturb you, tell me when they are. But at night, you're mine."

Holding his gaze in challenge, she angled her chin. "Fifteen minutes every hour on the hour until I have two complete hours."

She almost made him grin. "So I'm popping in and out? No, sweetheart. A hundred and twenty consecutive minutes."

She pouted. He'd not seen her with such a mulish expression. It seemed out of character for her. Even when she'd realized what an arse her brother was, she'd not pouted at his treatment of her. Been devastated by it, but not pouted.

"I don't know. I'm being stubborn. I don't need two hours alone. I suspect I'll have too many as it is. I'm not certain how I'll fill them."

"By preparing for my arrival."

"As I suspect you'll mostly want me with my clothes off, I don't see how that will take much time."

He narrowed his eyes. "What do you know about how I'll want you? Your brother swore you were a virgin."

He didn't think she could turn any redder. "He told you that?"

She was horrified, not that he could blame her. "He told all of us."

"Oh, dear God." She buried her face in her hands. At least she was no longer clutching the sheets. They floated down. The cotton of the borrowed nightgown was not provocative and yet he was intrigued by what was hidden behind those twelve buttons. He imagined slowly releasing them, pulling aside the cloth, pressing kisses over her flesh.

She lifted her head, peered at him over her fingertips. "Can you stop referring to him as my brother? I think he more closely resembles the devil. What else did he tell you?"

"That you were well read and played the pianoforte." He studied the blue velvet canopy. "I didn't pay a lot of attention as I wasn't really there for you."

She dropped her hands into her lap, obviously not aware that the sheet no longer covered her. He imagined her sitting there without the nightdress. He had a good idea regarding the size of her perky breasts. "Why were you there?"

He wondered why his gaze didn't linger on her chest, why he was compelled to gaze into her eyes. The pale light prevented him from being able to fully appreciate the shade, and yet he couldn't look away. "I've made my fortune by taking advantage of other men's weaknesses. I was there to explore opportunities."

"Instead, you discovered a weak woman to be exploited."

"I don't consider you weak."

"Don't you?"

She seemed truly surprised. He was quite astonished himself with the realization regarding how he viewed her: certainly not meek. "You are in an unfortunate circumstance, but hardly weak. If you were, you'd be curled in a corner weeping about your lack of options and the road before you. Instead you're going to make the most of the situation, give your bro—" She arched a brow, gave him a pointed look, and again almost had him smiling. "Wortham cause for regret. You're a survivor, Eve. I think you'll do quite well for yourself once you're rid of me."

"How long do you think it'll be before I'm rid of you?"

He did smile then. He couldn't help it. Just a quick flash of teeth, but he held back the laugh. "Not long."

"What if I'm never ready? What if I'm never comfortable with you, Rafe?"

She might as well have bludgeoned him in the midsection. She'd never before uttered his name and it struck him with the force of a battering ram, nearly doubling him over. Women had said his name before, often in the throes of passion. Then the words she'd spoken ahead of his name slammed into him. Unacceptable. Completely and utterly unacceptable. He wouldn't force her, but by God he would have her, and his patience was quickly running out.

"Then I shall just have to ensure that you do become comfortable."

To Evelyn, the words sounded like a challenge. But then from the moment she'd awakened to find him standing in her bedchamber, she suspected that something was going on that she didn't quite understand. Geoffrey had always stayed out all night at his clubs. She'd assumed Rafe, as owner, would be occupied until dawn. But then perhaps as owner he had underlings to do the work. She suspected he was a man who did whatever he wanted when he wanted.

Just as now, in a predatory manner, he moved to sit at the foot of the bed, his back against the post, which couldn't be very comfortable. He lifted his legs onto the bed, and she couldn't stop her eyes from widening. His feet were naked. Large and naked, with rough soles that looked as though he might have run through the streets with no shoes at all. The intimacy of it almost had her crawling out of the bed and going to stand by the window.

She didn't know why she was so surprised. He wore only his familiar linen shirt and breeches. She was fairly certain that he'd recently bathed because his hair curled at the ends and appeared damp. But his feet . . . good God. She couldn't recall ever seeing a man's feet before. Like the rest of him, they seemed powerful. He crossed one ankle over the over and settled back as though he intended to stay the night.

"Don't look so alarmed," he said, his voice low and somehow sensual. "I've told you that nothing will happen tonight."

"I'm not alarmed. I'm simply . . . it's not proper for me to see your bare feet."

He released a dark chuckle. "Sweetheart, nothing between us is going to be proper."

She supposed announcing that he shouldn't be on the bed with her would result in the same response. "Will we often have these midnight encounters?"

"It's long past midnight. Closer to half past two now."

He'd deftly avoided answering her question, no doubt because he thought the answer would unsettle her. But she had made her decision to become his mistress. She wasn't going to back out, even if he did look decidedly more dangerous at that moment. She imagined him unfurling that magnificently toned body of his and prowling toward her like a large predatory cat—one of the panthers she'd seen at the zoological gardens.

"You keep rather odd hours," she said.

"Sin seldom runs on a schedule."

She began plucking at the blanket, belatedly realizing that it had pooled in her lap at some point and was no longer covering her. Her first impulse was to snatch it back into place, but the action would only make her appear skittish. She would meet her fate with him with as much dignity as possible, much as a condemned woman might face the gallows.

"Tell me about your life in St. Giles," she prodded.

He studied her for a long moment before giving a

careless shrug. "There's little to tell. It was hard, unpleasant. And I was determined to get out of there
as quickly as possible, to do whatever it took."

She leaned forward a bit. "What did it take?"

"Even more unpleasantness."

He gave her one of his wicked grins, the one that
seemed to say, "You don't really want to know, do
you?" She found herself wanting to see a joyous
smile. Did he even have one in his limited repertoire of facial expressions? He was so guarded, so
careful not to reveal a hint of vulnerability. Would
she adopt his method of dealing with the unpleasant aspects of her life?

"In a few hours you should shop for hats and
shoes and all the other little fripperies that women
require," he said. "Take Lila with you to assist as
needed, and a footman to carry your packages."

"Makes it a little difficult to shop for hats and
such when I'm unclear as to what the clothing will
look like. Items must go together. A woman doesn't
simply purchase a hat to have a hat."

He narrowed his eyes. "You're upset about the
clothing."

"About the high-handed way you handled it, yes."

"You wanted only black, and I, daresay, items that
buttoned up to your chin."

She *had* considered putting button makers in
demand.

"Virginal clothing will no longer suit," he told her.

"I'm well aware of that," she snapped, then closed
her eyes tightly. She refused to become a shrew
simply because of the circumstances. "I apologize—"

"Don't. I like a bit of fire."

Opening her eyes, she found herself in the midst

of a conversation she never thought to have. Because of the low flame in the lamp, she couldn't see him as clearly as she'd like. He was more shadow than form. She was half tempted to reach over and make the flame brighter, but then it would reveal more of her as well. At that particular moment, she preferred the gossamer darkness. "Yes, well, I can show you quite a lot more temper if you like."

A corner of his mouth slowly rose. "I said a bit of fire. Besides, you keep your temper on too tight a leash to release it completely. Why is that, I wonder?"

"You don't answer my questions. Why should I answer yours?"

He tilted his head to the side. "Thought you believed we needed to know inconsequential things about each other."

"There are no inconsequential things if you care for someone. That's what my father told me. Do you like me at least?"

She didn't think it was possible for him to grow any more still. He didn't blink. He didn't seem to be drawing in breath.

"It's important for you to be liked," he said slowly.

Another question that would go unanswered. He would test the patience of a saint. She wished she could read him as easily as he seemed to read her. She did want to be liked. As a little girl, she thought if she were good enough, behaved properly, her father would do more than give her dolls, he would take her with him. And when he finally had taken her—after her mother's death—she thought that if Geoffrey would like her, he would become a true brother. Now, she supposed she was silly enough to think that if Rafe liked her, she might become more than a mistress. But he wasn't going to like her. He didn't seem to like anyone.

Then she remembered something else he hadn't liked.

"Why are you truly here, my lord?"

Although he didn't move, she felt the fissure of temper roll off him. "You're never to refer to me in that manner."

His voice was flat, but sharp. He could slice a man to death with it. Had he used it on Geoffrey? Dear God, she hoped so, but what sort of cruel person did that make her?

"Why?"

He gazed toward the window as though the answer lay beyond it. "That's not part of my life now."

"But you told Madame Charmaine of your heritage."

His jaw tightening, he shifted his cool eyes back to her. "Yes."

"You used it to curry her favor and you're unhappy that you did."

"Quite."

Had he done it for her, so Madame wouldn't look down her nose at Evelyn, or had he done it for his own pride? Not his own pride. It would have had him storming from the shop. She didn't think he was a man who bowed before anyone.

"But you are a lord—"

"I am my own man. I built myself up from the squalor in which my brothers left me—"

He came up off the bed with a speed that had her pressing back against the headboard, even though he moved away from her, presenting her with his back. She could see the tenseness in his shoulders, the corded muscles of his neck.

"We won't discuss this matter, Evie."

He turned back toward her, no evidence of any emotion. He might as well have been snuffing out a candle. With two strides, he returned to the side of the bed, stood there as his gaze slowly roamed the length of her. Of their own accord, her toes curled as though they wished to hide from him. Reaching out, he closed his fingers around the covers and began pulling them down.

With a tiny shriek, she grabbed the bedding, jerked it up, and glared at him. "What are you doing?"

"Taking steps to make you more comfortable with me."

"This isn't the way to go about it."

"Neither is talking apparently. You're not going to want to hear this, but I want you, Eve. I won't take you tonight, but by God, it needs to be soon."

His voice was rough, ragged, and made her toes curl even tighter. She shook her head.

"You've seen my bare feet," he said. "Shouldn't I see yours?"

"You saw mine last night." Had it only been one night since she'd made the bargain with this devil?

"I haven't seen them in bed."

"They don't look any different."

"Then why be shy about it?"

She felt as though he'd led her into a trap.

"Loosen your hold on the covers. I won't hurt you."

"And if I don't loosen them?"

He slammed his eyes closed, then slowly opened them. "I won't hurt you then either."

"Finally, a question you didn't neatly sidestep." Swallowing hard, she slowly, slowly unfurled her fingers.

He wanted her flat on her back, with her legs spread. He wanted to be buried deeply inside her, thrusting, thrusting, until the pleasure carried away the pain of memory. He'd almost told her everything, the dark secrets that he'd never shared with anyone, that he'd begun carrying with him since he was ten. He'd accumulated more over the years, each one weightier than the one that came before.

But if he told her, she'd choose the rookeries over him. She would know the blackness that was his soul, the horrors that haunted him, the desperation that had once filled him with dread.

Now that desperation was turned toward her. He'd never wanted a woman as he wanted her. If only some of her innocence could wash over him, but it was more likely that his darkness would rub off on her. He hated the thought of touching her, of destroying the light in her eyes, but he hated more the thought of never possessing her.

He waited, his patience barely tethered until her fingers were no longer clutching the blankets. Then ever so gradually, he dragged the covers down. The cotton of the nightdress hid her well. He was having a new nightdress sewn for her, one that wouldn't leave much to his imagination. The blankets reached her waist and slid down to reveal her hips.

She didn't avert her gaze, but he saw the silent challenge there. She wanted him to stop. He almost did. But he would take her in the dark. Without gentleness, without care. Without the tenderness she deserved. He would hate himself afterward, but he'd long ago learned how to live with hating himself.

He eased the blankets over the small lumps that were her knees. Just a little farther—

He lifted his eyes up to hers, surprised to find her watching him so intently. Her obstinacy, her anger were gone. Now she appeared curious and fighting to draw in breath.

"Do you desire me?" she rasped.

"Very much."

"Because I'm a woman."

"Obviously. I don't generally go about desiring men."

She rolled her eyes. "I meant it's simply because I'm a woman. It wouldn't matter who was here."

If only that were true. But it did matter. For reasons he couldn't fathom, it mattered that it was her. "I could have been with any woman tonight. Instead, I'm here."

"So you must like me a little."

He could have told her that he didn't have to like her to desire her. He could have told her to stop asking so many bloody questions. Instead, he told her the truth. "I like you more than is good for either of us."

And then because he knew another question was on the tip of her tongue and he didn't want to have to deal with whatever it was, he pulled the blankets down all the way, revealing her tiny perfect feet. Yanking them back, she raised her knees and covered them with her nightdress.

"Want me to remove your nightdress next, do you?"

Her eyes widened. "No! Absolutely not."

Drawing the cloth taut at her ankles, she bared her feet. Not a callus to be seen. He imagined the rest of her would look as smooth and silky. He desperately wanted to wrap his hand around her foot and skim his fingers over her ankle, her calf, her knee. He wanted to unbraid her hair, press a kiss to the pulse at her throat, begin unfastening those infuriating buttons.

But he knew she would stiffen, and he wanted her pliable. "You do know what happens between a man and a woman."

She nodded jerkily. "Geoffrey showed me once."

Fury, immediate and swift, rampaging through him, he took a step toward her. "He touched you?"

She scooted back, nearly curled into a ball, shaking her head riotously. "No, no. He showed me a pair of hounds mating."

Spinning away from her, he plowed his hand through his hair. He'd been contemplating murdering her bastard of a brother. And all he'd done was show her a couple of dogs rutting, but it irritated the devil out of him that he'd exposed her to that.

"I must say," she began timidly, "that it didn't appear that the girl dog enjoyed it overly much."

Oh dear God. Suddenly an unfamiliar sound echoed through the room. It took him a moment to realize it was his laughter. Abruptly he stopped, peered over his shoulder at her. She was smiling and, with regret, it occurred to him that when he was done with her, she might never smile that sweetly again.

"You'll enjoy it, Eve, I promise you that."

He strode from the room before he did something rash. He was torn between taking her at that moment and letting her go. Maybe he should flip a coin, but as he'd told her, fate was seldom a friend, and he wanted her too much to take the chance.

Evelyn heard Rafe prowling about in his bedchamber. Perhaps he was right. Best to just get it over with. She took immense pleasure in his kisses. She could only imagine the pleasure she might find in his bed.

He wasn't Ekroth of the pudgy fingers, Berm of the rancid breath, or Pennleigh of the wrinkles in the wrong places. She furrowed her brow. Where precisely were the right places?

It didn't matter. Rafe would not have wrinkles. He was young and firm and powerful. She would want to hold him, caress him, stroke him. Lying there like a fallen tree was going to be difficult. Perhaps she should come up with a few rules of her own.

She slipped out of bed, padded toward the door, raised her hand—

But couldn't quite bring herself to knock. Once done, she would not be able to retreat. She understood that. Such a bold move would result in an even bolder one from him.

The thing of it was, though, she had become more comfortable with him. She'd seen the terrifying look on his face when he thought Geoffrey had touched her, yet she had not been terrified. His anger hadn't been directed at her. She'd known that, but that he could care so much, so passionately that she might have suffered at Geoffrey's hand, had caused the misgivings about this arrangement that she'd been harboring to drift away as though tossed on the outgoing tide.

She had little doubt that had Geoffrey abused her, Rafe would have killed him. Or at the very least made Geoffrey wish he were dead. Probably the latter.

She should be horrified that Rafe was a man who would take such dreadful actions, but instead she felt remarkably safe. He would defend her, he would protect her. Had he not been doing so all along? First from the *gentlemen* who had come to call, and then from Geoffrey. Of course it came with a price, but it was one she was willing to pay.

It was his laughter that had won her over, that had reached deep down within her, reverberated through her heart. It had sounded rough, like the rusty hinge on a door being opened after such a long period of disuse. He seemed as surprised by it as she was.

She wandered to the window and gazed out on the night. He had revealed only bits and pieces of himself but she was beginning to gain a sense of the whole. Like her, he had been left with no one to see after him. But he had managed to make himself into a successful man. He had not relied on his heritage, but on himself. He was to be admired.

Perhaps someday she would meet a man who would respect her for doing what she had needed to in order to survive.

Chapter 10

The following morning Evelyn enjoyed a solitary breakfast. It seemed Rafe had left for his club. He didn't return that evening or the next. Or the one that followed. No word from him. Was this the uncertainty that would be her life?

Curiosity had gotten the better of her one night and she'd attempted to open the door to his bedchamber, only to find it locked. She'd tried both doors, the one that led into her room and the one in the hallway. She wondered what secrets he harbored in there, what she might learn about him. He was so mysterious, and if he wasn't returning to the residence, how was she to come to know him better?

She knew all he desired was the bedding. Unfortunately she dreamed of more.

On the fourth afternoon, following a midday meal, she sat in a chair beneath the shade of a towering elm, near the brick wall that bordered the massive garden of the property beside this one. From a window at the end of the hallway in the wing where her bedchamber was located, she had been able to gaze out and see the large residence with its immaculate surroundings.

As usual, she had spent her morning wandering through the residence, imagining it as her own. She decided that she would convert it into a shelter for women who found themselves in a circumstance similar to hers. She would provide lessons in order for them to acquire skills that would allow them to secure gainful employment, so they were not dependent on others as she was.

Although it was quite possible that he was already done with her. She'd not heard a word from him. Had she done something to displease him? He seemed the sort to point out flaws. Perhaps she should visit a bookshop to see if she could find that book regarding the laws of mistresses. She felt quite ignorant about the whole affair. She supposed she should try to be seductive, but how did one go about that?

On the other hand, if he never bedded her, she'd never be ruined. She scoffed at that absurd thought. Living in a man's residence was ruination enough. No one would believe that a man as virile and masculine as Rafe Easton had not taken her to his bed.

She heard the childish gleeful laughter that had made her smile on other afternoons. This had become her favorite time of the day.

"Lord Redley!" a woman called out. "Come here, child."

More laughter, and she envisioned him running beyond the reach of his nurse. Based on the squealed pitch of his laughter, he couldn't be more than a couple of years old.

She fought not to regret that she would have no children running about these grounds. As she was only two and twenty, she supposed if Rafe released her while she was still young, with all she would obtain from him, that she could secure a husband and perhaps have children. But she couldn't stay here.

She was surprised that Rafe would situate his mistress beside a noble family, but then he did not seem to follow convention. She had considered introducing herself to the neighbors, but how would she explain her position here? She suspected they wouldn't be at all pleased to know a woman of such questionable moral character resided within easy reach.

So she stayed in her own garden, sipping on her tea, alone with not even porcelain dolls to keep her company.

She watched as Laurence strode toward her. He was incredibly kind. Perhaps she could convince him to join her for a bit of tea. If she was going to be an unconventional woman then she could treat the servants unconventionally.

"Hello, Laurence."

Stopping before her, he bowed slightly. "Afternoon, miss. Several large boxes have arrived from a Madame Charmaine. I've placed them in the parlor to await your inspection."

"Oh." She popped up out of her chair. "My wardrobe." Already? She could hardly believe it. Nor could she believe her excitement at the prospect of having something to wear other than her one black dress. If Laurence didn't have such long legs, she doubted he'd be able to keep up with her. She was fairly skipping over the lawn.

"Is it usual for Mr. Easton to stay away so long?" she asked.

"Yes, miss. Sometimes I wonder why he even bothers to have a residence. I believe he prefers his club."

She peered at him out of the corner of her eye. "Have you ever been there, to his club?"

"Once or twice."

His answer seemed a bit evasive, and she couldn't help but wonder why. It seemed everyone associated with this residence held secrets.

He opened the door to the small sitting room and she skirted past him into the hallway. "Send Lila to me."

"Yes, miss."

Laurence veered off, while Evelyn carried on until she reached the entryway. She swept into the parlor and stumbled to a stop.

Rafe lounged in a chair near the window, with sunlight pouring in to bask him in its golden warmth. One leg was outstretched, the other bent at the knee, one elbow resting on the arm of the chair, a tumbler of honeyed liquid near his lips. Lips that had taunted and teased her, warmed her, sent plea-sure whirling through her.

Pleasure very similar to what was thrumming through her now at the sight of him. He was so large, so very masculine, so incredibly beautiful even though it was obvious that he'd not bothered to shave in some time. But the stubble only served to make him appear more sensual, more enticing.

She clasped her hands together to stop herself from reaching for him. She feared she'd find not being able to hold him torturous in the days and nights to follow. Because if she couldn't hold him, he in all likelihood wouldn't hold her. And that seemed almost a sin.

"You've returned." Her voice was raspier, throatier, and sounded quite breathless. From the scurrying to get here, no doubt. Not as a result of any joy emanating from the fact that he was here, because his presence always brought with it the possibility of total ruination.

"It would seem so, yes," he said, his gaze shuttering whatever he might be feeling upon seeing her again. Probably nothing at all. It saddened her to think that he might never view her as anything more than a tumble. He waved his glass toward the boxes. "Some of your clothing is completed. The remainder should be finished by the end of next week."

She glanced over at the myriad of boxes before returning her attention to him. They seemed inconsequential now that he was here. She wanted to ask him where he'd been, what he'd been doing, why he had stayed away, if he was well, although she doubted he'd answer. "You went to the trouble to pick them up."

He shrugged. "I was passing by. Take a peek, see if the items are to your liking."

She desperately wanted to tell him that he couldn't just leave her here, languishing, worrying over him—but she didn't want him to know that she had been worried. Were men likely to become volatile when they lost a good deal of money? She had disquieting visions of him being accosted by someone who had lost at cards at his club. Someone like Geoffrey.

She wanted to inform him that she expected certain considerations, but an image stuttered through her mind—one she'd not thought of in a good long while. Her mother sitting by the window, dressed so beautifully, gazing out.

"What are you doing, Mama?" Evelyn had asked.

"Simply waiting for the earl, darling."

In retrospect she realized that her mother had spent a good deal of her time simply waiting. Now it seemed living in expectation of Rafe's arrival would become her lot in life. But waiting on him was preferable to waiting for Geoffrey to come unlock her bedchamber door.

She also remembered how her mother would rush out the door the moment she spotted the earl's carriage. How she would be in his arms as soon as he alighted. How after he patted Evelyn's head and gave her a doll, he would go up the stairs with her mother. She wondered if she'd ever experience such delight in Rafe's arrival. Delight, not relief because she suddenly thought that she should do more than simply stand there like a ninny reveling in his physical perfection when it was obvious that seeing her stirred nothing at all in him.

Self-conscious of her role in his life, she turned to the first box, lifted the lid, and dug through the tissue until she found the dark blue riding skirt with its white shirt and its blue jacket trimmed in silver piping. It was elegant, yet sedate. She'd expected the clothing he purchased her to be risqué, to proclaim loudly and clearly what she was, but this was the sort of outfit that a highborn lady would wear. She peered over at him, certain he hadn't moved a single muscle.

"Thank you. It's lovely."

With the hand holding his tumbler, he indicated a circular box resting on a settee. "The hat that goes with it."

It was the same shade of blue. White chiffon wound around the brim and was gathered into a bow at the back. "It seems you have superb taste."

"I have you, don't I?"

She jerked her head around to find him studying the liquid in his glass as though it had spoken rather than he, and he was castigating it. She couldn't recall him ever issuing her a compliment, ever admitting that he found her attractive or enticing. He'd wanted her because other men had, and he'd found them unsuitable. Or so she thought.

She reached for another box. Inside was a gown very similar in shade to the purple she'd worn the night that Geoffrey introduced her around, but the cloth was silkier, a finer quality. Slipping it over her body would cause her nerve endings to dance.

Within each box was a surprise: a black mourning dress, plain and yet elegant. She'd not expected him to provide her with something to wear when he wasn't around, something that would allow her to continue to honor her father.

A deep green gown for dining. It would bare her décolletage. One of soft pink that had a frothy bodice. A silk dressing gown of violet. A gossamer nightdress of white. Even gathered up, when she ran her hand behind it, she could see her skin. It would leave nothing at all to his imagination.

As she placed it back in the box, she couldn't look at him, didn't want him to see the fear and trepidation that raced through her with the reminder that he would bed her, and he wanted her to be enticing when he did.

Among the scattering of box lids and tissue, only one box remained. She knew what it was before she'd fully pushed the paper covering it aside. The vibrant red could not be hidden. When she pulled the gown out of the box, she gasped, her breath caught.

She hated it . . . because it was so beautiful. It was silk and lace, satin bows, and elegant flounces. Clutching it to her bosom, she wished she knew how to knock that smug self-satisfied expression off his face.

"It's . . . it's exquisite." She balled it up, stuffed it back into the box. "But I still shan't wear it."

A corner of his mouth quirked up. "You've a bit of stubbornness in you."

She didn't know why she was being so obstinate about the red. She just wanted something in her life that she had some say over. "I should probably take these upstairs and try them on, make sure they fit properly."

"Start with the riding habit," he said, tapping his glass with one finger. "We'll go for a ride through the park."

Her breath hitched, and while she knew it was quite possible that he had a stable filled with horses, she couldn't stop herself from asking, "You have Snowy?"

He lifted his glass in a salute, downed the remainder of its contents.

"That's where you've been, what you've been up to."

Tilting his head slightly, he studied her. "Where did you think I was?"

"At your club. I thought you were giving me time to become accustomed to you."

"A bit difficult to become accustomed to me if I'm not here."

She released a slight self-conscious laugh. "I'm not certain I shall make a good mistress. I didn't like not knowing where you were or when you might return. I didn't like waiting about, not knowing what I should be doing. I realize that you don't have a care for me and that I'm to serve only one purpose, but—"

In a motion as quick as it was powerful, he shoved himself out of the chair and crossed over to her. His gaze wandered over her face, and she felt it almost like a touch. "It did not occur to me that you would worry. Rather I thought you would welcome the reprieve that my absence offered." With the knuckle of his forefinger, he grazed her cheek. "I can't always know when I can be here. My business, sometimes it will keep me away."

"But it didn't this time."

He skimmed his thumb over her lower lip. "You are part of my business now."

Before she could respond or read whatever might be in his eyes, he turned away. "Let's go for a ride, shall we? I went to a great deal of trouble to bring that horse here."

He had suggested they go for a ride because from the moment she had walked into the parlor, he wanted nothing more than to lift her into his arms, carry her up the stairs, and ravage her. Like the barbarian London accused him of being.

His desire for her had only worsened as he'd watched the delight play over her features as she'd viewed one item of clothing after another. And the red—she would wear it. He had seen the temptation of it in her eyes before she shuttered it. He could not have been more pleased with her reaction to his gifts.

But when she had seen the horse—

Something inside of Rafe had felt as though it were being torn asunder. He wanted her to look at him with the same joy, the same pleasure, the same . . . he wasn't quite sure what the emotion was. She liked the horse, deeply. Favored it. She had stroked it and murmured to it and smiled at it.

He wanted her to smile at him.

Not look startled and apprehensive when she walked into the room and saw him sitting there.

As he kept his horse plodding along beside hers, he didn't want to contemplate that he might be jealous of the creature because it held her affections.

He didn't know what was wrong with him. He'd returned to London, stopped by the dressmaker's to see what had been completed, and then he'd gone to his residence. Not his club. From the night he'd obtained it, it had always held sway over everything else in his life. In his absence, it could have burned down for all he knew, but he had hardly given it a thought. His entire focus had been on seeing her again.

He had not missed her, because he was not in the habit of missing people. But he had thought of her constantly, continually. He had dreamed of her naked and writhing beneath him. He had dreamed of her wrapping her arms about him—and his not breaking out into a cold sweat, his breathing not becoming erratic, his heart not pounding unmercifully. In his dream, he had merely sunk down into her as she had tightened her hold, until it was impossible to tell where he ended and she began.

But that was fantasy. Reality would be much different. He knew that. Accepted it.

He couldn't stop his gaze from wandering back over to her. The clothing fit perfectly, hugged her bosom, her ribs, her narrow waist. She sat a horse well. As they entered the park, her eyes widened.

"There are so many people," she murmured softly.

"This is the time of day when anyone who is anyone promenades about. Have you not been to Hyde Park before?"

She suddenly took great interest in the reins, running the leather through her gloved fingers. "My father brought me here once, in a carriage, early in the morning. I can't recall seeing more than a dozen people. Will the people here know what I am to you?"

He wished he'd taken her father's tact and not brought her during the height of the late afternoon. "I doubt it. The men you met that night—of course, they will know, but it serves them no purpose to tell others about what took place. As they did not leave with you, it makes them appear weak."

"Yet here I am without a chaperon. That says a good deal about my morals, doesn't it?"

"A good many ladies come unchaperoned—only because there are so many people about. Besides, it doesn't matter what they think."

"No, I suppose it doesn't. Not anymore anyway." She straightened her shoulders, lifted her chin. "After Mother died, Father took me to his country estate. I'd not returned to London before this year."

"You remained at the country estate."

Nodding, she patted the horse's neck. "I liked it there."

He imagined she did. From what he'd been able to determine, it was remote, quiet, green. So very green.

"Why did you return this year?"

"I think Father intended to marry me off, but then he took ill—so swiftly, so unexpectedly. His health declined at an alarming rate. The physician said he'd had cancer of the blood for some time. I thought that I might be attending balls." She glanced around, guided her horse with an expert hand. "I realize now it was a silly dream. If he'd not have brought me to the park during a time when everyone else was about, he'd not have bothered to garner me an invitation to a party."

He could see the realization dawning that her father might not have been as proud of her as she'd always imagined. Anger, quick and sharp, surged through him. He fought to keep his tone flat, uncaring. "It wasn't because your father didn't value you that he didn't bring you for the promenade. I suspect it was because he cared for you so much that he wouldn't wish to see you hurt. The people prancing about now can be cruel when they put their minds to it."

"You don't think much of them."

"No, and neither should you. They're not important."

"What of the people who live in the residence next to yours? The ones with the little boy. Do you know them?"

"They're not important."

She twisted her lips into an ironic smile. "Is anyone important to you?"

You are. The sentiment made absolutely no sense. His rush to the residence in order to see her again, his prolonging their time together by bringing her here. He couldn't remember the last time he'd come to a park. It had been for a lady, and they had parted ways soon after. "I've been on my own for too long, Eve, for anyone else to matter."

"Will I feel that way, do you think? After a time?" She shook her head. "I hope not. I find it very sad. And I should think it would be very lonely."

"Not if you like your own company."

"And do you like yours?"

Not very, but that was beside the point. He ignored her question, allowed the silence to stretch between them.

"Will we see Geoffrey out here, do you suppose?"

"Not if he sees us first."

She smiled, a bright cheery smile that reached her eyes and made them sparkle. Something in his chest tightened. The damned waistcoat was much too snug. He shouldn't have indulged in a sweet. It didn't take many before his clothes needed altering. He'd discovered that quickly enough years ago.

"Did he give you much trouble over the horse?"

"He named a price and I paid it." He'd considered simply taking it, but he knew the money would end up back in his pocket anyway, and he had decided angering Wortham further would only serve to increase his resentment toward his half sister. He didn't think Eve would ever see him again, but one never knew.

"Did he take advantage, do you think?"

He laughed darkly. "Eve, no one takes advantage of me."

"I can't decide if you're confident or arrogant."

He met and held her gaze. The color of her eyes was darker, not quite so violet. It was the blue of the riding habit. He should have gone with a violet, but he couldn't deny the grace that it added to her form. Nor did he understand what had prompted him to purchase an item of clothing that covered so much of her.

Wasn't a mistress supposed to be daring and bold in what she revealed? Eve looked absolutely innocent. Young. So very young. "How old are you anyway?"

"What difference does it make?"

The difference was that out here, content on her horse, relaxed, with no worries that he would demand of her what she certainly was not yet ready to give, she looked more girl than woman. "None at all. Simply curious."

"Four and ten."

Swearing harshly, he reached out and grabbed her reins, jerked her horse and his to a stop. He dragged his gaze over her. The delicate features, the slope of her neck and shoulders, the curve of her bodice, the narrow waist, the flare of her hips. "You're not a child," he ground out, because he didn't want her to be, he didn't want to have this utter fascination with someone he would have to wait years to possess.

She angled her head slightly. "If I were?"

"I don't take children, and you're lying."

"Teasing more like. I thought you a man without a moral compass at all. I'm quite relieved to discover you're not completely wicked."

"How old?"

"Two and twenty. An old lady by most standards, I believe. Quite on the shelf. That's why I thought . . ." Sighing, she shook her head.

"Thought your father intended to marry you off."

She nodded, skewed her lips into annoyance. "And Geoffrey. When he said he wished to introduce me to gentlemen—I assumed marriage. What of you? Is there someone you fancy?"

"Marriage is not for me." He released his hold on her reins. His fingers were beginning to ache from the tight grip. The thought of not having her for years—

"Don't tease me," he ordered before urging his horse on.

"I enjoy teasing."

"Yes, well, that's a habit you'll have to break while you're with me."

"I don't think I want to be molded into something I'm not." She sighed heavily, glanced around. "Although I suppose that's happening, isn't it?"

He refused to feel guilty because of her father's poor planning.

"Are there other mistresses here, do you think?"

"I suspect there are, but they're cleverly disguised as ladies."

"Much like me."

Not like you, he thought. In all of England, he doubted there was a woman to compare.

Evelyn knew she was babbling, talking about nothing of consequence or importance. It irritated her that she worried what people thought, that she felt as though she moved about with a great big M sewn onto her chest. She saw many couples parading about. Surely they weren't all married.

And surely if her father had not been ashamed of her, he would have brought her when the park was teeming with people. She didn't doubt that he loved her, but she was beginning to realize that he might not have been as proud of her as he'd always claimed. He'd never taken her into a dressmaker's. He'd never ridden by her side through a park.

She supposed Rafe Easton did it without any embarrassment because he was notoriously scandalous himself. She couldn't deny that he epitomized what she imagined fell into line with most ladies' dreams—tall, handsome, with just enough aloofness to be intriguing. He would make the women come to him. She wondered if he would expect her to initiate their coming together. She very much doubted it.

If he waited on her to be ready, he would find himself waiting a good long while. Although perhaps not as long as she'd originally thought. She didn't like knowing that he was such a loner. No one stopped to speak with them, no one shouted greetings. Rather people seemed to make a point of avoiding them as though they were in danger of catching the plague from them if they got too close.

Her initial reaction had been that it was because of what she was to become—a woman of low moral character. Yet she was coming to realize that it was more the wall surrounding him that kept people away. He didn't smile, he didn't greet, he didn't acknowledge. He was a lord, and yet he wasn't treated with the deference of one. She wanted to tell him that it didn't matter to her that his business dealings rendered him not quite respectable. He'd made something of himself, and yet it was obvious that all his hard work had not returned him to the bosom of the aristocracy, had not returned him to where he should have been.

Swearing harshly, he grimaced. He must have tightened his hold on the reins because his horse sidestepped and had to be brought back in line.

"Whatever's wrong?" she asked.

He gritted his teeth, shook his head. "We're about to be put upon."

"By whom?" Glancing around, she spotted the couple on matching bays trotting toward them. They were near enough that there was no hope for escape, but as they got closer, she had suspicions regarding who the gentleman might be. His eyes gave him away. The pale blue that resembled ice over a lake—but they weren't cold. Rather they were warm and inviting, twinkling with amusement that matched the smile worn by the lady riding beside him. Her hair was such a pale blond as to be almost white. Her eyes were a molten silver. Evelyn would not have described her as a great beauty, and yet there was a nobility to her bearing that graced her and made her unforgettable.

They brought their horses to a halt as Rafe and Evelyn did the same.

"Brother, I never expected to run across you here," the man said.

"Is Sebastian about?"

"Somewhere. Mary insists he make appearances." He shifted his attention to Evelyn. "I don't believe we've been introduced."

"Allow me the honor of introducing Miss Evelyn

Chambers. Evelyn, Lord Tristan Easton and his wife, Lady Anne."

Lord Tristan swept his hat from his head. "A pleasure. You're Wortham's sister."

"Half sister, yes."

"So sorry for the loss of your father," Lady Anne said.

"Thank you." She was acutely aware that she was not dressed in mourning and she should be.

"She'd be in black, if I didn't insist otherwise," Rafe said. "It's a horrendous shade on her. Does nothing to flatter her complexion."

"I think we go to extremes on the mourning attire," Lady Anne said kindly. "I say that as someone who wore black for two years."

"You lost your father as well?" Evelyn asked.

She smiled softly. "No, he is quite well. Like so many, I lost my betrothed during the Crimean War. Tristan and I met when I hired him to take me to Scutari to visit Walter's grave."

"Tristan was a boat captain for a bit," Rafe said.

Lord Tristan growled in a manner very similar to Rafe's when he wasn't happy. "*Ship* captain. There is a difference between a ship and a boat."

"They both float on the water."

"And there, the similarities end. If you would go sailing with us, I could demonstrate the difference."

"You still have your ship?" Evelyn asked. She could imagine how wonderful it would be to be able to go wherever she wanted, whenever she wanted.

Lord Tristan gave her a kind smile. "No, I sold the *Revenge* to a gent who I knew would appreciate it and care for it. But I'm designing and building yachts. I suspect yachting will become quite the thing in a few years. We'll be taking the first one out for a testing next week. If Rafe joins us, you're more than welcome to come along."

"I've never been on the sea."

"I found it quite exhilarating," Lady Anne said.

"If you're testing it, then there's a good chance it might sink," Rafe said.

Lord Tristan laughed. "Do you think I would dare risk my wife on something I wasn't sure of? Besides, I know you swim."

"That's not the point. Although it hardly matters. We won't have time for the boat."

"Probably for the best because if you called it a boat while you were on board, I'd heave you over the side."

"I'd like to see you try."

Evelyn had never seen two men glare at each other in such anger. Were they going to come to fisticuffs? She'd never witnessed a fight before. She suspected what was hovering between them had nothing at all to do with the ship or the boat. It went much deeper. Lord Tristan was one of the brothers who had left him, gone on without him.

Lady Anne revealed her mettle by reaching across and squeezing her husband's arm. "I fear we must be off."

Lord Tristan closed his eyes, released a long slow breath. When he opened them, they were once again filled with the teasing glint. "Whether you like it or not, you're part of the family. I hope you'll change your mind and join us on the *boat*." He settled his hat on his dark head. "Pleasure, Miss Chambers."

Then he and his lady were trotting away as though no dark clouds had been in danger of forming.

"Don't say anything," Rafe muttered before turning his horse about and sending it into a lope, back in the direction from which they'd come.

She almost didn't follow. Only she knew what it was to feel as though she wasn't wanted. As much as her father had spoiled her, Geoffrey had never embraced her presence. So she urged her mare into a trot, grateful when he slowed his horse to a walk and allowed her to catch up. He was breathing heavier than his gelding. Her father had never spoken harshly to her, had never shown her anger. She didn't know how to respond to it, how to diffuse it.

"I didn't much like him," she finally said.

He jerked his gaze over to her, his brow furrowed deeply. She wondered what he would do if she reached across and smoothed it out. Although considering the distance between them, she'd probably topple from the saddle before she reached him.

"Lord Tristan," she clarified in case he had doubts.

A corner of his mouth eased up. "You're loyal, I'll give you that. But I don't dislike him."

"Then why not go on his boat?"

"Ship." His lips hitched up higher. For a moment she thought he might laugh, but the hint of a smile disappeared. "I'm not like them. Tristan and Sebastian. Sebastian, the duke, he fought in the Crimea. Was gravely wounded trying to save someone. Tristan sailed the seas. I've heard he rescued a boy from sharks. They're good men and I'm not. We have little in common. They've moved back into Society, while I inhabit the darkest corners farthest from it."

He kicked his horse into a quick trot that made it impossible to carry on a conversation.

Still she followed, curious about these dark corners of his, silently questioning why he would prefer them, and wondering if a time would come when they would swallow her up as well.

Chapter 11

He took the first punch because he deserved it.

He'd seen Eve's face alight with Tristan's invitation, and he knew within the depths of his soul that it was probably the first one that she'd ever received from a noble. Her father, for all his love for her, had kept her in a gilded cage, one so beautiful and filled with such kindnesses that she'd not even realized it surrounded her.

And Rafe was going to deny her the pleasure of accepting it because if he spent time in his brothers' company, he had little doubt that they would see into his dark soul and know the things he'd done in order to survive.

He ducked as Mick took his next swing. Then he delivered a quick jab to his man's ribs.

"You're in a foul mood," Mick quipped.

If only he knew the half of it. As soon as he'd seen Eve delivered safely to the residence, he'd taken himself to his club to spare her his presence. In the boxing room, he was stripped to the waist. It was the one place where he didn't have to hide his aversion to wearing clothing. If only he could remove his trousers as well, he'd be in paradise.

Bouncing on the balls of his bare feet, Rafe danced around Mick. He was angry at himself for revealing to Eve that his brothers were good men and he wasn't. It was something he acknowledged in the darkest recesses of his soul, but he'd never voiced it aloud. He'd been so proud of his accomplishments, so proud of what he'd obtained.

He'd planned to show them both . . .

Instead, they had shown him that they were men of honor, that they had not turned their backs on their heritage, that they had done nothing to bring shame to the family name. While he had managed to commit one offense after another.

He didn't think about his sins, didn't let them get past the wall to his conscience. Under the same circumstances, he'd do it all again.

He swung out at Mick, missed, and the bastard took advantage to land a blow to Rafe's midsection that nearly doubled him over.

"You're off tonight," Mick said.

Rafe straightened, lifted his fisted hands. He never spoke of his past, he didn't confide, he didn't trust anyone to look beyond their own self-interests. It was the world in which he'd grown to manhood, one in which to survive, he never looked beyond his own needs, wants, desires. Finding himself concerned about what Eve might want unsettled him. He didn't want to keep her in a gilded cage, but taking her away from it meant moving about in circles where he was far from comfortable. "Do you ever think about how we came to be here?"

He swung. Mick ducked and scurried back. "You've heard the rumors, too, then."

"What rumors?"

Mick jabbed, Rafe blocked with his right and delivered a solid punch with his left. Mick staggered before regaining his balance and saying, "That Dimmick's not dead."

Dimmick, previous owner of the Rakehell Club, Rafe's mentor as well as his tormentor. A more vile creature had yet to be born. The man had supposedly jumped from Tower Bridge a few years back, although the bloated remains that washed up along the shores of the River Thames were hardly recognizable. It was the distinctive ring that Dimmick always wore on his left hand that had been used to identify him.

Avoiding a punch to the jaw, Rafe feinted one way before dancing back to the other. "It would be like him to fake his own death, and then lay low for a while."

"Six years?"

Dear God, had it been six years since he'd coerced Dimmick into signing the Rakehell Club over to him? He'd been fourteen when he'd begun working for Dimmick. Three years later he'd become his most trusted henchman, breaking bones without remorse, threatening without compunction. "You have the conscience of a corpse," Dimmick had once told him. "That's why you're so good at what you do." He took his orders and carried them out, because he'd learned too late that Dimmick wasn't the sort of man to whom he should be in debt.

"Dimmick always had patience." His mantra had been that if you're going to destroy a man, do it so you destroy him completely.

"If he is alive, he's going to be coming after you." Mick jabbed Rafe's shoulder.

"If something happens to me, go see a solicitor named Beckwith. He has my will and the papers for this place. Upon my death, the Rakehell Club goes to you."

Mick froze, stared at him, and Rafe—from a long ingrained habit of never failing to take advantage of a weakness—rammed his fist beneath Mick's chin and sent him spiraling backward and to the floor.

Damn. That was going to end the sparring. He knelt beside the man who had scurried around behind him when he was younger, taking whatever scraps Rafe was of a mind to toss his way. Not many, but it was enough to keep Mick loyal. When Rafe had acquired the gaming hell, he'd offered Mick a place. It didn't make them friends. Their only association was the business. Mick managed it, and looked out for things when Rafe wasn't here. Which until recently had been seldom.

"Not that I'm planning for anything to happen to me," he assured Mick when the glazed look left his eyes.

"Why would you leave it to me?"

"Who else would know how to manage it?"

"I can manage it without owning it. Surely there is someone better to leave it to."

"If there is, I've yet to meet him. But as I said, I plan to be around for a good long while yet. Still, send out some runners, have them ferret around, see what they can learn. If Dimmick is alive, it's to my advantage to get to him before he gets to me."

"*Wake up, wake up*," his mind whispered, but he didn't dare say the words aloud. He wasn't certain he wanted her to know that he was there, leaning against the bedpost at the foot of her bed, watching her sleep again. While he was away, he'd thought of the night before he left, when he'd observed her while she lay sleeping. Every night he wanted to be back here, his gaze honed in on her face, the sweet expression of it.

All the women he'd known intimately had been coarse and hard, shaped by life into something impossible to break. She could break. In all likelihood he would eventually destroy her, unless he found the strength to let her go.

He admired her stubbornness, enjoyed sparring words with her. He would think he was winning, and then she would slip in beneath him and deliver a quick jab that left him flummoxed. Sometimes, only a few times, when he was in her company, he caught shadowy glimpses of the man he might have become had fate been kinder. A man who deserved to have her for the remainder of his life.

Her eyes fluttered open, and she smiled. "While you were away, I woke up every night expecting to see you standing there."

He'd stayed awake every night, wanting to be here. Dangerous, so dangerous. She could become an addiction. He was well aware of what happened to men who could not get enough of gambling, liquor, or opium. He had to put a stop to his growing obsession with her, of wanting to be in her company.

"I missed you during dinner," she said, and something in his chest clutched. Words, they were merely words. Something someone said when another person wasn't about. She hadn't meant that she'd truly *missed* him. She would have to care for him to yearn for his presence. She was here only because she was forced to remain. If he let her go, he'd never see her again.

That thought was intolerable.

She started shoving herself into a sitting position, stilled, and narrowed her eyes. "What happened to your face?"

He shrugged. "I was sparring."

"You mean fighting?"

"For sport. I have a boxing room at the club."

"Sport? Why do gentlemen find it entertaining to be hit?"

"Not to be hit. To do the pummeling."

She rolled her eyes as though exasperated, jerked on the bellpull, threw back the covers, and scrambled out of bed.

"What are you doing?" he asked, alarmed by her actions. She wasn't thinking of hugging him in comfort, was she?

"A man of your wealth no doubt has an icebox. We're going to get you some ice for your wound."

"It's hardly a wound. Mick doesn't have that hard of a punch."

She stood before him, rose up on her toes, and studied his face as though it was a curiosity, something unusual that should be on display. She lifted her hand, he grabbed her wrist. She furrowed her brow. "It's bruising and swelling."

Releasing his hold on her, he gingerly touched his

fingers to his tender cheek, near his eye. "It's not that bad."

A knock sounded at the door.

"Sit in a chair by the fire," she ordered with authority before heading for the door.

He stood exactly where he was. No one ordered him about. No one.

Opening the door slightly, she spoke to the servant on the other side. When she turned back into the room, she pressed her lips together and pointed toward the sitting area. "Sit!"

She walked to the washbasin, picked up a cloth, and dipped it into the water. He looked at the sitting area, looked at her. Where was the harm? He wasn't following an order. He wanted to sit. That was the reason that he ambled over and dropped into a stuffed high-backed chair.

As she strolled toward him, he watched the movements of her nightdress in fascination. He caught glimpses of the outline of her legs. He wanted to run his hands over her thighs, then send his lips on the same journey.

She knelt before him, lifted the cloth. "This will suffice until the ice arrives. The water was cool."

"I can do it," he said, reaching for it.

She yanked it back and glared at him. "I'll do it." She waited a heartbeat. "Please. You've done so much for me, and I've done nothing for you. I can give you this small courtesy."

It had been so very long. He didn't know how to accept kindness graciously. It was the reason that Tristan's gift had nearly unmanned him.

He didn't answer, but neither did he object or pull away when she very gently touched the cloth to his cheek. He watched her instead: the concern in her eyes, the tiny furrow between her brows, her concentration—as though if she didn't do it just right, she would cause irreparable harm.

"I don't understand men fighting," she said quietly. "Did you get the better of him?"

He experienced a strange swelling of pride in his chest. "I felled him."

"Why would you hurt a friend?"

"He's not a friend. He works for me. He got in a good jab or two."

She sighed. Another knock sounded on the door. "Hold this in place."

Another order. As she got up to answer the door, he realized he was going to have to have words with her about this ordering him about business. He wouldn't tolerate it. But when she returned, took the cloth from him, and placed ice shavings in it, he said not a word. As she gently laid it against his cheek, he thought he'd never felt anything so sublime.

"Are you hungry?" she asked. "I could have the cook prepare something."

"No, I've eaten." He wasn't accustomed to having someone asking after his welfare. It was unsettling.

"Why would a gambling den need a boxing room?" she asked, her eyes focused on her task. She was positioned in such a way that from time to time, with an intake of a breath or an adjustment in her posture, one of her breasts brushed against his arm. It was almost his undoing. His mouth went dry. It would be so easy to roll out of the chair onto her, take her to the floor, lift the hem of her nightdress—

No, he'd not lift it. He'd rip it asunder. He wanted

to see her in all her naked glory, and he had no doubt that she would be glorious.

"Men have frustrations," he said, finding himself being tied up into knots at that moment with those very frustrations. "They need a place to work it off, so I have a room where they can box or wrestle. And sometimes—" He stopped. He wanted her comfortable with him. Not knowing the truth about him.

She peered up at him. "Sometimes . . . ?"

"I take men there and teach them a lesson."

The cold ice left his face as she sat back on her heels. "What sort of lesson?"

"Things that belong to me are not to be abused."

Her brow furrowed. "What sort of things?"

Why had he started down this path? Perhaps because he needed her to know some of the worst things about him, so she wouldn't care whether he'd eaten or was hungry or had a bruise forming on his cheek. He didn't want to fall into the allure of being tended. "The women who work for me—some do so on their back. Their choice," he added quickly. "They plied their trade on the streets, but in my place they have it better. They're clean, the rooms are clean, the customers who visit them are clean. But from time to time those gents can forget where they are and get a bit rough. When they hurt one of the girls, I hurt them back."

She blinked. "You personally?"

"Yes, me personally. There's nothing more frightening than facing a man who doesn't give a bloody damn."

Something soft touched her eyes. It made him want to squirm. He despised discussing any aspect of his life. He shouldn't have come in here to look in on her.

"You told me that you would make Geoffrey regret the manner in which he'd treated me. Are you going to do it in that room?" she asked.

"No, I have something else in mind for him."

"What precisely?"

"I haven't worked out all the particulars yet. I'll let you know when I do." Rafe had long ago learned that the best revenge didn't involve physical pain. Hurts healed. The memory of agony diminished over time. Better to arrange something that was a constant reminder of failings or misjudgments.

"Thank you for that, for seeing that Geoffrey will have regrets."

The gratitude in her eyes almost had him asking her to make him promise her something else. No one had ever looked at him like that. He was accustomed to instilling fear, but for the first time in his life, he thought there might be something stronger than fear. He wasn't certain what it was, but it scared the bloody hell out of him.

Rising back to her knees, she carefully placed the ice enfolded in the cloth on his darkening bruise, and her nearness distracted him from his irritation. Her breast rested firmly against his upper arm now, and he could feel the taut nipple through her nightdress, through his sleeve. He wanted to circle his tongue around it, once, twice, then over—

"I should like to visit your gambling establishment sometime." Her voice seemed raspier. Did her thoughts travel in the same direction as his? He doubted she was even aware of the liberties a man would take with a body such as hers.

He scoffed. "Ladies are not allowed inside."

"But then I'm not a lady, am I?" She held his gaze

with a challenge. He wanted to deny her words, but he couldn't.

"You wouldn't much like it. It's mostly black and green. There's always a smoky haze. It smells of rich tobacco, fine liquor, and finer women."

"Still, I should like to see where you spend so much of your time."

Before she'd entered his life, he'd spent all his time there.

She set the cloth aside, and with a featherlike touch moved his hair back. He couldn't remember the last time he'd known a caress that was as light as a cloud. Yet even for its faintness, it was powerful.

"I wish he hadn't hurt you," she said.

"I've known worse."

Her eyes shifted over to his. "Yes, I presume you have. You live in a very rough world. Do you ever think of leaving it?"

"It's where I belong."

"But you're the son of a duke."

"If he were alive, he'd disown me." Never mind that if he were alive Rafe would have never been in a position to do the things he'd done.

"I suspect my father would do the same, knowing the decision I made to stay here. Although I suppose in truth, he never really owned me."

"Don't give too much weight to a trip to a park."

"But you're not keeping me hidden away. You're not ashamed to be seen with me."

He cupped her face, grateful she hadn't realized that his knuckles were also lightly bruised and slightly swollen. They bothered him more than his cheek, but when he touched her, the pain eased, as though she were a balm. He wanted her now, this moment. He wanted all the hurts to cease. What a fanciful thought. Some were embedded so deeply they'd never be touched, comforted, eased. He would take them to the grave.

He skimmed his thumb over her cheek. He had promised to give her the skills she needed to survive on her own. He had yet to begin teaching her about investments, but he knew now that she needed something more. "How tired are you?"

Her eyes widened slightly, her skin flushed, and he knew by her reaction where she thought he was going with his question. "I'm fully awake."

He heard the slight tremble in her voice, but at least she hadn't lied. She was growing more comfortable with him. He thought about taking her to bed, but he wasn't at his best tonight. Too many dark thoughts were tumbling through his mind. Faces he'd beaten, bones he'd broken. On Dimmick's orders. At first he'd been too young and frightened not to obey the ruthless orders. Disappoint Dimmick, and there would be hell to pay. Then for a time he'd begun to enjoy it. Smashing people up, throwing his weight around, being feared. Until he'd been passing by a shop one day and caught sight of a thug in the large mirror that was on display behind the window. It took him a moment to recognize who the brute was—it wasn't until he'd looked into the icy-blue eyes that he'd known, and his stomach had roiled with the realization of what he'd become.

He shoved himself out of the chair. "Get dressed. Your hideous mourning attire should do nicely. We're going to the club."

"Now?"

"You're less likely to be seen at this hour." And

at the club, he was less likely to tumble her onto the
bed and turn his attention to a sport that had little
to do with fisticuffs.

Evelyn fought not to be disappointed. When they'd
first arrived, he'd brought her downstairs, and she'd
thought they were heading for the dens of deprav-
ity. Instead, he'd led her into a room with a roped-off
square in the middle and benched seating stacked
along the walls. She imagined people sat there to
watch what occurred within the boundaries of the
rope.

She was hoping to see the gaming room, to view
the games that men lost fortunes playing, especially the one that had put Geoffrey into debt to
Rafe, the one that had caused him to invite the
gaming hell owner to his night of entertainment
when he'd sought to foist her off as some man's
mistress. She didn't like to contemplate where she
might be now if Rafe hadn't been there.

"Remove your cloak," he ordered, and she
glanced over to see he was shrugging out of his
jacket. She did wish the man wasn't in the habit of
ordering her about without first explaining where
his directives would take her. Still, she unfastened
her cloak, slipped it off her shoulders, and draped it
over a bench.

When next she looked at Rafe, his waistcoat was
gone and he was dragging his shirt over his head.
He tossed it aside. She stared in wonder at his rippling muscles, his washboard stomach. He moved
as though he were comprised of poetry, smooth and
flowing. She had visited a museum with her father

once and seen statues of the gods. But even they were not as lean, as firm, as beautifully sculpted as Rafe.

"Am I to remove my clothing?" she asked.

He jerked his gaze over to her. "What? No, of course not. That would be distracting, give you an unfair advantage." He pulled up one of the ropes, creating a small archway. "Come on. In you go."

"What are we doing here?"

"Eventually you'll be on your own. Someone might try to take advantage. You need to know how to defend yourself."

"You're going to teach me how to box?"

He shook his head, locks of his dark hair falling forward, making him appear both younger and more dangerous. "I'm going to teach you how to fight."

"I could punch Geoffrey."

"If you like. I'll hold him for you."

"That wouldn't be fair."

"I don't believe in fighting fair; I believe in fighting to win. Now come on. Into the boxing ring you go."

She could hardly countenance this, or the exhilaration that fissured through her. She suspected not all the excitement had to do with what he was about to teach her, but with the fact that the sight of him without a shirt was causing something rather giddy to occur in her stomach. As she got nearer, she spied the darkened flesh over his ribs. "Oh my God, you're bruised."

Without thought, she reached out and touched it with her gloved hand. Stiffening, he took in a sharp breath, the air hissing between his teeth.

"Why didn't you tell me? I would have tended it."

Wrapping his long fingers around her wrist, he

moved her hand away. "I'm on a short tether here, Eve. If my shirt had come off in your bedchamber, your nightdress would've as well."

She looked at him through widened eyes. "Surely not when you're hurt."

"When I'm hurt, when I'm ill, when I'm on my deathbed."

"Is it that way for all men?"

He gave her an expression of pure exasperation. "I have no idea. I don't discuss this with men. I only know what it's like for me. Now, into the ring you go."

As she ducked beneath the hemp, she doubted he discussed anything with anyone, but as he was more worldly than she, she suspected he thought a great deal about what it might be like between them. She was finding her own thoughts turning in that direction more often. She didn't want to find herself attracted to him, but she couldn't deny that he was a fine specimen. She didn't want to stare at him, but it was so very difficult to look away. His arms were firm and muscled. Sinewy. While he didn't want her arms around him, she realized she would very much enjoy having his arms around her.

"—bring him to his knees."

"Pardon?" She realized he'd been talking while she'd been lost in thought.

He sighed. "Pay attention, Eve. I was explaining that a man is most vulnerable between his legs. Kick him there and you'll drop him like a felled tree."

"I see."

"With your skirts and petticoats, it's unlikely that you'll be able to kick high enough—"

"Well, unless he's a dwarf. Then I should be able to manage it quite well."

He stared at her, then released a sharp bark of laughter. It made her smile to hear the sound echoing around her. "If he's a dwarf, you should be able to outrun him, so let's assume he's not a dwarf." He moved nearer to her and she folded her fingers against her palm so she wouldn't reach out and touch him again. "You want to allow him to get close." He curled his hands over her shoulders. "All the while looking innocent—"

She widened her eyes, blinked them.

He grinned. "Well done. He'll be arrested by your eyes and not notice when you slyly position your leg between his. Then bring your knee up as quickly and as hard as you can."

She did. Growling, he released her and dropped down to all fours, breathing heavily, head bent. "You . . . weren't . . . supposed to . . . do it."

She knelt. "How am I to learn if I'm doing it properly? Are you all right?"

"Just give me a moment."

She dearly wanted to comfort him, to rub his back and shoulders, to lean in and kiss his forehead. When had she begun to stop wishing that calamity would befall him? Uncomfortable with the thought that perhaps she wanted to be *with* him, she glanced around. "Suppose while I'm waiting for you to recover, I could take a look about, peek in at the gaming rooms."

"No."

"After you teach me to fight, will you teach me to gamble?"

He peered up at her. "No."

"You rather fancy that word, don't you?"

With a deep breath, he sat back on his heels. "Why

would you risk losing on the turn of a card what it is going to cost you so much to gain?"

"It does seem rather senseless, I suppose."

"Yes, it does." He shoved himself to his feet and pulled her to hers. "Now make a fist."

She curled her fingers around her thumb, tucked everything up against her palm. Taking her hand, he unfurled her fingers. "You want your thumb on the outside, covering your first two fingers. And you want to keep your fist level with your wrist, braced so it doesn't go up or down. Less likely to break your bones that way." He held up his palms. "Now punch a hand."

"I'll hurt you."

"I'll be fine."

Hearing the slap of her fist against his palm, she didn't much like it.

"Good," he said. "Again."

She punched, the awful sound of flesh being hit echoing around her.

"Harder and faster," he ordered.

She did, again and again. He began backing around the ring and she followed.

"If you really want to hurt someone, punch him in the nose. Stings like the devil. If you can break his nose, all the better. If he turns away from you, strike him in the kidney. It'll take him down like a kick to the groin."

"Where's the kidney?"

With her next punch, he quickly folded his large, powerful hand over hers, capturing it as though it were nothing, and she had a sense now of why he might have given that knowing smile the night she had threatened to scratch out his eyes. She'd have not stood a chance against him.

He moved his other hand around her and drew a small circle on her back. "There. And on the other side. Can momentarily paralyze a man if you do it just right."

"Do you do it just right?"

He nodded. "Little point in doing it if you're not going to do it correctly. That's the thing as well, once you commit to fighting, commit fully. Never back down, never give quarter. I've seen many a small man take down a larger one simply because he had the determination to win."

"You've seen a lot of fighting then." She couldn't recall ever witnessing any. Certainly neither her father nor Geoffrey had ever come home bruised and bloody. She'd never held a damp cloth to a man's face, had never begun counting a man's whiskers because she feared if she continued to gaze into his eyes, she might become lost within their depths.

By his words and actions, Rafe gave the impression of a man who cared about little save himself, but tending to him she knew there was far more to him. She just wasn't certain if she'd be wise to explore it.

"I've seen a lot of people striving to survive," he said. "It's generally not pretty."

"Seeing it probably affects a person as much as experiencing it."

"Not as much as," he said quietly, his gaze roaming over her face as though he wished to *experience* the silkiness of her skin, the taste of her lips. He cleared his throat. "Now then, if a man comes up behind you and puts his arms around you—" He spun her around, cupped his hands on her shoulders. "—bow your head forward, then slam it back with as much force as possible, hit him in the nose. Within any luck, you'll break it."

"I don't think you're close enough for me to reach."

"I prefer to avoid this demonstration if you don't mind."

"I won't do it hard, but it seems I should have a sense of it."

With his thumbs, he stroked the corded muscles on either side of her neck. His arms didn't come around her, but she felt his warm breath wafting over her nape. "I'm near enough."

His voice was low, seductive. Her breathing went shallow, her stomach tightened. She thought for her own self-preservation she probably should slam her head back. But the thought of hurting him made her nauseous. "Will I know if I've broken his nose?" she asked in a dry rasp.

"Yes. You'll hear a loud crack."

A circle of damp heat caused dew to form on the sensitive flesh near her left ear. It was all she could do not to turn into it. He slid his mouth to the other side. Her eyes slammed closed, and she thought of rainy mornings buried beneath a mound of blankets.

"What if he doesn't let me go?"

Silence followed, thick and heavy, and she wondered if like her, he was trying to decipher whether she was still referring to an attacker, or if she was asking about the man who now stood behind her, trailing his lips so lightly, so slowly along the nape of her neck, causing the fine hairs to rise.

"He will," he finally said, and she could have sworn she heard regret in his voice. He moved away from her. "I think you have the gist of things now."

She turned around to see him slipping beneath the rope and going toward his clothes. "We didn't practice overly much. It hardly seems worth it to have gone to the bother to come here."

He snatched up his shirt, shoved his arms into the sleeves. "The flooring is softer within the ring, there is no clutter or trinkets that can be broken, and you were less likely to get hurt if we took things further."

"Why aren't we? Taking things further, I mean. I think I was beginning to get the hang of it."

He didn't bother with his waistcoat or jacket. Just clutched them in his hand. "Are you that naive?"

She could see the strain in his features, the white of his knuckles as he fisted his free hand. He strode over and lifted the rope as though he'd like to use it to strangle someone.

"This was a bad idea," he said. "We need to go."

"I thought it was a rather good idea." She slipped beneath the rope. "Now I know how to punch Geoffrey the next time I see him."

"Just remember to keep your wrist level. I shouldn't like to be inconvenienced by your being hurt."

She wished he'd smiled when he'd said that so she'd know whether he was joking. "Since we're here, may I have a look around?"

He studied her for a moment. "I suppose no harm would come from a quick peek."

She followed him out of the room, up two flights of stairs, and down a hallway with several rooms. She might have thought this was the bordello portion except that the doors were open. The walls were papered in burgundy, with gold vines. More tasteful than she would have expected. Gas lamps flickered along the walls. Glancing through a doorway into a room they were passing, she stopped.

"This is your office; it's where you work." She strolled inside. It was Spartan. A desk. A chair in front of it, and another behind it. A table with decanters. The windows were bare, looking out onto the night.

"Why do you say that?" he asked.

Looking over her shoulder, she saw him leaning against the doorjamb, his arms crossed over his chest. "The globes."

They were sprinkled about numerous shelves on three walls. "There must be a hundred of them."

"A hundred and two to be exact."

Astonished, she twisted around. "Does that include the ones at the residence?"

"No."

"Why do you collect them? What's your fascination with them?"

He just stood there, staring into the dimly lit room.

"Is it because you were planning to travel the world and you wanted to study where you might be going? You can confide in me. I won't tell anyone."

"You have no one to tell."

"I suppose that's true enough. I collected dolls when I was a child. Not by choice, but rather it's what my father always gave me. So perhaps I wasn't so much collecting dolls, as I was collecting symbols of his love. Maybe that's why I smashed so many of them. I was angry, and I couldn't very well smack him." She turned away from him. She hadn't wanted to travel into her own life. Rather, she wanted to journey into his.

"They gave me hope."

Her heart hammering, she jerked back around. Just a glimpse. She wanted only a glimpse into his soul. She waited. Surely there was more. And then her patience was rewarded.

"They gave me hope that there was someplace better than where I was."

"So you collected all these when you were a child?"

"No, Eve, I still collect the damn things." He shifted back into the hallway. "Did you want to see the gaming hell or not?"

He was still searching for someplace better than where he was—just as she was. She didn't want to be a mistress, she didn't want to live in a house that belonged to a man who wanted her only for sport. She wanted something better: a husband, a family, a home.

His residence would never be a home.

Nor would his office. It didn't satisfy him. As comfortable as he appeared, nothing here—except the globes—reflected the man. She had thought she'd make some small discovery about him that would explain him, but even here he was very careful to reveal nothing about himself.

"Yes, I want to see it."

Maybe there at last, she would come to understand him.

Rafe had an unsettling suspicion that he hadn't brought her to the club in order to teach her how to defend herself. That he'd used it as an excuse—to himself of all men, someone who had no tolerance for excuses—because he wanted her to see his establishment. Not the sins perpetuated within it, but rather what he'd managed to make of it, something that ensured he would never again be in another man's debt, that he would never suffer, that he would never be forced into doing what he had no desire to do.

She could learn from him. Yes, for a time she would be unhappy, but when she was free of him, she would have the means to do whatever she wanted. Between now and that time, she needed to come to understand exactly what she wanted. He suspected that as soon as she was handed her first doll, the only thing she had envisioned for her future was becoming a wife.

Just as he had spent his first ten years believing that he would be a gentleman.

As he escorted her down a darkened hallway to the shadowed balcony, he drew forth a memory that he had long ago locked away. Sitting on his father's lap at his father's desk, watching as he carefully turned the pages of his atlas, and pointed out all the places that Rafe would someday visit.

"Pembrook brings in a fine yearly income so you'll have an allowance. No army or vicarage for you. I know it troubles you when Sebastian and Tristan go off without you, but someday you shall travel the world, while Sebastian will be forced to remain here."

In the end, they'd all been forced to leave.

He drew back the thick heavy curtains, inhaled Eve's rose scent as she walked by, and followed her onto the balcony. She went to the very edge, wrapping her hands around the carved railing. Even there, though, the shadows kept her hidden from those on the floor below. No one would ever know she'd visited. Although he suspected her phantom scent would haunt the hallways through which they'd walked. It was a mistake to bring her here, to risk having a memory of her within his club. When he let her go, he wanted nothing of her to linger. He wanted no recollections outside the bed.

Yet here he was enjoying the vision of her profile, while she studied everything spread out before her like a feast of sin. He could hear the cards being shuffled, the dice being thrown, the wheels being turned. He could hear the exclamations of joy and the groans of despair. He didn't have to look onto the gaming floor to know what he would see.

"There's so much activity. It's very much *alive*, isn't it?"

He didn't have to ask her to explain. He knew too well what she meant. It was a pulsing room of activity. Always something was happening. A card turned, a die tumbling to a stop, a ball dropping into a slot.

"What appealed to you about this place?"

Had he ever known a woman who asked so many questions? Had he ever known another woman who made him want to answer? Inquiries irritated him. They were bothersome, intrusive. Yet when she questioned, a small kernel of something in his soul snapped to attention and wondered, foolishly, ridiculously, if she cared.

"The money I could rake in."

She peered over at him, gave him what he suspected she thought was a knowing smile. "You could also lose it."

"The house always wins in the end, Eve. It wouldn't be unusual for a million pounds to exchange hands tonight, and most of it will go in the Rakehell's coffers."

She spun around, her eyes wide. "You're joshing."

He gave a small shake of his head.

"That's obscene."

"There are worse obscenities."

She scrutinized him, and he wished he'd kept his mouth shut. "Such as," she finally asked.

Using children for labor. Sending them down into the mines, in the dark, alone—except for the rats, and the roaches, and other multilegged creatures that bite—expecting them to sit still, open and close a door as needed for the horses and wagons. Sending them deeper into the pits, crawling into tiny spaces where they barely fit, having the dirt cave in on them until they thought they'd suffocate.

But he couldn't tell her any of that. It wasn't meant to be brought up to the surface. It needed to remain buried as deeply as the coal.

"Wortham for one," he said flatly. Perhaps the other lords who had been there that night as well. He was ready to move on. "I think we're done here."

She had thought he would escort her out to the carriage. Instead, they trudged up another flight of stairs.

She had to admit that Geoffrey was an obscenity, at least the manner in which he'd treated her. However, she didn't think for a single moment that Rafe had been considering Geoffrey while she'd waited for his answer. His facial features had not moved at all, but within his icy blue eyes she'd seen something— only a flicker—yet it was deep, powerful, and haunting. Something from his past perhaps, an incident, a person, a place that had been part of the process that had forged him into the man he was.

For a moment she'd thought he was going to share it. She didn't know if she wanted him to. She had a keen desire to understand him, but she was beginning to think it would come at a high price—that his nightmares might become hers.

At the top of the stairs, in the middle of the hallway, he opened a heavy mahogany door. She stepped through into a large living area, not quite as sparsely furnished as his office but he obviously cared nothing at all for knickknacks. She could see hallways branching off on either side of it and assumed they led to other rooms, bedchambers perhaps.

"My living quarters."

"Why do you have these when you are in possession of a lovely residence?" she asked as she wandered over to the large bare windows. She looked out on the street below. The fog was rolling in, giving an ominous feel to everything around which it swirled.

"I prefer here. The residence . . . I acquired it because it was within my power to do so."

She peered over at him. "This is where you'll reside once the residence is mine."

"In all likelihood, yes. Although perhaps I'll purchase another before that happens." He leaned against the edge of the window.

"You don't fancy draperies."

"Why put glass in a wall and then block the view you've obtained?"

She turned her attention back to the street. She could see gentlemen coming and going. "No one leaving has quite as lively a step as those arriving."

"When they first get here, they think Lady Luck sits on their shoulder."

"I suppose they soon discover that she doesn't."

Reaching out, he tucked a few loose strands behind her ear. A warm shiver flowed through her, but she kept her gaze focused on the street. It might prove very dangerous to look at him just then, with other rooms—bedchambers—nearby.

"She doesn't exist. She's merely a figment of some poor fool's imagination. Do you know the worst thing that can happen to a man the first time he visits a gambling hell?"

"He loses everything?"

"He wins."

She snapped her gaze over to him. He was watching her intently, but she was coming to realize that he always studied her as though he wished to decipher every aspect, every nuance, of her. She had journeyed through life paying little attention to anything of importance, while he allowed nothing to escape his scrutiny. He survived while she stuttered along, striving to find her way. She could learn from him.

"It's the winning that causes the obsession," he said. "That momentary exhilaration as though you're on top of the world, unbeatable, invincible. You experience it once and you never forget it. No matter how often you lose after that, you keep seeking that elusive thrill that for a time made you forget all the troubles in your life."

"So which was I, that night at Geoffrey's? Something to possess because you could? Or something to win for the momentary delight it would bring?"

He moved nearer, took the strands that had again worked themselves free, and sifted them through his fingers as though he'd never seen them before. "Some day some gent will win your heart, and the elation will far exceed anything he will experience with the turn of a card or the roll of the dice. He won't care that you're ruined or that your father never married your mother." His knuckles grazed her cheek before he slid his hand around to cup her chin. With the roughened pad of his thumb, he painted sensations over her lower lip.

She realized that he'd neatly avoided answering her question by filling her with hope that she might still possess all for which she yearned. "Will you ever marry?"

The words came out on a whisper of air. She didn't know why it mattered if he took a wife, but suddenly it did. Would he bring his lady here, teach her how to defend herself, show her his apartments? Would he allow her to put up draperies?

He shifted his gaze up to her eyes, and she saw the resignation and the truth there before he spoke.

"No."

A simple word that left no doubt, that allowed no space for the unexpected.

"What if she wins your heart?"

"She would first have to find it."

His mouth covered hers, with purpose, his tongue impatient to dance with hers. The intensity had her swaying, reaching up to wrap her arms around him for balance, to keep her knees from buckling and carrying her to the floor.

He grabbed her wrists before her hands grazed his shoulders, brought her arms back, shackled them in one firm grip, all the while continuing to plunder her mouth, to somehow keep her near even as he sought to put some distance between them.

Why would a man as sensual as he was, with such voracious kisses that threatened to devour her, have such an aversion to her holding him? How could he remain so aware of every small movement she made when she was lost in the frenzy of his coercing her to respond in kind, to deepen, to explore, to savor?

In the farthest recesses of her mind, she remembered that she was standing in front of an uncurtained window and that surely they must be providing entertainment for those arriving and leaving, but she didn't care. She. Did. Not. Care.

The realization slammed into her with frightening resolve. She wanted this kiss. His kiss. She wanted his mouth on hers. She wanted the taste of him, the rasp of his bristled jaw against her soft skin, the echo of his groans surrounding her.

Or was she the one moaning and sighing?

When had she begun to anticipate his kissing her? When had she begun to anticipate being in his presence? When had she decided that she desperately wanted to unravel the mystery of him?

He had no heart. He was not kind. He would never marry.

He was the absolute worst person for whom she should develop any sort of feelings, and yet there they were. Only seedlings now, but they would grow, and then where would she be? A woman broken in body and spirit.

Only she didn't think he'd break her. He was taking too much care not to, not rushing her, not forcing her before she was ready.

He tore his mouth from hers and, breathing harshly, he studied her as though she confounded him. Slowly, so very slowly, he released his hold on her, one finger unfurling at a time. His gaze slid over to the hallway, and he looked as though he were measuring how many steps it might take to get her there and beyond—to his bedchamber.

"Not here," she said quietly. She didn't know why it mattered, but it did. She didn't want him to take her in a place of sin and vice and debauchery.

His gaze came back and landed softly on her, the icy blue not quite so frigid. "No, not here."

They left then, with him escorting her down the stairs and along the corridors until they reached the back door, the one through which they'd entered what seemed an eternity ago.

"Was it all that you imagined?" he asked as he shoved open the door.

"I thought it rather dull and plain, actually. I don't know why I expected more excitement."

She walked down the steps to the carriage waiting in the mews for them. A footman opened the door. Rafe handed her up, but didn't follow her inside.

"The driver will see you home safely," he said.

"You're not coming?" She wondered why she was disappointed.

"I have some things to which I must attend."

"When will you return to the residence?"

"I'm not sure."

After shutting the door, he walked to the steps and stood there, watching the carriage, watching her. She could see him clearly through the window.

The carriage rocked and was off. It turned and she lost sight of Rafe. She didn't know if she'd ever seen anyone who looked so alone.

Chapter 12

The clock on the mantel was veering toward eleven when she awoke. She never slept in this late. She supposed that was what happened when one entertained gentlemen at all hours of the night.

She climbed out of bed, rang for her maid, walked to the window, and drew back the draperies, not surprised to discover it was a dreary overcast day. Although it hardly matched her mood. One of these nights he would come to her and they would do more than talk. It was the terms to which she'd agreed. She would honor them. She might not have much left to her but she had her word.

The door opened and she glanced over her shoulder at her maid. The air in the room didn't take on an energetic charge, seem to shrink in size, or become more alive with her entry.

"I shall want fresh linens on the bed today."

Lila seemed surprised. "Yes, miss. We put on fresh linens every day."

Of course they did.

Lila went to the wardrobe and retrieved the

mourning dress in which Evelyn had arrived that
fateful night. It seemed an eternity had passed. Suddenly Evelyn despised the thing.

"No, the newer one. I have an errand to run. I'll
want you to accompany me, and we'll need three
strapping footmen to come with us."

"Yes, miss."

"I shall want to meet with cook. I need to look
over the menu for tonight's dinner. I want it to be
something special."

The maid blinked, and Evelyn realized that she
didn't need to reveal her entire schedule to the girl,
especially as she'd only just determined that she
was taking the day and night in hand as much as
possible.

It was early afternoon by the time she was in the
carriage, heading toward her destination. It struck
her that within the space of a sennight her life had
changed immeasurably. She had never called for
a carriage while at her father's residence. She only
went out when he accompanied her. She never instructed servants regarding her preferences on
meals. She had never served as mistress of a household.

She'd learned something valuable about Rafe in
the shadows of her room last night. He'd said that
he didn't give a bloody damn, but he did. Far more
than he realized and was willing to admit, even to
himself. If he didn't care, he'd not take to task any
men who hurt the women in his establishment, he
wouldn't have given her lessons on how to protect
herself. While she had suspected from the first that
he'd not hurt her physically, she was now certain
of it.

What he might do with her heart, however, was another matter entirely. She feared that unlike him, she didn't have the strength to keep it locked away. It was easily found and bruised. She had even allowed Geoffrey to cause her pain. He had never given her cause to think he cared for her, but she had never realized that he despised her. Her father's unconditional adoration had allowed her to embrace the fantasy of being special. Geoffrey had most cruelly torn her whimsy into shreds.

The carriage turned down a drive and finally came to a stop in front of a residence that no longer looked as elegant or impressive to her as it once had. The carriage door opened, and a footman handed her down. Once the others were gathered around, she said, "When the door opens, you may have to shove your way in as I've been told that entry is barred to me. But I want to enter."

She marched up the path, up the steps, and tried the door. To her immense surprise, it opened. Obviously they had expected her to never return. She swept inside, with her entourage on her heels. Manson came scurrying out of one of the hallways. His eyes widened, his mouth gaped before he got control of himself. He rushed forward.

"I'm sorry, miss, but—"

One of her footmen blocked him. She turned for the stairs and headed up them. "I won't be long, Manson. I just need a few things. Feel free to alert his lordship that I'm here."

At the landing, she turned into the corridor that branched into the east wing and went to the room located at the corner. Her bedchamber. Placing her hand on the knob, she hesitated a moment before shoving open the door. She strode in with purpose and staggered to a stop. The vanity, the bedside tables, the dresser—they were all bare of her things. The few dolls that remained after her smashing spree were nowhere to be seen. She walked quickly to the armoire. It was empty. The lush purple gown that she had purchased in hopes of wearing to a ball, the one Geoffrey had insisted she don on the most humiliating night of her life, was gone.

She heard the tread of footsteps pounded in anger. Surprised by the calm that settled over her, she faced the door. Geoffrey barged through, his face a mottled red.

"Now, see here—"

He'd taken but two steps when two of the footmen grabbed him. He tried to shake them off but they held firm. Finally he stopped struggling and glared at her. "You have no right to be here."

"You packed up all my things. Where are they?"

"I sold them."

The words slammed into her like a hard fist to her stomach, but she refused to show any reaction. She could be as stoic, as unrevealing as Rafe. "I see."

"Everything in this residence belongs to me now. I shall do with it as I please."

Did she hear guilt, remorse? She couldn't be sure but she was done with giving him the benefit of the doubt. His gray eyes were shooting daggers at her. His behavior saddened her for so many reasons. "I always admired you so much. My older brother, the future earl. But at this moment I don't like you very much. Father asked you to see to my care, and you did a rather poor job of it. You led me to believe you were seeking to find me a husband."

"I never said that. I told you that I was going to introduce you to some gentlemen."

"But you knew what I thought."

He sneered. "You were always a little fool."

"I find you remarkably sad."

"Don't you dare pity me."

"Oh, I don't pity you. You told Father that I would have had all I deserve. Eventually, Geoffrey, I shall be a very wealthy woman. You, on the other hand, will be insignificant."

"I'm a lord and you're a bastard."

How could he be so hateful? How could he despise her so much? She was wasting her time. He would never listen, never truly understand what a wretched creature he was.

"We're going to leave now and if you make a fuss, my footmen are going to pummel you. So please don't make a fuss."

With her head held high, she strode from the bedchamber that had once been hers, where she had once been happy. She supposed she would soon discover if happiness was to be found in another bedchamber.

In the late afternoon Rafe stood at the window of his office, looking out on the street, watching as people bustled by.

He didn't know why he'd not returned to his residence with Eve. He'd wanted her, God how he'd wanted her. Standing there in his apartments with the lights from outside, and the dim glow inside casting her in shadows that ebbed and flowed with her movements, she'd been a seductress. Her smoky voice and her throaty laughter had added to the allure.

His eyes slid closed as he remembered the kiss. She was becoming quite masterful at parrying. He'd almost given her rein to wrap her arms around him, almost. He'd felt the brush of her hands, craved the touch as much as it repelled him. His chest had tightened, sweat had popped out on his forehead, and he'd known that he'd shove her aside, possibly hurt her, so he'd snatched her wrists before any damage was done.

He didn't want her first time to be in his den of iniquity, or in his carriage, or in the streets. He wanted her in a bed, properly—or as properly as it could be with a man who had an aversion to being held.

He wondered how Sebastian would feel if he knew the truth of workhouses. He hadn't then, of that Rafe was certain, but perhaps he did now. Articles had been written about the deplorable conditions, the brutality and cruelty of the owners. Mr. and Mrs. Finch had been particularly ruthless. Their workhouse had been overflowing. Boys slept on pallets on the floor in a locked room. No candles, no light save for what the moon and stars provided.

Sebastian had told him to tell no one who he was, but he was a lord and lords did not sleep on the floor. So the second night he'd demanded a bed.

Mrs. Finch had dragged him to a tiny room. It contained a bed. A hard wooden bed with no mattress, no ticking. And they'd tied him down to it.

Rafe pressed a balled fist to the glass, fighting back the memories, the sense of hopelessness, the fear that he would be left there to die. It was only one of their punishment rooms, but it did its job. The next night, he didn't ask for a bed.

He slept wedged between two other boys.

A sound at the doorway had him glancing over his shoulder. Mick strutted in, his swollen and bruised jaw stirring guilt within Rafe, but then considering how swollen and tender his eye was, the guilt quickly diminished.

"A message was just delivered for you," Mick said, holding out an envelope.

Rafe took it. He didn't recognize the handwriting of flowing script that was his name. It wasn't from anyone who'd written him before.

"Your coachman delivered it," Mick said as though he could see the confusion Rafe was experiencing, despite knowing he'd not moved a muscle. He was skilled at never revealing a reaction.

Now, with the knowledge that Eve might have penned him a note, he said flatly, "That'll be all."

Not until he was alone did he trace his finger over the elaborate curls and swirls. She had fine penmanship, while his was fairly atrocious. He was more comfortable writing with his left hand— "The mark of the devil," Mrs. Finch had declared before she ordered his left arm tied behind his back during lessons in the evening. He'd never mastered writing with his right and when he'd made his way to London, he reverted back to what came more naturally—in applying pen to paper at least.

He opened the envelope, removed the small folded sheet of paper.

Miss Evelyn Chambers.
Requests the Honor of Your Presence
For Dinner Tonight.
Eight O'clock

He couldn't help but smile at her formality. Did she fear he might put in another long absence? Did she crave his company?

What an insane thought. No one *craved* his company. He never went out of his way to be pleasant. He didn't give quarter, he didn't care about anyone else's needs save his own.

He studied the script again, imagined the slow movement of her hand as she worked to make each letter precise, the crease that would form in her brow as she sought to select each word, so as not to give the impression that she was inviting him for anything more than a sampling of the fare. She would bombard him with questions all evening, no doubt, killing desire, striving to delay the inevitable.

The hell of it was he yearned for the sound of her voice almost as much as he craved the heat of her flesh. The way her lilting speech tipped up and down as though she feared the answer to the question, but was compelled to ask anyway. Sometimes he wanted to tell her, say aloud the things of which he'd never spoken. How, as soon as Sebastian and Tristan were out of sight, Mrs. Finch had grabbed Rafe by the collar and dragged him into a room. With the help of her husband who'd held him down, she'd shaved his head so he wouldn't get lice, then stripped him of his clothes and ordered him into a tub of water. Standing there before her, trying to shield his most vulnerable parts from her sight, he'd refused, demanded she return his clothes.

Then the cane had come out.

Whack! Against his shins.

Whack! Shoulders. *Whack!* Back. *Whack!* Buttocks.

No one had ever struck him before. He was a lord, the son of a duke. He was not to be touched.

The only way to escape her menacing swinging arm had been to climb into the tub. So he'd climbed. The water had been frigid, and he'd almost immediately shriveled up, begun shaking. Then she'd attacked him with a hard bristled brush, scrubbing, scrubbing, scrubbing until he'd feared she'd remove every inch of his skin.

When it was all over, when he was dry, she'd handed him his trousers along with a shirt and jacket made of rough cloth that was patched in places and didn't fit properly. It wasn't until he was living on the streets of London that he understood she'd taken his shirt, jacket, and waistcoat because the buttons were valuable. She'd no doubt removed them and sold them. Then sold the clothing as well. What did it matter if they came without buttons? The material was the finest. Buttons could always be bought—perhaps not as fancy as what had been there originally, but serviceable.

But at the workhouse, he'd still had lessons to learn and had spent the remainder of the night locked in a room with other boys who were sleeping. Rafe had merely curled into a tight ball, trying to gauge exactly how quickly time would pass before he saw his brothers again.

The next morning after a meal of milk porridge—

all meals were milk porridge—he'd been led to a shed with several other boys and charged with picking apart old ropes, down to the smallest fibers. The tinier they were, the more likely they were to cut into fingers as they were pulled. Hands bled, but none of the boys complained.

Because the cane was always waiting.

Once again, he trailed his fingers over Eve's delicate script. Only this time he noticed as well the faint crisscross of scars where the most minute strands had bitten into his fingers. It seemed almost an abomination that hands such as his would touch her. Not because of the scars, but because of what they'd eventually become. Weapons used to do another's bidding.

Rafe stood in his library savoring his Scotch. Upon arriving, he had been informed by Laurence that Miss Chambers had indicated that Rafe was to wait in the library.

He was to *wait for her.* That was not the way of mistresses. Though he had no one to blame but himself. He'd been remiss in providing her with a complete list of his rules.

The door opened. She glided in and he nearly swallowed his tongue. His fingers tightened around his glass and he suspected if it wasn't so thick that it would have shattered. Miracle of miracles, the black was gone at last. She wore the purple gown, the one he'd had sewn for her. Her upswept hair caught the light, causing it to flicker over the pale locks, captivating him. The necklace her father had given her sparkled at her throat, tempting him to kiss over it, beneath it, along it until he reached the shell of her ear where he could nibble lingeringly.

She exuded confidence.

Yet as she neared he saw the doubts, the insecurity. He wished he were a man of poetry, but poetic words had been stripped from his soul. Besides, poetry was the domain of lovers, and the one thing he would not do was be dishonest with her. He had no heart with which to gift her, and he didn't want to give her false hope that he might suddenly obtain one. Although for a fleeting moment, he thought if he could purchase one for her, he would.

Turning toward the table that housed his spirits, he uncorked a bottle of wine and concentrated on pouring it generously into a glass, grateful his hands had steadied so he wasn't making a mess of things. "Do you have any idea how beautiful you are?"

"A mistress is supposed to make herself presentable, isn't she?"

He extended the glass toward her, watched in fascination as her fingers curled around the stem. Why were his senses heightened? The anticipation of soon having her, he supposed. "A mistress is not to go to her bro—to Wortham's—without me."

She angled her chin. "I took Lila and three strong footmen with me." She took a sip, touched her tongue to her lips. He wanted that tongue touching his. "The night when everything happened, the butler—Manson—told me he was sorry that he couldn't let me in, but seeing him today, the way he looked at me as though I should be used as an object upon which to wipe his boots, made me realize that it was only training that had him telling me he was sorry. He wasn't really. I told my lady's maid, Hazel, that she was welcome to come with me if she wanted. I rather missed her."

She sipped again, taking in more. "But she declined my invitation, as though it were beneath her. All my life, I knew what I was, but my father provided a shield for me. I never comprehended the extent of it. With his death, and my visit today, I realize I was not as well liked as I assumed."

All his life, he'd known what he was as well, but it had not shielded him. At times it had served to make situations worse. "They don't matter," he grounded out. "They're nothing."

"Is that how you carry on? By pretending no one matters?"

"I don't pretend, Evie. They don't matter." He wouldn't allow them to matter. "Why did you even bother to go there?"

"There were a few things that I decided I wanted, small things: a pearl comb for my hair, gloves, a brush that had belonged to my mother—he sold everything. Walking into that room, I saw no evidence at all that I'd ever even lived there. He simply wiped me away, as though I'd never been born, which I suppose is what he always wished."

It angered him beyond measure that she should feel less because of this unplanned visit she'd made today. Wortham was going to pay, and pay dearly—eventually. But for now Rafe needed someplace to vent his fury. "If you want something, then purchase it for God's sake. Here." He removed a folded sheaf of paper from beneath the blotter. "Did Laurence not tell you about this? It's a letter I wrote for you. You take it to any shop in London—in Great Britain for that matter—show it to a shopkeeper, and your purchases will be charged to my accounts."

Her chin came up with such force that he was surprised he didn't hear her neck pop. "I'm not going to spend your money."

Proud stubborn woman. How she infuriated and intrigued him. Seldom did anyone stand up to him, and that this small woman continually did so astounded him. "Have you not eaten since you've been here?"

"I beg your pardon?"

"Have you not had meals since the night you came here in the rain?"

"You know I have."

"Do you use the gas lights? Do you leave an oil lamp burning by your bed? Have you taken a warm bath? Have you had a fire going in the fireplace in your bedchamber on a chilly night?"

"I don't—"

"You're already spending my money, Eve. It's ridiculous to split hairs as to whether you're walking into a shop and purchasing something that you want or burning oil late into the night because you wish to read. I pay for the gas, the food, the salaries of the servants who see to your every need. If you want a blasted comb for your hair, purchase a comb."

Devastation swept over her features. "I hadn't thought of all that, all the myriad ways to which I'm already indebted to you."

Turning away, she walked to the window, and he wanted to kick himself for not considering that she might have experienced a sense of control in her life when she'd penned her invitation to him that afternoon. With a few blunt words, he'd effectively managed to plunge her back into reality concerning her place in his life. He didn't know what to say, how to make things right, how to return the smile to her face or the ease in her posture with which she had walked into the library.

"Evie, I'm—" *Sorry.* When had he ever apologized? But then he could hardly remember the last time that he'd been wrong.

She took a sip of the wine, held the glass with two hands as though she needed it to balance herself. "Of course, I know and understand that items are purchased, that nothing is free, but I never considered *everything* that must be bought." She faced him. "It was just always there. Father provided it. He never spoke of paying for it. I never thought to ask how it all worked." She sighed in frustration. "I'm not saying this properly. I understood that items were purchased. I just never contemplated precisely how much it might cost if I burned a log in the fireplace or used coal. The minutia, you see. I never considered the minutia. My God, I must owe you a fortune already."

He tossed the paper onto the desk and walked over to where she stood. He inhaled her fragrance, glad that he was near enough to smell it. "Hardly a fortune, and I told you before that I'm not keeping tally. So if you need something, purchase it, or send Laurence or one of the servants out to fetch it."

"So we're talking an allowance here?"

"If you wish, if you're more comfortable assigning a name to it."

"For what amount?"

He couldn't stop himself from grinning. "Now you're talking like a mistress."

"As you professed to have never had one, I'm not certain how you know that."

"When men gamble, they do one of two things: they either grumble or they boast. And both are exaggerated. Nothing is as bad as they seem to make on that it is, and none of them excel at whatever they're talking about to the extent that they would have one believe. But often the topics revolve around their wives or their mistresses."

Reaching out, she touched a fold in his cravat, her fingers working to right what he wasn't certain needed be righted. His gut tightened as though she'd gone further and actually removed the blasted neckcloth, in anticipation of removing everything.

"You didn't answer my question regarding how much," she said.

"As much as you like."

She lifted her gaze to his, and he was grateful to see a bit of spark there. "I'll put you in the poorhouse."

"I think that highly unlikely. Shop all day every day if you wish."

"You're too generous."

"Don't mistake my spendthrift tendencies with generosity. A generous soul gives his last and only ha'penny to someone else. You saw my gaming establishment. Trust me when I tell you that as long as men believe that they have a chance of winning fortune rather than earning it, I shall never have a last and only ha'penny."

She gave him a self-effacing smile. "Well, this is certainly not how I'd planned for the evening to go. All this talk of money. I'd hoped for the evening to be about us."

Us. It had been years since that word had been part of his vocabulary. He almost told her that they should only think of him and his needs, but if that was part of tonight's plans, he wouldn't be standing there in a damned waistcoat, jacket, and cravat, feeling on the verge of suffocating. He'd done it for her. He was beginning to realize that he was doing a great deal for her. Giving her leave to spend as much as she wanted? He'd never been a spendthrift. His coins were too hard-earned. He certainly never did without anything he wanted, but what he wanted most was more coins.

Taking her empty glass, he set it aside. "Let's go to dinner, shall we? I've been anticipating it ever since your invitation arrived."

They ate in the sitting room that looked out on the garden. She'd had her father's portrait removed earlier. She would have it returned tomorrow. But for tonight she wanted the intimacy of a smaller room. The dining room was too large, too formal, too cold.

Candles flickered. Servants brought in the food, one course after another. She barely touched anything, was aware of his constant gaze. Whether he was eating or sipping on his wine, he was looking at her.

She had clung to a vain gossamer hope that things between them would not progress, that she might become more of a companion than a mistress. Talking of inconsequential topics over dinner, reading to him as he'd asked that first morning. But the extent to which she was already in his debt astounded her. She'd given no thought to the small things.

"That's how men lose fortunes, isn't it? They lose a little bit at a time, hardly giving it any credence—then suddenly they look about them and everything is gone."

He studied her over the rim of his wineglass. "Usually, yes."

She could sense a tension building on the air, like a dark storm sweeping over the moors. She'd known when she penned her invitation where things tonight might eventually lead, that she would end up playing the part of seductress. It had been her intent to ease the loneliness she sensed in him, to give him more than he required, to be more than the bargain demanded.

"You went to a great deal of bother to arrange things for this evening," he said quietly.

She nodded, touched the necklace at her throat. "It just seemed that a mistress should ensure that the evenings are rich with flavors and fragrances. I know you're not wooing me, but I thought I should create an atmosphere in which it appeared you were." She didn't know how to explain it without sounding like an absolute ninny. "I came to the realization last night that you're not such an awful sort—"

"High praise indeed."

Darkness hovered at the edge of his grin, and she wondered if he would ever bestow upon her a smile of pure enjoyment. Ignoring his interruption, she continued. "This afternoon I came to understand that with my father's passing, I lost everything. I was simply too overcome with grief to fully comprehend the extent to which my life had changed. I'm here until you tire of me, so up to that moment I shall strive to make our arrangement pleasant for both of us. I thought I could read to you after dinner. Or play the pianoforte, if you prefer."

"Surely, you can think of another entertainment."

His gaze was hooded as he sipped at his wine in a manner that made her think of him sipping at her mouth, slow and leisurely, taking all until he'd had his fill. She knew what he wanted her to offer—bed sport, but she wasn't going to make giving up her maidenhead as easy as all that. Yes, she owed him, yes, she'd promised. But he could damned well do his part to entice her into the bed. "Would you prefer a game of chess? I'm rather good. I played with my father quite often."

His lips curled up into a smile that promised wickedness. "We'll begin with a reading."

She suspected they were going to end with a tumble. "It's going to be tonight, isn't it?"

She was extremely pleased that her voice didn't quiver.

"I've been more than patient."

"I daresay you've been as patient as a saint."

"I'm hardly a saint."

A sinner, and soon she would be one as well. "I'm trying not to get nervous."

"Drink some more wine."

She did, savoring the flavor on her tongue, the warmth swirling through her, the light-headedness taking hold. "I can't think of anything to talk about."

"Then don't talk. You don't have to entertain, not tonight."

She furrowed her brow. "Will I on other nights?"

A corner of his mouth curled up. "I doubt it. I suspect once I've had you that it will be awhile before I've had you enough."

Had it been that way with her mother and father? She didn't want to think about them tonight, but she heard herself saying, "My father loved my mother, more than he loved his wife."

His wineglass was halfway to his mouth when he stilled. "I'm not your father."

She released a quick burst of laughter. "Thank God for that."

He studied her intently. "I meant, Evie, that I don't love. Don't begin to think that what happens between us is more than it is."

She nodded. He had emphasized often enough what she would be to him. Still, she found herself hoping for more. "Have you never loved any lady that you've . . . *been* with?"

Slowly he shook his head. "It is not within me to love."

Sadness swept through her. *What a lonely person you must be.* She didn't say the words aloud. She didn't want to travel any conversational path that would lead them away from enjoying the night. "You're right. We shouldn't talk."

He studied her for a moment as though he were memorizing every line and curve of her face. She wondered if he would study her as thoroughly during breakfast in the morning, if there would be differences for him to note. How much would she change tonight? Would anything about her remain the same?

"If I were the sort to spout poetry," he finally said, "I would spout it for you."

She didn't know whether to weep at his sincerity or laugh at the words he'd chosen to use. She settled on a soft smile. "*Spout* poetry? You don't think very highly of poems."

"I have a difficult time following them. Words don't always mean what they are supposed to mean. They're not always in the right order. They circle about."

"You prefer things straightforward."

He gave a slow appreciative nod. "I do."

"I enjoy poetry. Even when I can't figure out exactly what the poet is saying, I like the way the words flow, especially when read aloud. I believe poetry must be read aloud in order to be truly appreciated."

"Perhaps if you read it to me I'll grow to appreciate it."

She smiled, accepting the challenge. "I suppose we'll find out, since you've already agreed that we'll begin with a reading."

She didn't recall ever seeing a gentle smile on him before. It looked at once out of place, and yet so very natural. Leaning over, he tucked a finger beneath her chin, pressed his thumb to her mouth. "Don't be nervous."

"It's a little hard not to be." She couldn't manage to quiet the romantic in her. She wanted more than this. He was going to bed her and she would never be the same again. Her stomach was twisting and turning like the strings of sugared candy that she'd watched being pulled in a confectioner's window once.

He shoved back his chair, stood, and pulled her to her feet. "We'll have the reading in the library."

A reprieve. She hardly knew whether to be grateful or annoyed. She settled for grateful.

Chapter 13

In the library, Rafe stood by the fireplace and drank his best Scotch, one glass after another, while she sat in a nearby chair, her posture perfect.

In the end, she didn't read him poetry but some story about windswept moors and haunting love. But he wasn't listening to the words as much as he was the lilt and smoky cadence of her voice. The raspiness of it had intrigued him from the beginning. She could recite the letters of the alphabet and hold him enthralled.

Dangerous, so very dangerous.

He wanted to sweep her up into his arms and carry her upstairs, even knowing the hell that holding her so close would bring. Watching her, he could almost forget his limitations, that there was so much he could not give her, and for the first time in his life, his inadequacies filled him with regret.

He was vain enough to acknowledge that on the surface he was a handsome enough fellow. It was what lay beneath that would turn her away. The dark parts, the secrets, the things he'd done. If she knew of those, even the surface would not be attractive to her. And then she'd wash her hands of him. She wouldn't send him invitations, dress becomingly, have a lovely dinner prepared, offer boring entertainments such as reading and music.

She would leave him, and he would once again be alone with only his thoughts to keep him company.

Her voice was growing lower, raspier, more seductive. He wanted her with every breath he took. He drained his glass, set it on the mantel.

Before he went truly mad, he walked over to her, reached down, closed the book, and set it on the table beside the chair, beside the glass of untouched Scotch that he'd poured for her earlier. He brought her to her feet, watched as she focused her gaze on the black onyx stickpin in his cravat.

"You're the most beautiful woman I've ever seen. I thought it was your skin or your hair or your eyes. But it's more than that." Dear God, how much had he drunk? He couldn't seem to stop his mouth from opening and uttering words. He cradled her face, tilted it up, because he wanted to gaze into the violet depths of her eyes. "I'll hurt you, Eve. It's what I do. I hurt people. I have for so long that I don't know how not to. I want you with a desperation that"—damn near had him on his knees, but he wasn't going to tell her that, give her power over him—"consumes me. I don't want to hurt you."

"Then don't."

She made it sound so simple. "I should let you go."

"I don't want you to."

He told himself it was because of all she would gain by becoming his mistress. When he was done with her, she would have wealth, power—and if she played her cards right—influence. And the freedom to do any damn thing she wanted.

"Make me your mistress in truth," she rasped, and the wisps of her smoky voice swirled through the charred remains of his blackened soul.

A deep feral groan hung on the air as his mouth blanketed hers before she took her next breath. Her arms were almost around his shoulders before she recalled his first rule and dropped them to her side. Oh, she wanted to touch him, hold him, secure him to her because she was in danger of melting into the floor.

No gentleness, no kindness. He would not bestow those upon her, but the dark and needy way in which he devoured her heated her blood, weakened her knees, sent pleasure cascading from her head to her toes.

She wasn't exactly sure when she'd decided that she wanted him, that she cared little about her ruination. She only knew that she desired him. They were two lonely souls cast aside by Society. Surely they could find solace within each other.

He drew back, and the ice that was usually in his eyes was gone, replaced by smoldering embers. The blue was a richer hue, like the hottest flames at the base of a fire. "I must have you, Eve," he growled.

Nodding, she licked her lips, tasted his Scotch and him lingering there.

"Just remember my rule."

"I won't hold you."

He swept her into his arms and began marching from the room. She wanted desperately to wind an arm around his neck, to stroke his jaw. "What am I allowed?"

"Nothing." He strode down the hallway. "Just take the pleasure, don't try to give it."

"What if I leaned in and kissed your neck?"

He gave her a quick glance, his eyes clashing with hers, before he started up the stairs. "No."

She wanted to ask him why, to uncover what had happened to make it so he couldn't bear her touching him—no, not her, anyone. She realized now with resounding clarity that the night he had carried her through the rain, he hadn't been urging her on as she'd originally thought. He'd been urging himself on. Whatever had happened to him? But now was not the time to poke, pry, and prod. But she would. After tonight, this distance between them could not remain. After tonight, everything would change.

He shouldered open the door and made his way inside, kicking it closed behind him. Gently he set her on the bed as though she were capable of breaking. Then he began tearing at his clothes. She heard linen rip and buttons ping as they scattered over the floor. She thought she should be frightened by the frenzy, but instead she was fascinated that she could elicit such a reaction from a man. That he was fairly mad with wanting her.

It was a heady realization as she rose up on an elbow to watch him. He pulled his shirt over his head and tossed it aside. He balanced on one foot, jerked off his boot, cast aside his stocking, before moving on to the other side.

He freed two buttons on his trousers before he stopped, looked at her. Her mouth had gone dry; her heart was beating as though it would fly from her chest. He was breathing heavily. She could see a fine sheen of sweat forming on his brow.

"Close your eyes if you like." His roughened voice caused prickles to form over her skin.

He was flawless. Skin and muscle tight on bone. Shaking her head, she dared to say what she hadn't the courage to reveal the night before when he'd taken her to the boxing room. "I think you're beautiful."

He released a huff of air that might have been a laugh. Then his fingers made short work of the remaining buttons and he shoved down his trousers. Desire nearly swamped her. She wanted to touch. All of him. Badly. She thought she should be frightened by his jutting manhood. It was the only term she knew, but it somehow seemed wrong when applied to Rafe. His required a stronger, more powerful word. Yes, he could very well hurt her, but she wasn't afraid.

His legs were long, corded muscles—a puckered scar on his right thigh. She sat up. "What happened there?"

"Later," he said, walking toward her. "I'll tell you later."

Would he? Would he finally start talking to her in truth, telling her everything about him, his past, his present, his dreams for the future? Did he have goals and ambitions? She had so many questions, but they could wait, they could all wait.

When he reached the bed, he brought with him the fragrance of male, perhaps of sex, musky, not unpleasant. With a hand on her shoulder, he guided her back down to the pillows. He closed his fists around the top of her nightdress, then ripped it asunder from collar to hem, spreading it wide, until she was as exposed as he.

"Oh, dear God, I knew you would be . . ."

His voice trailed off, and she wondered what word he might have used, but based on the appreciation that lit his eyes, the faintest upturn of his lips, he was pleased.

"Shall I roll over now?" she asked, her voice thready.

His gaze came back to hers, his brow furrowed. "I'm not taking you from behind." He gave her the smallest of smiles that warmed and touched her heart. "We're not dogs, and I promised you would take pleasure in our coupling."

Still standing, he bent at the waist, lowered his head and kissed her, his mouth working the familiar magic to which she was becoming accustomed. Strong sweeps of his tongue that encouraged hers to respond in kind. She desperately wanted to comb her fingers through his hair, hold him near. Instead she raised her arms and clutched the pillow. It was a poor substitute, but it served to anchor her.

She felt one of his hands gliding leisurely from her knee, along her thigh, halting at her hip to massage gently, before skimming along her side until he was cupping her ribs. Another hesitation. Then the flat of his roughened hand was curving around the underside of her breast. Kneading tenderly as though he feared bruising her. His thumb—she thought it was his thumb—circled her nipple. It puckered. She moaned.

He dragged his mouth from hers, along the column of her throat, along her collarbone, nibbling, nipping, soothing with his tongue. Opening her eyes, she gazed down on his bent dark head. He hovered over her, only his mouth and hand touching her. She wanted to feel the press of him over the full length of her. Was that the way it should be done? She didn't know. She only knew that she desired him, all of him.

The room was growing warm, as though they'd built a fire at its edges. But perhaps it was only she heating up, as passion—as he—licked at her skin.

He trailed his mouth lower, lower, over the swell of her breast, lower still until it replaced his thumb and his tongue was swirling, taunting. He closed his mouth over the tautened peak and suckled. She sighed a raspy note that came from deep within her, and twisted toward him.

"Do you like that?" he asked, blowing on the dampened skin, driving her to madness.

"Yes. Why can't I hold you?"

"Because you can't."

It wasn't an answer. She wanted to disobey him, but would all these lovely sensations dissipate if she did what he commanded her not to? Just one little touch, she wanted to beg, just one little stroke of her fingers over his back. Not a hold really, but she dared not risk it.

His hand traveled down, came to rest between her thighs. His fingers stroked, circled.

"Oh. Rafe—"

"Shh. Just enjoy."

Enjoy? She thought she might take flight. She wasn't certain how she remained anchored on the bed.

Slowly, slowly, he slipped a finger inside her most intimate place.

"Dear God, but you're already so wet, so hot . . . so damned tight." He turned his face toward her then, and she could see the strain in his features. "I've never known such tightness."

"Is that bad?"

He gave her a wolfish grin. "Not for me, but I fear you'll find it unpleasant."

"It's not been unpleasant thus far. I don't want you to stop."

"Selfish bastard that I am, I want you too badly now to stop." She didn't believe him. She thought if she said no he would cease his attentions, but then she thought she might die. She loved having his hands and mouth on her, loved all the sensations he was stirring to life.

Placing both his hands on her inner thighs, he spread her legs and bent his head.

And kissed her there.

"Oh God."

He remained standing. It seemed a terribly awkward uncomfortable position for him, but he seemed not to mind at all as his mouth slowly began to follow the path his hand had taken. Another kiss, a swirl of his tongue, a gentle suckling. Over and over. The attentions changed, but the outcome remained: an intense pressure that built and built until she thought she might scream.

She rolled her head from side to side, reached for him, remembered that she couldn't touch him, and dug her fingers into the sheets instead. She wanted him. It was torment not to touch his firm flesh, not to feel his warmth while he worked so diligently to increase hers.

Her breaths began to come in pants. She heard

little cries, coming from her, small sounds that she couldn't hold in, couldn't control. Madness, this was madness.

One hand tiptoed up her torso, covered her breast, squeezed, pinched, touched lightly. All the while his mouth worked feverishly. The pressure built, her body tensed—

"Oh, my word!"

Pleasure shot through her, out of her, as her body convulsed, her back arched. Crying out, she yanked on the sheets, needing to hold onto something to keep her anchored. Breathing harshly, she sank back down, unable to believe what she'd just experienced.

He moved swiftly, wedging himself between her thighs, hovering over her, his arms on either side of her shoulders, straight, the muscles bunched, his once icy eyes a fiery blue. "Forgive me," he rasped, before thrusting forward.

The pain was sharp, intense, quick. She bit her lip to keep from crying out as he stared down on her, his arms quaking now.

"I'm all right," she assured him.

She thought he might have nodded, and then he was rocking against her, with long powerful strokes. Fast. Furious.

He emitted a deep-throated growl, threw his head back. His body jerked, stiffened, thrust once more. Then he stilled, breathing harshly, staring at her as though he didn't quite know who she was.

She couldn't stop herself from reaching up and gently combing the damp locks of hair from his brow. His breathing began to even out, his eyes never straying from hers.

"I was supposed to leave you," he said, his voice

hoarse as though he'd been screaming.

"Pardon?"

"I was supposed to spill my seed in my hand, not in you."

"The next time then."

He released what sounded like a weary burst of laughter. "You want a next time."

She smiled at him. "Yes, I rather think I do."

He bent his arms, and managed, without his body touching hers, to give her a quick kiss on the lips. Then he was easing off of her.

"Are you leaving?" she asked.

"Not yet. Wait here."

As though she had a choice, as though she weren't lethargic and her limbs were naught but jelly. She studied him as he walked over to the basin stand. She liked the shape of his buttocks, the way the muscles flexed with his movements. She was a mistress now. She could probably enjoy the male form without feeling guilty about it. It was her job.

He washed up, then returned to her with washrag in hand. Sitting on the edge of the bed, he began to gently swipe at the inside of her thighs.

"There's not as much blood as I thought there would be," he said.

"Am I your first virgin?"

He lifted his gaze to her, and for the span of a heartbeat, he appeared younger than he usually did. He nodded, before returning to his task. "Did it hurt very badly?"

"It wasn't too awful."

"It won't always hurt."

"The pain was worth it for what came before."

He gave her a small smile and she wanted to keep

it there forever. "You liked that?" he asked.

She nodded. "Yes, I did rather. You're more skilled than the hounds."

He stared at her for moment, his brow furrowed, and then he laughed. A deep rich sound. It didn't last long, but it lasted long enough for her to fall in love with it.

"I should bloody well hope so."

She gnawed on her lower lip, trying to decide if she should say the words aloud. She mentally flipped a coin. It didn't work as well as flipping a solid one, but she wanted him to know. "I'm glad it was you."

He went totally still, studying her as though she'd spoken gibberish.

"My first."

She watched his throat muscles work as he swallowed, his Adam's apple slide up and down. Standing, he brought the sheets and covers over her, before skimming his thumb along her chin. "Sleep well."

Sadness engulfed her. She wasn't ready for him to leave. It seemed that there should be more. It was the holding, she realized. Afterward they should have held each other. She remembered once being frightened and going into her mother's room when the earl was there. Her back had been against his chest and his arm had been around her. So close they had reminded her of two spoons in a drawer. But then they loved each other. Rafe didn't love her. She wasn't quite sure how she felt about him.

"You're leaving?" she asked, trying not to be hurt, to take offense.

"Yes. I probably should have told you earlier. One of my rules. I'll never stay in the bed with you."

"Why?"

He only shook his head, reached out, and lowered the flame in the lamp. "I won't be here when you wake up in the morning."

"Where are you going?"

"A mistress is not supposed to question everything. You accept what I say."

She heard a hint of irritation in his voice. She didn't want this night to end with them getting out of sorts with each other. "Will I see you tomorrow evening?"

"Yes. Wear the red." Bending down, he picked up his clothes, riffled through the torn garments until he found the pocket of his waistcoat. He dug out a key, went to the door between their chambers, inserted it, opened the door, and disappeared through the doorway without another word. After the door closed, she heard the bolting of the lock.

She fought not to feel saddened, disappointed, abandoned. From the beginning, he had warned her that there would be rules, that things had to be done to suit him. She'd known he wasn't the warmest of creatures. But for a short time she'd actually considered that something special existed between them. Rolling to her side, she stared at the window. An entirely different life waited for her beyond it.

The problem was that she suddenly very much wanted this one—or at least a good many parts of it. And she couldn't help but believe with time, she might want all of it.

Rafe pressed his ear to the door. He couldn't hear her weeping. He didn't know whether to be relieved or alarmed. But then other than the night Wortham had turned her out, she'd not shed a tear. She was made of stern stuff, his Evie.

He'd wanted to give her so much more, had nearly begged her to touch him. A hand on his shoulder, her fingers through his hair. But he couldn't risk it. In the throes of passion she might forget his aversion to holding, she might wrap her arms, her legs, her entire body around him—

Turning, he flattened his back to the wall and slid down to the floor. A gaslight burned, it always burned, relegating the demons to lurking in the shadows, waiting, waiting to spring forth. Tonight they would be there if he slept. He felt it in the very fabric of his being. He needed to go to the club, to hear the constant noise of life, the activity, the spin of the roulette wheel, the clack of the dice, the whisper of cards being dealt. He couldn't stay here.

As badly as he'd wanted to lie beside her, to watch her drift off to sleep, he'd been unable to risk falling asleep himself. If the nightmares came, he didn't want her to be near enough to hear his screams.

"I'm glad it was you."

He doubted she would be as glad if she discovered that she had been taken by a madman.

Chapter 14

Even if he hadn't told her that he'd be gone when she awoke, she would have known. The residence took on a different feel when he wasn't about. She couldn't quite explain it, but it seemed emptier, less vital, more plain.

After Lila helped her dress, she stepped into the hallway just as a rather short and podgy servant was opening the door to the bedchamber across the hall. Ironed shirts were draped across his left arm. She tried not to stare at the clawlike gloved hand that seemed to be frozen in a most uncomfortable position. He stopped and gave Evelyn a quick bow. "Good morning, miss. I'm Mr. Easton's valet. Bateman."

Evelyn forced herself to smile so he wouldn't read her mind. She was wondering how a one-handed valet could possibly see to his duties properly. He must have known what she was thinking, however, because he explained, "My hand got smashed when I was younger. It never healed properly. Still aches a bit, especially when the weather is cold and damp."

"I'm terribly sorry, but I'm certain you're a marvelous valet."

He straightened his shoulders. "The master never complains."

"Those are his shirts I assume?"

"Yes, miss. I was just putting them in his room. His tailor delivered them yesterday. He likes them washed and pressed before he wears them."

At a quick glance, Evelyn estimated a half-dozen shirts. New shirts. So many. Although after last night's encounter, he certainly needed to replace at least one.

Evelyn felt rather self-conscious pointing at the room next to hers, but it was part of her responsibilities to see that everything was taken care of properly for him. "But that's his room."

Bateman blinked. "No, miss. This is the room where I dress him. That room there, no one is allowed in there."

"How is it cleaned and tidied?"

"As far as I know, it isn't."

"I see." Only she didn't.

"Will that be all, miss?"

Evelyn nodded. "Yes, carry on."

After the valet disappeared into the room, she walked over to the door that she knew was locked. What secrets was he hiding in there?

The jewelers on St. James was one of the finest in all of London. When Rafe walked through the door, he wasn't surprised to see a duke standing at one of the glass cases. He only wished it wasn't that particular duke.

Due to the positioning of the door, and his limited sight because of the eye patch he wore, his brother had to turn almost completely around to see who was entering. "Rafe."

"Sebastian." He jerked his chin up. "Sorry. Keswick."

Keswick shrugged. "Sebastian works. This is the very last place I expected to run into you."

The clerk wasn't about. Rafe considered leaving, but it had been a good many years since he'd felt the need to try to avoid the unpleasant, so he closed the door and walked over to the case. "Where's the shopkeeper?"

"Retrieving a necklace that I had created especially for Mary. We're hosting a ball in a couple of nights. Our first in London. She's a trifle nervous about it. The one we held at Pembrook before Christmas went well, but you know how it is in London. Things are scrutinized a bit more closely."

"She shouldn't care what people think."

"If not for our son, she probably wouldn't. She married me, after all." He turned his attention back to the jewelry case, which meant that he could no longer see Rafe. Rafe thought that perhaps he should move to the other side of him, but it was Sebastian's choice to look where he wanted. "Did you get the invitation?" Sebastian asked quietly.

"To the Christmas affair? Yes, I sent my regrets."

"To the ball we're having this week."

"I did. While I appreciate it, I won't be able to attend that either."

"It would mean a great deal to Mary if you would."

"Yes, well—"

"And to me. To have us all in the residence, as we once were."

Only Rafe wasn't as he once had been, and because of that, he said, "I'm sorry, but business will keep me away."

Sebastian merely nodded, and Rafe began studying the pieces in the case. He wanted to find something that matched the shade of Eve's eyes, when he had risen over her and was gazing down on her face. Passion deepened the violet. He wanted to be able to show her what he saw when he looked into her eyes. It wasn't like him to have such fanciful thoughts. As with the chocolate, giving her jewelry would be a mistake, would make her think that he cared for her in a way that he didn't.

He was providing her with necessities. He didn't need to provide her with frivolities. He should leave now, before he did something to make a fool of himself.

The curtains to the back room parted, and a man with a shiny pate ringed with white hair stepped out and smiled. "Good day, sir. I shall be with you in a moment. Here you are, Your Grace. I think your duchess is going to be most pleased with this." He set a velvet box on the counter, and opened it to reveal a necklace with green stones interlaced with diamonds. A jolt went through Rafe at the realization that he and his brother were both seeking to acquire necklaces that matched a lady's eyes.

"What do you think, Rafe?" Sebastian asked. "Will Mary like it?"

"I suspect she'd be pleased if you chained daisies together to put about her neck."

The clerk drew himself up. "I daresay, she will

not find another piece in all of London as much to her liking as this."

"My brother's a cynic, Mr. Cobb, so don't take offense."

Rafe grimaced as the clerk jerked around to look at him. "My apologies, my lord. I didn't realize—"

"No apologies needed."

"Lord Rafe is correct, though," Sebastian said. "The duchess would be happy with daisies. But I know she will be happier with this." Rafe thought if his brother still possessed two eyes he might have winked. "Add this to my account please."

"Yes, Your Grace. Without delay."

Sebastian slipped it into his pocket, turned to leave, and halted to hold Rafe's gaze. "I have it on good authority that a gentleman can never go wrong purchasing a lady pearls."

"You didn't purchase pearls."

"Not this time, no, but I have on other occasions. I'll let Mary know that you've sent your regrets."

Rafe thought if the clerk weren't standing there, Sebastian might have said far more. Instead, he walked from the shop without another word spoken.

The clerk bustled over to stand before Rafe. "So, my lord, how might I be of service this afternoon?"

Rafe hesitated but a moment before saying, "Show me what you have in pearls."

Evening was approaching. He would be here soon. Or so she thought. Hoped.

She wanted to be waiting on the terrace, but a misty rain had settled in so she sat in a chair near the window in her small sitting room, not certain

when she had begun to think of it as hers. She still
didn't truly believe he was going to give her the residence. She could only hope that it would be a long
time before she found out. Although a part of her
worried that now he'd had her, he'd be done with
her. Anyone could lie beneath him as he slaked his
lust. What difference did it make if it was her?

He didn't care for her enough to linger beyond
the mating.

"You didn't wear the red."

Coming up out of the chair, facing the doorway,
she despised the joy that nearly consumed her because he was here. She was surprised by how tired
he appeared, as though he hadn't slept. She wondered if he'd had to deal with trouble at his club.
What did he do there all day, all night?

"No, I thought in order to hold your interest that
it would be best if I weren't predictable." The pale
yellow had arrived that afternoon and so she'd decided to go with it.

"The last thing I would consider you to be is predictable."

"More so than you. I wasn't certain when to
expect you."

He walked over to the fireplace. Shouldn't he
come to her, kiss her, take her in his arms—

"I wasn't going to come until midnight, but I
couldn't force myself to stay away that long."

A small thrill of happiness went through her. "I'm
glad." She wondered how he would react if she confessed to missing him. Would a mistress say such
a thing? Had her mother? She'd told Evelyn often
enough that she missed the earl, but had she ever
told him? She hated that she didn't know exactly

how she was to behave. On the other hand, he'd never had a mistress before so he probably didn't know how a mistress should behave either. If she made a mistake, he wouldn't know, would he? She knew only that she wanted to matter, and she suspected that she didn't.

"Shall I ring for dinner?"

"No." His voice contained a tightness, and she realized then that his knuckles were turning white where he gripped the mantel. "I want to have you now, before we dine."

Not exactly poetry, but then he had no need to woo her. Their arrangement didn't require that he make any effort to lure her into his bed.

"Yes, all right. Shall we go to my bedchamber then?" Because surely he wasn't thinking of taking her here, beneath her father's portrait.

"I brought you something to wear."

Before she could make any sort of inquiry, he reached inside his jacket, removed a nicely crafted leather box, and held it out to her. She stared at it. Her father had given her a similar appearing box once. Inside had been a sapphire necklace.

Rafe gave it a quick wave. "Take it."

Her fingers trembled slightly as she did so. As though something might jump out and bite her, she opened it with extreme care. Inside, resting on velvet, was a pearl necklace. Smiling, she said, "It's beautiful."

He looked so terribly self-conscious, as though he were anxious that he might displease her. For all his gruffness and his rules and his distance, she found something incredibly touching about him.

"That's all I want you to wear," he said. "Tonight."

"I shall require fifteen moments to change."

"Ten."

"You are quite dictatorial."

"If you knew the restraint I was exhibiting not to have you on the floor at this precise moment, you'd already be on your way out the door."

"You want me that badly?"

"I'm dying here, Eve."

While she knew that it was probably not her specifically that was driving him to madness—but rather only the thought of having a woman—she did take some satisfaction in his suffering. "Twelve minutes."

Before he could protest, she was hurrying out the door.

Rafe turned, gripped the mantel, and stared at the clock. He was ignoring his own rules for her. He didn't live his life counting minutes, but he had spent most of the day doing precisely that, striving to determine how soon he could appear without giving the impression that it had been torment to be away from her. It was only because he'd taken her but once last night, out of concern for the soreness she was no doubt feeling. But tonight, hopefully, she would experience no pain, and he could have his fill of her and this awful need to see her smile, to inhale her fragrance, to hear her voice would dissipate.

The necklace had taken her by surprise. It gave him satisfaction that it had, that she'd not been expecting it. She'd been pleased by it. Tomorrow perhaps he'd bring her a matching bracelet. The next night earbobs. Then he would move on to diamonds, rubies, emeralds. She would have a collection to rival the queen's.

A minute had gone by. Bloody hell. He'd stopped keeping track of time when he was at the workhouse. Minutes ticked by at an infernally slow rate. It was torture. Best to just exist, not to think, "I have a thousand more moments of this hell." Counting them down was not a relief. Counting them not at all was better. Time had begun to have no meaning—until the night when he was waiting for Sebastian and Tristan to return. It had been the longest night of his life.

The minute hand on the clock jerked. He'd given her enough time. If she wasn't prepared for him, he'd speed things along by helping her get ready.

He stopped in the bedchamber where he kept his clothes, where the servants were allowed to see to his needs. After removing his jacket, he tossed it onto a nearby chair. His neckcloth, waistcoat, and shirt followed. He sat down and removed his boots. Warm water was waiting in the washbasin. He'd ordered it sent up before he went in search of Eve. He washed quickly, considered shaving when he rubbed his hands over his rough face, but he didn't have the patience for it. He'd probably nick his jaw or worse, slice his throat. No, better not to risk it.

He headed across the hallway, opened her door without knocking, and came to an abrupt halt at the sight of her lounging against the pillows on the bed, her hair cascading around her. The only thing she wore was the necklace. He'd expected her to be obstinate about it—the way she was with the red gown. He'd thought she'd be in a nightdress, her chin angled high, daring him to find fault.

Even when she did what he commanded, she was unpredictable because he didn't know if she would heed his words. Oh, she was skilled at this mistress game. If he didn't know her history, he'd have thought she was a trained courtesan. Although perhaps her mother's influence had rubbed off on her.

She'd left but one lamp burning low, and it cast her in provocative shadows. He liked that she wasn't modest, that she was already comfortable enough with him that she felt no need to be coy.

"Please, do close the door," she said, and only then did he realize that the sight of her had stopped him dead in his tracks, his hand gripping the door handle. He closed the door, shed his trousers, and strode over to the bed. Her second time should be gentle as well, he thought. But it wasn't going to be. He had envisioned her beneath him for hours now. He craved the feel of her hot velvety tightness closing around him.

When he was near enough, he cradled her jaw, lowered his head, blanketed her mouth with his, and came very close to losing all control. The taste of her made him more heady than his finest Scotch. His body cried out for him to whisper the words, "Touch me," but he didn't dare, for fear that the madness would come upon him and he would cause her to suffer. The last thing he wanted was to hurt her, and yet he knew that he already had. Selfishly, he had carried her onto the path that made it unlikely that she would ever have the husband and children she wanted.

Children. Damnation! He'd brought sheaths with which to cover himself, to ensure he didn't give her the children out of wedlock that she didn't want, but they remained in his jacket. He should return for them but he couldn't bear the thought of leaving her at that moment.

He skimmed his hands over her, parted her thighs, felt the molten heat, and realized she was anticipating what was to come. He'd done so little, yet she was ready. Her moans and sighs echoed around him.

Her hands skimmed through his hair, and he groaned with the sensation of her scraping her nails over his scalp. *Stop her, stop her.* But he didn't. One minute more. But it wasn't long enough. When had time become so short? Why did it encompass an eternity when he wasn't with her, yet hurtled along as fast as a train when he was? He wanted to slow it down, make it last forever.

Her fingers flexed, tightened, pressed—

Grabbing her wrists, he broke off the kiss. Locking her wrists together with one hand, he carried them over her head as he climbed onto the bed and positioned himself at the core of her heat. He kissed a trail along the top of her necklace, then below it. With his free hand, he balanced himself over her and slid into the molten recesses. He almost closed his eyes with the marvelous sensations that swelled up within him, but that would have denied him the sight of her.

Rocking against her, he knew the moment that pleasure took hold for her, the wonder of it traveling over her face. Her thighs squeezed his hips. He bore it because he wouldn't deny her the journey. He was grateful that she was so responsive, quick to settle into the rhythm of their mating.

Lost in the wonder of her, he rode her fast and hard until she was crying out and arching against him. Only then did he let himself go, give the myriad burgeoning sensations the freedom to rip through him, take his breath, his reason, his thoughts. To consume him.

Evelyn feared her wrists might be bruised in the morning. She knew he hadn't realized how tightly he was gripping her when he bucked against her with his final thrusts. Locked in her own web of passion, she hadn't noticed it either until she'd gotten up to clean herself and fetch the silk robe that he'd had sewn for her. He'd slipped into his trousers, and now sat with his back against the headboard, his ankles crossed, as he ate a meat-filled pastry. The tray of food rested between them on the bed. At least he hadn't left immediately. Although based on the way he watched her, she suspected they'd have another rousing round before he did.

"I like the necklace," she said.

"I'll bring you another tomorrow."

He said it as though there was nothing special about it. It was simply a thing to be given. As she was just a woman to be taken.

"You've given me so much already, you don't have to give me jewelry."

He stopped chewing, studied her as though seeing her for the first time. "Mistresses are supposed to want things."

"Rafe, I'm not here to get things out of you. I'm here because I want to be."

"What do you mean, you want to be?"

"I like being here. I like the residence. I like the servants. I even like you, as impossible as that may sound."

Averting his gaze, he reached for a strawberry. "I've given you no reason to like me."

"I suppose that's true enough." Only it wasn't. He'd rescued her from Geoffrey, protected her, always seemed intent on ensuring she had what she needed, even if he did it in a high-handed manner. Even that high-handed manner was becoming endearing to her.

"What do you do when you're not here?" she asked.

"Purchase you jewelry."

She rolled her eyes. "I assume you go to your club. What do you do there?"

"Boring things. Look over ledgers, calculate the money coming in, the money going out, make adjustments so always more is coming in than going out. Decide the liquor to be bought, the games to be added, the ones to be taken away. Determine which lords need to be spoken to about their debt."

"Did you speak to Geoffrey? I know he owed you."

He nodded. "That's the reason I was in attendance that night. He wanted to demonstrate his plan to ensure that he paid off his debt. I was there to only observe, but when you walked through the door . . . you fairly took my breath."

She sat up. "You barely gave me the time of day."

"Never let anyone know how badly you want something. It gives them an advantage."

She tried not to give more credence to his words than they deserved. He meant that he wanted to bed her, not that he wanted her for herself. "You didn't tell me how you came to have the scar on your thigh."

"It doesn't make for a very entertaining story."

"I'm not interested in entertainment. I long to know about you."

He picked up the nearly empty tray and carried it over to a table. When he returned to the bed, he stretched out on his back, shoved one arm beneath his head, and stared at the canopy. Rolling onto her side, she studied his profile.

"It happened after my brothers had made their way back to London. Sebastian had reclaimed the title, returned to Pembrook with his new bride, and asked me to look after the London residence. One night I saw a silhouette lurking about, so I went to confront the intruder. He fired a bullet into me before I realized he had a pistol."

It took her a moment to understand that he thought he was finished telling the story. "So then what happened?"

He turned his head to the side and looked at her. "You asked how I came to have the scar. That's how I got it."

"But how did you get away? Why was he there?"

"Our uncle hired him and his two mates to do away with us. They came out of the shadows. I beat them to a bloody mess until they were unconscious."

"While you were wounded you managed to overcome all three of them."

"I was angry. They tried to murder Sebastian. If he dies, Tristan becomes duke. He's killed? I become duke. I don't want to become duke."

"I think you would make a marvelous duke."

He scoffed. "I have no patience with Society and it has none with me. But you on the other hand—" He rolled onto his side, slipped his hand inside the silk, and cupped her breast. "I have quite a bit of patience for you."

"I don't know about that. Things went rather quickly earlier."

"They will again, I suspect," he murmured just before he leaned in and kissed her.

He tasted of strawberries this time, and she couldn't determine if she preferred the fruit over the heady taste of his liquor. The spirits seem to suit him more; the other seemed far too innocent for one such as he.

Without breaking off the kiss, he deftly unknotted her sash and spread her robe wide so he could have easier access to everything he wanted, and it appeared he wanted everything. She had to admit that he was a considerate lover. With an understanding now of how things were between a man and a woman, she was well aware that he could have taken his own pleasure without giving any to her. While she thought it would increase her enjoyment to be able to engage him fully—holding him, climbing over him, rolling about with him—she couldn't fault him for giving her what he could.

She didn't want her hands clamped together this time so she refrained from reaching out to touch him, but it was difficult, so difficult not to touch, not to feel the warmth of his flesh, the softness of his hair.

He lurched from the bed, and she bit back the cry of protest. Of course, he needed to rid himself of his trousers. While he was about that, she worked her way out of her robe completely and tossed it onto the floor.

When she turned back to him, he was standing there magnificently displayed, the flickering flame in the lamp sending light and shadows dancing over him. She rose up on her knees, sat back on her heels, and simply appreciated the sight of him, of what she longed to touch.

With a devilish grin, he crooked a finger at her. With widened eyes, she wondered if he'd managed to read her thoughts, if he knew her deepest desires resided in sharing more with him. "What are you thinking?"

"Just come here."

She scooted to the edge of the bed, made to get off of it, and he stopped her with a hand on her shoulder. "Lay back, your legs dangling over the edge."

She'd be so extremely exposed, and while he'd seen all of her, touched all of her, to do as he asked made her feel vulnerable. Yet how could she deny him, and she wondered when his wants and needs had begun to take precedence over hers. She did as he asked, lay back, and stared at the canopy.

He skimmed his warm roughened hands over her, and she slid her gaze down to his. At least he allowed her to hold his gaze.

"You're perfect, you know," he said.

"Careful. You're beginning to sound like that poetry you abhor."

"You're far more comfortable with me than I'd ever hoped you would be."

She was far more comfortable with him than she'd ever expected to be. But she sensed that he was not nearly as comfortable with her. Oh, when it came to the physical, certainly he had no qualms about baring his flesh to her, but it was his soul she longed to see, his heart she yearned to find.

Kneeling, he gently parted her thighs and buried his face against her soft curls. She sighed in bliss. She dearly wanted to rub her soles up his back, over his shoulders. Instead, she pressed her tongue against her upper lip and fought to concentrate on her own escalating pleasure instead of what she might give to him.

With his tongue, he worked his magic, circling and stroking. Oh, the wicked, wicked man. Welcoming the sensations rioting through her, she dug her fingers into the sheets. Glorious, glorious. She wondered if he was spoiling her for any other man.

She thought she might be beginning to understand why a woman was ruined if she was bedded before she was wedded. Having known one man, would a wanton forever compare the next to the one who'd come before?

With his hands, he kneaded her breasts, and the sensations tripled, quadrupled, threatened to overwhelm her, to bring tears to her eyes. It felt so good. She shouldn't allow it to be so, but she could no more deny herself the gift he gave her now than she could deny the acceptance of the pearls.

When she thought she could stand no more, her body folded in on itself, raising her back off the bed before slamming her into a whirlwind of pleasure that had her crying out. Through heavy-lidded eyes, she watched as he rose to his feet like some sort of god emerging from desire, his face set in a mask of determination, his nostrils flaring, his eyes burning with want, want of her. Cupping her thighs, he brought her nearer before plunging into her with one bold sure stroke.

She was fascinated by the pumping of his hips, the undulating of his flat stomach. She could see him so much clearer from this position: the tautening of his jaw, the clenching of his teeth, the flopping of his hair against his brow. The muscles bunching in his arms as he adjusted her position, held her legs.

Throwing his head back, he growled low, slamming into her with his final thrusts. His body was coated in a fine sheen of sweat. His eyes were closed tightly, his lips parted, his breathing harsh. While she thought it inconceivable, he'd never looked more beautiful—in a barbaric sort of way. Untamed, uncivilized. Fierce.

When he finally opened his eyes, they shone with the victory of a conqueror. He took a deep breath before slowly extricating himself from her. Her legs weak, she scrambled back. He fell onto the bed, stared at the canopy, his breathing still labored. She thought if she were allowed to place her hand on his chest that she would feel his heart pounding, fast and furiously.

One of them should say something. Instead, she remained silent, curled on her side, and simply watched him, wondering all the while what sort of musings traveled through his mind.

She was going to be the death of him. She was different from the others. He tried to convince himself that it was because of her innocence, because she was his mistress, because she was supposed to be different.

But it was her, the essence of her, not whatever label he'd given to her to make her less dangerous. It was the manner in which she trusted him, the way she opened herself up to him, the unaffected way she responded. She was honest, pure, even now.

He feared he would come to care for her. Along that path lay disaster.

Rolling his head to the side, he discovered she'd fallen asleep. As gently as possible, without disturbing her, he reached down, grabbed the blankets, and brought them slowly up over her. She released a soft sigh, and snuggled in against them.

He experienced a sharp pain in his chest as though his heart had ceased its beating. How desperately he wanted her snuggling against him, her hand furled on his chest, her breath stirring the fine hairs.

What a fool he was. He needed to stop this mooning about. She was nothing more than a convenience, a very lovely one to be sure, but the means to an end, not the end itself. She was spoiling him, however. When he was done with her, he would acquire another mistress. He discovered that he rather enjoyed the expediency and accessibility of having a woman at his beck and call. When the need struck, she was there.

The problem was, with her at least, the need seemed to strike with increasing frequency. He wasn't spending nearly as much time at the club as he needed to. Tomorrow night, he vowed he would not return here until midnight.

He would regain control of himself, of the situation.

Chapter 15

Because if anyone saw her, they might think she was mad, Evelyn slipped out of the residence and into the night without telling a soul—other than her lady's maid, who'd assisted in dressing her—of her plans. The lights in the garden were not flickering, but remained dark, so it was only the moon that guided her steps to the far wall. When Rafe had left that afternoon, he'd told her he would be late so she was not expecting him until well after midnight.

The nights were usually the loneliest. During the day the air filled with the rattle of carriages and the clop of horses' hooves. She would hear the din of people passing by, children running about in the distance and laughing. But when darkness fell, everything became quiet and she merely passed the time, like an ornament set on a mantel waiting to be taken down and admired, studied, touched.

But tonight the loneliness was worse because there *were* sounds. So many marvelous noises. Carriages were lined up on the street, and when she'd looked out one of the windows of a bedchamber upstairs, she saw them turning into the long drive of the residence next door. They were hosting a ball.

She could catch only glimpses of the people attending in their finery. They were too far away for her to discern any details. Bereft, she turned away from the window. She would never attend so glorious an occasion. She would never receive invitations. She would never be welcomed into proper homes. She would always be an outcast, for no matter how much she might gain in possessions, she could not change the circumstance of her birth. It would continue to overshadow every other aspect of her life.

Because these maudlin thoughts threatened to take a stranglehold, she marched to her bedchamber and rang for Lila. An hour later, within the shadows of the garden, she listened as the music wafted on the breeze. She imagined the doors that led onto the terrace were open, allowing the air to cool the guests as they waltzed over the polished floor. She was tempted to retrieve a ladder, place it against the wall, and peer over into the neighbor's domain, but she was no longer a child who didn't know how rude and intrusive it was to spy through holes in fences. So she merely listened and imagined it.

She could hear people talking, quiet whisperings and murmurs mingled with soft sighs. Lovers meeting for a tryst no doubt. Lovers were acceptable, mistresses were not. It hardly seemed fair, but then allowances were made when the heart was involved. The music drifted into silence. She missed it, missed it terribly. Perhaps she would hire an orchestra to play for her and Rafe one evening. He didn't seem to care one whit how she spent his money. His concerns revolved around only what occurred in the bedchamber.

The lilting strains of a waltz floated over the wall. Swaying with the gentle music, she raised her arms as her dancing instructor had taught her, resting one hand on an imaginary tall gentleman, envisioning him placing his hand on her waist, squeezing slightly, a secret shared, that something intimate existed between them. He held her other hand and began to lead her in swirls about the garden, his eyes on hers because he was too infatuated with her to look away.

She dipped one way, twirled around, and her imaginary gentleman took form, a solid hand at her waist, a warm one holding hers. Rafe. Without missing a step, he guided her over the lawn in perfect cadence with the music. She didn't remember dropping her hand to his shoulder. Perhaps because it was already the perfect height for him to slip beneath. Holding his gaze, she smiled softly. "I wasn't expecting you until midnight."

"I hadn't planned to return until *after* midnight."

"Yet, here you are."

"Here I am."

"You must think me quite the ninny to be dancing in the garden."

"I think you're beautiful dancing in the garden, with just enough moonlight to make you mysterious." His voice was low, sultry. He smelled of tobacco and whiskey. "You're wearing the red."

"I was hoping you wouldn't notice."

"You like it."

"I love it. Blast you. You knew I'd wear it."

He grinned, his teeth pearly in the moonlight. "I had hoped. It suits you as I thought it would."

The music stopped, and when the next tune began—a quadrille—they continued to waltz. So like him. Determined not to conform, but to do exactly as he wanted, and he obviously preferred waltzing.

"I've never danced with a gentleman before."

"You're not dancing with one now."

Only she was. He saw himself as a rogue, a scoundrel, but threads of goodness were woven through the coarse fabric of his character.

"I've never been to a ball," she told him. "Do they have many next door?"

"This is their first in London."

"They seem to have drawn quite the crowd."

"Because they're a curiosity."

"Who are they?"

He merely shook his head and studied her intently. "Did you wish to go?"

To the bedchamber. It was where they were inclined to spend all their time now, and while it was lovely when he was with her, sometimes she wanted more. "A few more moments before we go indoors."

"I was referring to the ball. Would you like to make an appearance?"

A shiver of anticipation raced through her, before it crashed into reality. "What do you plan? Climbing over the wall? You can't simply arrive. You must be invited."

"I received an invitation."

She nearly tripped over her feet. His hold on her tightened as he steadied her. Naturally he'd been invited. He was a lord. An available one at that. The mamas would be all over him, striving to match him up with their respectable daughters. She shifted her attention to the wall, thinking of the glamour that rested beyond. It was a world into which she'd hardly been allowed to peer. Stepping away from him, she walked into the deeper shadows. She had so often dreamed of attending a ball, but the price now . . .

She shook her head. "They'd not welcome me."

"They would or they'd deal with my wrath." He glided his finger along the nape of her neck, then across her bared shoulder. "Evie, if you want to go, I'll take you."

As she turned around, his finger remained on her skin until it came to rest in the hollow at her throat. "People will know I'm your mistress."

"When will you learn that they don't matter? None of them matter. Besides, it's not as though you'll be announced as such. You'll be announced as Miss Evelyn Chambers. That I accompany you might raise a few eyebrows but that will be because of my reputation, not yours. The gents who were at Wortham's aren't going to say anything. They're not likely to admit that they didn't end up with the prize."

If she was going to become infamous, make Geoffrey regret his treatment of her, she supposed tonight was as good a night as any to begin. "Yes, all right. Let's go."

His finger dipped down to touch the chiffon that began just below the swell of her breast. "The red is for me. I suggest you change into the purple."

She had planned to do exactly that. The red was gorgeous but incredibly scandalous with its frightfully low neckline. She expected at any moment to pop right out of it. "I shan't be long."

"Take all the time you need. I have it on good authority that this particular ball shall go on forever."

Or at least it would feel as though it was going on forever, Rafe mused while his valet assisted him as much as possible into his formal attire. Rafe buttoned the blue silk brocade waistcoat because the dexterity required was beyond Bateman's skills. When finished, Rafe slipped his arms into the black swallowtail coat that his man held for him.

"Can't remember the last time you dressed so formally," Bateman said, masterfully brushing the lint off the jacket.

He wished he wasn't wearing it now. He didn't know what had possessed him to tell Eve he'd take her to the damned ball.

He'd not planned to return to the residence until late, but he'd been at the club no more than an hour before he found himself thinking of her, wondering what she was doing. He'd found her in the garden waltzing. Alone. He didn't even remember striding across the lawn. He knew only that suddenly she was in his arms and they were moving in rhythm to the music.

Her touch was light, so very light upon his shoulder that he'd barely felt it, and therefore he'd been able to endure it. With little regard to consequences, he'd almost told her to tighten her hold, to close her fingers around him. Would it be different with her? Could it be different with any woman?

He didn't know. It didn't matter. He wouldn't risk it.

Because there was far too much of himself that he

couldn't share with her, he had decided to give her this ball.

Evelyn had often crouched at the top of the stairs and watched as the countess, dressed in her finery, descended to the foyer where the Earl of Wortham waited for her. She'd always thought that her father was the handsomest then, when he was accompanying his countess to a ball or the theater. Rafe quite literally put her father's handsomeness to shame. When he was dressed in evening clothes, he was devastatingly gorgeous. She suspected the ladies would be clamoring to dance with him. With the thought, a fissure of jealousy went through her. They would be the sort whom he would marry, and when he did, he would no doubt dispense with her. If not, she would leave, in spite of everything her leaving would cause her to give up. She would not share him with another who warmed his bed. She almost told him that she'd changed her mind: she didn't wish to attend the ball. Almost. But she had wanted to experience one for far too long to give up on the dream now. Besides she might never have another opportunity.

She was not yet infamous, but once she was, doors that had never been opened to her would be bolted shut forever.

She had always imagined seeing pleasure rippling over her own husband's face as she descended the stairs to meet him, but Rafe was not her husband, and as he stood in the foyer, his expression gave away nothing. He merely studied her with heavily-lidded eyes.

She wished she could hide her thoughts so well, but she suspected that her eyes were shining at the sight of him. Even in his black tailcoat with every strand of hair perfectly combed, he appeared dark and dangerous, someone no one would want to meet in an alley late at night. His broad shoulders filled his jacket nicely. His black trousers hugged his long legs. He tugged at his white gloves. Hers went up over her elbow, fit so snuggly that her fingers would no doubt be numb by the end of the evening. But she didn't care. She was going to attend a formal affair.

As her slippered feet took the last step and settled on the marble in the foyer, he took his top hat from Laurence and settled it on his head. When she reached him, he extended his arm. He'd only offered that courtesy to her once, the night they'd walked through St. Giles, and she'd assumed he'd done it then as a means of protecting her. Was he thinking he needed to serve as her protector now? She smiled brightly before placing her hand on his forearm.

"I can't believe I'm going to attend a ball," she enthused.

"I'm confident you'll find it dreadfully dull," he said drolly.

"Nothing you say will diminish my excitement."

Laurence opened the door and they swept through into the night. She was surprised to see a carriage waiting for them. "It's not that far a walk," she said.

"Far enough."

A footman opened the door, and Rafe assisted her inside. As she settled onto the soft cushion, she supposed walking would have given her a dirty hem and slippers, but the carriage meant enduring the long line of arrivals. She was afraid if she had time to give all this too much thought, she would lose her courage.

Rafe took his seat across from her, bringing with him his glorious male fragrance of cigar, sandalwood, and bergamot.

"Have you attended many parties?" she asked.

"Enough to know I don't much like them."

"Then why are we going?"

"Because you shouldn't be dancing in a garden; you should be dancing in a ballroom."

Nothing he could have said would have pleased her more. "Are you certain they won't mind that you've brought a guest?"

"Sweetheart, they'll be so flummoxed that I arrived at all that they would not object if I walked into the ballroom naked."

She laughed lightly. "I daresay they would object to that."

He tilted his head. "Perhaps I overstate things. You look beautiful, you know."

She pressed her fingers to the pearls he'd given her. "So do you."

He laughed, just a quick burst of sound that reverberated around them.

"I mean it," she said, slightly offended that he didn't seem to believe her. "You are quite possibly the handsomest man I've ever seen. I thought that the first night I met you. I kept stealing glances at you when I was talking with the other gentlemen." She interlaced her fingers tightly, hoping the pain might stop her from opening her mouth. "I don't know why I confessed that. Nervous, I suppose."

"You have no reason to be nervous, I assure you,

but I should warn you that our host is not such a handsome fellow. He was gravely wounded during the war. His face is rather scarred. It can be disconcerting when you first see the extent of the damage."

"He's a soldier then, not a lord." She felt a sense of relief. She would not be mingling about with the upper crust. But what of the little boy? Was he only visiting.

"He's a duke."

Her stomach knotted. "Perhaps we should reconsider."

"I never took you to be cowardly."

"I'm not afraid, but I don't wish to create scandal. You said this was their first ball. I don't want to ruin it for them."

"You won't."

The carriage rocked to a halt. The door opened. Rafe fairly leapt out before extending his hand to her. Taking a deep steadying breath, she placed hers in his. His fingers closed around hers, strong and purposeful. She alighted, taking in the sight of so many footmen scurrying about to assist the guests as they arrived. She thought everyone would be here by now, that they would be the last, but she supposed people came and went all night. The residence was as large as Rafe's, perhaps larger.

As he escorted her up the steps, she said, "They have a son. I hear him playing in the garden sometimes."

"He's but two. He'll be abed."

"You seem to know them very well."

"Not so well."

They stepped through the doorway, and he handed his hat to a servant while she took in everything. It was gorgeous. Family portraits adorned the walls. Something about them was familiar. It was the eyes she realized. All the gentlemen had such pale blue eyes.

But before she could give it much more thought, Rafe was escorting her down a hallway where a few couples waited in line. They looked at him but said nothing, and she wondered if they knew who he was.

"Do you suppose Geoffrey will be here?" she whispered.

"I doubt it. He was lost in the cards when I left the club."

She was glad of that. He'd no doubt make a fuss, although she suspected Rafe would put a stop to it quickly enough. She did wish now that she had purchased some pearl combs for her hair, but she couldn't bring herself to spend his money, to place herself more in his debt.

Then they were through the doorway, and her breath fairly escaped her body. It was all that she had imagined. Stairs led down into the enormous parlor. Candles flickered in the chandeliers. A mirrored wall reflected the guests milling around the edges of the dance area. The fragrance of the abundance of flowers scattered about permeated the air with a heady aroma. The ceiling was so high up that the room contained a balcony where the orchestra played. On the opposite side from where she and Rafe stood, the doors were open onto the terrace.

Leaning over, Rafe said something to the liveried servant standing there. Then he placed his hand over hers where it still rested on his arm.

"Miss Evelyn Chambers," the man announced

in a booming voice that nearly stopped her heart. "Lord Rafe Easton."

She had assumed he would come here as a lord, but still it was disconcerting to hear him announced as such. It was so easy to forget that he inhabited this world, while she had only skipped at the edge of it. At the foot of the stairs, a couple jerked up their heads and Eve saw the scarred visage of the duke. Even Rafe's warning had not prepared her for the massive threads of thick skin that resembled molten wax easing out from around the black eye patch and down to the man's jaw. In contrast, the woman beside him was perfection, with bright green eyes and flaming red hair. She smiled warmly as Evelyn and Rafe descended.

As they got nearer, Evelyn realized the man's remaining eye was the same shade as Rafe's, ice over a clear blue lake. She fought to keep her mouth closed, to not look stunned. She didn't want him to think it was his face that so startled her, rather than the realization that she was on the verge of meeting Rafe's other brother. She was sure of it. If she blocked out the scars, he looked very much like the man she'd met in the park. She was half tempted to smack her fist against Rafe's arm. Why hadn't he confided in her?

As they came to a stop before the couple, Evelyn took a deep curtsy. "Your Graces."

The duke merely studied her, probably seeing more with his one eye than most people did with two.

"Miss Chambers, it is a pleasure," the duchess said. "And you—" She slapped her fan against Rafe's shoulder. "How wicked of you not to tell us you were coming."

"I wasn't certain I'd be able to find the time."

"But then he caught me dancing in the garden—"

"Our garden?" the duke interrupted.

Taken aback by his brusque tone, Evelyn shook her head. "No, his garden. On the other side of the wall."

The duke glared. "You live in that monstrosity on the other side of the wall?"

"No. Miss Chambers resides there. I live in the rooms at my club. And now if you'll excuse us, I hear a waltz starting. I promised the lady a dance."

Before anyone could respond, he wrapped his long fingers around her arm and was propelling her toward the dance floor.

"That was remarkably rude," she muttered.

"We didn't come here to talk. We came here to dance."

"Why didn't you tell me whose affair we were attending?"

"What does it matter? You wanted to attend a ball, and you have. One dance and we leave. Enjoy it, sweetheart."

Within the mad crush of dancing couples, he took her into his arms and glided her over the polished wood. She wanted to remain irritated with him, but decided to lock it away until later. She didn't understand his relationship with his brothers—except to think that he didn't truly have one. But for now, she was at a ball dancing with a handsome gentleman. She wouldn't have it ruined.

"Why didn't you let him know that you lived beside him?" All right. Perhaps it would be ruined.

"It never came up in conversation."

"You can be the most infuriating man—"

"Who brought you to something he despises so you might find some enjoyment."

That knocked all the fight out of her. "Do you really despise it?"

"Only because it reminds me of my roots, and they were dug up long ago."

"But roots always return to where they were, don't they? They return to the soil."

"Oh, my little philosopher, can you not see that they are as uncomfortable with me being here as I am with being here? Many of these gents frequent my club. They owe me a good deal of coin. A few even spend time with my girls. I know their darkest indiscretions."

"Which gents?"

He gave her a sardonic smile. "Would you have me lose my value as a keeper of secrets?"

The music drifted into silence and the disappointment hit her. They would leave now. She supposed she should be grateful for the time she had. Only he didn't escort her from the dance floor, and when the strains of another waltz began, he led her into it. She smiled up at him. For all his gruffness and complaining, she doubted he was going to whisk her away, back to his residence, as quickly as he'd said. He was going to give her this night until she was tired of it. She was sure of it.

"Madame Charmaine told me that you and your brothers have only been known in London for three years. Surely you've had your club longer than that."

"I acquired it when I was seventeen, but I used the name Rafe Weston."

"Clever. East. West. But no one recognized you?"

"I was ten when we . . . disappeared, as it was

so gently put. No one looked for us. No one tried to find us. The most popular tale was that we were eaten by wolves. Wolves, Evie. One of us perhaps, but all three of us? The other two wouldn't have stood around, twiddling their thumbs waiting to be devoured. Yet people believed it."

He sounded so incredibly offended. She supposed that she could hardly blame him. "But surely once you returned, they were glad to see you."

"Not as glad as you might think. Uncle had made friends. We weren't very polished, but mostly, this isn't the world in which I grew up. I'm far more comfortable walking through St. Giles."

Which she found so very sad. He should have been comfortable here. She wouldn't ask him to stay any longer than this dance. So she decided to make the most of these few precious moments. A month ago, a week ago, she would have looked around, taking in all the beautiful gowns, the well-dressed gentlemen. She would have noticed hairstyles and jewelry. She would have watched the orchestra playing, the flames flickering in the chandeliers. Now she merely focused on him. The way his ice-blue eyes remained on her, the set of his mouth and how she longed for it to curl up into a smile. The weight of his touch at her waist. The gentleness with which he held her hand. The feel of her palm curved around his strong shoulder. The heat in his gaze. The promise she saw there that the night would end with pleasure in her bed. She had never wanted to be a mistress, but she did acknowledge that she wanted to be with him.

When the final strains of the song drifted away, she knew she would remember them always, and the gift he had given her of waltzing in a ballroom. "We should leave now, I think."

His gaze intense, he gave her a quick nod. Then he did something he'd never done. He laced his fingers through hers. The small act seemed almost as intimate as being in bed with him. Wending their way through the throng, he guided her around the couples until they reached the outer edge. His hold on her hand tightened as Lord Tristan, Lady Anne beside him, stepped into their path.

Lord Tristan smiled broadly. "Heard you were about. Thought you might join me for a drink in the library."

"We're leaving now."

"So soon?" Lady Anne asked, clear disappointment in her voice. She looked at Evelyn. "I thought we might get a chance to visit, just for a moment. We have so much in common."

Evelyn wasn't quite sure what to say. "I'm not certain we do."

"We're both on the arm of a Pembrook lord. I find it terribly challenging. We could discuss it. You don't mind, do you, Rafe?"

"One drink," Tristan said. "Just to be polite."

"Being polite is not what I'm known for."

"Don't be stubborn. Five minutes is all we're asking."

Evelyn didn't want to interfere. This matter was between Rafe and his brothers, but neither did she want a lovely evening spoiled for everyone simply because he'd given her the gift of dance in a ballroom. She squeezed his hand. He looked down at her and she smiled. "I'll be perfectly fine with Lady Anne if you wish to join them."

He sighed heavily. "I don't wish it, but I suppose a few minutes delay will cause no harm." His fingers released their hold on hers. "I won't be long."

She watched him stride away with his brother. They cut fine figures, both tall and broad-shouldered, dark hair shining almost blue in the candlelight. She could see people turning to observe them.

"They gather attention wherever they go," Lady Anne said.

"Yes, I've heard they're a curiosity."

"Oh, there is that, but mostly I think it's because they're so devilishly handsome and they strut about with such confidence. They intimidate a good many."

Yes, Evelyn could see that.

"Will you join me on the terrace for some fresh air?" Lady Anne asked.

Evelyn was surprised by the invitation. Obviously Lady Anne didn't truly understand Evelyn's role in Rafe's life. "That's very kind but—"

"Don't even think of refusing me." She slipped her arm through Evelyn's and began strolling toward the open doors. "I know what it is to be a curiosity myself. I mourned my fiancé's passing for two years. When I finally returned to Society, everyone was scrutinizing my behavior. It was quite irritating. We tend to judge far too much I think."

They walked onto the cobblestone and crossed over to the railing that bordered the terrace. From here, Evelyn could make out the rooftop of Rafe's residence in the distance. With the brick fence and the trees and shrubbery, it was impossible to see into the next yard, and each house sat on a lovely plot of land that put distance between the residences.

"I can't believe that's Rafe's property," Lady Anne said. "We didn't know."

"I live there. You really shouldn't befriend me."

"Why? Because you're his mistress? None of us are completely pure. Would you feel more comfortable with me knowing that Lord Tristan and I were lovers before we married?"

Evelyn knew her eyes widened. Fortunately she was able to keep her mouth from gaping open.

"I only tell you," Lady Anne began, "because I can see what you mean to him. I was rude enough to watch as you were dancing. He never took his gaze from you. I think he cares for you, so I want you to feel at ease with us."

Evelyn blinked. "I'm quite sure I don't know what you're talking about."

"Rafe's a loner. Yet here you are. With him."

"It's not what you think," Evelyn assured her. She couldn't risk thinking that it might be more, because she knew he could very easily break her heart.

"Forgive me then. I'm just a romantic. Oh, and look, Mary's coming to visit with us. She knows the Pembrook lords better than any of us. She grew up with them."

"They're not the boys I knew," the duchess said as she joined them. "But I'm ever so glad Rafe is here tonight." She smiled. "I suspect you're responsible for that."

"I only wanted to dance."

"Well, perhaps you'll get another dance before you leave. Sebastian shouldn't keep him overly long, but as it's been a good long while since Rafe has been to the manor when Sebastian was here, he couldn't pass up the opportunity to speak with him."

"I understand they separated when they were boys."

"They had no choice." And Mary began to tell her the tale.

"**H**ow long have you lived there?" Sebastian asked.

They were in his well-appointed library. He sat on the edge of his desk, Tristan lounged in a nearby chair, and Rafe leaned against the fireplace. They each held a glass of whiskey.

"Three years longer than you've lived here." Rafe shrugged. "It allowed me to keep a watch over Uncle."

"Why didn't you tell us? Everyone is of the belief that Lord Loudon lives there, although he's not been to town in years from what I understand."

"I didn't want Uncle to know I was there, so Loudon and I handled the transaction very quietly. I pay him a yearly sum to maintain that he still owns it. The fact that he doesn't come to town means that no one calls, so no one learned differently." Although now he supposed he could dispense with paying the man.

"But you could have told us," Sebastian insisted.

"As I said, I normally stay at the club. It's just a bit of property. Besides I don't really consider my properties to be any of your affair." And he hadn't wanted Sebastian popping over or interfering with his life, and he'd feared he do that if he knew that their residences were in such close proximity. Besides he liked that people—even his brothers— knew so little about him.

"How wealthy are you?" Tristan asked.

"Wealthier than you, I'd wager."

"And this woman you brought here tonight," Sebastian began.

"Miss Chambers."

"She's your mistress?"

"You say that as though you disapprove. Considering the scandal that resulted in your marriage, I'd rethink my tone if I were you."

"I'm not finding fault. I'm simply trying to understand—" Dragging his hand through his hair, he sent his eye patch askew, scowled as he straightened it. Rafe had never considered that after all this time, his brother wasn't completely accustomed to the changes the war had wrought. "Why must you keep your distance, be so secretive? You're our brother. We might not have been there for you for twelve years, but we can be here for you now."

"I don't need you now."

"One always needs family," Tristan murmured, staring into his glass.

"Don't take it personally. I was on my own—"

"We were all on our own."

"Not like I was. Sebastian had his comrades in arms, you had the crew of your ship." *I had no one. I was completely, absolutely alone.* "I'm not discussing this."

"I want to know what your life was like, what happened while we were away," Sebastian said.

Rafe shook his head. "No, Sebastian, you don't."

Sebastian downed the remnants of his glass. "I've been reading troubling accounts in the newspaper about some of the workhouses and the conditions there. Did they beat you?"

"What does it matter?"

"They did then."

Rafe sighed. "Does it make you feel better knowing that? At least none of the punishments left scars. Tristan can't claim the same thing."

"I wouldn't have left you there if I'd known what truly took place within its walls. I thought it a place that took care of orphans and abandoned children. Not abused them."

Rafe had never wanted his brothers to know what he'd suffered. It had made him feel weak that he'd not been able to stand up for himself, that even the heritage of which he'd been so damned proud carried no sway within the confines of the workhouse. It had only made things worse because no one believed him. They ridiculed him and made his punishments harsher. Everyone had only served to reinforce his suspicions regarding why his brothers had left him behind: because he was inadequate, unable to be of any value in helping them escape. He was a deterrent, a burden, incapable of carrying his own weight. "I truly see no point in traveling this path. It only serves to bring to the surface what is best left undisturbed."

Sebastian studied him for a moment, while Tristan contemplated the contents of his glass.

"As you wish," Sebastian finally said. "We won't talk of the past then. But we can move forward. I want my son to know you, to know both his uncles, to understand that what he inherits, he does so only because you and Tristan were willing to fight with me for our birthright. He needs to fully comprehend the legacy that is being passed down to him."

Rafe almost responded, "No, he doesn't. Not my legacy at least." Instead, he said, "Once I left"—

escaped—"the workhouse, and made my way to London, not everything I did was within the law."

"You think that everything I did was?" Tristan asked. "I wasn't serving in her Majesty's navy, you know. I was on a ship captained by a man who thought laws only applied when he was on land— and then only when he was in the mood to heed them. On his ship, he was Caesar. We didn't always come by our spoils honestly."

"But when you were captain of your own ship?"

Tristan swirled the liquid in his glass. "A ship I won at cards. Cheated to obtain it, if you want the truth. Because I was desperate to have it, to be in control. My point is that we have all done things with which we must live, but at least we are here to live with them. I for one am glad of that. Even arguing with you is better than not having you around to argue with."

Rafe looked over at Sebastian. "Does he always talk this much?"

"Afraid so, but every now and then he does say something worth listening to."

"I wouldn't have to carry the weight of the conversation if you weren't so melancholy. It's the horrors he faced in the war," Tristan added for Rafe's benefit. "The one thing you can say is that we've not led boring lives. Perhaps we should consider that Uncle did us a favor."

"No," Sebastian growled at the same time that Rafe said, "Never."

Tristan appeared very pleased with himself, as though he'd just proven that for all their differences, they did have commonalities. "Join us on the ship Friday."

Begrudgingly Rafe said, "I'll consider it."

"Well, then we're making progress." Tristan downed his drink and stood. "Now, if you gents will excuse me, I need to dance with my wife."

Rafe watched him stride from the room, before setting his own glass on the mantel. "I should be off as well."

"He's not as unaffected as he acts," Sebastian said. "Did you know that I sold him?"

Rafe hadn't known, but before he could respond Sebastian continued. "For a pouch of coins so I could purchase my commission. He never said a word. After we reached the wharves. He just remained stoic and silent. It always haunted me."

"Unlike me, who blubbered and begged."

"You were only ten. It tore me apart to leave you behind, but it was either the workhouse or settling you with gypsies. I didn't know how else to protect you. And in spite of the hardships I suspect you suffered, I'm extremely proud to call you brother. You not only survived, but you've done very well for yourself."

Rafe didn't know what to say, how to respond. "I need to make sure that Evelyn is carrying on all right."

"Off with you then."

Rafe was halfway across the room when he stopped and said over his shoulder, "You're a better man than I am. You *and* Tristan." It was all he could give his brother for now, but perhaps it was a start.

Chapter 16

She was in her nightdress by the time she heard him leave his bedchamber. She expected him to come to her, but instead his footsteps echoed in the hallway, growing fainter as he retreated down the stairs. She considered crawling into bed, but had decided this mistress business involved more than what happened between the sheets. He might not want it to be so, but it was. For whatever reason, he was estranged from his brothers, and while he might not admit it, it caused him considerable pain.

Grabbing her wrap, she slipped into it and belted it firmly at her waist before heading out of her room and following the path she was certain he had taken. He might have gone to his club for all she knew, but she hoped not. She knew it was his place of solace, when she dearly wanted to play that role in his life. She wasn't certain when she'd developed such a fondness for him. He was obstinate, moody, and didn't possess a frivolous bone in his entire body, but for the moment at least, he was hers.

Until he tired of her, she intended to have some purpose in his life other than looking presentable and being available for him to slake his lust upon. Because it was after midnight, the servants were already abed, so she opened the door to the library herself, not even certain why she knew that she would find him there—if he were still in residence.

He was. Dressed in his loose linen shirt and trousers, one arm raised, pressed to the mantel, while the other held an almost empty tumbler. He was staring into the barren hearth before glancing back at her, heavy lidded.

"Go on to bed, Evie. I won't be bothering you tonight."

Her belly clutched painfully, and her chest filled with a sadness that nearly cracked her ribs. Was that how he viewed things between them: that his coming to her was a bother for her? Did her cries of pleasure mean nothing? Did he not understand that she had come to cherish him? Did *she* mean nothing at all to him?

She wandered over to the table, removed the stopper from a decanter, and lifted it.

"What are you doing?" he asked.

"I'm of a mind to have something to drink." She filled a glass. With decanter in hand, she walked over to him and poured the amber liquid into his glass. She could feel his speculative gaze on her, but didn't dare bring herself to look into his eyes. They could easily dissuade her from her purpose. She returned the decanter to the table, took her glass, and made herself comfortable in a nearby chair, pulling her legs beneath her. She lifted her glass. "Cheers."

She downed a good bit, let the warmth swirl

through her, igniting her courage. "They didn't want to leave you, you know."

He released a strangled laugh. "I know." He turned his attention back to the empty hearth.

"I understand that it doesn't make it any easier, though. The knowing," she said. "When I was a little girl and my mother was still alive, the earl would come to visit us. Every time he left, she sat by the window and gave herself leave to cry for two minutes. Then she would stop, wipe her nose with her silk handkerchief, and say, 'He doesn't want to leave us, Evelyn, but he has no choice. Duty and all that rubbish.' I thought there must be something that would allow him to stay, and then my mother died, and I was able to be with him."

He snapped his head around, penetrating her soul with his focus. "You didn't make your mother die."

"I know, but still it was a silly thing to wish for. Do you think either of them had it easier than you?"

"No." His attention was back on the hearth. "But I don't think either of them had to do what I did to survive."

She swallowed more Scotch before tightening her arms around her legs. "What did you do, Rafe?"

Slowly he shook his head. "You don't want to know, Evie."

"Do you do those things now?"

"No." He glowered at her. "Absolutely not."

"Then perhaps they don't matter." She took another sip. Amazing how relaxed she was becoming. "Would it be so awful do you think to go on the boat with your brother?"

"Ship."

She giggled, then sobered. "Their wives seem very nice. Did you know . . ." She looked at her glass, wrinkled her brow. "Oh, it's empty."

In long strides he went to the table, retrieved the decanter, and refilled her glass. He took the chair opposite her. "Did I *know*?"

Lowering her voice so revealing a confidence wouldn't seem quite so wicked, she said, "Lord Rafe and Lady Anne were intimate before they married."

"Yes, I knew. All of London knew. Even though he denied it later, I think everyone recognized his denial was a lie, a wish to protect her when it was far too late."

"Oh." Pondering, she took a long sip of the Scotch. "Why are mistresses looked down upon then? If others do it without benefit of marriage."

"I suppose it has to do with love."

"Have you ever loved anyone?" Looking at him over the rim of her glass, she sipped again. It was a funny thing but the more she drank, the more she wanted to drink.

"My father. Never knew my mother. She died when I was born." He rubbed his thumb over his lower lip, a lip she wanted to kiss. What would he do if she got up, crossed the distance separating them, bent over, and placed her mouth against his? "I suppose she was the first person I killed."

His words slowly registered through her lethargic haze. "What? No. It's not your fault she died. It simply happened."

"She gave birth to twins without dying. So why was I so difficult? I don't believe my father blamed me, but still I reflect on it sometimes."

"You shouldn't. Not like that. She loved you, I'm sure of it. She'd want you to be happy."

He chuckled low. "After everything that's happened to you, how can you remain so damned optimistic?"

"I wouldn't much like being the other way." She squinted. "You need to stop drinking. You're becoming blurred."

He smiled, a real smile, she thought, but it was so difficult to see. The room was growing dark around the edges, and she was having a devil of a time keeping her eyes open.

"I believe you're the one who's *blurred*," he said, and she could have sworn she heard the amusement in his voice.

"Who was the other person you killed? You said your mother was the first."

"I don't know his name."

"He deserved it, though. You wouldn't have killed him otherwise."

He tilted his head to the side as though to see her more clearly. "Are you not appalled?"

She fought to shake her head forcefully, although it seemed to want to loll about on its own. "I wanted to kill Geoffrey, although he didn't really deserve it. But I should have smacked him I think."

"I can arrange that if you like."

She heard laughter. As his mouth was closed, she supposed it was coming from her. "I've decided I feel rather sorry for him. He's weak, not to be admired. Not worth the effort of me slapping. Besides, I don't think I can get out of the chair."

"Yes, I assumed that when you dropped the glass."

She looked at her hand, her fingers. "I was holding it, wasn't I?"

"I think you're quite into your cups."

She lifted her gaze to find him hovering over her. Reaching up, she trailed her fingers over his lips. "Do you like me?"

"Very much. That's your misfortune. I thought I'd be done with you by now."

"I thought you would as well. I don't think you quite appreciate yourself."

"And you, my sweet, are drunk."

He lifted her into his arms and she rested a hand on his shoulder. "I won't hold you, but this is like when we were waltzing. I liked waltzing."

"I'll take you to another ball."

She was vaguely aware of his long strides taking them out of the library.

"I should like to go on your brother's boat."

"You shall have to call it a ship."

"I will, I promise. So will we be going on it?"

"I don't know. I've not yet decided."

"Have you a coin?" she asked.

"What has that to do with anything?"

"Have you a coin?" she insisted.

"Yes. The same one you used before."

"Then set me down."

"You'll fall on your face."

"No, I won't. Set me down."

He did as she ordered, and her feet settled on the cold marble. They were in the foyer. She wobbled around a bit, before he set his hands on her shoulders and steadied her.

"All right, take out your coin. You'll be the one

to flip it. Heads we go on the ship, tails we don't. Agreed?"

"I don't believe in giving fate—"

"Trust me. Are we agreed on the terms?"

He narrowed his eyes at her. "Agreed."

"Toss it in the air, but don't look at it when it lands."

"How will I know—"

She placed her fingers against his lips. "Don't think about it. Just do as I say." She forced herself to concentrate on his face, his eyes. "Toss it."

He flipped it up, it spiraled down—

"There," she said, putting her hand up so he couldn't see the coin as it clinked with its landing, rolled, and fell onto a side. "There, that split second before it landed, what did you think?"

"That this is ridiculous."

He started to move away, and she stayed him with a hand on his arm. He glared at her. There was a time when the fierceness of his glower would have sent her cowering up the stairs, but that was before she knew him. "My father taught me that when you flip a coin, there is always a second, just before it lands, when you think either heads or tails. And that's when you truly know what you want the outcome to be. So what did you think? I saw it in your eyes. I know you thought one or the other."

"The first night you were here, you flipped a coin."

"Yes, but I didn't tell you if heads meant I stayed. And actually, tails meant I stayed, so I lied to you and said it was heads. But you see, that's the beauty of it. It doesn't matter what lands. What matters is what you hoped would land. And that's your answer. So what did you want, Rafe?"

"Doesn't matter what I want." He swept her into his arms. "We'll go because you'll harp about it if we don't."

Suddenly exhausted, she rested her head against his shoulder. "When have I ever harped?"

Rafe set her down gently on the bed and unknotted the sash of her robe. She barely stirred as he worked her out of it. Bringing the covers up over her, he was incredibly tempted to slip beneath them with her. But it had been years since he'd been able to stand the weight of covers lying heavy on his body.

She didn't harp, she didn't complain. The more he came to know her, the more he realized she'd have not ended up in St. Giles as he'd originally assumed. She possessed a determination, a strength of will that would have had her finding a way to avoid the rookeries. She'd taken the path of least resistance by staying with him, but it had also been her smartest move. Smarter yet to make him think that she'd allowed fate to decide when she'd done it all along. She was here because she had chosen to be. Which meant she could just as easily choose to leave.

He broke out in a fine sheen of sweat. He didn't care if she left. She meant nothing to him. He hadn't enjoyed dancing with her. He hadn't taken pleasure in seeing her in the red. He wasn't glad she'd worn his pearls. He was ready to leave her now, to get on about his business. Yet he stood there, watching her sleep, thinking that she deserved to have a man holding her tightly, his breath wafting over her neck while she dreamed.

And he found himself desperately wishing he could be that man.

After extinguishing the lamp, he left the room and returned to the foyer. His coin was still on the floor, tails winking up at him. His father had given him the coin one blustery morning. "Go into the village and purchase some humbugs. We'll share them tonight when I regale you with tales of our hunting." Then his father had mounted his horse and gone off with his younger brother, Lord David. Rafe had never made it to the sweet shop. It was a cold day, so he'd lounged by the fire instead, playing with a carved wooden horse he'd stolen from Tristan. He didn't like going to the village alone. He'd planned to convince his father to go with him when he got back.

But his uncle was the only one to return. Servants were sent out to retrieve his father and to put down the horse that had thrown him.

Rafe rubbed his fingers over the coin. He didn't know why he'd kept it all these years. There was many a time when he could have used it to purchase food to fill his belly. But he had held onto it.

He would never admit it to Eve, but he had hoped for heads. During that one second, just before it landed—*heads*, his mind whispered. As much as he hated to acknowledge it, he was curious about Tristan's yacht. Rafe had been disappointed that Tristan had sold his ship before Rafe had a chance to sail on it. If he hadn't avoided his brothers, if he hadn't isolated himself—

He'd always known, deep in his gut, that they'd had no choice except to leave him behind. But he also knew that if he'd been stronger, sharper, quicker they might have taken him with them. It was what was lacking in him that had forced them to abandon him. He was tired of clutching to the past. Yet it was so damned hard to let go.

Chapter 17

The following night, standing in the shadows of the balcony, Rafe decided that he was going to stay at the club until dawn. Simply because he so desperately wanted to be with Eve. This need he had for her—

He shook his head. He didn't need anyone. Only himself. He wouldn't need anyone. He'd learned that lesson soon enough when he'd first arrived in London. He was a quick study. When taught a lesson once, he mastered it. He was giving Eve too much power, allowing her to have too much influence over him. Did he really want to go on Tristan's boat? Or was it that *she* wanted to go, and he wanted only to please her? When had he ever wanted to please anyone other than himself?

He didn't like the little game she played with the flip of a coin. He believed in knowing his own mind. If she flipped a coin, she should leave it to fate. She shouldn't have stayed with him. That had been fate's answer. Go.

Eventually she would. Everyone did. Everyone left.

Except for Wortham, it seemed. The man was losing at an astonishing rate. "How much is he into?"

"Eight thousand quid," Mick said from farther back in the shadows.

Rafe scoffed. "What an idiot."

"He thinks the cards will turn in his favor. They all do. That's the reason they play."

And the reason that Rafe didn't. A man had control over the cards only when he cheated. Rafe had done that on occasion when he wanted something badly. His residence, for one. It assuaged his conscience little that once he'd taken ownership, he'd invited the lord to a private game in which the lord had walked away with the majority of the take. The lord had then retired to his country estate. He'd cancelled his membership at Rafe's club.

Wortham should do the same.

"Think I shall have a word with his lordship," Rafe murmured.

"In your office?"

"No, on the gaming floor should work well enough." He didn't expect much of a protest from Wortham. The man had no backbone. He needed to leave the table until his debt was again paid in full.

Rafe made his way down the darkened stairs. His club was made up of more shadows than light. That's where sin was best carried on and sinners were most comfortable. He strolled among the tables. Once this was the only place he wanted to be. It irritated him that he now longed to be elsewhere. It annoyed him further that the one place he wished to be most of all—in Eve's arms—was the one place he would never be. But sometimes he wondered: could it be different with her?

He came to a stop beside Wortham's chair, watched as the last hand was played out, and the chips were taken from Wortham. "Now would be the time to leave, m'lord. While you still have a few chips to cash in. Your credit here has reached its limit."

"You fuck my father's daughter—"

Fisting his hand around the man's neckcloth and collar, Rafe yanked him to his feet. "Do not speak of her."

"Or what? You won't allow me to breathe any longer? Perhaps it's you who will cease to breathe."

As fire burst through his side, Rafe slung Wortham away. A knife clattered to the floor one second before Wortham joined it in a sprawl, his eyes wide, his face ashen. Rafe suspected the man had never poked another.

The dealer straddled Wortham and drew his fist back.

"No," Rafe barked. "He's not worth it." One didn't go about striking the nobility without suffering dire consequences.

"He knifed you," Mick said.

"It's just a nick, but get him out of here. I don't want to see him in here again." He tugged on his waistcoat when he dearly wanted to rip it off. "Back to your games, gentlemen. The entertainment is over."

Leaning down, he picked up the knife, pocketed it, and began striding for the stairs that would take him to his office and a back exit.

Mick caught up to him. "Judging by the blood on that knife—"

"See that things are tidied up and everything returns to normal. I'm going to my residence."

To Eve, a small voice whispered, *to Eve*.

He had yet to show. It was unusual for him, even though he always claimed he would not see her before midnight, he had never held to that claim. As Evelyn waited in the sitting area of her bedchamber, she tugged on the sash of her silk wrap. Beneath it, she wore a silk nightdress that shimmered over her skin whenever she moved. She saw no reason to dress formally, when he would have her out of the clothes almost as soon as he walked through the door. She supposed she should be glad that he had such a driving need to possess her, but sometimes she did wish they had time to savor each other a little more. Although she wasn't going to complain. He had taken her to the ball after all. She thought if she asked that he would take her to the theater. She had seen an advert—

The door burst open. He took two steps in, halted. "Why weren't you waiting for me downstairs?"

"I was waiting for you here." She'd never seen him look so disheveled. He was breathing harshly, his neckcloth askew, his waistcoat open, his shirt unbuttoned. She slowly came to her feet. "Dear God, is that blood? Did you kill someone?"

He laughed darkly. "At least you know me well enough to know what I'm capable of."

He tore at his jacket. She heard material ripping before he had properly removed and discarded it.

"We must send for a physician," she said.

"Laurence is seeing to it."

Working to get off his waistcoat next, he took a step, staggered, then made his way to the bed. He sat down heavily and hung his head. She hurried over, stared at him, at the red-soaked spot on his shirt. "Oh, my Lord. Is it all *your* blood?"

"Afraid so, but don't worry, pet. My solicitor is well aware that should I die, you gain all. Except the gaming hell. That goes to Mick."

"Do you honestly believe that is what is on my mind at this moment?"

"If you're smart, you'll start praying for my demise."

"Then I must be exceedingly stupid, because what I'm praying for is the physician's hasty arrival."

He studied her as though she were a new species of butterfly to be pinned to a board and examined. "After all you've endured, how can you think of others before yourself? Do you not see how important you are? That you are all that matters?"

"I'm not *all* that matters. It would be a rather sad world if I were." As carefully as she could, she worked his arms out of his waistcoat. "What happened?"

"Idiot didn't like that I wasn't going to give him any more credit."

"You were attacked at your club?"

He shrugged, grimaced.

"What sort of clientele do you serve?"

"Wortham's a member. That should give you a clue."

She began gathering up the hem of his shirt. "But he wouldn't do something like this."

He was silent as she began to lift. She stilled, horrified by a thought. "Say it wasn't him."

"It wasn't him."

Relief coursed through her. Cautiously, as he raised his arms, she pulled his shirt over his head. Then she saw the ghastly gash oozing blood. She thought she might be ill.

She rushed over to the washbasin and grabbed a towel. After returning to the bed, she pressed the cloth against the gaping wound. She heard his sharp intake of breath.

"It isn't bad," he assured her. "It's long, but not deep. He didn't strike any organs."

"How do you know?"

"Because I'd be in a good deal more pain. Idiot didn't know what he was doing. He just struck without thought or aim. A few stitches should do the trick. You could probably sew me up."

"My stitching is atrocious. I'm always having to undo it and redo it. I'd probably end up sewing your side to your thigh."

He released a short burst of laughter. "Then I suppose it's a good thing I didn't take you to be my tailor."

"I told you I have no skills." She lifted her gaze to his as realization dawned. "You live in a very violent world, don't you?"

"Not as violent as it once was." He averted his gaze. She thought perhaps he was studying the lamp. She could see the flame reflected in his eyes. "I know he didn't hit any organs because I know what the inside looks like. When I was fourteen, I worked for a nasty fellow. He went by the name of Dimmick. He would do favors for people or lend them money, but what they owed him was a good deal more. When it was time to pay up, he would send a couple of us to collect. 'His boys' he called us. 'Don't want me to be sendin' me boys 'round.' Before he sent us on our first job, he took us to a morgue, cut open a cadaver, and showed us how to strike to cause the most pain, where to strike to kill."

"You mentioned that you'd killed someone. Did you do it for him?"

He brought his gaze back to her. "Not for him. But I hurt people, badly. I'm not proud of it, but at the time I felt I had no choice if I was to survive. A couple of years later, he found himself in a bit of a bother. One of his boys could read and write, you see. He kept very good records of the man's activities." He gave her a devilish grin. "In exchange for not taking them to Scotland Yard, I wanted his gaming hell."

"That's how you came to have your club."

He nodded slowly, thoughtfully, and she wondered how much longer before he clammed back up. It was unusual for him to reveal so much. He had to be trying to distract himself from the pain.

"What happened to him? Where is he now?"

"He sent someone to kill me. I broke the bloke's arm, told him I could teach him a better way to live."

Knowledge dawned. "Laurence?"

He nodded again. "Word spread that I was a fairer sort. Those who once worked for him began to work for me. He had a lot of enemies, and soon there was no one to protect him. Heard he jumped off Tower Bridge one night."

"You shouldn't feel guilty."

"I don't feel guilty about anything. There's nothing to be gained by it."

"Why did you tell me all this?"

"So if I die, you'd know not to come looking for me when you get to heaven."

She felt compelled to carry on with the farce that neither of them was worried about the wound. "I wouldn't anyway."

He grinned. She heard the door creak as it was opened further. Rafe looked up. "Ah, Graves, I'm in need of your skills."

Evelyn put her faith in Dr. William Graves because he had the countenance of an angel. Rafe seemed to have an inordinate amount of confidence in the man's abilities as he cleaned out the wound—which was far deeper and ghastlier than Evelyn had originally thought—and sewed it up.

After Graves left, tiny tremors were still coursing through her. She was half tempted to take a dose of the laudanum that the doctor had left behind. It had certainly worked to put Rafe asleep. As he didn't stay with her after they—she didn't know how to think of it. They weren't making love, yet it seemed to be more than just bedding, at least to her; she doubted it was to him. But because he didn't remain, she'd never had the opportunity to watch him sleep. With the medication carrying away his worries and burdens, he appeared vulnerable, young.

And so damned proud. Not allowing the servants in to see to his needs. What if he'd not had her? Would he have suffered through all this alone, with no one to watch over him? She knew the answer before she'd completely asked herself the question. He would have. He kept himself isolated from others. He fought not to need anyone. Not even her.

She provided surcease for his physical needs, but his heart, his soul remained distant, untouchable. He did things for her because they were expected of him—a man bought jewelry for his mistress and so he bought it for her. Because she was his mistress, not because he held any tender regard for her.

She was a fool for wanting to mean something to him. But then, unlike him, she seemed to have little control over her heart. Perhaps she was more like her mother than she realized. Surely if she'd had a choice, her mother would have fallen in love with a man who could marry her, instead of one forced to steal moments with her. Evelyn would be mistress to but one man. When he was done with her, she would find a way to make herself presentable. She would leave the aristocracy behind, London as well. She would go someplace where she wasn't known and she would find love. Or at the very least a man who placed her happiness above his own. He would intertwine his fingers with hers when they strolled along. He would wrap his arms around her when they watched the sunset. He would carry her into the house because his strides were longer than hers and he was impatient to be with her.

With a sigh, she brought the covers up higher over Rafe's still form and tucked him in. A chill haunted the air tonight, and she didn't want him falling ill. Dealing with his wound would be troublesome enough. Dr. Graves had told her to expect a fever and explained how she would know if the stitched-up gash became infected. He gave her instructions to send for him if he was needed. Lowering her head, she pressed a light kiss to Rafe's forehead, aware that it was clammy. She hated seeing him in agony. She would get a damp cloth and gently pat his face.

Turning away from the bed, she spotted his clothing strewn over the floor. As she gathered it up, her gut clenched at the sight of his blood staining the white, and marring the beautiful brocade. The material was ripped beyond repair not only from the knife—she shuddered with the image—but from Rafe's haste to rid himself of his clothing.

Starting to bundle it up, she realized that something was in the pocket of the waistcoat. Gingerly, she dug her fingers into it and retrieved a key. It very much resembled the one in her door, one she never turned because a mistress shouldn't lock out her lover. And then she knew. This brass object provided entry into *his* room. Clutching it to her breast, dropping the clothes, she snapped her head around to stare at the bed.

He was still there, had not moved a single muscle. Sleeping soundly.

She turned her attention to the door separating their rooms. What was behind it that he protected so fiercely?

As quietly as possible she crept toward it, her heart hammering, her breathing unsteady. Reaching the door, she unfurled her fingers and stared at the blood smeared over the brass. His blood.

She would not feel guilty for wanting to know everything possible about him. It was unconscionable that they were intimate physically and yet he held secrets. What might be behind that door had been taunting her. Now she would know. It wasn't as though she was really doing anything awful. She would see the room when the house became hers exclusively. So where was the harm in seeing it now?

She peered over at him to make certain he was still asleep. Deeply based upon the snores he was beginning to emit. She didn't know he snored. She didn't know so many things about him. It was the reason that she wanted to take a peek into his room. Just a peek. Was the bedding dark? Was the bedchamber filled with globes?

Once she opened the door, she couldn't unopen it. She looked at him again. If he trusted her, if he cared for her, he wouldn't remain so mysterious. He would bare all. By opening the door, wasn't she indicating that he couldn't trust her? Even if he never found out, she would know.

Placing her hand on the knob, she moved the key nearer to the keyhole—

They were holding him down, beating him, monsters with hideous smiles and cackling laughter. He wanted to kick at them, strike out with flailing fists, but he had no arms, he had no legs. Nothing. He could do nothing, not even roll. Everything was pressing in. His chest was going to cave in. He couldn't breathe.

He heard the whimpering, the fading cries for help. They were coming from him. They weren't coming from him. They stopped, and that terrified him even more.

"I'm a lord! You can't treat me like this! I'm a lord! My father was a duke! My brother's a duke!"

But they only laughed louder, pushed harder, wrapped more tightly. They were putting him in a cocoon, like the one he'd once seen a caterpillar create. Being inside it had changed the insect into something else, something beautiful. He'd seen it emerge. But he knew he wouldn't emerge

*from this. He was going to suffocate, die. He could feel
less and less of himself. He was disappearing while the
monsters loomed larger. When he no longer existed, he
wouldn't be free of them. They would follow him into hell.*

*He had to escape, he had to fight. If only he could
breathe. He could regain his strength, he could fight them
off. He had to show them he was strong, that they couldn't
beat him. But his lungs were going to explode.*

*Air. Air. There was none to breathe because all the
space was filled with screams.*

The screams woke her. She shot out of the chair
near the bed, disoriented and groggy. She'd meant
to watch over him, not fall asleep. She was horrified
to see him thrashing about as though caught in the
grip of a horrendous nightmare.

Climbing onto the bed, she fought desperately to
grab his wildly flailing arms. "Rafe. Rafe! Wake up!
It's only a dream."

"Get it off! Get me out of here!"

His wayward fist smashed into her face and sent
her reeling backward off the bed, slamming against
the floor, jarring her teeth. Pinpricks of light danced
in front of her eyes, her head spun. With determination she struggled to her feet.

"Rafe?" Dear Lord, her jaw ached.

He glared at her with an unholy feral gleam in his
eyes, like those of a cornered animal she'd once seen
at the zoological gardens. He was a man possessed,
battling the covers, as though they were the enemy.

"Oh, dear God." His rule slammed into her with
the impact that his fist had only moments earlier. He
didn't like to be held, and she had tucked the covers

in snuggly around him. When she was ill, she drew comfort from being nestled beneath a mound of them. But he had to feel as though the widest arms on earth were holding him. Grabbing the covers, she began jerking them free. "Calm down, calm down. I'll get them off."

As their hold loosened, so he began to still. When she had dragged the last of the dampened sheets to the floor, he scrambled off the bed. Breathing heavily, he glanced around wildly. She could see blood seeping through the bandages.

"Where are my clothes?" His voice was rough, harsh.

He was still in his trousers. Surely he wasn't planning to go out. "They were ruined. I had one of the servants take them to a rubbish bin."

"My key. I have to get—"

"I placed it on the bedside table there. I found it in your waistcoat pocket."

He spun around, pinned her with an accusatory glare. She knew what he assumed, and she was so grateful that she could speak the truth.

"I didn't use it. I didn't go into your room." She'd not been able to bring herself to open the door. Everyone had secrets. She had decided he was entitled to his. "Please, lie back on the bed so I can tend to your wound."

Ignoring her, he snatched up his key and staggered to the door. She didn't know if it was the pain, the final throes of the nightmare, or the lingering effects of the laudanum, but he was having a devil of a time putting the key into the keyhole.

She darted around the bed, hurried to the door. "Allow me."

"No."

"Rafe, I want to help you."

"Then leave me be." He finally jammed the key in, turned it. "Go away, go away now." He opened the door, slid through the narrow opening.

"You need help. You're bleeding again," she said, determined to help this obstinate, proud—

She staggered to a stop in muted disbelief.

"Well, now you know the truth of it," he said, his voice laced with anger, resignation, shame. "You're the mistress of a madman."

Chapter 18

Evelyn glanced around at the disarray of clothes strewn about, the buttons littering the floor, the mattress stripped bare, the curtainless window, the dust-coated floor.

"Please leave," he muttered, hunching over slightly, pressing his hand to his side, no doubt suffering excruciating pain from his wound. But she saw more: his humiliation at her discovery of his secret.

The strong man who had protected her, provided her with sanctuary appeared defeated, and it tore into her soul.

"Don't be ridiculous. Sit in that chair by the fireplace while I get sheets for the bed."

"I don't want sheets. I can't stand them." Gingerly, he eased himself into the chair. "They make me feel as though I'm smothering."

And she had tucked them in securely around him. Quietly, she walked over, knelt before him, and lightly placed her hands on his knees. Holding his gaze, she said, "You're not mad."

"Look about you. Of course, I am."

She could argue until she was blue in the face, but he was obviously past the point of listening. "Please, let me tend to your wound."

"The bandage wrapped so tightly is killing me. I need to get it off. And my trousers. I need you to leave." She watched his throat muscles work as he swallowed, his gaze on a distant spot on the wall. "Please go, Eve."

The rough, ragged plea nearly sliced open her heart. Tears stung her eyes. "I can't. I can't leave you alone, not like this. I'll take off the bandage and your trousers. You can lie on my bed. We won't put the covers back on, but I can stop the bleeding. Then you can rest."

Reaching up, she tenderly combed back the hair from his brow. He grabbed her hand. She expected him to fling it aside. Instead, he turned his face into her palm, and pressed a kiss to its center. He closed his eyes, and she thought he might be drifting off to sleep, holding her like that.

"I just need a few moments in here," he whispered.

Bending down, she picked up a shirt. It was ripped, several buttons missing. "I can mend—"

"I don't want them mended. I gather them up occasionally. Take them to a poorhouse. They can mend them."

If he wasn't having the clothes repaired, then he was purchasing new. She supposed he didn't want the servants or anyone else questioning how his clothing came to be so tattered. "Your tailor must absolutely adore you."

He chuckled low, the sound vibrating against her hand where it rested against his throat. "He does."

He was breathing less erratically. It appeared

the bleeding had stopped. An intimacy was weaving around them, something deeper than anything they'd shared in bed. She was loath to bring an end to these moments. "People aren't usually born feeling as though they're smothering. What happened?"

He lowered their hands to his lap, hers cradled within his, her palm upturned. It was as though he were studying all the lines, searching for the answers, or perhaps merely the words to explain the unexplainable.

"I won't tell," she whispered. "I promise."

His eyes slid closed, his voice raspy when he finally spoke. "Promises hold no sway, Evie. They can be broken."

"Not mine," she said with conviction.

He opened his eyes, but still didn't look at her, his finger tracing over her palm. He released a long slow sigh. "My brothers left me at a workhouse. Horrid people owned it. But it costs money to manage a place like that, and the people inside certainly haven't the means to pay. So they had an agreement with the owners of a nearby coal mine. Before the sun rose, we were woken up, fed our milk porridge, and marched off to the mines. We worked there until long after the sun set. It got to the point that when I did see the sun, it hurt my eyes."

He trailed his finger over one line and then another as though he were etching his story on her palm.

"I was a coal bearer. I carried the coal that others dug up from deep in the pits. Backbreaking work. Sometimes I wondered if I'd ever be able to stand up straight again. Then one day several of us were gathering up our burdens, when someone shouted at us to run. I wasn't very nimble. In spite of the fact that I'd lost weight, I wasn't as slender as I would become. Not then. So I was slow. Another lad and myself. The ceiling and walls caved in on us. We were pinned there. In the dark. The lanterns had gone out.

"I was fortunate. My head, shoulders, and one of my arms were free. I started to try to dig myself out. Then I heard the other boy. In the pitch black, I couldn't see him, I couldn't find him. I could only hear his cries, his whimpers, then his silence. His silence was the loudest of all. As impossible as it seemed, it had echoed around the cavernous pit, through my mind, straight into my soul. I knew he was dead. And I was alone again, certain that death was going to claim me as well. I could find no air to breathe."

She desperately wanted to wrap her arms around him. "But someone came and rescued you."

"Eventually. I don't know how long I was there. Hours, days, weeks. Perhaps only minutes. I knew only that the weight of the dirt and the coal and the beams would crush me, just as it had the other boy. I don't even know his name. I don't know why it didn't flatten me. I was digging frantically when I wasn't fighting off the rats who wanted a nibble."

"Did they send you back there, to the pits?"

"Oh, yes, the next day. We had quotas you see, and there were always more children to be found. It was a few weeks before I managed to escape and make my way to London. As frightening as it was to be on my own, it was better than being in the pits."

"I hate that you went through all of that."

"The cave-in was the start of it I think, my aversion to being confined. Sometimes I lose my sense of calm. Before you were here, when I came to the residence, the first thing I did was come to this room to strip off my clothes and prowl through it until I regained my composure."

Now he came to her room and stripped off his clothes. It was an improvement she supposed, but still she wanted to weep for the child he'd been, the one who thought death was coming for him, who had heard it snatch away another.

"You think you'll lose your calm if I hold you?"

"I know I will. I struck out before at someone who tried to hold me." He trailed a finger around her face. "I won't risk hurting you."

"You should have explained all this to me sooner so that I would have understood, could have helped you with it."

He scoffed. "Explained what? That I would be naked all the time if it were acceptable? Even my servants aren't allowed in here. It's my dark secret. I share it with no one. I certainly had never planned for you to find out." He angled his head, studied her. "Did I strike you?"

Gently, she touched her fingers to her cheek. "It's more that I got in the way, I think."

He slammed his eyes closed. "Ah, Eve." When he opened his eyes, she saw the remorse and regret mirrored there. "I've tried to be so damned careful not to lose control."

"It's not as though you did it on purpose. You were locked in the throes of a nightmare."

"Can you not see that I'm mad, that if I don't keep a tight rein on myself, I risk becoming a barbarian?"

"I can see that you're a man who's battling

demons. That's not the same thing. And you don't have to fight them alone. Let me help you."

He shook his head. "I can't."

She couldn't blame him for his hesitancy. He'd been alone for so long now. But there could be so much more between them. She was certain of it. Yet it would require patience. He'd told her far more than she'd ever expected him to, but she was left with the notion that he had failed to reveal everything. "Please, come to my bed and let me tend to you." Rising to her feet, she held out her hand and waited. She could see the indecision crossing his face as he warred with himself. Where would he seek his sanctuary? Here alone, or with her? She prayed he would choose her. Finally, he placed his hand in hers and came to his feet, sending the smallest spark of hope through her that more would eventually exist between them.

"Perhaps," he muttered, "we're both mad."

Rafe awoke, momentarily disoriented by the silken sheet beneath his back and the velvety canopy above his head. He was as bare as a newborn babe, his wound uncovered. The stitches pulled when he rolled onto his hip. And there she was, turned on her side, a hand resting beneath her cheek, her long lashes lying gently against her skin. Her knees were drawn up, her nightgown having gathered at her calves. Her toes curled and unfurled as though she were dreaming of skipping over green fields. He inhaled her fragrance with each breath, watched her rhythmic breathing.

She'd left a lamp burning just low enough that

he could see her clearly, and yet the shadows still formed a gossamer layer over her. He almost found himself envious of the shadows. He remembered how gentle her hands had been as she'd tended him, careful to touch him as little as possible. During that time as her hands had moved so tenderly over him, he'd experienced an unfamiliar sensation: of being loved. And the feelings he felt toward her had very nearly scared the bloody hell out of him. He'd wanted to ask her to never leave him. No, not ask. Plead. Beg.

She'd not been appalled by what she'd discovered in his sanctuary. She'd understood his aversion to clothing, had not thought him mad, had almost succeeded in convincing him that he had nothing of which to be ashamed. She was the most remarkable, kind, generous woman he'd ever known. And she was his.

Until he tired of her or she began to look elsewhere for protection. Not that anyone else could provide her with the security of which he was capable. As long as he was the one to call things off, she stood to acquire a great deal, would become an independent woman.

In the deepest recesses of his soul, the corners that he refused to acknowledge, he wished that the relationship between them was different, that she was here because she wished to be, not because of what she would gain. But then if not for the reality of their arrangement, she wouldn't be here at all.

Opening her eyes, she gave him a soft smile that was nearly his undoing. "Hello there. How are you feeling?"

"As though I've had far too much cheap whiskey."

"I doubt you know the taste of cheap whiskey."

"I didn't always have so much." Once he'd had nothing at all. "Why didn't you unlock the door when you found the key?"

She sighed, stretched like a cat that had just woken up in the sun. "Because it was something you wanted to hold secret, and I thought a mistress should respect your privacy."

A mistress. Always that was between them. That she was here not by choice.

"Your wound is red."

"I suspect it'll be angry for a few days. I'm barely aware of it."

"Only because you've suffered worse. I might have had a similar life if you hadn't taken me in."

He hadn't taken her in. He'd offered her sanctuary, but at an incredible cost. He hadn't considered it then, hadn't thought of anything beyond his own wants and needs. When had he become such a selfish bastard, thinking only about himself? He was not the sort of man into which his father would have shaped him had he remained alive, had he been able to assert his influence. Sebastian and Rafe were closer to the lords that they all should have been. Of course they were older, had their father in their lives for more years. Still, he could not help but believe that his father would be disappointed in him.

She rose up on an elbow. "I've been thinking."

"Thought you were sleeping."

"Before I drifted off to sleep. What if I didn't hold you, but just touched you? I dream about it all the time, you know? Stroking my hands over your shoulders and your back."

He slammed his eyes closed and growled, "Eve, don't."

"You must think about it as well. Just light touches, as though we were waltzing."

He swallowed hard, before he opened his eyes. "I'll hurt you."

"No, you won't. I trust you."

"You're a fool." Rolling from the bed, he was light-headed. He took a moment to regain his balance before walking to the window and gazing out. He should go to the bedchamber with the stripped bed, where he slept with no danger of getting tangled in sheets or blankets. He didn't cry out in there, but he was loath to leave her.

He heard the hushed padding of her bare feet, didn't look down when he sensed her presence beside him.

"Why are you so certain?" she asked softly.

He didn't want to travel this path. It was as ghastly as listening to a boy die in the mines. But she needed to understand, even if it put her at risk of leaving him. His darker secret, the one that ate at his soul.

"I'd not been long in London. I scavenged for food, sought shelter wherever I could find it, usually in an alleyway, beside rubbish, in a dark corner. One night, I woke up to find a man holding me down, tearing at my clothes . . . he told me to stop fighting, that it wouldn't be so bad if I'd stop struggling."

"Oh my dear God."

He couldn't look at her, as much as he wanted to, he couldn't. "I don't remember how I got away from him, but I did. Before he got my clothes off, before he did what he intended to do. I don't remember beating on him, but I did. I beat on him until I killed him, until he would never again touch another boy."

He felt her fingers, trembling, touch his hand, wrap around it, squeeze. "I'm glad," she rasped.

He jerked his head around then to look at her. Tears were in her eyes, tears that he'd wanted to shed that night, tears he'd wanted to shed when the boy had died in the tunnel with him, but he'd feared that if he gave them their freedom they'd never stop, that they would confirm that he was weak, that they would serve as further evidence that his brothers had been right to leave him behind.

"I'm glad," she repeated. "I'm glad you killed him. He was the worst sort, to hurt a child."

"You don't understand, not completely. All I saw was red. I don't remember doing what I did, but I know I did it because no one else was about. He was holding me, and I was suffocating again, and I did what I had to do in order to get him away from me."

"And you've been afraid of letting anyone hold you ever since?"

"Because I know what I'm capable of. If I lose control—"

"You won't with me."

"Eve—"

"You won't with me," she repeated with conviction. "You won't with me."

He should tell her the remainder of it, but she gave him hope, and it had been so terribly long since he'd embraced true hope. Perhaps with her it *would* be different. He felt something when he was with her, something he'd never felt with another, as though he'd found a part of himself that had been missing, as though all that he could be was possible.

Very, very slowly, she moved her hand toward his bare chest.

His mind shouted, *"No! No! No!"*

But his body was separate from it, holding still, waiting, waiting. She held his gaze, challenging him to trust her while at the same time issuing promises that she wouldn't hurt him. He wasn't afraid of pain. He'd suffered through enough to know that when it ended, he'd remain. What she didn't know was that she had the power to destroy him.

She meant something to him. He wasn't exactly sure what, but he knew she mattered. That's why he had been devastated that she'd seen his madman's cell. That's why he refused her touch. He could hurt her and when he did, she would leave. She was strong enough that she would survive without him. He didn't want to survive without her.

Terrifying thoughts that sent a shiver through him just before her hand came to rest above his pounding heart. He could feel the pad of each finger, the warmth of her palm. If he were a kinder man, a gentler man, he might have wept. He had yearned for so very long to be touched, stroked, held.

His baser instincts allowed him to bed her, but beyond that he dared not risk hurting her.

So slowly that he was barely aware of the movement, she glided her hand up his chest, over his shoulder, down his arm.

"Tell me if the pressure is unsettling," she whispered in a low voice, similar to the one he used when calming his horse.

Unsettling it should have been. He should have tossed her back by now. That's what had happened the first time he'd been with a woman. She had held him, and he had shoved her off. He hadn't hit her as he had the man in the alley, but he'd been trembling as though someone had thrown him into an icy river. She had told him he belonged in Bedlam. He'd been sixteen and he'd believed her. He'd not let a woman hold him since.

Eve's other hand came to rest on his chest and she took it on a similar journey as the first, along the other side. Wherever she touched, he felt as though he was being set ablaze, but not with fire. With passion. It felt so good, so good.

Touch all of me. All of me.

Her hands traveled back up his arms, over his shoulders, down his chest. "I don't think I'd ever get enough of this."

Leaning in, she pressed her mouth to the center of his chest. It was his undoing.

"Eve." The guttural sound was that of a man dying, and he was. He plowed his fingers through her hair, tilted up her face, and took her mouth as though he owned it, as though he were the only one who would ever experience the taste of her. It drove him mad to think of anyone else ever knowing her as he had.

Her hands traveled along his neck, up into his hair, over his scalp, and back down. Always open, always nonthreatening, never closing around him. Long smooth strokes. No holding, no squeezing, no restraining.

Liberating. How had he ever survived without this? How had he ever thought it was enough to touch her, and not let her stroke him?

Her hands glided over his back, over his buttocks. He growled low, as he began gathering up the hem of her nightdress. She broke off the kiss, unbuttoned the garment, shrugged out of it. It shimmered along her body and pooled on the floor. She stepped over it and came in close, pressing her body against his, her breasts flattened against his chest. He groaned, while she released a throaty sigh.

"Yes," she breathed. "I've wanted this so badly."

He circled his arms around her. It had never occurred to him that he was denying her pleasures, that she would *want* to touch him, caress him. He thought if she didn't know what was lacking in their coupling, she wouldn't miss it. He held her, just held her, while she held him.

Marveled at the wonder of it. So much skin against skin. Silk to satin. Velvety warmth. If not for the wound in his side, he would have picked her up and carried her to the bed. Instead, he took her hand and led her to it.

She lay on her back and he covered her.

Not like before, raised on his arms, allowing himself to touch her only for what was required for the act to reach completion. With a sultry smile, she tiptoed her fingers along his back and over his shoulders. Skin on skin, more than he'd ever experienced. It was intoxicating, addicting. With her, he experienced no sense of suffocating.

"Press harder," he commanded.

She did, and he felt the indentations along his skin where her fingers traveled. He arched his back, curled it forward. It wasn't enough. It wouldn't be enough until he was buried inside her, until her velvety heat was surrounding him. He'd probably rip his stitches, but he didn't care. He was lost in the sensations she created, lost in her. The blue of her eyes, the blond of her hair, her bodily fragrance mingled with rose perfume.

A wicked gleam came into her eyes and she lifted her head slightly, pressing her lips to his throat. Hot moisture dewed along his skin. "Ah, Evie."

She pushed on his shoulder, nudged him. "Off," she ordered.

He rose up. "Am I'm too heavy?"

"No." She smiled. "I want you on your back."

Then she was raining kisses over him as though he were covered in confection that she needed to gobble up. His hand became tangled in her hair. He was desperate for the connection, to be touching her as her tongue swirled along skin that had never known the caress of a woman. Had she required the connection as well? Had what they shared been less because he had denied her this?

Before now, he had never felt adored, wor-shipped . . . worthy. He had kept so much of himself frozen, behind stone walls, impenetrable. With each stroke of her tongue, each sweep of her hand, she was loosening the stones, she was warming the frigid center of his being.

And it hurt. God help him, it hurt to know that he had gone so long without this. That he had denied himself ultimate pleasure. Lower she went, lower and lower, her hair spread out over his chest like gossamer. So faint as to barely be there, but for a man who had not known another's caress in years, it might as well be a woolen blanket, he was so aware of it.

His senses were coming alive as they never had before. Pleasure began rippling through him. It didn't matter where she touched, it was everywhere.

Lower still, she went.

"Evie," he rasped.

She lifted her sweet face and gave him the softest of smiles, and yet in her eyes he saw the determination. He wouldn't deter her from her goal. "I've wondered what you taste like."

Then she bent her head and wrapped her velvet mouth around him, and he nearly wept from the pleasure of it. His hand tightened its hold on her hair while his other hand fisted in the sheets. He groaned low, a beast being set free.

All this time, he'd thought he was acquiring pleasure, but it was nothing like this. To be receiving so grand a gift. He'd always thought it was enough to simply give. But now he understood that the taking was also a form of giving. She may have been innocent in her ministrations, perhaps even unskilled, but having never known anything else, he was convinced that her enthusiasm was more than he would ever find elsewhere. She spoiled him with her endeavors. She brought him more acceptance than he'd ever known.

He wanted her more than it was wise to want, but he had ceased to care about wisdom. He was like a man addicted to games of chance. Life was filled with more disappointments than successes, more bad cards than good, but when fate smiled, nothing else mattered but that one moment of victory.

He felt vulnerable, exposed, but it heightened the adventure, the moments with her.

"Evie." He urged her up and onto her back. Kissing her, he thought he tasted himself on her tongue. He was humbled by how much she wanted to do for him, how much she desired him. Deepening the kiss, he wedged himself between her thighs, surprised to find her so moist, so ready.

Rising up, he plunged into her and then sank down until his chest flattened her breasts. Her arms came around to rest lightly on his back. He should have been sweating by now, trembling, feeling the familiar tightness in his chest, but all he felt was her. He began rocking against her. Her legs came up, pressed against his hips. He should have objected, but it felt so marvelous to be enclosed within the cocoon of her warmth.

He quickened his pace. Never before had the pleasure been so intense. Never before had it encompassed all of him. She was riding the crest with him, her cries echoing around him, her body spasming beneath his. He could feel her muscles undulating. Never before had he been so close to someone physically. He thought a shadow could not slip between them.

As she arched against him, her arms tightened around him, and the force of his release ripped through him. If he wasn't lying on the bed, it would have dropped him to his knees.

Resting on his elbows to keep from crushing her, he turned his head and pressed a kiss to the underside of her ear.

"I knew it could be like this," she whispered softly.

Her words stung his pride. "Did you not enjoy it before?" She'd certainly given the impression that she was quite pleased with his performance.

"It's always lovely. You make it so. But it's also lonely, as though we're each drawing pleasure in our own little worlds. This time it was as though we

shared the same world. I liked being able to touch
you, to feel your muscles bunching and straining
with your efforts. I liked thinking that perhaps you
found some joy in my touch."

"Joy? Evie, you damned near killed me."

He felt her jerk beneath him and lifted himself
back up so he could look into her eyes. "That's a
good thing. It's never—" Dear God, he couldn't believe he was actually talking about this. The next
thing he knew, he'd start wearing skirts. He combed
her hair behind her ear. "It's never been as fulfilling
for me. I found it lonely as well."

He wished he hadn't admitted that, but he seemed
unable to keep from telling her anything.

"Your wound?"

"The stitches held." Although how they had managed to do that under the circumstances, he hadn't
a clue. He rolled off her and onto his back—and
damned if he didn't miss the nearness of her.

She snuggled against his side and placed her
hand on his chest. "I won't hold you, but feel free to
hold me."

He brought his arm down and around her. He
held her there. Eventually, he heard her soft snoring
and stared at the canopy. There was a tightness in his
chest. He feared it was the stone wall around his heart
crumbling.

Without it, how the hell would he protect himself?

Chapter 19

The yacht sliced through the water, with Eve of all people at the helm. Some scrawny lad stood slightly behind her and guided her. Her smile was so bright as to be blinding. Her laughter was carried by the breeze, and sitting at the end of the boat, Rafe fought not to growl. He also fought to keep his stomach from heaving.

While they had missed the planned christening of the yacht, he had sent word to Tristan that the next time he took it out, Eve would like to join them. He had thought it would be weeks before he was forced to go sailing, but Tristan had promptly shown up at his club with a devilish smile. "Tomorrow. I'm not going to give you a chance to change your mind."

So here he was, impressed with the beautiful woodwork and craftsmanship. Tristan had taken them on a tour when they'd first arrived. Below deck, he had shown them a library, a sitting room, three bedchambers, and Rafe had known that one was for him, that Tristan had designed the yacht hoping that all three brothers would take a long sojourn together. The thing was large enough that a man would be comfortable sailing the world in it.

Tristan sat on the bench beside him, placed his elbows on the railing, and stretched out his legs. "If you harm Mouse, you will have to deal with me."

"Thought you introduced him as Martin." He didn't see any point in pretending he wasn't contemplating taking his fist to the lad.

Tristan shrugged. "While he served under me on my ship, he was Mouse. Hard habit to break. He's only become Martin as he's become interested in the fairer sex. He thinks it's a disadvantage to be named after a creature that makes women scream and leap onto furniture. Suppose he has a point there. But he's a good lad, which is why I don't want to see him hurt. He's enjoying Eve's company, but he won't pursue her, so you've no worries there."

"I'm not worried."

"Ah, you just glower for the hell of it then."

Rafe scowled. Tristan could irritate the devil out of him in short order.

"How's your stomach holding up?" Tristan asked. "You seemed a bit green when we started out."

"Nothing wrong with my stomach."

"I spent the first six weeks hanging over the side of the ship."

"Why didn't you get off?"

"Have you not studied your globes adequately? When you're on the water, land isn't always within easy reach. So you suffer in silence, and hope you survive until you see land again. Eventually you get used to the roiling, but when you're onshore, you find it odd not to have the constant movement beneath you."

"Do you miss being out on the sea?"

Tristan smiled at his wife, who was standing near Mary. "Not really. The choice was the sea or Anne, which meant there was really no choice at all. I like Evelyn."

Rafe scoffed. "As though I care what you like."

Looking over at him, Tristan grinned. "Come on, Rafe. You know you care. You wouldn't be here otherwise."

Before Rafe could come up with an appropriate comeback, Sebastian wandered over and leaned his hip against the railing. "Much nicer vessel than the one I took to the Crimea."

"Or back to England," Tristan added.

Rafe had given little thought to how his brother had traveled to war.

"I barely remember the journey back. Sick most of the time."

"You were recovering from your wounds," Tristan reminded him.

"I suppose." He looked at Rafe. "You have to admit it's rather fine out here. Better than London anyway."

"You don't like London?"

"Despise it. I'd remain at Pembrook if Mary didn't insist otherwise."

"Plus there's the little matter of the House of Lords," Tristan muttered. "Don't know why Uncle wanted that responsibility."

Sebastian sighed. "Hard to believe it's been fifteen years since he tried to do us in."

"Fifteen?"

Rafe was surprised to see Eve standing there, her expression one of absolute astonishment.

"Since you all became . . . lost?" she added.

"Since we first left Pembrook, yes," Sebastian confirmed. "Fifteen. Give or take a few months. It was winter."

She shifted her gaze over to Rafe. "You told me you were ten."

He shrugged. "I was."

"You're only twenty-five?"

"How old did you think I was?"

"A good deal older than that."

He felt older than that. Sometimes he felt as though he were a thousand, weighted down with years.

"It is difficult to believe how truly young we all are," Sebastian said.

"Age is measured by how the years are lived, not by the time in which they pass," Tristan mused.

"Ah, is my husband spouting philosophy again?" Lady Anne asked as she sat down beside him. His arm immediately went around her shoulder, bringing her in close.

"You like my philosophies."

She smiled softly. "Indeed I do. They are part of the reason that I love you."

Rafe felt as though his clothes were beginning to restrict his breathing, even though all he wore was a shirt and britches. Tristan had insisted they dispense with proper attire when on board. Maybe it was that the bench had suddenly become so crowded. Rafe shot off it, nearly lost his balance, regained it, and covered the short distance to stand by Eve.

Mary joined Sebastian, and he held her near.

Rafe suddenly felt self-conscious not placing his arm around Eve, but she wasn't his wife or the love of his life. He didn't want her to misinterpret her place. "You seemed to like steering the ship."

"Martin did most of the steering," she said, and he heard no laughter brimming in her voice, when only moments before she'd been overflowing with the joyous sound.

How could that scrap of lad bring her such joy with so little effort?

"Land-ho!" the boy yelled.

"Thought we'd picnic on an island," Tristan said, getting to his feet.

"Which island?" Eve asked. "I see several."

"As you're our guest, you get to pick."

Eve was smiling so brightly that Rafe wished the gift of the choice had come from him.

The blankets were spread out with each couple having their own upon which to sit, and wicker baskets filled to the brim with food and bottles of wine. The couples were all near enough to each other that they could carry on a conversation if they wanted, but it seemed most were wont to murmur among themselves.

At least the other two couples were murmuring. Evelyn and Rafe seemed to have fallen into an awkward silence. She enjoyed the company of the others, but being in their presence reminded her of what she wasn't: loved.

Married.

With the prospect of children.

She was grateful that they didn't shun her, make her feel less, but a small part of her wished she'd stayed on the yacht with Martin.

"You're quiet," Rafe said, his voice low, as though he had no more desire to disturb the other couples than she. He was stretched out on his side, wineglass in hand. "You were laughing earlier with that Martin fellow."

She smiled in remembrance. "He was sharing some of his adventures with me." Stammering while he did it until he came to realize how much she was enjoying the tales. Then he had begun to relax. A shy lad, but she suspected he'd win over many a heart. "I can't imagine seeing as much of the world as he's seen."

"Yet you're sad now. Is it because you must stay in London?"

It was because she was a mistress and not a wife, but now wasn't the time to get into a discussion on that matter. "I was surprised you're so young."

"That's the reason behind your melancholy?"

She wanted to reach out and press flat the furrows between his brows, but they'd not touched since they boarded the *Princess*. The lack of bonding signified a difference between the couples, and as much as she wished it didn't, it caused an ache in her chest.

Perhaps if she'd known what Geoffrey had planned for her, if she'd had some forewarning, she might have found another way. In the past few weeks she'd lost all her innocence, felt as though she'd aged beyond her years. At the time her decision had seemed the only way to go. She'd been frightened, disoriented, taken unawares by the path that Geoffrey had flung her on. Her father had done her no great service with his shielding of her. With Rafe, she'd become stronger, more confident.

Now, she knew not only what she wanted, but what she deserved.

"Life forced you to grow up very quickly. Early on, you learned what you wanted and what you didn't. You didn't let people take advantage of you. I can't say I've done the same."

For a moment there she thought he might have ceased to breathe. "You think I took advantage?"

Dear God help her, but she believed he had, that he was the sort of man who would. Was he really the sort of man worthy of her love? "I believe I'm going to take a walk."

"I don't wish to walk."

"That works out perfectly then, as I prefer to go alone." He didn't try to stop her, for which she was immensely grateful, as she pushed herself to her feet and walked to the edge of the beach where the water lapped at the shore. She had removed her shoes earlier so they wouldn't become filled with sand, and now she waded out until the water swirled about her ankles. She didn't care if her hem got wet. It would dry.

She understood Rafe, knew much of what had shaped him, what had caused him to build a wall around his heart. She was slowly chipping away at it, but even if she did find it, he was a lord and she was the illegitimate daughter of an earl. She was a fallen woman, a mistress.

"It's lovely out here, isn't it?" Lady Anne asked.

Evelyn turned and smiled at her. "It's peaceful."

"The breeze sounds different here; the water has

its own song. Tristan and I often picnic on various islands. He needs the sea."

"But he gave it up for you."

Lady Anne laughed lightly. "I was going to give up the land for him. In the end, I think we compromised. Neither of us feels as though we gave up anything at all."

"You've been very kind to me."

"It's not easy to love any of these Pembrook lords. They've all led harsh lives. They all became misguided as to what should be held dear. Keswick, as I understand it, thought that only Pembrook was significant. For Tristan, the sea was his mistress and she was the only thing of importance. I don't know Rafe well enough to know what he believes matters."

He believed that nothing mattered. Or at least it was important to him that nothing—no one—mattered.

It was nightfall by the time they returned to their residence.

Evelyn wasn't surprised that they immediately retired to her room, and that Rafe had discarded his jacket, waistcoat, and shirt within minutes. It had been a week since she'd discovered his aversion to clothing, a week during which time his side had begun to heal nicely.

She was a bit slower at loosening her buttons. She was more interested in studying the man she thought she was coming to know. She'd thought he was well past the age of thirty. Instead he was merely three years older than she.

She'd known he'd had a difficult life, but it had never occurred to her how hard he would have had to have worked to acquire everything he now possessed in such a short span of time.

"Would you rather be with him?" Rafe asked gruffly.

She was taken aback by the question. "With whom?"

"The lad. Martin. Mouse. Whatever the deuce his name is. Were you thinking of him when you went to the water's edge?"

"I was thinking of you," she admitted.

That brought him up short.

"I was thinking of us. We're very different from the other couples."

Leaning forward, he planted his elbows on his thighs, narrowed his eyes on some point on the far wall, the window maybe. "I never lied to you. I was always honest about what would exist between us."

"But we've shared so much, I began to convince myself that things might change. I saw potential for what might be. I dared to want what I never thought to hold."

He shifted his gaze over to her.

"I still dream of being a wife." *Of being your wife.* She wasn't certain when she'd begun to entertain that thought. She held his gaze for a moment, trying to read something there, to see if he was appalled by the notion or perhaps receptive to it, but his emotions were shuttered. The night he'd been wounded he'd lowered the wall, but during the nights that followed he'd put it carefully back into place. Although he continued to allow her to touch him, and he held her while she slept, still something was missing, the loneliness hadn't dissipated completely. He never told her that he loved her—or that he even liked her for that matter. She didn't know quite how to broach the subject. "Your brothers and their wives have been very kind to me, but it's only because they don't wish to create more distance between you. I'm still a scandalous woman. I doubt they'd welcome me into their home if you weren't about."

"They know a bit about scandal. They had their own."

"But it's forgiven when love is involved. Then it becomes romantic, the stuff of books, something to be sighed over by young girls who don't yet realize that not all scandal ends well."

"Yours will end well. You'll become a woman of independent means."

Eve stared at this man tugging off his boots. Her stomach tightened, she felt a small tremor cascade through her. "Do you care for me?"

He slowly set aside his second boot. "I give you jewelry, do I not? I took you on the blasted boat, didn't I?"

"But you didn't hold me." She slapped her hand over her mouth, fighting away the tears that stung the back of her eyes. "The entire day, distance existed between us. We might as well have been strangers. Martin paid me more attention than you did."

"Perhaps you think you'd be happier with him."

"Of course not. I know only that I'm not completely happy with you."

He shot to his feet. "What do you want of me, Eve? I've given you everything."

Her heart sank to the bottom of her soles. Slowly, she shook her head. "No, you've only given me what can be purchased."

Wearing naught but his trousers, he strode over to her. "Surely you didn't think there would be more between us. I explained that the first night. It is better without sentiment."

"Is it? Truly. You said it wasn't so lonely when I touched your skin. Do you not think it would be remarkable to have your heart touched?"

He began the task of undoing her buttons. "I have no heart to touch. I haven't for a good long while. And I'll not feel guilty about it."

He removed her dress and petticoats, discarding them on the floor. Her shoes, her stockings. Her limbs seemed to be moving of their own accord; she had no control over them. "So this is all that will ever be between us?"

He stilled, studied her, held her gaze. "Those were the terms of the arrangement between us."

"And if I don't like them anymore?"

"Then I shall have to work harder to convince you that the terms are to your liking."

His mouth came down on hers, hard and hungry. Tears pricked her eyes. She was vaguely aware of his carrying her down to the bed, his hands and mouth trailing over her. She felt like the porcelain dolls her father had given her, easily broken.

"Touch me, Eve," he rasped. "Touch me."

Only she couldn't, not when she had no hope of reaching his heart. She realized with astounding clarity that from the beginning she had hoped for more between them, had thought that perhaps he would fall in love with her. That she would acquire the happy ending that her mother had never known.

He rose up over her. She could feel his hardness

nudging, intimately, seeking entrance. "Respond to me, Eve."

For the first time in her life, nothing mattered. "What is the purpose in life if there is no hope for love?"

He cursed harshly, nuzzled her neck, kissed her breasts, taunted and teased her nipples. "There is purpose in this. Respond to me."

She stared at the canopy and imagined the roiling of the yacht as it glided through the water. It could carry her away from here. She would let it take her someplace far, far away. That first night, she had wondered if she would possess the wherewithal to distance her mind from her body. She was discovering that it was quite easy to accomplish when one's heart was little more than shattered remains.

With a feral growl, Rafe came off of her, off the bed, and glared at her. "You knew what the arrangement was. It's too late to have regrets."

"Unfortunately, I fear it's never too late."

"You're being unreasonable."

"I deserve more."

"You damned well won't find it out there," he said, pointing toward the window, before storming into his bedchamber, slamming the door in his wake.

She wrapped her arms tightly around herself, let the warm tears wash down her cheeks, but they couldn't wash away the ache in her heart.

Rafe pressed his back to the vibrating door. He'd not needed his key because it was no longer kept locked. He should have been familiar with the room by now but it still took him off guard. All his clothing was gone. Every torn shirt, waistcoat, jacket. Every pair of trousers. Every scrap of remaining neckcloth. Every discarded bit of attire that had once offended him, threatened to suffocate him. Gone.

Eve had gathered them up and taken them to the poor.

The bare mattress upon which he'd once slept when the thought of sheets or blankets would make him break out in a sweat was no longer visible. It was covered by violet velveteen. The recently hung draperies were drawn aside to let in the night. Not a speck of dust was to be seen. The wooden floor was polished to a fine sheen.

The room smelled of beeswax and polish. The room smelled of her.

She had done this. She had chased back the demons. She had returned to him the magic of touch. She had helped him conquer the madness.

He strode over to the window and gazed out, when everything inside him told him to return to her room, to apologize, to make her smile. More to make her laugh. That was what had upset him today, seeing that a lad had the ability to bring forth her laughter with such ease when he couldn't recall a single moment when he had managed to accomplish such a remarkable feat.

He braced his hands on either side of the windowsill.

"Do you care about me?" she'd asked.

With every breath I take.

For a heartbeat, he had been that small boy standing beside his father's coffin, the one who had watched his brothers ride away, the scruffy lad who had been terrified and alone in the dark.

She would leave him. If he gave her power over him, she would leave.

There wasn't enough goodness in him to make her stay, and she knew his secrets.

He wasn't supposed to care about her. She wasn't supposed to matter.

But she did.

Reaching into his trousers pocket, he rubbed the coin. She would tell him to flip it, but he didn't need to in order to know his own mind.

He'd never needed anyone or anything. Not since that night when their uncle had tried to kill them. He didn't *need* her, but it didn't stop him from wanting her.

He didn't know how long he stood there, rubbing the coin, recounting every moment he'd spent with her. He considered lying down on his bed, the one that now looked as though it belonged to a sane man, but he didn't want to sleep alone.

Turning from the window, he strode back toward the door.

She was his mistress. He made the rules. He would sleep with her when he damned well wanted to, and he wanted to at that moment. He wouldn't make love to her—

The thought staggered and stumbled through his mind. When had he begun to think of what happened between them as making love? When had it ceased to be merely bedding? When had it become more with her than it had ever been with any other woman?

He pressed his forehead to the door. All he could hear was the silence on the other side. Was she asleep by now? Had she wept? He hated the thought that he might have caused her to cry. She deserved so much better than him. He should walk away, leave, announce the terms met. The residence was already in her name. He'd seen to that before he'd left to retrieve the horse. In truth, she was within her right to toss him out on his ear.

She was a woman who wanted more than he could give her. He could purchase her anything she desired. The problem was what she truly yearned for could not be bought, and well he knew it. He also knew that he hadn't the means to give it to her.

He wanted to crawl into the bed, have her scoot over, and scrunch up against him. He wanted to feel her pressed against his side, her head nestled on his shoulder, her hand curled on his chest. Once more, just once more, then perhaps he would set her free.

So as not to disturb her, he quietly opened the door and stepped into her bedchamber. Immediately he felt her absence. It was as though all the life, breath, joy had been sucked from the room. He didn't have to look to know she wasn't in the bed. He didn't have to look to know she wasn't in the residence.

But still he stormed across to the armoire and nearly tore the door off its hinges as he opened it. All the gowns were there: the red, the violet, the yellow. Every dress, every wrap.

All except the hideous black dress and the matching black cloak in which she'd arrived.

"No."

It was a strangled sound, the cry of disbelief. He hurried over to her vanity, to the jewelry box. Every piece he'd given her was nestled on velvet, winking up at him mockingly. Only the two pieces that her father had given to her were missing.

He felt as though something inside of him was ripping and being torn asunder. She wouldn't leave him. He wouldn't allow it.

He tore out of the room and down the stairs. "Laurence! Laurence!"

Somewhere a clock was chiming—once, twice, thrice. It was the bloody middle of the night. Where could she go?

His hair untidy, his jacket askew, Laurence appeared in the entryway just as Rafe reached it.

"Did Eve have a carriage brought round?"

"Miss Chambers, sir? No."

Then she was on foot. Where was she going?

He rushed out the door and down the steps. He couldn't see her on the drive. He couldn't see her in the shadows of the night. He almost screamed her name, but his pride wouldn't allow him to do it, to let all of London know that once again, he'd been left behind.

Chapter 20

Rafe was standing at the window of his apartments at the club, watching the people coming and going, trying not to remember how much they had fascinated Eve. To not think of her was proving a fruitless endeavor. Everything reminded him of her.

When he walked through his residence, he inhaled her fragrance. He could no longer tolerate being there, not even for a moment. Every room held a memory of her.

It was equally as difficult being here, at his club.

When he boxed with Mick, he thought of Evie enduring his lessons in the ring.

When he looked out over the gaming floor, he saw it through her eyes.

When he went to his office, he regretted that he'd not shown her the globe that Tristan had carved for him, that he'd not told her that he was afraid to be grateful for it. If he truly cared for something, it would be stripped away. The best recourse was not to care.

Then he was immune to hurt.

So why was he now in so much blasted pain?

Because he adored her, dammit. That was the reason he was in such agony now, why he wasn't seeing after his club, why he didn't care how much money was being raked in, why he didn't care that some men owed him more than they'd be able to repay in ten lifetimes.

She'd had no one, nowhere to go. Yet she had managed to disappear like smoke caught on a wayward breeze. If he didn't know better, he'd consider that she might be a figment of his demented imagination.

He should leave her be, stop worrying about her. She had made her decision. She had left.

But she had done so without knowing how he truly felt. She had departed believing that he didn't care.

What a jackass he was.

Would it have killed him to tell her that she mattered?

He removed the coin from his pocket, studied it, remembered how warm it had been when his father had placed it on his palm. He didn't believe in fate, luck, or good fortune. He believed that a man created all three, sometimes from nothing.

He turned the coin over, once, twice, thrice. He wouldn't play her silly game. But he would flip it. Heads he would let her go. Tails he would search for her.

Tossing it up, he watched as it reached its apex, turning end over end, before beginning its descent. He was halfway to the door when it clattered on the floor. He realized with everything deep inside him that it didn't matter how the coin had landed.

He would search for her until he found her or drew his last breath.

He hurried down the stairs and toward the back door. He wasn't quite certain where he would start. The rookeries he supposed. She certainly would not have returned to Wortham, and if she'd had any-place else to seek sanctuary, she'd have not stayed with him that first night.

He'd told her where to sell her jewelry. He'd shown her where to seek shelter. Yes, the rookeries. That was where she would go.

Stepping outside, he locked the door behind him and headed down the mews. He'd sent his carriage home, because he'd had no plans to return there. It was a miserable place without her. The small things about her brought him such delight. No one had ever fascinated him as she did.

He turned into an alleyway, intending to make his way to the nearest street to hire a hackney, but six hulking men closed in around him. He had nei-ther the time nor the patience for this nonsense. "If you know what's good for you, gents, you'll back off and let me be on my way."

"And if ye know what's good for ye, ye'll sign me club back over to me."

Rafe watched as the group parted and Dimmick stepped through, and while the light was dim, it was clear that he was as ugly as ever. "Ah, Dimmick, I'd heard that you were dead."

"Best way to lay low for a bit. Found a bloke around my size, bashed in his face, dressed him in my clothes, and let the fish nibble at him for a bit. Then paid a fine fellow to say, 'By God, that's Dim-mick.' Bobbies don't look too hard at our sorts. But now I've risen from the dead and I want me club back. And yer fancy residence. That'll cover the interest."

Rafe's stomach tightened with the thought of Dimmick walking into the residence that belonged to Eve. Lord help the servants if Dimmick recognized any of them. Some had owed him money, and Rafe was to have dispensed with them. Instead, he'd given them new names and a place to live where they were unlikely to cross paths with the man who wished them harm. "Afraid I like both a bit too much to part with either easily. And as I am familiar with how you operate, you should know that upon my death, the club goes to Mick. All nice and legal. My solicitor has my will and the deed to the property, all properly signed."

"Sorry to hear that. All right, fellas, you know what to do."

They rushed in, fists flailing. Rafe fought them off as long as he could. At least one, maybe two, went down, but they were a skilled lot, and he soon found himself trussed up and laying on the ground.

Dimmick crouched low. "You'll give me what I want, one way or another."

As Rafe was hefted to his feet, he thought, *No, I won't. Not if it means there is any chance in hell that you'll ever learn about Eve.*

He found himself in an empty room in a large building. A warehouse perhaps. Every movement—shuffling of feet, grunts, breathing, scurrying rats—echoed. Rafe was tied to a chair, the rope wound tightly around his upper torso, arms, and legs. His hands were free, resting on a low table. On it were a pen, an inkwell, and a sheaf of paper.

"Now," Dimmick began, "you're going to write a new will, leaving your establishment to me. In exchange for which, I'll give you a quick death. You're well aware that I can give you a slow painful one."

Rafe glanced around, taking in his situation. Half a dozen men surrounded him. One was holding a large hammer. He knew what that was for. If he could break free of his bonds, he could probably get to two of them, but all six was going to be a trick. He almost laughed. When had he become an optimist to think anything good was going to come of this? Optimism was Eve's domain. He regretted immensely that he'd never see her again. Just once more. To gaze into her eyes, to see her smile, to tell her . . . Sweet Christ, it was an unfortunate time to realize that he loved her.

And had for some time. For much of his life he had worked hard to ensure that nothing mattered. She mattered. She was all that mattered.

When she left he had lost a part of himself, perhaps the last bit of himself that was of any worth.

He lifted his right hand, wiggled his fingers, as much as he was able with the ropes digging into him. Dimmick moved the pen closer. Rafe picked it up, dipped it in the inkwell, and set the tip on the paper, watching as the ink slowly spread over the parchment. Looking up, he winked at Dimmick. "Don't think I will."

"Right. Charlie, smash his left hand."

"But you always have me smash their important hand, their writing hand."

"Use your head. He needs it to write."

"Oh, I see. All right then."

Two other men moved in. One wrapped his arm around Rafe's neck and forced his chin up, while the other held his left wrist so his hand was splayed on the table. Rafe remembered the first time that Dimmick had told him to break someone's hand.

"Break his hand or I'll break your arm."

Rafe had broken the man's hand. He'd never forget the sound of cracking bone and the man's painful wail. His hand had never healed properly, which made him one of the most ineffectual valets in all of London.

Rafe kept his gaze on Dimmick. If he managed to get out of this, he was going to see Dimmick hanged. Nice and legal. He wouldn't be coming back from a hanging.

Out of the corner of his eye, he saw the hammer going up. He braced—

The immeasurable pain shot through him. He wanted to be stoic, but he couldn't hold back the guttural cry. Both men released him. Breathing heavily, he glared at Dimmick, who was smiling with satisfaction.

"Now, write the will or I'll have him hit your hand again until the bone is naught but tiny bits."

"Gonna be . . . a bit difficult. I'm left-handed, you see."

He heard Dimmick's roar, saw the hammer was now in his meaty hand, swinging down—

The pain carried him into the depths of darkness.

Evelyn thought that she should be hungry, especially as the dinner set before her was one of the finest she'd ever seen, but everything tasted of nothing. She ate tiny bites because it made things more palatable.

"Is it not to your liking?" Mary asked. "I can have Cook prepare something else."

Evelyn smiled at her. "I have no appetite. That's all. You've been so kind." They'd taken her in the night she'd walked out on Rafe. She hadn't known where else to go, but she'd learned early on that the duchess was an extremely compassionate sort. She'd held Evelyn while she wept and blubbered. She'd passed no judgments on Rafe except to say that Evelyn had been right to leave him.

But if that were the case, why did she hurt so badly? Why did she sit in her bedchamber and stare out the window at the residence across the way, hoping for a glimpse of Rafe? Was he well? Did he miss her at all?

Sometimes she considered returning to him, but she wanted so much more than he could give her. She yearned for the essentials that couldn't be purchased: love, family, happiness.

She'd moped about long enough. It was time to move on.

"I can't continue to take advantage. I thought tomorrow to start searching for employment." How long had she been here now? Even the passing of days, nights held no meaning.

"We'll help you find something. What are your skills?"

Before she could begin to list her limited talents, the door to the dining room burst open as though by a tempest and Tristan Easton strode in and, without preamble, announced, "I suspect Rafe might be in trouble."

The duke was on his feet so fast, with such force, that the table shook. "Why do you think that?"

"He hasn't been to his club or his residence in three days. No one knows of his whereabouts."

A sense of dread and foreboding tore through Eve. "It's not like him, to stay away from his club."

"Have you a notion as to where he might be?"

She shook her head. "His club is the only thing about which he cares."

"I very much doubt that," the duke said, and the look in his gaze told her that he thought she was important to Rafe. She wasn't going to argue the point. "Do you think he might have gone to Pembrook?"

"It seems unlikely to me," she told him, "but then I don't believe that I truly knew him very well."

"I went there," Tristan said. "When Anne and I had our parting of ways. It helped me to overcome the past but I'm not sure Rafe's demons reside in Pembrook."

"If they live anywhere at all, they live in the workhouse or in St. Giles," Evelyn said. "Laurence might know. He tried to kill him once."

"His butler tried to kill him?" the duke asked. "What the devil was he thinking to hire the man to run his household?"

"Doesn't matter," Lord Tristan said. "I'll have another chat with him."

Evelyn came to her feet. "I'm going with you."

As she walked with Tristan and the duke—who had insisted upon coming as well—to the house next door, she knew that Rafe wouldn't fancy his brothers learning the truth about the life he'd led while they'd been away. But if he was in trouble they might be in a position to help him, and that was all that mattered now. Finding him, ensuring he was safe.

She didn't know why she cared so much. Yes, she did. It was that little irritating fact that she loved him, in spite of his gruffness, his walls, and his distance. He was a better man than he gave himself credit for. She'd caught glimpses of that man.

She didn't bother to knock when they arrived, but simply walked in as though the residence was hers. Laurence emerged from a doorway, stumbled to a stop, and smiled. "Miss Chambers, you've returned. The master will be relieved. I'll send word round to the club."

"He's not there," Tristan said. "He left his club three nights ago. When I was here earlier, you told me you hadn't seen him in three days."

"Yes, that's correct. He's not been here, but then for him that's not unusual. Before Miss Chambers arrived here, he might go a month or two without popping by."

"So if he isn't at his club or here," the duke began, "where might he be?"

Laurence shook his head. "There is nowhere else. Except for St. Giles. But he wouldn't stay there for any length of time. He quite abhors the place."

"Where should we begin looking?"

Laurence hesitated, no doubt from long association with a man who harbored secrets.

Evelyn gave him an encouraging smile. "Laurence, you should answer the duke. He and Lord Tristan are Mr. Easton's brothers."

"Ah, yes, I can see the similarities."

"Tell him what you know."

"He could be anywhere in St. Giles. I'll send the servants out to see what they can uncover."

"No need," the duke said. "We're off for there now."

"With all due respect, Your Grace, are you familiar with St. Giles?"

"I've been through there, yes."

"We all have lived there. If something is amiss, we can ferret it out."

"All of you are from St. Giles?" Evelyn asked, not surprised to discover that Rafe had taken them in.

"Indeed, miss. If I might so bold, I suggest that you also have a word with Mick at the club. He remains a bit closer to the unsavory element than I."

"Thank you, Laurence, for your advice," Evelyn said. "We'll heed it."

"Let's head to his club," the duke said, turning to the door.

Evelyn spun on her heel to follow him.

"Miss?"

She turned back to Laurence.

"He spent a good deal of his life surviving those streets. One doesn't do that without making some enemies, but he's not one to go down easily."

"You agree with Lord Tristan, you think he's in trouble?"

"If he's not at the club, then I fear it is the case. But we'll find him, one way or another."

She didn't want to consider that "another" meant finding him dead.

"Disappeared?"

Standing in the balcony with the duke and Lord Tristan, Evelyn watched as the manager of the Rakehell Club, Mick, crossed his arms over his chest and glared at them as though they were responsible for the disappearance.

Tristan explained what Laurence had told him. Mick swore harshly beneath his breath. " 'Tis true that he never is long from this place. But of late he's been spending more time away, so I thought nothing of it. You should make inquiries of Lord Wortham."

"What might my brother have to do with any of this?" Evelyn asked.

"He stabbed him one night, right in the gaming area, in front of everyone."

She stared at him. "What? No. Rafe told me—" She slammed her eyes closed, remembering the exact conversation.

"Say it wasn't him."

"It wasn't him."

She blurted a very unladylike invective, and opened her eyes to find the men staring at her as though they thought women were incapable of uttering obscenities. "He never referred to the man who stabbed him by name. Only referred to him as an idiot. I should have known. He has a very low opinion of Geoffrey."

"One well deserved," Mick said. "Although for the life of me I never understood where Wortham got the guts to do what he did. A more cowardly man I'd never met."

"Maybe someone else is responsible for his sudden backbone," Keswick said. "I'm of a mind to have a word and find out."

As Evelyn followed Manson down the hallway, with Tristan and the duke behind her, she was amazed by how differently she viewed the residence. She had once considered it *home* but now she realized that it was her father who had made it home, not the walls or the portraits, the furniture or the decorative pieces—although there seemed to be far fewer of those. She wondered how many items Geoffrey had sold in order to relieve his debts.

When they walked into the library, Geoffrey shot out of his chair and hurried around his desk. "Your Grace, Lord Tristan, this is an expected surprise."

She couldn't fail to notice how he had ignored her.

"You know Miss Chambers, do you not?" the duke asked.

Geoffrey's face turned a mottled red. "Yes, of course."

"You would be remiss in not greeting her as well."

He gave her a perfunctory nod. "Miss Chambers."

"My lord. May I say that you're not looking well?" He had lost weight, much as she had after the death of her father. His skin had an unhealthy pallor to it. Dark half-moons had taken up residence beneath his eyes.

"Your Grace, how might I be of service?" he asked, once again giving her a cut direct.

"It has recently come to my attention that you attacked Lord Rafe with a knife."

If at all possible, Geoffrey looked even more ill. Sweat suddenly beaded his forehead. "He provoked me."

"In such a way that killing him would have been acceptable?"

"It was—" He turned away, his hand shaking as he plowed it through his blond hair.

"It was?" Lord Tristan prodded.

"An unfortunate misunderstanding."

"Where is he?" the duke demanded to know.

Geoffrey spun around, his expression one of incredulity. "I haven't a clue. Dimmick doesn't confide in me."

Evelyn felt a jolt of unease and took a step forward. "What do you know of Dimmick?"

"Who is he?" the duke asked her.

"He owned the club before Rafe," she told him. "He's supposed to be dead."

"If he was, he rose from the grave," Geoffrey said, his manner superior as though he relished the thought of knowing something she didn't.

"What's your association with him?" Lord Tristan asked, menace reverberating through his voice.

Geoffrey stepped back as though he were in danger. "I . . . I borrowed some money from him."

"How much?"

"Too much. He threatened to kill me. You must understand . . . that's why . . ."

"Why what, Geoffrey?" she asked, marching forward until she stood toe to toe with him. "Does he have anything to do with you hurting Rafe?"

"I was supposed to kill him. Then my debt would have been forgiven."

"You were going to kill him because of money owed?"

"It was either him or me. This Dimmick fellow is a nasty bit of business."

"You bastard!" Without thought or planning, the anger roaring through her, she bundled her hand into a fist the way Rafe had taught her, brought it back, and plowed it into Geoffrey's face. He landed like a felled tree, blood spurting from his nose.

Lord Tristan knelt beside Geoffrey. "Looks like you broke it, sweetheart."

"What do we do now? How do we find Rafe?"

"We'll take him with us back to the Rakehell Club. He might be able to give us some clue that Mick will understand."

"**I** don't know where to find Dimmick, I don't know how to get word to him. He just shows up out of the fog," Geoffrey whined, sounding as though he were holding his nose. It was red and angry looking, and Evelyn could see his eyes were bruising. She thought she should have felt remorse. Instead she wanted to hit him again.

They were back at the club, in Rafe's office. Geoffrey sat in a chair while Mick and Rafe's two brothers glared at him.

"I'd heard rumors that Dimmick hadn't died," Mick said. "Didn't want to believe they were true. He holds a grudge. Makes sense that he might be responsible for Rafe's disappearance."

"How are we going to find him?" Evelyn asked.

"Not to worry. Got the best ferreters in the world at my fingertips. This way, Miss Chambers, gentlemen."

Leaving Geoffrey where he was, with a huge hulk of a man watching him from the doorway, Mick led them out of the office to the balcony where they'd been earlier. Reaching up, he jangled a bell. All activity below ceased. Everyone glanced up. "Gentlemen, I must ask you all to leave. We have a bit of cleaning up to do here. When we reopen you'll find your accounts wiped clean of debt. But you must leave now, as quickly as possible."

A bit of grumbling echoed over the floor, but soon the only ones standing about were those who worked for the club.

"All right, listen up," Mick said. "Seems Mr. Easton has gone missing. Spread out through St. Giles, see what you can uncover. Let me know as soon as you hear any whisperings, especially if they involve a bloke named Dimmick. Many of you know him, some of you don't. Be grateful you don't. Let it be known that there is a five hundred pound reward to the man or woman who can tell us exactly where Mr. Easton might be found. Off with you now."

Everyone began to scatter.

Mick turned back to them. "That should do it. I suspect we'll have something before the night is done."

"They're all from St. Giles," Evelyn said.

"Every last one of us. He always takes the hungriest, the filthiest, the worst off of the lot—gives us something better. Not a soul out there wouldn't die for him."

"You've known my brother for a long time," the duke said, not really questioning, but affirming.

"Ever since I was a scrap of a lad, fighting to make my way about the streets. He had no patience for me, was constantly telling me to bugger off, to leave him be. But he was always there with a ready fist when the bullies began picking on me, taught me how to raise my own fists and deliver a good solid blow. When my belly was aching, he'd toss me something to eat, even if it was all he had. He has a heart surrounded by stone, your brother. But inside that stone is a far better man than even he knows he is. I'll go down fighting for him, and if it is Dimmick who is responsible for you not being able to find him—God help your brother, then God help Dimmick once I get my hands on him."

"You'll have to stand in line," the duke and Lord Tristan said at the same time.

They'd left him bound tightly in ropes. Without food, without water, without solace. He didn't know for how long. Days, weeks. Time had no meaning. The only thing he was aware of was the constant agony in his hand.

They came for him, took him back to the almost empty room, placed him in the chair at the table, secured him to it. Only this time, Dimmick was sitting as well, scrawling on the paper.

"When I'm finished here, ye'll just sign it as best ye can," Dimmick said. "Then yer hell will be over."

Rafe doubted it. He'd not gone mad with the binding. He simply pretended that they were Eve's arms, wrapped around him, holding him close, as she whispered words of encouragement. *All would be well, everything would turn out fine.*

Lies. A man could survive on lies. So could a boy.

"Did you already forget that I write with my left hand?"

"I don't forget nothing. I don't forget how ye blackmailed me." He lifted his gaze and stared pointedly at Rafe, with one eye closed and the other hard and accusing. "I don't forget how you turned my own lads against me. Even those who owed me coin stopped fearing me, thought you'd watch over them."

Rafe wouldn't go so far as to say that he watched over anyone. He had no stomach for bullies, and Dimmick had been one of the worst. That Rafe worked to undermine the ruffian brought him a great deal of satisfaction. That was why he offered better things to those upon whom Dimmick depended. Not for what they received, but for what it brought him.

Everything was always about him. His world centered around him.

Until Eve. Then the center had shifted, and nearly toppled him.

Dimmick returned to his scribbling. "I, Rafe Easton, bein' of sound mind and body, do hereby . . . how do you spell bequeathed?"

Dimmick looked at him again. Rafe simply looked back.

Dimmick sighed heavily. "You are a stubborn one. Charlie, the hammer."

"B," Rafe began, "e-q-e-t-h-e-d."

"Thank you kindly."

Rafe hoped that Mick or a solicitor would recognize with the misspelled word that Rafe had not in fact written the will. It might not make any difference, but perhaps—

"Bequeath to Angus Dimmick the Rakehell Club—"

Rafe was vaguely aware of a commotion, the sound of a door crashing open, the rush of feet. The air suddenly filled with shouts and yells. Dimmick was scrambling out of his chair, a blurred figure rushed by and grabbed him by the throat.

"You dare to harm my brother?"

Sebastian? What the bloody hell was he doing here? Had the pain caused Rafe to hallucinate? Was all this a dream?

Rafe watched as he took Dimmick to the floor and began pounding him as Rafe had longed to do ever since he'd found himself bound.

"Oh, my God. Help me get the bindings off him. Quickly. Quickly."

Eve was suddenly kneeling beside him, touching his face. "My love, we'll have them off in no time."

"Eve," he rasped.

"I'm here now."

Mick and Laurence were cutting the binding, he felt it loosening, felt as though he could finally breathe again. When his good hand was free, he cradled her face. "I want to make you laugh, Evie."

"I'm not quite certain you understand the concept. This isn't the way to go about it. Oh, my Lord, your hand. It's so terribly swollen and bruised. We must get you to a doctor."

"Later. First, you must know that I love you, Evie. I want to marry you. I want to give you children and the family you so yearn for."

"You're in pain, Rafe. Your poor hand. You don't know what you're saying."

"I know exactly what I'm saying. I wanted to tell you before. But I couldn't find you."

Tears welled in her eyes. Because her answer would be no or yes?

"Sebastian, stop now," Tristan ordered, and Rafe glanced over to see him trying to move an unconscious Dimmick out of the path of his brother's flailing fists. "You're going to kill him."

"Do you think I bloody care? Did you see what he did to Rafe?"

"He's alive. That's all that matters."

Sebastian slumped down onto the floor. "It's not all that matters. I'm supposed to watch out for him, for you and Rafe. I didn't do it fifteen years ago. By God, I should be able to do it now."

Rafe wanted nothing more than to take Evie into his arms, kiss her soundly, and then lead her someplace where they could be alone. But he'd been doing a lot of thinking the past few days, as he had nothing else to do except think. He stood on unsteady legs and walked over to where his brothers were hunkered near Dimmick.

Sebastian looked up at him. "I'm sorry, Rafe."

"I don't need you to watch out for me."

"Rafe—"

"Hear me out. I don't need you to watch out for me because I'm completely capable of watching out for myself. Even if he'd killed me, it would have been on my terms. You had no choice except to leave me all those years ago. I've always known that. Didn't make it more palatable but there it was. Because you weren't there to coddle me, I made something of myself—something I'm not always proud of—"

"You might want to rethink that," Tristan said. "The being proud of what you are. How do you think we found you?"

Rafe hadn't had time to give any thought to how they'd known he'd been taken, by whom, and to where. His brothers didn't know the dark side of London, not as he did.

Tristan jerked his chin to the area behind Rafe. "You've got quite the loyal following."

Rafe turned then, stunned by the sight that greeted him. His servants, his staff at the Rakehell Club—they were all there, down to every man and woman. And Evie, standing apart from them, and yet part of them. But more, so much more.

She smiled softly. "I knew they would help us to find you."

He'd never felt so overwhelmed. Never felt as though something inside of him was crumbling. He'd not cried since the night he was left at the workhouse, but something thick and hot was clogging his throat.

Tristan slapped him on the back. "Seems you're not as alone as you always thought."

"God, Rafe, your hand," Sebastian said.

"It'll heal. You and Tristan have had worse." And for the first time in his life, he recognized that perhaps they had.

Mick and Laurence wandered over.

"What do we do with the maggot?" Mick asked.

"Haul him down to Scotland Yard, hand him off to an Inspector Swindler. Tell him I'll be down with some information in a day or so." Rafe knew James Swindler because he, too, had grown up on the streets. He knew he could trust him with the journal he'd written that described Dimmick's activities.

"Right. And his lads? Same as always?"

Rafe looked around at Dimmick's pitiful followers. He knew what it was to fall in with the wrong sort. He nodded. "Give them their choice: service work or the club."

As Mick and Laurence took over, issuing orders, having Dimmick carted out, Rafe turned his attention to Eve. She was still standing there, studying him.

Sebastian cleared his throat. "Tristan and I will be waiting outside for you."

Just as he'd once been waiting for them. Two long years of wondering if they were dead. During the ten that had come before, it had never crossed his mind that he wouldn't see them again. But the last two of waiting for them had been the longest of his life.

Finally, it was only he and Eve. "I meant what I said," he told her. "I want to marry you." He took a step toward her. "I know I don't deserve you, and that I can never be the kind of man who does deserve—"

"I need to hold you," she cut in.

He felt as though his chest might cave. "Dear God, Evie, I need you to hold me. But more than that, sweetheart, I *need* to hold you. Desperately."

In the next breath, her arms were locked tightly around his neck and she was sobbing against his chest. It nearly broke his heart. When had he acquired one?

He folded his arms around her. "Oh, Evie, sweetheart, don't cry."

"I was so afraid you might be dead."

"I'm too much of a bastard to die young, so if you do marry me it'll be for a good long while."

She leaned back slightly. "You do know that you're only giving me the illusion of choice. How can I not marry you when I love you so much?"

He felt as though she'd picked up the hammer

and slammed it into his chest. No woman had ever loved him. "Say it again."

"I love you, and yes I'll marry you."

He covered her mouth with his. Soon, he thought. Very, very soon. Before she had a chance to change her mind.

Chapter 21

The boxing room was more shadows than light but then it usually was. Most of the light focused on the ring where Lord Ekroth stood, as he kept glancing around at the other men surrounding the roped-off area.

Rafe had called the meeting, invited Ekroth into the ring. It had appeared he was going to decline the invitation until Mick ushered him in with a gentle prodding and the lifting of the rope. Splints kept Rafe's left hand immobile and it was far from being completely healed, but he could pack quite the wallop with his right.

He wondered if Ekroth recognized the significance of the group of men who were in attendance. If any of them realized why they had been singled out for this particular lesson.

"Don't keep us in suspense, Easton. What's the meaning of all this?" Ekroth asked.

"Lord Rafe."

"Pardon?"

"Not Easton, but Lord Rafe Easton. That's how I should be addressed."

"I didn't think you much cared for your noble heritage."

"I've had a change of . . . heart. So in the future, you will address me with the respect that my father passed down to me."

"Simple enough. Consider it done."

"Splendid. Now on to more important matters. Do you know what you all have in common?"

Each one looked at the others. Some squirmed. Some shook their heads. Some averted their gazes.

"You were all at Wortham's the night that he decided to send the earl's daughter to her ruin."

"You were there as well," Ekroth said accusingly.

"Indeed I was, and so I'm well aware of what you'd planned for the woman who is to become my wife. And it doesn't sit well with me. Doesn't sit well with me at all. So, gentlemen, tonight I give you a choice: you can see your debts to me come due and your status within Society ruined, or you can let it be known—without going into specifics—that you know Wortham to be unsuitable for any man's daughter, sister, or cousin. You will ensure that he is reviled, considered the scum of the earth, and shunned by all who are proper. Do that, gentlemen, and with the exception of Ekroth, all your debts to me will be wiped clean."

"What of me?" Ekroth demanded.

"Of you I require a bit more. You wanted to put your hands on her, humiliate her, ruin her with your vile touch, while promising nothing in return."

"I promised five hundred quid."

"Her worth cannot be measured."

Ekroth jerked up his chin. "So what do you plan, *my lord*, in order for us to be even?"

"I plan to beat you bloody."

Geoffrey Litton, Earl of Wortham, strode into his library, frustration gnawing at his heels. Today should have been the day when everything was once again set right. Angus Dimmick had been publicly hanged that afternoon for committing several murders. The man was a frightening piece of work, and Geoffrey was grateful to be no longer in his debt. He'd witnessed the hanging, then gone to a tavern to celebrate with a few tankards. When the tavern closed he had headed home. What he truly wanted was a game of cards, but every club he visited barred his entrance, informed him that he was not welcome. He had expected it of the Rakehell Club, but the others made little sense. He'd yet to run up a debt elsewhere.

Something was amiss.

Tomorrow when his vision wasn't quite so blurred and his head wasn't swimming, he'd go round to the clubs again and talk to the owners about his membership.

The room was mostly shadows. One lone lamp burning low on the desk guided him to his liquor cabinet, where he poured himself a hearty helping of Scotch. He lifted the glass and inhaled the heady aroma. He tossed back a long swallow, turned on his heel, staggered back, and to his everlasting mortification, squealed like a piglet that had just had its tail pulled.

Rafe Easton sat sprawled in a chair near the cold fireplace.

"What are you doing here?" Geoffrey asked, despising the high pitch of his voice, though he seemed unable to lower it.

"Come to settle our debts."

"It wasn't my fault," Geoffrey said. "That Dimmick fellow. He said he would erase my debts if I knifed you. I would become a permanent member of the club when he regained possession of it. He's to blame. Now he's dead. You have nothing to fear from me."

"I never had anything to fear from you. And I don't give a damn about the knifing. What I do care about is the atrocious manner in which you treated your father's daughter."

"But you're marrying her. I saw the announcement in the *Times*. So she's come out of the situation smelling like roses."

Easton slowly rose from the chair. Ominously. "But what if I hadn't been there that night? What then? You were going to give the lords freedom to rape her."

"No." He backed up, hit the table, glass decanters tinkled. "No, no. Only examine her, touch her. Not actually fu—" He remembered the last time he'd used that word in relation to Evelyn. "—bed her. She would have lost her value if she were no longer a virgin. It's all moot now."

"Hardly. You're going to see after her welfare as you promised your father you would." He tossed some papers onto the desk. "You're going to sign those."

Geoffrey tried to see them without getting too close to Easton. "What are they?"

"Transfer of all property that is not entailed, including this residence, to your beloved sister."

"What? No. Never." The man had gone mad.

"Consider it a wedding gift to Eve. Sign the papers and I'll not beat you to within an inch of your life."

"You dare to threaten me?"

"Not only do I dare it, I enjoy it. You lost your membership to my club, and you've no doubt discovered that no other club will have you."

Red flashed before Geoffrey's eyes. "You arranged that?"

"Oh, I've arranged a good deal more than that. There is not a lord in all of England who will give you leave to marry his daughter. You will die without issue, and your cousin Francis will inherit the title and estates when you are dead. Until that time, for the aristocracy, you no longer exist. You will be invited to no balls, no dinners, no parties. You will have no choice except to live out your life on your ancestral estate, alone, with nothing to sustain you except regret for the unkindness you showed Eve and the knowledge that I am always watching. You won't see me, but rest assured that I shall be aware of every breath you take."

"You'll not get away with this."

Easton gave him a devilish grin. "I already have. Sign the papers."

Geoffrey crept toward the desk. "At least allow me back into your club. I shall go mad with no cards to entertain me."

"Try managing your estates."

"But the cards, you see, they are my passion."

"A misguided passion. They led you toward the path to ruin, but it was your choice to step on the road the night you offered up Eve to anyone who wanted her."

"You must give me something for signing these papers."

"I'm giving you your life."

But what a miserable life it would be. "I'd rather you'd kill me."

"That can be arranged."

Geoffrey saw the hard coldness in Rafe Easton's eyes. Yes, he thought, he could arrange it. But it wasn't what Geoffrey truly wanted. He would find a club willing to take him in. Tomorrow. Tomorrow he would find a way out of this mess. Dipping pen in inkwell, he signed every document, then watched as Easton gathered them up and slipped them into a satchel.

"You missed an opportunity, Wortham, to claim a wonderful woman as your sister. You sought to take everything that matters away from her. It seemed only fitting that I take all that matters away from you. Leave London before the sun rises or you'll find yourself in debtor's prison."

"But I just paid my debt to you."

"No, you paid the debt you owed Evelyn. Your debt to me remains open, my lord, and as I am now in possession of the markers you signed to Dimmick, your debt is considerable."

When Rafe Easton left, Wortham placed his head in his hands and wept for all he had lost, for the lonely life that would stretch out before him.

Chapter 22

Studying his reflection in the mirror, Rafe tugged on his light gray waistcoat. It took an inordinate amount of time to dress these days. His hand had healed but the mobility in it wasn't what it had once been. Dr. Graves had set the bones together as best as he could. Rafe was grateful for that, at least. He hadn't lost his hand completely. And he was learning to write with his right.

In retrospect, he supposed he could have told Dimmick from the outset that he was left-handed, so he would have broken the right, but he was familiar enough with the man's tortuous ways to know that a time would come when he would have signed anything the man put before him in order to stop the pain. And he'd be damned before he gave the man anything that belonged to Evie—or to Mick for that matter.

So damned he was.

But not as much as Dimmick.

During the three months since his rescue, Rafe found himself spending more time with his brothers, and he wondered why he had resisted being in their company for so long. Late into the night, they would drink Scotch and share stories from the years they were apart. Rafe liked hearing about all the various places Tristan had visited, the different people he'd met, the cultures he'd encountered. Sebastian's stories were less entertaining and more reluctantly recounted, but they gave Rafe a view of war that made him appreciate his brother's bravery and sacrifice more than he might have otherwise.

He held out his arms as his valet helped him into his black morning coat. "Did you see that the gift was delivered to Miss Chambers?"

"Yes, my lord."

Rafe no longer grimaced when his servants here or those who worked for him at the club addressed him as such. He was the son of a duke, the brother of a duke. He was proud to claim his family heritage, his birthright. Besides, he wanted there to be no doubt that Miss Evelyn Chambers, illegitimate daughter of an earl, was marrying a lord.

The very wealthy lord of a very powerful family.

Mary had insisted that Eve continue to live with them until the wedding. It had never occurred to Rafe that Evie had found sanctuary next door. It was the last place he would have looked for her. And she'd known it. At the time, he'd never have gone over there willingly.

Unlike now, when he went every day. He courted Evie as she should have been courted all along. With flowers, books of poetry, and chocolate. He escorted her on rides through the parks, danced with her at balls, dined with her every evening. He had much to make up for, and he was looking forward to spending the remainder of his life ensuring that she never regretted, not for a single second, that she became his wife.

Evelyn stared at her reflection in the cheval glass, hardly able to believe the beautiful handwork on the pearl-beaded ivory gown she wore. No quiet wedding in a country church, no secreting away. In two hours she was to be married at St. George's, and all of London had been invited.

Except Geoffrey, as he was no longer in London but had returned to the family estate—after signing over all the properties that were not entailed. She suspected Rafe might have been responsible for that, but when she asked him about it, he said only, "He's keeping the promise he made to your father."

As she had no use for another residence in London, she was going to convert it into a sanctuary for unfortunate women, a place where they could acquire skills so they wouldn't be dependent upon the kindness of strangers.

"You look lovely," Mary said, standing near Anne.

Evelyn turned to face the two women who would soon become her sisters by marriage. "It seems I should be nervous but I'm not."

"Because you know that you're marrying a man who loves you," Anne said.

"Yes, he does rather, I think."

A slight rap sounded on the door. Mary opened it and retrieved a small package from the servant. She held it out to Evelyn. "For you. From Rafe."

She took it and walked over to the window for

a bit of privacy. Sunlight streamed in through the glass. It was going to be a beautiful day.

She opened the note that had been tucked beneath the ribbon. She read the uneven awkward scrawl, and knew it had been written with a great deal of effort.

Something I hope you dearly will not need today.

After untying the ribbon, she lifted the lid. Inside rested a coin, and while she had seen many like it, and thousands existed, she knew she had held this coin once before in her hand, on a long-ago night when she'd thought she had no options.

Taking it out, she realized another note resided beneath it. She unfolded it.

My father gave me this coin shortly before he died. This morning I flipped it. Heads I would marry you. Tails I would take you as my wife. For me, Eve, there is no choice to be made. I love you more than life. I want to spend whatever years are left to me proving that to you. But if you have doubts, my love, I will let you go. Nothing means more to me than your happiness.

With a deep sigh, Evelyn pressed the note to her chest. Then she flipped the coin.

When the carriage drew to a halt, it was nearly dusk. Evelyn watched as her husband—her husband!—alighted, and when she went to step out, he caught her up in his arms. With a squeal, she wound hers around his neck.

It had been a lovely wedding, a lovely day.

The duke had escorted her down the aisle to the altar, where Rafe had been waiting with Tristan by his side. When the duke gave her into Rafe's keeping, he had stepped up to position himself beside Tristan. Tears had welled in her eyes at the sight of the three brothers standing there, the lords of Pembrook finally together as they should have been all along.

And following their habit of going against convention, as usually only unmarried men stood at the altar with the groom.

Rafe carried her up the steps. The door opened. Laurence bowed his head slightly as they went past. "Welcome home, my lord, my lady."

My lady. She almost laughed. As Rafe began climbing the stairs, she said, "Who would have thought the illegitimate daughter of an earl would one day be a lady?"

"You were a lady the moment you were born."

"You once told me I was ruined the moment I was born."

"That was before I knew you. I was a foolish man then."

Not so foolish, she thought. Cautious, rather. Not daring to care for anything that he might lose. He had lost her once. He would never lose her again.

The door to his bedchamber was open, and he swept her inside, kicking the door closed behind him. When he set her on her feet, she knocked aside his hat and ran her fingers up into his hair. "Oh, I have missed this, missed you."

"Mary and her silly rules about respectability." Bracketing his hands on either side of her face, he looked at her seriously, his ice-blue eyes intense. "Did you flip the coin?"

"I did. Heads I would marry you. Tails I would become your wife. I didn't need a coin to tell me what I wanted. I never did."

He kissed her then as though she were everything, as though she were all that mattered.

Clothes were removed piece by piece, in haste. It had been so long, so very long. She'd often thought of sneaking over here, had sometimes hoped to find him climbing in through the window of the bedchamber where she slept next door. But her scoundrel, her rake, her rogue had remained a gentleman. He had shaken off the mantle of the streets that he had worn for far too many years, and embraced his place within Society.

And Society had embraced not only him but all the brothers, as though together they were more formidable, more respected, more elevated. It had been an interesting phenomenon to watch. As his place had become more secured, so had hers.

She saw the envy on ladies' faces when he rode with her through the park, saw the admiration when he danced only with her at balls. She received invitations because it became quite clear that if she wasn't invited, none of the Pembrook lords or their wives would attend, and their disapproval was not something that the others in Society wished to garner.

When all their clothes were gone, they tumbled onto the bed, a tangle of arms and legs. She was grateful that he didn't feel a need to lock her wrists together, to restrain her movements. She longed to touch all of him, every firm muscle, every bit of taut flesh. It seemed appropriate that their life together as man and wife should begin here, in this room, where he had once fought his demons. He had conquered them all, and the man who had emerged from the fiery depths of hell was one that she would love until she drew her final breath.

When he joined his body to hers, she'd never felt so complete. When he rose up above her and gazed down on her, she thought his eyes had never looked more beautiful, filled with the love he held for her. She imagined him looking at her in the same manner when they were old and withered, fifty, sixty years from now. They were both so young. They had a long lifetime ahead of them.

She skimmed her hands over his face. She could see his youth now, tempered by the years, but still there. She wished he had not journeyed through life as he had, but it was that journey that had brought them together. To wish for a different path for either of them would be to wish they had not landed here, for how else would they have ever met—had he not been the purveyor of sin, and she sin's daughter?

"I love you, Evie," he whispered. "I doubt I'll say it much, but tonight you should know."

"I do know. And I love you. With my heart and my soul and my body."

He began to rock against her, not protesting when she wrapped her legs about him. Not flinching when she wound her arms around him. She held onto him tightly, as the pleasure spiraled beyond the bounds of flesh to encompass her soul, her heart, her very being.

Their gazes remained locked, their breaths matched tempo. He led, she followed, they twirled in rhythm to lilting strains that only they could hear. The sensations built, rolled through her from head to toe, over and over, reaching out, stretching—until they could go no farther, and then they burst through her, carrying her to heights she'd never before ascended.

She was aware of his final hard thrusts, his body jerking, his jaw clenching, and she saw the wonder of it all in his eyes. As magnificent for him as it had been for her.

Gently, he lowered himself, burying his face in the curve of her neck. "Damn, but I have missed you."

"You saw me every day."

"Not like this."

"I love holding you."

"I love you holding me." He kissed her chin, her ear, her temple, and then was once again gazing into her eyes. "You're going to be very glad you married me."

Smiling, she arched a brow at him. "Oh, you think so, do you?"

He gave her a devilish grin. "Oh, I know so. It would have been a colossal mistake not to."

Her laughter was abruptly cut off by his kiss. Oh, the arrogant man. How she did love him.

Epilogue

Pembrook Castle, Yorkshire
Winter 1864

Tonight was the night they were to have died. Instead, they would make love to their wives.

But for now, in the late wintry afternoon, they sat upon their horses, at the top of the rise, looking down on Pembrook Castle. From their vantage point, they could see the remnants of the tower that had served as their prison so many years before. Sebastian had been slowly tearing it down, his sledgehammer against one brick at a time.

"Difficult to believe it's been twenty years," Tristan said.

"I should hire men to raze it completely, get it done," Sebastian said.

"I think you should leave it as it is," Tristan replied.

"What of you, Rafe?" Sebastian asked. "What do you think I should do with it?"

"Rebuild it, make it grander than it was." He thought it a symbolic gesture, but feared he'd come off as a fool if he explained how Uncle had torn *them* down, reduced them to their bare souls, and that each of them had survived and built themselves up into something—someone—better than they might have been otherwise. So he said instead, "You'll be around for a good long while. Your heir will need someplace to reside before he inherits the title."

"You might be right. He seems to fancy the place. I'm always finding him exploring it. Perhaps that's what I'll do. Don't suppose I need to decide today. It's not going anywhere."

"Unlike us," Tristan said. "I suppose we need to return to the manor. I've heard your wife has prepared quite the feast to celebrate the night she rescued us."

"She rescued me twice, once from the tower, and once from myself."

Rafe felt as though he were still being rescued, every morning when he awoke to find Eve in his bed. It always amazed and humbled him to find her still there, still in his arms, smiling at him, making him laugh, giving him sons—two so far. She told him that the next time she was giving birth to a daughter. He suspected she would. She had a habit of achieving what she set her mind to do.

Using the house she'd obtained from Wortham, she had established a sanctuary for women who had no one, no place for refuge. She saw that they were taught skills, and found them gainful respectable employment. She had convinced him that the women who worked for him should manage his games rather than mattresses. It had created quite a stir the first time a woman had sat down to deal cards at one of his tables. But over the years his memberships had doubled; his earnings had tripled. Seemed a gent paid little attention to how much he was losing when he was receiving smiles and encouragement from a woman.

His brothers were as quiet as he, and he wondered the paths their thoughts traveled. He had yet to tell them that he loved him. He couldn't voice the words, but Eve assured him they knew. He attended all their little gatherings, had been out on Tristan's yacht so many times that he no longer dealt with illness when on board. He and his family were always here for Christmas.

He thought if his father knew that, he'd be pleased.

"We'd best get back," Sebastian said. "They'll be waiting for us."

Without hesitation, they wheeled their mounts around as one and galloped down the rise toward the manor. Rafe could see the three women waiting on the front lawn, in spite of the cold. Then his gaze homed in on the one he loved more than life itself.

Her smile was bright, her hand raised in greeting.

His horse had barely slowed when he dismounted, took her into his arms, and kissed her deeply as she wound herself securely around him. He might have been self-conscious if he hadn't known his brothers were greeting their wives in the same manner. No, he thought. He wouldn't have given a damn what they were doing. He was too glad for her welcome, yearned too much for her touch.

Sweeping her up into his arms, he began striding toward the manor.

She laughed. "What are you doing?"

"We have a bit of time before dinner. Want you to myself for a while."

She settled her head against his shoulder. "I love you, Lord Rafe Easton."

"Not as much as I love you, Lady Eve."

When she began nibbling on his ear, he laughed. Such a wicked woman. He intended to make love to her before dinner, then after. He would never have enough of her.

For a moment in his mind, all the globes he'd collected over the years spun. More than a hundred, spinning, spinning. He'd been searching for someplace better than where he was.

He'd finally found it, the best place of all— wrapped tightly in Eve's arms.

USA TODAY BESTSELLING AUTHOR

Lorraine Heath

Pleasures of a Notorious Gentleman
978-0-06-192295-4

A shameless rogue, Stephen Lyons gained a notorious reputation that forced him to leave for the army. Upon his return he is given the opportunity to redeem himself, and Mercy Dawson will risk everything to protect the dashing soldier.

Waking Up With the Duke
978-0-06-202245-5

The Duke of Ainsley owes a debt to a friend. But the payment expected is most shocking—for he's being asked to provide his friend's exquisite wife with what she most dearly covets: a child.

She Tempts the Duke
978-0-06-202246-2

Sebastion Easton always vowed he would avenge his stolen youth and title. Now back in London, the rightful Duke of Keswick, he cannot forget the brave girl who once rescued him and his brothers from certain death. But Lady Mary Wynne-Jones is betrothed to another.

Lord of Temptation
978-0-06-210002-3

Crimson Jack is a notorious privateer beholden to none. But all that will change when exquisite Lady Anne Hayworth hires his protection on a trip into danger and seduction.

*Next month, don't miss these exciting
new love stories only from
Avon Books*

Any Duchess Will Do by Tessa Dare

Griffin York, Duke of Halford, has no desire to wed, but when his mother forces him to pick a bride, he decides to teach her a lesson . . . by choosing the serving girl. For Pauline Simms, tolerating "duchess training" is worth the small fortune the duke has offered her, even if it is just play-acting. But as Pauline inadvertently educates Griffin of the love within him, both must face the biggest challenge of all: Can a roguish duke convince her to trust him with her heart?

Surrender to the Earl by Gayle Callen

Audrey Blake just wanted a favor, not a fiancé. But when Robert Henslow, Earl of Knightsbridge, appeared on her doorstep willing to help her take ownership of her rightful property, she couldn't turn him down. Not even with a fake engagement on the line. Yet it's Robert who yearns to prove to her how much they have to gain by making it real—and convincing her to submit to the most blissful passion.

The Secret Life of Lady Julia by Lecia Cornwall

One kiss led to another for Lady Julia Leighton, but when the roguish stranger disappeared from her betrothal ball, her life was forever changed. Now seeing Julia again years later, Thomas Merritt is utterly bewitched, even if they can never be together. Now in a Vienna rife with political intrigue, Thomas harbors a perilous secret—and the only person who can aid him is the woman who has captured his heart.

*G*ive in to your Impulses!

These unforgettable stories only take a second to buy and give you hours of reading pleasure!

Go to *www.AvonImpulse.com* and see what we have to offer.
Available where ebooks are sold.

AVON